WESTERN NOVELS
BY G. R. HOWE

Fiction

No Time to Trust

Dragons of Fire

Crow Woman on Deadman

Tequila Promises

Short Story Collection

Short Stories Out Of Kane

NO CHANCE

G. R. Howe

Published in the United States by Allied Publishing, a Wyoming corporation.

This is a work of fiction. Names, characters, and incidents either are the product of the author's imagination or are used fictitiously. Any resemblance to actual persons, living or dead, events, or locales is entirely coincidental.

Acknowledgement

Thank you to the following individuals who have contributed so much time and effort in the editing and creation of this novel: Joy Howe, Rachel Montgomery, and Martha Howe. These individuals were marvelous and free with their time, generous suggestions and comments.

For Joy

CHAPTER 1

August 23, 1854
Eight miles north of the Sweetwater River
Central Nebraska Territory

Eli Tallasinius sat his sorrel horse, reining him in, but the horse wasn't liking it. He tossed his head, dancing sideways, shifting his weight from one leg to another, the oft twitching ears laid back listening as he wondered about the rider's inexcusable hesitancy. It was, after all, morning: time to go, time to be moving. In spite of the sorrel's impatience, Eli held him back, fighting the horse's impetuous desires. Sympathetic to the horse's quandary, he patted the sorrel on the left shoulder as he studied the ridge that rose on his right.

It was not high, a mere ten to fifteen feet higher than the creek bed, extending north a quarter of a mile. Beyond that the land leveled out until it reached the edge of the canyon and the dark blue mountain range beyond. Eli took a deep breath; something wasn't adding up. He felt it rather than knew it. It was far too quiet. It was as though the rocks, the leaves in the cottonwood trees, the branches of olive green sagebrush, and the stems of curing grass were holding their collective breath, waiting with a singular apprehension.

Several prairie chickens abruptly took flight a hundred yards up the ridge line. A rock dog began chirping incessantly. Strange chatter so early in the day. Something had alarmed it, roused it from sleep. Eli was conscious of the wagons lined up behind him, all twenty-four readying themselves for another day's journey northward, ten or fifteen miles if all went well. To Eli's right, a short distance along the ridge, centered on a flat red rock, a chipmunk doing its herky-jerky dance suddenly held itself still, eyeing him, its tail continuing to bounce and bob.

Something was amiss. He knew it from all the years of doing what he did. Frustrated and restless, Eli shook his head, his nerves popping. Even as he came to grips with the odd morning, he was scouting the trail north, looking for the easiest path through the

1

mountains or around them–maybe a little of both. He doubted the trail had changed since his last trip, but stranger things had happened.

Best to be sure.

Zeke had left camp before first light. Prior to his leaving, Eli had stood with him on the north edge of the night camp sipping hot, black coffee from a bent tin cup. Zeke held the reins to his black gelding and a packhorse saddled with an empty pack saddle. Together they'd studied the lay of the land, gazing at the stars that sprinkled the early morning sky. It had been quiet then, too.

Damn the quiet.

"I don't know, Uncle Eli," Zeke said, tucking the empty tin cup back into his saddle bag.

"Me, either," Eli replied, pausing. "Be careful, boy. Be extra careful. I'm feelin' real edgy. That ain't good."

"Uncle," Zeke said, "this is like waitin' for a horse to get himself uncorked--you sittin' in the middle waitin', the bronc restin', barely movin' a muscle, yawnin' like he ain't got no care. You know it's gonna happen. He knows it's gonna happen. But when? You don't know that. Or where?"

"Expect it'll be sooner than later, boy."

"Probably sooner."

Eli nodded in agreement. "Somethin' is goin' on. What, though? That's the question without the answer." Eli scratched his head. "Better get a move on, boy; see what you kin see. Maybe we kin figure it out 'fore it buries us. Probably nothin'." He stepped away from his nephew and the horses, moving a short distance. He breathed in the dank, night air, then looked back at Zeke. "I'm goin' ta alert the night watch. You be careful. See you this evenin'. If ya can, bring back a couple a mulies. Don't expect they'll be hard ta find."

Zeke laughed. "Not likely," he'd said.

The boy mounted the tall black, swinging into the saddle, finding the stirrup with his off foot. He glanced at his uncle, touched the brim of his hat with his gloved hand, then nudged the black into motion, the packhorse stretching his neck before reluctantly following, pulled by the lead rope. Eli watched.

Boy? Why do I think him a boy? Gotta stop that. Been too long. Too damn long. Ain't no kid no more. Full grow'd. Gots hisself a gal. Wonder if he knows he ain't no boy. He better. He sure as hell better.

2

That was earlier--three and a half long hours ago. Eli relaxed the tension in the reins, allowing the sorrel his head. There was no putting it off. Everyone was ready, waiting. Immediately the horse stepped forward. Eli waved his arm, motioning for the lead wagon to follow. Behind him he heard the lead teamster walking alongside his wagon talking to the oxen, slapping them on the butt. Whips cracked. Several wheels squeaked, needing grease. Eli made a mental note to find out whose.

Get that taken care of before it becomes a problem.

Wagon boxes creaked as teams leaned into their harnesses, the slack taken from loose trace chains. Eli Tallasinius rode out front and to the side, worried, suspicious, scanning the ridge's edge, the creek bed, and the country beyond. Somehow what he was seeing--the peace, the quiet--was lying to him and he knew it.

The company of emigrants began to stretch out along the leeside of the red ridge, moving between it and the brush that hid the creek. As if on cue a breeze picked up, bending the grass in brown waves. Eli turned in the saddle, looking back at the wagons, watching them falling into line as they moved forward.

In that instant he saw what he didn't want to see: Indians advancing out of the creek brush, moving swiftly afoot, running toward the creeping wagons and the unsuspecting emigrants. Without seeing them, he knew others were coming off the ridge on the other side of the wagons. It was a trap sprung in the morning mist, the dew still clinging to the drying grass. The first wave of hostiles was almost to the wagons.

Eli whipped the sorrel around. Pulling his Navy Colt from its holster, he fired at an attacker. Spurring the sorrel, yelling alarm, he charged the nearest man, striking him with the horse's shoulders, knocking him down before he was able to avoid the plunging horse. Eli shot him, too. He heard a shrill scream edged with panic, saw men in the seats above the jockey boxes turning, reaching for rifles. Eli fired again. Weapons discharged up and down the line of wagons. He brought the sorrel to a dead run, jabbing his spurs into its ribs. A warrior in front of him, running toward a wagon, stumbled, fell. Another took his place. Eli felt the pistol buck in his hands.

Eli Tallasinius rode another warrior down, shooting him in the head, the sorrel's forward movement knocking the warrior sideways. An arrow caught the sorrel in the chest in front of the cinch. He

3

reared. Eli stepped down from the saddle as the horse rolled, kicking frantically. He clubbed an attacker over the head with the pistol butt, then shot the man behind him, pulling a second pistol from his waistband. As an afterthought he shot the man he'd clubbed. The first pistol was empty, no longer any good. He threw it at a new attacker too far off to do any damage. The man kept coming.

Eli felt an arrow drive deep into his chest, instantly realizing there wasn't ever going to be "no never mind." This was it; he wasn't walking away, not from this one. He fired the second Navy Colt at his assailant, his fingers seizing the hilt of his knife. A warrior with a club charged him. Turning, Eli slapped him in the skull with the pistol in his left hand, then stabbed him with his long knife, driving it upwards deep into the assailant's body. Dimly, as if through a glass darkly, Eli saw two more warriors advancing, both running toward him. One fired an old Colt Dragoon, the molded lead piercing Eli's body, driving him backwards.

Eli got off two additional shots, firing at forms and shadows, firing until the hammer fell on an empty chamber. Cursing quietly, his teeth clenched, he dropped the useless weapon, and stumbled toward the sorrel, seeking the extra in his saddle bags. Before he could reach the horse, the light of his soul went out and he surrendered to the gray oblivion.

CHAPTER 2

May 1845
St Paul's Cathedral
St. Louis, Missouri

Zeke did not remember how long he'd lived with the nuns and the priest. It was quite a spell. He liked eating three meals a day. An older couple had picked him up outside of a small one-horse town called Columbus. He'd walked that far, choosing the open road over the Rawlins' regular beatings.

He'd been living with his mother and his grandparents when his mother died of a snakebite. Not long after, when his grandparents got consumption, the neighbors, a family named Rawlins, took Zeke from the sick house. The neighbors, if they could be called neighbors, lived twenty-six miles up the road from Zeke's grandparents. Zeke never saw his grandparents again. Mr. and Mrs. Rawlins did the neighborly thing and took the boy in permanently. They didn't ask; they volunteered. Mr. and Mrs. Rawlins were a bit on the severe side, holding to raising the boy by not sparing the rod. They beat the boy to keep him right with the world.

Zeke didn't take to being beaten, so one evening he walked out of their lives and made his way down the road. He figured that walking was better than being smacked around. He remembered being "gawd awful" hungry. "So hungry his back bone done rubbed a hole in his stomach" or so he felt. He "could've eaten a good sized horse and chased its rider to hell, then stepped down for a snack." That's what his grandfather had always said when he was hungry and wanted his grandmother to laugh.

The old couple that found him outside of Columbus fed him hot scones with butter and honey. Zeke thought they must have been really rich: eating like that. They took him to the priest in St. Louis, who had originally blessed him in Philadelphia. The priest didn't know who he was; he didn't remember the boy. Certainly Zeke didn't look the same as the day he was blessed. The priest was the only living person who could have known the boy's real name but he'd long forgotten it and didn't know that he ever knew it. For a skinny man dressed in a black robe, there were many names he was supposed to

5

remember and didn't.

At the boys' birth his mother had had him blessed in the Catholic church in Philadelphia. The priest, Patrick Monahan, inscribed the boy's name in the records as Ezekiel M. Penrose. The "M" might have stood for Morgan or Mitchell or Merriweather, or the way his grandfather explained it before he died: "for what the hell have ya." Nobody knew because his mother never mentioned it. She couldn't write and neither she nor the priest ever said. The record in the family Bible didn't carry the middle name spelled out. The paper that said he was blessed by the priest was lost when his grandparents moved to the countryside. It was found and lost again after his mother died. After his grandparents' deaths the cabin they built and lived in burned to the ground along with the family Bible and any records they had. No one knew why. It just did. Zeke was six years old when they died. As Eli would say in the telling of it: "it was one hell of a note, sure enough." Zeke wasn't altogether sure what that meant but apparently that is what it was: "sure enough." That being said, in spite of his mother going to the trouble of giving him a proper name that sounded important and substantial, she called him "Zeke." So did everyone else.

On several issues Zeke had every right to be confused. Eli Tallasinius was Zeke's mother's brother. To Zeke his Uncle Eli was "sort of Greek." "Sort of" because his uncle spoke English but his parents were Greek. Eli didn't speak Greek, but his parents did.

No one knew exactly how old the boy was which, at best, was sometimes a distraction. Years later Eli told folks the boy was fifteen and sometimes sixteen. He'd tell it that way because he couldn't remember how old the boy had been when he picked him up from the Catholic priest in St Louis. Part of the confusion started at that time. His exact age was a mess even then. Zeke and the priest weren't sure either, not that it mattered. Eli hadn't been present when the boy was born nor had he been present when the boy's mother died. He didn't know who the boy's father was because he hadn't been around then either.

Even Zeke's mother hadn't remembered the exact date of his birth. No mother would believe she didn't know the date, but she didn't. It was a particularly difficult travail. Toward the end she passed out and nearly bled to death. When she woke up days later, she had a baby and was delirious. In her mind, Zeke's birth date could have been any day of the week, any day of the month. She did remember that it was warm and must have been sometime in early summer. The exact date was forever lost.

Truthfully, Eli didn't know how old the boy was. And Eli was truthful most of the time. Not so much when he got himself wrapped around a jug of corn whiskey: those times he was a bit boastful, given to exaggeration. Consequently, the boy's numerical age sometimes hrunk as his height grew, making him six feet tall when he was "thirteen." It wasn't so but that is the way Eli told it. The fact was Eli didn't know. The first time Eli saw Zeke was when he picked him up from the priest.

CHAPTER 3

May 1845
St Paul's Cathedral
St. Louis, Missouri

Zeke remembered his last day in the convent: the stained glass windows, the morning sunlight casting colorful light patterns on the floor. He remembered standing in the doorway to the priest's office, waiting for him to finish writing. The priest was alone. And he remembered Sister Carlyle's hand on his shoulder and the cool stone floor on his bare feet. Mostly he remembered the long shadows cast by the morning light flowing through the high, stained glass windows.

The evening before, a roughly dressed man had stood inside the alcove of St. Paul's Cathedral, St. Louis, Missouri. He spoke with two nuns. It was an unusual picture: a frontiersman towering over two ladies of the cloth. The longer he stood talking with the two women the more animated they became. Outraged by his presence and his request, Sister Carlyle tersely addressed him.

"Please wait here," she said. "I'll get the priest. He'll know what to do. This is ridiculous. That's what I think."

"Thank ya, Ma'am," he said.

"Do you know your nephew's name?" the remaining sister asked. "How is it that you know he's here? We have twenty-eight children, you know. We get more every day. Do you know what your nephew looks like?"

"Ma'am, his name is Zeke. That ain't his given name, mind ya. That would be Ezekiel. His last name is Penrose. Best that I kin remember. I'm here ta get him. Why not trot him out? If you would be so kind. Save us both a lot of jawin'."

"I'm sorry but we don't just 'trot' a child out on anyone's say so. It's just not done. Besides, look at you."

"Look at me, Ma'am?"

She glanced down at his knee high boots, the holstered long barreled Walker Colt hanging on his right thigh, another stuck in his waistband (as if one wasn't enough), and the Bowie knife draped in a sheath that hung on a leather strap around his neck, the hilt in front of his left elbow.

The Colt looked heavy and worn to her. It looked used; he looked used and hard, unrelenting. It occurred to her that 'no' was a word he wasn't used to hearing. Pointing at the pistol stuck in his waistband, she said, "Why did you bring these merchants of death into the church? You know better."

"Ma'am, I came a hell of a long ways ta pick up a kid. I'm wearin' these 'merchants of death' because the good Lord put men out there that fully intend ta take my life. I aim ta stop 'em by shootin' 'em dead before they shoot me dead. Now, Ma'am, trot my nephew out here before I raise more hell than you've seen lately."

"My word, young man! Your mouth . . . "

"Get the boy fer me, lady."

"May I be of some assistance?"

The tall stranger turned to the voice. "Father," the stranger said, nodding, noting that the sister had returned with the Priest.

"What seems to be the trouble?"

"Ain't no trouble, Father. Got your letter. I'm here ta pick up my nephew."

"And you are?"

"Eli Tallasinius. My nephew's Zeke. I'm told he's here. I'm here ta take him off your hands. It seems I'm his last known, livin' relative. You might say I'm all he's got."

"And you're his uncle?"

"If Zeke is the boy you got here, I am."

The priest stared at the man dressed in fringed buckskin sporting a three day old beard and a wide brimmed hat with a flat crown. The brim shaded the man's eyes, making it difficult to see his face. He smelled of open prairie and cigar smoke. The priest wondered what response he'd get if he asked him to remove the hat; they were standing in a church, after all. But the priest didn't ask. He only nodded.

"There is a boy here who said his name was Zeke. Ezekiel, I believe. He said he had an uncle, 'Eli.' That he was a soldier. That must be you."

"I reckon it is."

"I wrote you."

"I got the letter."

"Good. Very good. Ezekiel is asleep or should be. Please come

9

back tomorrow morning, say 8:00 a.m. We'll have him ready."

The tall man nodded. "Father, tomorrow mornin' will be fine. I thank ya. I'll be here."

For an instant the frontiersman looked at the two nuns, then touching the brim of his hat, said, "Sisters. Thank ye kindly."

He turned to leave the building much as he had arrived, walking easily down the long hall, the fingers of his right hand brushing the walnut grip of the long barreled Walker Colt. The nun on the priest's right stared after him; her eyes followed his gait.

She said, "He's trouble, Brother Patrick. Are you going to let him have the boy?"

"Good question, Sister. Do we have a choice? Really have a choice? What are we going to do with him if we keep him?" The priest shook his head slowly. "We can't keep him. We have other children we must care for and we can't keep them all."

Neither sister answered.

"I sent out sixteen letters trying to locate the boy's uncle and this fellow shows up. At least he showed up. It's God's will," he said.

"Yes, but does God know what he's doing?"

"Sister Carlyle!"

"Excuse me, Brother Patrick. I misspoke." She turned and proceeded down the hall in the opposite direction.

In the morning the priest sent Sister Carlyle for the boy. It didn't take long before he heard a knocking at the door, not loud but persistent, like a small woodpecker with a rounded beak. Tap, tap, tap. The heavy door was opened. The priest looked up. He saw Sister Carlyle, her arm around a boy's shoulders, both standing in the doorway. The priest wondered if she'd been crying, noting the red hue to her cheeks.

Probably this morning, he thought. *These children, they certainly grow on you.*

"Brother Patrick," she said.

He looked across his paper littered desk at the boy. "Ezekiel. Young man, come in, please." Then, glancing at Sister Carlyle, he said, "Sister, thank you very much."

He turned to the lad, watching as he stepped inside the office.

"Good news. Your uncle . . .the gentleman you told me about . . . he's coming for you." The priest stood. "I believe you told me he's

10

your mother's brother. I spoke to him last night. He received one of my letters. You were asleep and I told him to come for you this morning. He said he would. Do I have this information correct? An uncle named Eli?"

"Yes."

"Well, you are about to meet him again. So get yourself ready. Do you have anything? Did you bring anything with you?"

"No. Yes. My clothes. I brought 'em 'cause I got 'em on."

"Good. Good."

The priest stared at him for what felt to the boy like a long, long time. "I don't know your uncle, Ezekiel," he said. "Not personally. What I do know is that he showed up in this place."

The priest glanced around him, at his desk, and then back at Zeke. "He didn't have to come. Understand? He could have ignored you and me, both of us, but he didn't."

The boy stood staring at the priest, waiting. The priest took his time, thinking.

"Let me back up. Let me try and say this differently. Ezekiel, your uncle has come for you. You'll be leaving us. I want you to remember this because it's important. This man, out of all men living has come for you, because of who you are to him. He has not sidestepped any issues; he has made no excuses. He didn't even ask any questions. He just showed up.

"I know he soldiered in Mexico. That's how I knew one of the addresses to write him. I know he is a westerner. No doubt, he has seen things that most civilized men will never see. I know he has used the weapons he carries. While I do not condone it, I know he is going to use them again and so does he. He is not a godly man but he is a man. Listen to him. Watch him. You'll be living with him," the priest paused, ". . . out there." The priest waved his hand to the west.

"It won't be easy. Living with his kind never is. I suspect this man will show you how to stand up in the face of danger, do what needs to be done. I'm reasonably sure he won't avoid trouble. I don't think your uncle even tries. I don't think he will lead you astray, at least I hope not. I hope he will help you make your own decisions. Listen to him, Ezekiel. That's the best advice I can give."

"Listen?"

"Yes."

"Okay."

11

The priest looked at him, nodded, took a breath, and for a moment was going to say something more but Eli Tallasinius stepped into the room bringing the smell of the prairie and cigar smoke. The sudden movement caught the priest's eye. He looked up and then at Zeke.

"He's here, Ezekiel. This is he. This is your uncle."

Afraid the boy hadn't heard his advice, the priest came around from behind the desk and knelt in front of him, grabbing him by the shoulders. "Remember what I said. Listen to him, Ezekiel. Listen. Hear me? Listen."

"Yes, sir. I will. Thank you."

"Good boy."

The priest stood up, acknowledged Eli Tallasinius, then looked at the boy. "You're welcome, Ezekiel. Get your things."

"I got my things. I'm wearin' 'em."

"That's right."

That was the last thing the priest said to him.

The first thing that his Uncle Eli said to him was, "Hungry, boy? Let's find ourselves some grub and get ourselves 'round a big steak, maybe some beans; a chunk of sourdough bread would be nice." Eli Tallasinius paused and looked down on the boy. "Where the hell's your hat?" he asked.

"I ain't got a hat."

"I'll be damned," he said. "No hat? Wonder the sun ain't put a scald on your brain. Shoes? Ya gots any shoes?"

"No, sir."

"I'll be damned twice," he said.

"I hope not, sir."

"Ya hope not?" Eli started to laugh, stopped. He nodded. "Well, let's put the 'rectify' on these intolerable difficulties."

That morning Zeke learned that 'rectify' meant 'solve the problem right now' and that waiting for 'resolution' wasn't something that Eli Tallasinius did. Zeke also learned that his uncle did not tolerate an empty chamber. His uncle had asked him if he could shoot. The subject of an empty chamber came up after the question.

"Ya never know," his uncle said, "and 'cause you never know ya don't take chances ya don't need ta take." Eli rubbed his chin as he contemplated the subject. "Don't tempt fate," he said.

Zeke wasn't sure what he meant. He expected that some time

12

he'd know. It was the last time he didn't have a hat on his head and boots on his feet. He remembered, waiting for the cobbler to measure his feet, Eli had said again for the third time: "Ya never know, boy." And then: "Take care of what you got then what you got'll take care of ya."

Zeke had glanced at the new heels the cobbler was nailing to his new boots, and then at his uncle leaning back in his chair.

Listen and remember, he thought. *I can do that. Nothin' to it.*

He remembered thinking that his uncle was the richest person that ever lived, and that he liked felt hats, the brim pulled down on his forehead making it difficult to see his eyes. And he liked tall boots, too.

It was a good day. Ezekiel M. Penrose was nine years old.

CHAPTER 4

April 4, 1854
Independence, Missouri

In 1854 Zeke was or was about to be eighteen years old. Zeke wasn't a scatterbrain or a slacker. He'd listened, he'd watched, and he learned to write his name when need be. He was handy around a wagon. He could grease a wheel, mend a spoke, hitch a team to a doubletree, and shoe a horse. He was capable with a rope, a rifle, and a short gun. His uncle saw that he was handy: that he could take care of himself, that he could sit on a wagon seat, drive a team out of a mud hole, and pull his weight. His uncle taught him to be good at getting by and so he was good at getting by. Fact was, if a man was handy, folks appreciated it. If he wasn't handy, he'd just be in the way, another mouth eating grub, cleaning out the larder.

To hear the dusty, traveling ladies, the wives, daughters and mothers of emigrants tell it, as they sat in the shade of a Cottonwood swatting mosquitoes and waiting to move farther west, Zeke was "easy on the eyes." Zeke wasn't sure what that was supposed to mean.

Zeke stood five eleven, weighed one hundred eighty-five pounds. There was something incongruent about him, something that didn't quite fit together, in the manner of teenagers who haven't grown into their bodies. In loose fitting clothing, he cut a skinny figure. He had a mop of black, unruly hair, teeth that were white and mostly straight, and a face full of sunburned freckles. He got along, managed to do his chores, and stayed out of everyone's way.

Eli Tallasinius was a wagon master and Zeke, his tag-a-long. Zeke went with his uncle when he hired on to guide emigrants to California, Oregon Territory, the new Nebraska Territory or wherever they wanted to go. From the beginning folks just naturally looked out for Zeke, especially when they discovered that he was motherless and fatherless with only an itinerant wagon master to care for him and meet the needs of a growing youngster. He didn't really need caretaking; Zeke could do for himself. But folks took him under their wings as if dutybound. The wives taught him to mend shirts, to cook, to read something besides trail sign, to write a letter and to cipher

14

numbers. The irony, if there was one, was that most of this learning took place between April 1 and August 15 while he was working for his uncle. While he was learning these things, he ate some fair tasting food. That wasn't bad, not the way Zeke figured it.

Eli Tallasinius began taking folks west in early April 1844. He got the boy from the Catholic priest the next year. In 1849 when folks wanted to go to California looking for gold, he guided them out west for a price paid in gold. There was a time when he'd work for a couple of dollars a month and board. He asked for two hundred dollars a wagon for taking parties west, or five dollars a head if you were walking, carrying what you owned on your back. Most folks paid less than the two hundred. The boy traveled with him, did a lot of the work, and was paid nothing. Eli hired another man to drive the wagon that contained their gear. Sometimes his fare was the passage west. Most often he was paid for driving the team of four horses, but not very much since he ate Eli's grub and slept under his wagon. Most men would have done it for free just to get to where they were going. Eli, however, didn't want to be beholding.

Zeke had never heard of the Thermo country and pointed that out to his uncle when he was asked if he wanted to go there. Eli rubbed the three-day stubble on his face and stared at the boy. Finally he said, "I'm surprised that these folks heard of it. It's wild country. Expect it still is. Last I know'd it was being fought over by the Crow and the Lakota. The 'who' that owns that country ain't settled. I ain't heard of nobody livin' there. The place they're wantin' ta go ta has these hot springs boilin' up out of the ground. Damn hot, too. Sorta spooky."

"Why you suppose these folks want to go there?" Zeke asked.

"Start a settlement, I expect. Get religion. God knows. They probably don't."

"We goin'?"

"I'm thinkin' no. I'm thinkin' no, we ain't."

"California, then?"

Eli nodded. He said, "I'm thinkin' the money is good and it ain't as dangerous." Eli paused and stared for a moment at the inside of the wheel the boy was greasing. "You know, folks still disappear up north. I don't like the thought of me disappearin'."

"And you like your hair," the boy said, smiling.

15

Eli glanced at him and nodded in agreement. "Yeah, and I like it on my head, not hangin' from some wickiup."

That was the way Eli thought, the way he saw things. Leastwise, that was the way he thought until he was offered more money and came face to face with his own greed. His opinion changed when faced with the thought of more gold coin bouncing around in the small wooden box he kept under the wagon seat. That box wasn't obvious to an untrained eye.

Eli had built a false bottom in the bed of the wagon under the seat and lined it with tin. He made the top out of old, worn floor boards from a wagon used too long and too often. The box was used for the coin and paper money that he didn't carry in his money belt. The belt was wrapped about his waist and protected by two Navy Colts, short guns with which he was well acquainted. Both irons were kept oiled and loaded. And as Zeke had learned, Eli had no use for an empty chamber.

Before the Navy Colts, he had Walkers. The Walkers he'd gotten new in 1847 from a soldier involved in a shooting war in Mexico. They were heavy, weighing four and a half pounds and were .44 caliber.

"Insurance!" That is what Eli called his pistols. "If you're good with 'em, you don't need no other." He'd pat the grips and look at Zeke. He'd say: "These babies . . . they keep the dogs at bay. Remember that, boy. Remember that nobody looks down the barrel of a .44 and blinks. They damn well know better."

In 1851 Eli obtained two Navy Colts from somewhere in Texas; the location varied depending on how much corn liquor he had had to drink when he told the story. They were lighter by half and not nearly as long. The Navy pistols were .36 caliber and not .44s. Eli kept his Walker Dragoons in his saddle holsters near to hand. Eli had thick wrists to handle them. He kept the Navies on his person.

Those Navy Colts weren't for show. He practiced with his pistols and later made the boy practice until his forearms ached and he smelled of burned gunpowder, sulfur, and saltpeter. It wasn't just common target practice. Eli Tallasinius felt that targets such as a tin can or an empty bottle didn't shoot back. They weren't realistic compared to an actual fire fight where shooting counted and being calm and efficient was the difference between staying alive and being dead. For this reason, he had his nephew practice shooting from every

16

conceivable position: squeezing the trigger efficiently; letting his body, legs and eyes bring the weapon to bear without closing an eye and staring down the barrel.

"No sense not bein' ready," he said. "Besides burnt powder smoke keeps mosquitoes away." That's what his uncle said and that's why Zeke was efficient with a pistol, though a man wouldn't expect it looking at him.

When it came to raising his nephew, Eli thought the boy should be "well heeled." "Well heeled" didn't refer to boots. Zeke carried weapons, more than most. Riding, he had one strapped to his leg, one tucked in his waistband behind his belt buckle, and two in his saddle bags, wrapped tightly in oil cloth. Folks aware of his shooting irons considered it excessive, especially for a mere boy. The men from whom Eli had removed what became the boy's pistols hadn't needed them any longer, they being dead from gunshot wounds. On that cloudy day, Eli took the Navy Colts from their still warm fingers and gave them to the boy.

"Waste not," he said. "Look through their panniers and saddlebags; see if they have a store of black powder, lead, paper cartridges, what have ya. You're gonna need 'em."

Zeke did as he was told never imagining his uncle would let him carry such beautiful creations, courtesy of Samuel Colt.

CHAPTER 5

April 4, 1854
Independence, Missouri.

Hooped wagons covered in thick gray canvas were stacked up in a long, irregular line on the east side of the Missouri River, a mile or so north of Independence. They waited for the river ferry to take them across to the west side. Mosquitoes, deer flies, gad flies, flying ants, gnats, horse flies, and a host of other nameless blood sucking insects, some hardly visible, made time drag and the waiting longer. Swatting flies, while sitting in the baking sun in the Missouri's hot, heavy humidity gave a Greek steam bath a new meaning.

More emigrants arrived daily, having made the six day trek from St Louis. Mules brought them in five days. Oxen took a little longer, but they were stouter than mules and in the long pull lasted longer. But a mule? Nobody knew exactly what they would do or when they'd do it. Folks used them anyway, for a mule is a fine animal, just not one to be entirely trusted. Thankfully, a mule, most of the time, would let an observer know of its pending recalcitrance. Men lived a lot longer and in less pain if they were vigilant observers while working with those long, floppy eared "bastards."

The iron rimmed wheels of heavy-laden wagons turn slowly. They don't turn at all when waiting for the ferry. By the late afternoon they sat stationary, bathed in the long red rays of the setting sun, the horses and mules unhitched for the day. Men and women busied themselves starting camp fires of buffalo chips and twisted rolls of prairie grass. They'd glance at the river, rubbing the small of their backs, stretching, pausing for a moment, thinking about tomorrow, for tomorrow they'd cross the river and see the other side.

CHAPTER 6

April 11, 1854
Independence, Missouri

Holding itself steady, its wings rigid in the wind, an old seagull rode the breezes and updrafts above the river. It watched the comings and goings as it had for many summers. It watched as its mother had done when the gull was nothing but a white egg resting amid the reeds on the edge of the Missouri river. It was old and had gleaned daily sustenance from the small part of the earth it knew, consuming grasshoppers, countless bodies of dead fish, and living minnows who ventured too close to the surface of the swirling waters. It had seen these things in its short life span and if it lived another season, it would see them again.

"Lexie, Lexie, look at that gull. See him hanging in the wind? I think he's watching us."

Alexandra Wakeford stopped mixing the flour and water, mindful that she hadn't added a pinch of salt. She glanced at the bird her mother was remarking about and watched it float effortlessly in the wind.

"Do you suppose it knows something we don't? Some secret it isn't telling?"

"Like what, Mother? It's a dumb bird. It barely knows when it's hungry."

"It's remarkable how it just hangs in the wind, don't you think?"

"I guess so, Mother."

Alexandra stared at the white and gray bird, then looked over the broad expanse of river to the other side so tantalizingly close. The ferry had already transferred most of the Wilcox Company to the far bank. There were six wagons left; then it would be their turn. Finally.

Tomorrow we'll be over there, she thought.

She returned her gaze to the seagull; she marveled as it floated in the air. It did seem to be waiting, perhaps to tell them some marvelous message. Her mother was right. Alexandra wondered what stories it had to tell. She chuckled to herself. More than likely it was

19

waiting for a crumb of bread: a handout on a sultry afternoon, something to keep it from starving. She added the pinch of salt and continued mixing.

"Hi, Lexie," Alexandra looked up at the sound of Colleen's voice.

"Colleen, what are you up to? No good?"

"I wish I was. Hoping that we'd get across before it got dark.

"Didn't happen."

"Sure didn't."

"What were you and your mother looking at just now?" Colleen asked.

"A dumb bird."

"A bird?"

"Yes, a seagull flying above the river's water." Alexandra said.

"Oh. I guess she's bored. I can see that. I'm a little bit bored myself. A bird, huh?"

"Yes. A seagull."

"What are you cooking?" Colleen asked.

"Biscuits. We're fixing biscuits and gravy. My mother says your family is coming for supper. That right?"

Colleen nodded. "Yes, your mother asked us. Sounds delicious."

"That'll be fun," Alexandra said with a smile.

Colleen returned the smile and said, "Oh, thanks for saying that."

"It's true."

"Where's your father?"

"He crossed the river with Mr. Billings. They're looking for a wagon master. Said he'd be back this evening. He won't miss supper. Not if he can help it."

CHAPTER 7

April 13, 1854
Independence, Missouri

The subject of girls came up innocently enough. The first time was in the evening. Zeke never knew anything could turn out to be so complicated. He had spoken earlier with each of the wagon owners who wanted his uncle to guide them west to the Thermo country: land of hot, bubbling water and dry red hills. Eli hadn't formally agreed to do it, but he was thinking about it and thinking about it was the same as agreeing to do it.

Zeke had taken his uncle's checklist to each of the settlers, making sure each wagon was supplied, that they had the requisite amount of ammunition, salt, flour, pepper, and the like, and that wagons were only loaded down with what mattered. The Laramie plain, though far from Independence, already had enough abandoned furniture. It didn't particularly need any more. Zeke had been there. He'd seen the heavy oak chests of drawers, hickory bed frames, and hardwood sideboards sitting alongside of the road, weathering in the ceaseless wind, bleaching under the overhead sun, freezing in the long winters.

"Might as well have those folks unload what ain't needed and stock up on what is," Eli said. "See to it, boy."

Zeke saw to it, not that he didn't get complaints about unloading "great grandmother's" chest of drawers. Most of those conversations ended with him saying, "Mister, all the Sunday go to meetin' clothes ain't gonna be a hill of beans, if you be needin' .44 lead and black powder but all you got is an oak cabinet." Or sometimes he'd say, "What are you goin' to do? Kill a griz with a sack a socks? Fight off a hundred Injuns with a corset and a kitchen table made of cherry wood?"

If that didn't convince them, his uncle got right to the point. He'd say, "Suit yourself, Pilgrim, but ya ain't goin' with me. I don't take folks west ta bury 'em fer bein' stupid. It hurts my tender sensibilities." His Uncle Eli didn't have any "tender sensibilities" but he said it just the same. Zeke didn't get in the way of him saying it. His uncle's rule was "if a feller don't need it ta stay alive, he don't need it at all."

If the choice was between a piece of furniture and a rifle, take the rifle. Take lead, black powder, caps. Take a sack of oats and five cans of Schaeffer's Black Beauty wheel grease. If the settlers got a little out of hand, Eli dealt with them, which was all right with Zeke. Most of the men he dealt with considered him too young to know much of anything. Who was he to argue? He supposed he was ignorant and young, but he wasn't fifteen like his uncle said when he got to tuggin' on a jug of corn whiskey. That much he did know.

While sitting around a fire, eating baked beans, corn bread and venison, his uncle laughed and said to him, "Zeke, twice I seen 'em lasses givin' ya the once over."

"What?" he said, not knowing what his uncle was talking about.

"Them girls lookin' ya over. I saw it. Got me ta wishin' I was young, full of buckwheat, Black Strap sauce, and vinegar." His uncle sighed wistfully. "But I ain't. That was thirty years ago when I was stupid and didn't know no better. Ain't goin' there."

Zeke said, "I didn't notice. Should I? What do you think they wanted?" He knew that sounded stupid as soon as he said it.

"A little polite conversation, I reckon." Eli stood looking at Zeke for a moment. "Wake up, boy," he said, "smell the sunflowers. There are some things, things you'll find interestin' 'cause they are. Things better than a broom-tailed nag and a thirty-dollar saddle. Better than a Volcano repeatin' rifle. Hate like hell ta say it." Eli paused. "Soon as ya finish up, find me. I got a list of things fer ya ta do."

After his Uncle Eli was gone, Zeke sat wondering about what he'd said, who had been looking at him, and what did they want? Later, as he was walking to where the Jeffersons had parked their wagon to see if Mr. Jefferson had lightened his load, he found himself watching to see who was watching him. It was "innocent enough." A girl in the company of her mother was walking toward him. She looked right at him. He said, "hello." She smiled and said "hello" in return. She'd passed by and he couldn't help himself; he turned to look back. She was looking at him, head turned, her hair lying down her back. When she saw Zeke looking at her, she smiled again. Her face lit up.

A week later he would remember the encounter as though it had just happened. And all of the days that followed, like they had just happened, too. That first time he saw her face--right then is when his girl troubles began. No matter what he did, her face, her smile, the very thought of her was in his head. None of it made a whole lot of sense to him.

Zeke saw his uncle the next morning; he had just walked across the flat between the wagons of the Johnson company and those of the Wilcox company as they were forming up. Teamsters were shouting at obstinate mules and horses laboring in harness. Riders were passing by. He had been helping a fellow grease the wheels of an already loaded wagon. They were planning to join the Wilcox Company heading for Oregon.

"Zeke, we'll be leavin' day after tomorrow," his uncle said, pushing his hat back on his head, watching him work the wheel off the hub. "Maybe the day after . . . if we're not ready when I'd like ta be."

Zeke stood, pushed the wheel to the side, leaning it against the wagon box. He turned to his uncle as he looked for a rag to wipe the Black Beauty axle grease from his hands. Eli nodded at the fellow Zeke was helping. Zeke introduced the two. "Uncle Eli, this is Buster. He's fixin' to be with the Wilcox company. Buster, my Uncle Eli." Zeke was still looking unsuccessfully for a rag to wipe his hands.

"Howdy." Eli continued, "Zeke, we'll be travelin' ta the Thermo country. Takin' nineteen, maybe twenty or twenty-one wagons."

Zeke glanced at his uncle and smiled. "Not California? Thought we'd be goin' to Auburn or Sacramento or Sutter's Mill."

"No. Not this time. Not California. The sonstabitches offered me too much gold. What kin I say?"

"And you took it."

"I took it."

"Nineteen, maybe twenty-one wagons? That ain't many. Will it be enough to make it worthwhile?"

"I'd say so. We'll drop in behind Wilcox. Stay with 'em 'til just before South Pass up there on the divide. There we'll turn right. Maybe we'll do a hundred mile alone. On the outside, ten extra days the way I see it. If we're careful. We'll be all right." His uncle paused. "Not ta worry, boy. We'll be careful. Suit ya?"

"Sure," Zeke said. "I ain't never been there."

"Good. We work it right we'll get two short trips in this season."

"Two? How's that gonna happen?"

23

"I don't know. I'm just sayin' it."

Zeke had just taken a rag from Buster, wiped his hands of black axle grease, and re-seated his hat down on his forehead when she walked by. Not alone. There were two other girls and an older lady. He tipped his hat, said "Ladies" like he'd done a thousand times before. Buster tipped his hat and Zeke stepped back to give the women room and she looked right at him. It was just a glance, the mere turn of her head, a smile through perfect teeth. She had dark piercing eyes, sandy-blonde hair, and two braids hanging off her shoulders.

At that moment there hadn't been a "girl" thought in his head; he'd practically gotten over yesterday. Zeke glanced at her receding figure, the grease rag in his hand, thinking about hot springs that flowed right out of the ground, hot water that didn't need to be put to a fire, and noting the way her dress moved as she walked. He didn't suppose he'd ever watched anything like that before. Not ever.

His uncle said something to him, twice. Zeke didn't hear him. He was spellbound. Her dress had a rhythm to it that singularly caught and held his eye, holding his rapt attention way too long.

"Are ya listenin' or watchin' a girl?" his uncle said.

Zeke turned to his uncle's voice. "What?" he said. Buster and his uncle stood grinning at him.

Buster said, "You ain't gots anything important to say, Eli. Least not to this boy."

"I see that," Eli replied.

Zeke's face reddened. The two men laughed. Zeke wanted to crawl under a rock. He would have except there wasn't a rock large enough nearby.

That was the second time, same girl. Up until then girls simply hadn't mattered: certainly not to him. After that, he wasn't sure. Skirts and a pretty face certainly came to mind more frequently.

24

CHAPTER 8

Spring 1854
Immigrant trail
Independence, Missouri to South Pass, Nebraska Territory

The green grass of spring fades first, increasing in the dog days of late July when it turns from green to yellow, yellow to brown. The color change occurs more quickly in the land away from the coolness of the Missouri river bottom and the blood sucking swarms of mosquitoes and deer flies. It was especially evident looking west beyond the river toward the distant rolling hills that had harbored the Teton Lakota for ten thousand years. Out there it became one color, a vast ocean of light brown moving in the ceaseless wind: brown waves as far as you could see in any direction.

On the bench country, westward beyond the river, the prairie grass grew thick. As of yet the vast herds of buffalo hadn't tromped it down in giant swaths miles wide nor had the fearsome prairie fires turned the country to gray-black ash. Away from the river the buffalo grass grew tall, reaching above the hanging stirrups of a good sized horse standing seventeen hands. The country rose steadily, not all at once but gently, one step at a time, not noticeable at all. In the distance was the promise of mountains so far away they looked like clouds rather than snow-capped peaks, offering a promise, something unspoken, chilly, cold, unforgiving. It was the high country where the Lakota summered.

In the time of spring rains the grass was light green. A mixture of prairie flowers standing in patches and swarms of color grew. Later in the heat of summer the flowers, too, turned brown, their leaves wilting, their seeds dropping: some drifting in the wind, others swallowed by birds and carried away to be replanted. Their brittle stalks became roosts for meadow lark and snow bird. Under this sea of waving vegetation smelling of curing grass, the killdeer and prairie chickens hid their tiny eggs, hiding their young from the hungry eyes of hawk, magpie, crow, skunk, badger and raccoon.

Later in August and toward the end of September the grass would become dangerous, a menace, a tinder box. In those days every living thing held its breath waiting for the grass to burst into flame, knowing that sooner or later fire always came. Sometimes it started under a dark, boiling thunder head. Lightning would streak across formidable black skies, striking a rolling hill, sending sparks flying amongst rock and tree. Moments later, fanned by a gusting wind, there'd be a whiff of smoke. The smoke would hide an ever growing line of orange flame whipped by wind. Soon flames would be eating the dry grass in giant gulps, leaving in its path a black blanket of smoking ash. Before the advancing flames fled deer, elk and buffalo. It consumed everything in its path, the undertaker for all.

If the grass remained from one year to the next, temporarily untouched by flame, the menace increased. Sooner or later it would burst into flame, orange and hot. It was then that the wildfire took life, its very existence creating the windstorm that drove it to the banks of the river. Sometimes the river stopped it. Sometimes not.

CHAPTER 9

April 17, 1854
Immigration Trail Head
Independence, Missouri

"Gather 'round," Eli Tallasinius said in his loud, raspy voice, coughing as though he was clearing his throat. The travelers congregated; he glanced about, studying their faces, not saying a word until the silence grew heavy. He waited until they began to fidget, looking at each other in discomfort.

A gust of wind picked up, rattling the leaves of the cottonwoods, shaking the branches with gusto before it fled. Several men and women standing on the outside drew closer, hoping to hear him over this sudden commotion. Forty-eight adults. More than twice that in youngsters. Zeke sat on the tongue of the Williams' Conestoga wagon that rested at the edge of the gathering. His work was done. He glanced at the iron rimmed wheel, listened to the canvas rattle about the wooden hoops and waited in the shade of the black walnut tree.

He'd heard his Uncle Eli's speech before. For the people who hadn't it would become a highlight, a beginning, words remembered far beyond this day and quoted ad nauseam. There was expectancy in the air. He could feel it as the emigrants stood, listening: see it in the women, their arms folded, no longer paying attention to their offspring running in and out of the gathering. There were quiet hushes, stern looks, but most of the attention was on Eli. Some of the younger children waited quietly but the others had too much energy and were unable to hold their small bodies still.

"Tomorrow we start," Eli began. "This ain't gonna be no picnic. Y'all have hired me ta take ya ta the Thermo country in what's the middle of Nebraska Territory. Up there in the tail-end of the Big Horn Mountains. I'm gonna tell ya what ya kin expect. Fact is we're gonna be travelin' 'cross some mighty rough country ta get where y'all want ta go. It ain't gonna be easy. I really can't say that enough."

Someone coughed, then cleared his throat.

There was a movement beside him. Zeke looked up and discovered that the girl he'd been thinking about was standing beside him. Two girls stood beside her. She smiled at him through perfect, white teeth, her hair tied neatly behind her ears.

Damn, he thought.

"Ma'am," he said, immediately thinking how inane that sounded. An anxious Zeke stood up and was surprised to discover she was shorter than he. He wondered if four inches would make any difference.

Difference in what? It was really weird.

His uncle was speaking. He turned his attention to him.

"Tomorrow mornin' come 4:30 a.m. ya'll hear the bugle blow. When ya hear it, get up and get yourselves movin'. You men will catch up your oxen, mules, horses: what have ya. You ladies will be buildin' fires, cookin' breakfast, gettin' folks ta eatin' soon as you're able. Mostly that will be coffee, bacon, side pork and hard tack. Ain't much time fer nothin' else lessin' ya make it the night before. We'll try an get ya'll some fresh meat where it's available. Don't go dependin' on it. Fer the first three or four hundred miles, ten miles on either side of the trail will be pretty much hunted out by those folks in front of us."

The girl leaned over and whispered, "You heard this before?"

He smiled.

"Yes," he answered. "A number of times. Uncle Eli gets better as he gets goin'."

Eli continued speaking.

"We'll start movin' a little before six. In spite of y'all unloadin' what ain't absolutely necessary, your wagons are ridin' heavy. Y'all need ta be walkin' wherever possible ta save your oxen, mules, and horses."

"Walking?" she said aloud. "Did he say walking?"

Zeke was thinking about the soapy way she smelled, her profile as she stared at his uncle, how she stood beside him, listening.

"Mostly," Zeke said acutely aware of the few inches that separated him from her.

This afternoon Eli spoke clearly. "Each day we'll be stoppin' around noon. Soon as we stop, see ta your stock. Give 'em a bait of oats if'n ya'all have oats. Water 'em. Let 'em graze. Anythin' ya kin do fer your animals will be a benefit in the end. They'll get ya there. Y'all find there ain't much difference in breakfast and dinner except if you're lucky, maybe ya'll have some beans. After we've gone ten or fifteen mile we'll hole up, circle the wagons. I can't say this enough.

Look ta your stock. Durin' the night we'll keep 'em inside the wagon circle. Keep 'em from runnin' off; keep 'em from gettin' themselves stolen. Now I can't stress how important their health is. Without 'em you ain't goin' nowhere.

"Fer the men, we'll need lookouts: men ta stand watch. We'll be needin' five or six, on all sides of the wagons, every night. Ya go ta sleep on your watch, I'll beat the hell right out of ya. Stunts like that will get us all kilt. We just can't have it. Everyones' lives depend on ya doin' your job." Eli paused. "Take care of yourselves. Ain't no one waitin' on ya. Durin' the day we need ta be movin'. Supper will be what ya ate fer breakfast and dinner, maybe a little fresh meat. Now ya gots ta be lookin', watchin' all the time. We can't have ya steppin' on no snake. Them bastards can kill ya dead. Stay awake. Folks die out here all the time even when they're careful. Make sure it ain't ya."

Zeke felt her eyes on him.

"Does he mean that? I mean, really," she asked. "Is it so . . . I mean is it that dangerous?"

"Yes, Uncle Eli means it. He never says what he don't mean. Folks get killed even when everyone is doin' what they're supposed to." Zeke paused, thinking about her question. "So, yes, I guess it is dangerous."

Eli looked out on the crowd. "Now, people, I don't mean ta scare the hell outta ya. I really don't, but as I say, this ain't gonna be no picnic. Most of ya are gonna wear out ten pair of shoes gettin' ta where ya are goin'. So take care of what ya got. Some sorry man with nothin' ta do figured that two in every twenty emigrants die on this trip. Accident, mostly. Believe it or not fallin' under a wagon an' gettin' runned over kills a lot of folks. Add ta that gettin' runned over gettin' kicked, stepped on, gettin' snake bit, drowned, struck by lightnin', dragged by some sorry horse, kilt by Injuns. Any way ya kin find ta die, that'll be happenin'. So be careful if ya can."

He paused again, letting his words sink in. "Don't go wanderin' off alone. This country ain't forgivin' and it sure as hell don't give no second chances. Make sure someone knows where ya are all the time. Take someone with you ta watch while you take care of things."

"Oh, my," the girl said. "Is he serious? He's just trying to scare us, isn't he? I mean take someone with us all the time? Sometimes I need to be alone."

Zeke stared at her because he liked looking at her. "No. No, he

29

ain't tryin' to scare no one but he's serious. He's just tryin' to avoid what's gonna happen anyway. Last time out, some poor kid, maybe nine years old, fell under a wagon; it rolled over his head before anybody could get to him. We buried him right there in the middle of the road so the wolves wouldn't dig up his body and eat him. Uncle Eli ain't tryin' to scare no one. Folks get sick. Things happen. He figures if everyone is careful it might not happen so often."

All three girls were staring at him, their mouths open, their eyes large.

Eli's voice caught their attention. "To those of ya likin' the finer things like a bath there most likely ain't gonna be no bathin' 'cause there ain't gonna be no water. Not enough anyway. Besides there ain't no privacy fer you ladies and you're gonna end up wearin' the same clothes 'til they practically fall off. ta get where ya want ta go is gonna take the better part of five months. Y'all paid me. Right now, I frankly don't give a damn whether yal turn back or not. That's up ta ya. Ya got 'til four in the mornin' ta be decidin'. Fer some of ya it might be a good idea 'cause ya ain't gonna make it. I ain't sugar coatin' none of it. It's just the way it is and ya ought ta know it up front before we turn a wheel or hitch a team.

Eli paused, looked around, then continued. "If ya'all gots any questions, I'll try ta answer what ya got. If not, I'd suggest ya get ready. Four-thirty comes early even when you're expectin' it."

For a moment it was silent. "You aren't going to frighten any of us, Mr. Tallasinius. We're all going. That's why we're here." The voice was from Harry O'Reilly. He had organized the group and was one of the committee of five men who, with the help of Eli Tallasinius, had drawn up articles for the trail: a set of rules to live by, to govern the journey. He continued. "We'll all get where we are going. God'll provide like he always does."

"I didn't figure you'd be quittin', Harry. I reckon ya don't even know how ta spell it. You folks didn't get yourselves ta Independence 'cause ya was scared." Eli paused. "But ya need ta be scared. Fear'll give ya an edge. It'll make ya more careful. I've done told ya the way it is so you know this ain't gonna be no pony ride in no park." Eli Tallasinius hesitated. "I don't know God much. All the providin' and survivin' will be done by you folks. I know that. Of that I'm certain. Y'all get where you're goin' cause ya fought, clawed, refused ta give up, buried your dead and kept goin'. That is the way it is." He paused, waited, then said, "Any of ya gots any questions? I'll answer them."

There were none.

"Good. Make your preparations as ya see fit. Tomorrow comes early. Get some sleep while ya can."

The somber crowd began to break up, subdued, women whispering to their men, looking after their children, returning to their wagons and livestock to wait for the bugle to sound at 4:30 in the morning.

"Did you see that boy fall under the wheel? The one you talked about?" The younger girl's voice was soft. She looked a lot like the girl standing next to him, only not as tall.

"No, Ma'am. I did help bury him. That family had a lot of hard luck. The lady--she died of the cholera. 'Another women suckled her baby. Time they got to the Oregon Territory all that was left of 'em was her husband and two kids."

"Did a lot of people die along the way?" she asked.

"No. Most everyone made it." Zeke smiled.

"Just not all?" she said.

"That's right. Not all. I ain't been on one of these trips that someone ain't died. Someone always does that."

"What about Indians?"

"I ain't seen it but I've heard of 'em attackin' settlers, killin' folks, takin' their hair."

"But you have seen Indians? I mean up close?"

"Yes, ma'am. Where we're goin' it's their country. It's where they live. It's hard not to see 'em especially if they want you to see 'em. I've heard some of the stories. You know, Injuns killin' folks, but I ain't seen it. And I ain't seen nobody kill no Injun."

The youngest girl stared at him before asking, "You're not that old. How long have you been doing this?"

Zeke thought a moment. "Well, since Uncle Eli picked me up from the priest 'til now. So that'd be eight . . . ten years."

"That's comforting. I mean you know what you're doing." She glanced at the diminishing crowd. "If I had my way," the older girl said, "I'd have stayed home. I wouldn't be here. I don't need any western adventure. But my folks got religion and Horace Greeley, so here we are. My brother refused. He told Papa no."

"Horace Greeley? Who's that?"

"You know that man who said, 'Go west young man and grow

31

up with the country.' He's a newspaper man. Haven't you heard of him? He lives in New York, I think."

"Oh," he said, shaking his head. "I ain't heard of him." Zeke didn't care who Horace Greeley happened to be but thought he was glad the girl standing next to him hadn't stayed home.

A voice behind him called, "Beth."

Zeke turned to see who was speaking.

The shorter of the girls also turned to the voice.

"Beth, Beth, come. We have things to do."

The older girl looked at the woman. "Oh, mother," she said pausing, looking from her mother to Zeke. "Excuse me," she said to Zeke. "Mother, mother, this is . . . what's your name?" she asked.

"Zeke, Ma'am. I'm Zeke."

"Mother, this is Zeke." She turned back to him. "My name's Lexie. This is my sister, Beth and our friend, Priscilla."

The older woman looked at him appraisingly.

"Ma'am," he said again.

"Zeke, this is my mother, Mrs. Clara Wakeford."

Mrs. Wakeford said, "Pleased to meet you," her mind someplace else. She looked at the two girls and Priscilla, then said, "Both of you, we have things to be doing before we take our leave." She then turned her attention to Zeke. "It's nice to meet you, young man. Zeke? That's a strange name. I don't recall seeing you. Will you be traveling with us? Where's your mother? Which wagon is yours?"

"My mother's dead, ma'am."

"Oh, I'm so sorry."

"That's all right, ma'am. It was a long time ago. I was a baby when all that happened."

"Mother," Alexandra said, "Mother, he's with Mr. Tallasinius. That's his uncle."

"Oh," the woman said. She looked from Zeke to Alexandra, then to Beth. "You two find your father," she said. "He's looking for you. He has things for you to do."

Alexandra smiled at Zeke. "Goodbye," she said to him and walked away, taking the fresh soap smell, her younger sister, and Priscilla with her.

CHAPTER 10

April 18, 1854
Immigration Trail Head
Independence, Missouri

The shrill notes of the bugle broke across the early morning. Stars still dusted the sky. Everyone was awake and waiting prior to the bugle's sounding. The teams were hitched well before the horn sounded. Breakfast had been prepared: eggs fried, stacks of flapjacks darkened brown in the pan, and sidepork dished onto waiting plates. Minutes after the sound of the horn died, the Tallasinius company rolled out of Independence, Missouri in a single column.

For three consecutive weeks, excluding Sundays, they averaged fifteen miles a day. Wilcox was two days ahead. Johnson two days behind. Nothing happened on Sunday.

The order of travel changed when the column reached higher, dryer country and dust became a problem. As it was the first wagon picked up dust, the second more, until the fellow riding the oak seat in the last wagon could hardly be seen by the first. So in the hard dry dust country Eli Tallasinius doubled up the columns, shortening them so the last wagon wouldn't suffer nearly as much. Sometimes, depending on the direction the wind was blowing, he staggered the shortened columns in an effort to further eliminate the problem. Invariably, he kept the wagons together, the slower wagons in front setting the pace. It was safer. No stragglers could be picked off if there weren't any stragglers. Repairs, when needed, were made immediately. Each evening equipment was checked and rechecked. Repairs, if needed, wre made before they were reuired.

Commencing the first day, Eli sent his nephew ahead of the column of wagons. It was his job to keep him informed and bring him current information. Eli was especially interested in how much distance Wilcox Company made each day, whether Johnson company was catching up to them, the condition of the watering holes, and where trouble was hiding. If he could, where available, Zeke brought back fresh meat for Eli to share with those who didn't have any. Other men also hunted as the wagons moved west toward the North Platte river.

Fresh meat invariably became a rarity. The game, spooked and running, hid at the least provocation, having been hunted by Wilcox and whoever was in front of that company.

It was Zeke's plan to return to the wagon column at noon whenever he could for another mount and to advise his uncle. A fresh horse was a necessity. Things happened. Zeke never knew when he might need a horse with depth, the physical ability to carry him out of trouble. Each morning, early, he scouted ahead. In the late afternoon he hunted for game, the columns west of him. Between afternoon and evening, he rode both flanks, keeping out of sight, never introducing himself to trouble. Uncle Eli didn't believe in borrowing what wasn't there. As a practical matter it meant avoiding skylining himself, watching for riders, clouds of dust, thunder heads, taking note of the life patterns of antelope, buffalo, deer, studying them to see what they were avoiding, then discovering why. His Uncle Eli considered wild animals to be smarter than most men. "Make a note of that," he told his nephew. So Zeke did.

CHAPTER 11

Late April 1854
North Platte River
Immigrant Trail

Prior to meeting Alexandra, Zeke had never thought about a particular girl or girls in general. His life was simple. There was no need, no interest, no point. Many things occupied his thoughts. Not a girl. He had better things to do. After meeting her, life wasn't nearly so simple. Without any effort on his part, she came softly into his thoughts like shadows in the evening. He'd be turning over an idea, examining it, considering its ramifications and there she'd be, smiling at him. In retrospect it was surprising that with that girl banging around in his head he managed to get anything done. But he did. There was plenty to do, even with thoughts of her seeping steadily into the borders of his consciousness. Without meaning to be, that girl was trouble.

Even away from the rolling wagons where the edges of the ceaseless prairie met the blue cloudless sky, Zeke found her. He'd belly himself up to the edge of a ridge line, not wanting to skyline himself but needing to see what was there. He'd use his uncle's glass and search the country inch by inch. There she'd be, wafting into his thoughts with the smell of soap in her hair, a smile on her lips, mischief hidden in her eyes.

"Have a slice of fresh bread" she'd say or "Did you see that sunrise this morning? Oh my gosh!" He'd mentally thank her, looking into her incredible light brown eyes. Invariably he'd study the country again to see if he'd missed anything, remembering to cover up the front optics to prevent a glare that might give away his position. So far he hadn't missed anything but it bothered him how easily she interrupted his concentration and increased that possibility.

Sometimes in the afternoon, he'd be sighting down the barrel of his uncle's Sharp carbine at an antelope or a black tail deer. He'd fix his gaze on that spot just behind the front leg where the heart was hidden, then he'd see her walking toward him, her skirt moving gracefully. He'd have to take a breath and reaffix his attention before squeezing the trigger, killing it. So far he hadn't missed. His Uncle Eli's unspoken, unwritten rule was: one cartridge, one kill. That he'd been successful was a minor miracle, for there she'd be walking toward him in that blue dress her mother had made, bringing her smile, the smell of soap, and a warm greeting.

Early on, his dilemma did not go unnoticed. He had returned with fresh meat which his uncle immediately passed out to, among others, the Snyders. Sometime afterwards, Mrs. Snyder came to his wagon to thank him and his uncle. He and Bill Brothers, the teamster his uncle had hired, were fixing a late supper, sopping up grease from the skillet with crusts of bread, commenting that "there was nothin' like that." Both were happy to eat. Both were tired and hungry, not wanting to wait if waiting could be avoided.

Mrs. Snyder sat down in his uncle's chair with its worn slats and said to him, "I see you've taken a shine to that Lexie Wakeford. She's a cutie." She smiled at him knowingly. "You could certainly do worse, young man. A lot worse."

Zeke wondered what she meant. After she left Bill had looked at him from across the small fire, the coffee pot boiling noisily. He smiled and handed him a well-done, blackened leg of prairie chicken.

"Here," he said.

Zeke took it.

"Careful," Bill advised. "You'll be married to that sweet young thing before you know it, gettin' all settled down with a house full of kids and a plow to push."

It sounded like good advice but Zeke didn't listen, for all he could think of was Lexie. It was the small things that attracted him: the way she walked, how she said his name, the way her fingers brushed his as they stood together chatting, the smell of her. He'd never considered these things before. It was irritating. Sometimes when alone, the thought of her overwhelmed his mind. Inevitably, he wondered what it would be like to wake up each morning next to a beautiful woman, a woman like Lexie.

In those evenings when the clouds of the western sky burned deep red and orange, she taught him to dance to the tune of a fiddler playing *I Dream of Jeannie With The Light Brown Hair* written by a fellow named Stephen Foster. She knew things like that. Zeke had never heard of him. After the fiddler put away his bow, they'd sit on the tongue of her father's wagon and talk. He learned that her sister Beth's

36

real name was Bethany, that she was fourteen. He learned that Lexie's friend's name wasn't really Pris, but Priscilla. She was seventeen. Lexie was eighteen, his age. Hopefully, his age; he wanted to be older than her.

She turned his head by merely breathing, by wearing her blue dress, by walking toward him or away from him, by smiling.

"What is it you want?" she once asked him.

"Want? What do you mean? I didn't know I needed anythin'."

Taking her time, Alexandra looked at Zeke, then eastward where they'd been, then west in the direction they were going. She continued.

"I mean . . . you know what I mean. There isn't anything here. I mean, really. Just grass and emptiness. It's so lonely. Who could even live here? Who would want to?"

Zeke looked at the girl, watched her chapped lips moving, speaking to him with the earnestness of her soul. *She don't see it,* he thought. *There's so much. Today I saw a group of men ridin' their horses bareback, movin' southwest. I saw them. They didn't see me. They live here. Raise their families here. Hunt and die here.* He wondered how those men would feel in St. Louis, standing on a street corner watching white men walk in and out of stores. *Nothin' here, they'd probably say. Wouldn't want to stay. They'd say, Who could live here? Who would want ta?*

"Not much here? I guess you don't like it. Is that what you're sayin'?"

"Have you ever been to Boston, Zeke? I mean in the Spring or maybe the Summer? It's so pleasant."

"No, I ain't. I've been to St. Louis and Independence. Mostly in the Spring. I've been to Sacramento and Sutter's Mill. And a place called Frisco. I've seen the Pacific Ocean. It's pretty big."

"What are they like? Those places?"

"One horse towns. Folks that live there like it. I don't suppose you'd write home to mother about bein' there. They're just places. Not all that excitin', I guess. Personally, I can't figure what people do there. Nothin' I guess. Except live. They live and get by best they can. That's what they do."

She smiled, nodding her head, and said, "Boston's really something. I think you'd like it. It's progressive, you know. It has a medical school especially for women called Boston Female Medical School. Beth wants to go there. Me, too. I'd like to if I could. No more, though. I'm here." She paused, shaking her head, then looked at Zeke. "Boston has places like the Hay Market. The Revolutionary War started there. It has Bunker Hill. And Harvard School is across the river. Lots of famous people lived there. You know, like Paul Revere and Sam Adams and his cousin John who was President.

There are a lot of Catholic-Irish people coming in now. Some folks say that isn't good. Boston has great places to eat. There is a place called Hovey and Company where you can buy any kind of seed you can possibly imagine. And at J. B. Parker and Company you can buy anything from cigars to those coffee beans for that black coffee you like. That's where it comes from, you know. It's some place, I tell you."

"Why did you leave?"

"I didn't want to. My brother didn't, either. He told Papa he was crazy. That caused a big row. I guess maybe Papa read too much James Fenimore Cooper and got too much God. If you can get too much God."

"Who's that?"

"Cooper? He wrote books, you know. *Last of the Mohicans*, and *Leatherstocking*. Books like that. Haven't you heard of him? Have you ever read those books?"

"No. I ain't. I ain't heard of him."

"His books are about adventure on the western frontier. He's dead, you know."

"I didn't know."

"There are lots of things out there in the world to see and experience. So much."

"Not here?"

"There just isn't anything here, Zeke. For Pete's sake, look. It's just grass and nothing as far as you can see. It's a desert. The great American desert." She paused, staring south. "Who'd live here? You know what I mean? There's so much more. You have to want it or you'll never get it."

"It's not like I'm stuck here, Lexie."

"I'm not saying that. It's just there's nothing here. Nothing at all. I think that people who live here are stuck here. There's so much more. If you know what you're missing. If you want it more. Know what I mean?"

Zeke nodded his head following her gaze across the rolling

prairie.

Nothin' here? If she only knew. There's so much. I could tell her.

No. That ain't such a good idea. She's made up her mind. I don't think there's any changin' it. Too bad.

Too bad? Why? Why's it too bad?

She'll never be happy out here . . . will always want to be goin' back to some place with buildings, nice dresses, people walkin' up and down the street. Where you can buy coffee beans and read Last of the Mohicans. That ain't out here.

No, it surely ain't. I'd better keep my mouth shut. I'd better or she'll stop talkin' to me. That ain't good.

"You're so quiet. What are you thinking?"

"You can never catch a butterfly."

"What?"

"Nothin'," he said, smiling. But he didn't feel like smiling. Somehow he was losing. He wondered what. Lexie? He hoped not. But she turned his heart inside out and left him empty. It was as if he'd drunk too much ice cold water and wanted more, more, more. None of it made sense.

CHAPTER 12

July, 1854
North Platte River
Immigrant Trail

"Where do you go?" she asked once.

"Sorry?"

Alexandra was sitting so close, her skirts almost touching his trousers; it was difficult for him to think. He liked not thinking. He liked being close, her fingers playing with a strand of her hair.

She looked at Zeke to see if he was listening.

"When you leave in the mornings, where do you go? You leave so early. Today you left before sun up, before everyone was awake. I looked for you but you were gone. I could tell because your horse was no longer picketed with the others. Your uncle was standing out there beyond the wagons studying something. I don't know what. Sometimes he just stands out there."

Zeke smiled. He glanced westward, past a low-lying ridge, through a break in a solitary grove of trees. Clouds hung low and dark, threatening rain. His was an unconscious reaction to the question for he always rode west in the mornings. Pointing with his left hand, he said, "I go out there. I look around."

"Look around? Why every day? You've been out there before. What do you want to see that you haven't already seen?"

"Not me. Uncle Eli. He wants to know what's goin' on. So I take a gander. Things always change. Nothin's ever the same. It might look the same but it ain't."

"But doesn't he know? I mean he's the wagon master. He's supposed to know what's out there. You'd think he did. I certainly hope so."

"Uncle Eli knows. He knows what was there the last time we was here. He's been here enough," Zeke said. "But everythin' changes. Did you hear that thunder?" He looked at her.

She nodded.

"Maybe it will drop rain, maybe it won't. If it does, it could wash out the trail. Turn the road to mud. Maybe if we know about it,

40

we can go around. Avoid it. My uncle don't always know what will happen next. Nobody does. So I have a look. This country can change, hour to hour, every day. Folks live out there. Sometimes they're friendly. Sometimes they ain't." Zeke looked at her. "Is Lexie your real name?" he asked. "Is it a nickname? Like mine?"

"Lexie," she replied, "is short for Alexandra. My mother likes Greek goddesses, maybe it's Egyptian—she just liked it."

"Alexandra. That's pretty." He paused, then continued. "I . . . like I said everythin' changes, all the time. Water holes dry up. Creeks get flooded. Roads wash out. There's gully washers. There's fire. Sometimes we need to hole up for a day and rest. I give him an idea of how far we can travel. Our safety depends on those things. Hopefully there ain't no trouble we can't handle."

Alexandra looked at him. "You're alone! If something happens to you, what will you do?"

"I never think about it. What could happen?"

"Your horse could break a leg. What would you do?"

"I'd shoot him. Pull my saddle and start walkin'. Alone ain't bad. I don't feel alone. Don't feel afraid or nothin'. Somebody has to do it. Uncle Eli sends me 'cause I know what to look for."

"I'd be afraid. I mean to be really alone."

"It's not that bad. Just grass and more grass. Up higher there's trees and more trees. Hills and more hills."

"Sounds dangerous."

"Not really."

"It could be." She studied him. "You're just being brave. Trying to impress me."

"I ain't never tried to impress no one."

"You go out there alone. That's impressive. I'm impressed. My mother's impressed. So's my father. They don't think you should be out there. Not alone. Your uncle thinks we should take someone with us when we go out just a little ways from the wagons. He doesn't think we should be alone ever, but you're alone all the time."

"Well, thanks, I guess. I mean for bein' impressed. I didn't know you needed impressin'. I didn't know I was alone. I have my uncle. He'll always find me."

"Zeke, I don't need to be impressed. But I am. My mom thinks you are too young."

"Too young for what?"

41

"You know. To be out there alone without anybody."

Zeke took a while to reply. He was thinking about being young.

"I know you said your mom died," Alexandra said. "It's none of my business. I don't mean to be nosy, but what happened?"

"My grandfather said she was snake bit, timber rattler. Didn't make it."

Alexandra's hand went to her mouth. "Oh, I'm sorry, Zeke. I didn't mean . . ."

"That's all right. I hardly remember her. It was a long time ago."

"Your dad? What about him?"

"Never met him." Zeke smiled. "You are sort of nosy, ain't you?"

"I'm sorry. Really it is none of my business. I just wanted to talk, I guess. Most people have parents. I thought it was safe."

"It's all right. You are safe." He wanted to say "with me," but he didn't.

Alexandra thought for a moment, changing the subject. "You always bring back meat in the evening."

"I try."

"You must be an excellent hunter."

"I get by."

"My, my, how modest we are."

"I do get by."

"I know, but you don't have to say it. You're supposed to say, 'Thanks for the compliment.'"

"Oh. I am? What I said is really true. I get by. I just do the best I can. I don't brag or nothin'."

"I'm teasing you. Haven't you ever been teased before?"

"I don't think so. I guess not. I don't remember bein' teased. Except by my uncle--twice."

"Whatever did he tease you about?"

"Girls."

"Girls?"

"He said he caught some girls lookin' me over."

"Oh, really?"

"He teased me for lookin' at you."

Alexandra's hand went to her mouth. "Oh my goodness!" she

42

exclaimed. "You don't keep secrets, do you?"

"Should I? I mean, keep secrets?"

"Were you looking at me?"

"I was."

She paused. "What did you think?"

"You was very pretty. You was walkin' away from me with your mom, with Beth and Pris. I liked the way you moved with your dress."

"Oh my goodness!" she said.

"No. No, you're supposed to say, 'Thanks for the compliment.'"

Alexandra hit him on the arm. "You're teasing."

"I am," he said. "You're right about one thing. Things can happen. Things do happen. Things you can't possibly prepare for. Off the wall things." Zeke paused, looking at her for the hundredth time. "It's then I remember Uncle Eli's rules."

"Rules?"

Zeke smiled. "They are simple: First, slow down; Second, never quit." Zeke stopped speaking, hesitating a moment before continuing. "I guess they really ain't rules. You know what I mean? But if you quit, you're dead. It's over when you quit. So never quit. Never stop. Sounds sorta sappy. Maybe it is. But when I was younger, scoutin' for Uncle Eli the first time," he glanced beyond Alexandra, "it was actually right here." Zeke smiled, staring at the horizon again before looking back at her. "He said no matter what happens, never quit. He said, 'I will always come for you. Some things you can count on. Family you can count on.' That's what he said. I will always come for you.

"I didn't always listen. Came a time I thought I could take care of myself and that my uncle ought to mind his own business and let me. That changed in short order. More than once he showed me how not to skyline myself, how to keep off the horizon. He told me it was real important because skylinin' myself would attract attention I didn't want." Zeke smiled. "I pretty much ignored him, went where I wanted. He reminded me several times. I nodded my head fixin' to ignore him. Then I skylined myself once too often, just to show him I could take care of myself.

"Afterwards I found some boys waitin' for me--fixin' to take my horse and everythin' I carried. They knew and I knew they was

43

gonna kill me. So I ran, found a place where they couldn't get behind me. I was fixin' to shoot it out with 'em. They killed my horse but I made 'em pay a heavy price. I killed two of 'em, stole one of their horses, got plumb away. I was lucky. Maybe they just let me go. Afterwards, I remembered about not skylinin'. So when Uncle Eli says not to worry, 'I'm comin' for ya,' I count on it. I remember."

"You killed someone? I mean dead? That's a sin, you know. 'Thou shalt not kill.'"

"They was tryin' to kill me, Lexie. Not like I had a lot of choice."

"Did you feel bad?"

"No. No more than killin' a snake or a deer. It needed to be done. They needed killin'."

Alexandra stared at Zeke for what seemed to him the longest time.

"Zeke," she whispered, "if I'm lost will you come for me? Always?"

Zeke responded without hesitation. "Always, Lexie. Always."

She hugged him, standing on the lee side of her father's second wagon, the horses no longer hitched, the canvas flapping softly in the breeze, her mother a hundred yards away collecting buffalo chips for the evening fire. There they were: out of sight, out of mind, alone with time standing still, surrounded by the vast prairie extending forever in all directions.

"I know you will," she said softly.

Then she was gone, walking away, her right hand brushing something from her eyes.

It was a moment he remembered. It was a conversation he never forgot.

CHAPTER 13

August 13, 1854
Sweetwater River
Central Nebraska Territory

Each day took the Tallasinius Company farther from Independence and the slow-moving waters of the Missouri. In the ensuing weeks they traveled west along the south side of the North Platte: crossing the river at Fort Laramie, then moving west by northwest into central Nebraska Territory. They headed west toward the Continental Divide, South Pass, and the Sweetwater River. It was the Mormon Trail, the Oregon Trail, and the California Trail all rolled together. At the Sweetwater they rested three days, letting the Johnson Company pass them.

It was the deciding point for the Tallasinius Company: deciding whether to venture forward with their original plan, separating themselves from the steady trek west, turning north to the place of bubbling hot springs and sulphur mud baths. This thermal wonder was located at the north end of Wind River Canyon along the banks of the Big Horn River.

The trip west was fraught with danger. One in ten died, buried where they gave up the ghost, their bodies tucked away in the middle of the trail between the wagon tracks. It was a trail of tears for those left behind. Where possible the dead were buried deep, preventing coyotes and wolves from digging up the bodies and carrying away the bones. Each passing wheel packed the earth. The unmarked graves were lost permanently and forever. Thousands of travelers passed over them without knowing that the grass covers all, including the dead.

CHAPTER 14

August 16, 1854
Sweetwater River
Central Nebraska Territory

It was evening, the fiery red sun sinking into the Wind River range.

"It's decision time." Eli Tallasinius spoke to a man named Billings who was sitting across his fire with Harry O'Reilly, O'Reilly's dog beside him, his tail thumping the sod like it was a drum. "It's time ta decide if this is still what ya want ta do. If ya are of the same mind, I'll take ya right where ya want ta go. Understand this. The U.S. government has a treaty with the Injuns. Had it since '51. You're goin' on their land. It's theirs. All of it. If the soldiers find out, they're supposed ta remove ya: forcibly, if necessary.

"Ya gotta remember they ain't here ta protect ya. That ain't their job. Not on Injun land. Ya got that and the fact that the Injuns are lookin' fer some excuse ta kill the lot of ya. There's enough of 'em. They get all notional and you're dead. Ya could keep goin' and end up in California or Oregon. Good land there fer the askin' or as I said ya kin go ta the Thermo. Been there myself long ago. It ain't fer the askin'. Not then. Not now. Right now it belongs ta someone else and they ain't treatin' no white man kindly. I'll take ya there if that's what ya want. We'll leave on the morrow one way or the other. Goin' north there won't be no one in front of us and no one behind us. We'll be alone. North, it's just ya."

"You're trying to frighten us," Billings said. "Harry here said you would."

"Not really," Eli drawled. "I'm givin' ya facts. I figure ya have ta live or die with 'em. Your decision. I'm givin' ya that say so. That's all."

Billings glanced at Harry O'Reilly. "Thoughts?" he asked.

O'Reilly patted his dog on the head. "You know what I think, Billings." The dog growled. O'Reilly glanced at him. "What?" he asked. "You got something to say? Say it." O'Reilly laughed; the dog thumped his tail.

"I say we go like we planned. The Army won't be bothering us."

Eli Tallasinius cut a piece of chewing tobacco from a lump he carried in the left pocket of his shirt and worked it inside his mouth, between his cheek and gum. "Suit yourself," he said. "It ain't gonna make me no never mind. Y'all done paid me."

August 17, 1854

On August 17, 1854, the Tallasinius Company left the Emigrant Trail and headed north. They'd rested the livestock for three days on the Sweetwater River.

South and a little east about one hundred-ninety-six miles on the North Platte, a Mormon cow wandered into Conquering Bear's encampment. High Forehead, a visiting Miniconjou warrior, shot the cow dead. His friends ate it. It was a good joke. The old cow tasted . . . well, old. It had walked from Nauvoo, Illinois and was tough, sore footed, and worn out. Even on a good day, with plenty of rest, it never would have made it to Emigrant Canyon and the Great Salt Lake Valley. Now, it was dead, reduced to a stack of drying bones soon hauled off to be chewed on by camp dogs.

August 19, 1854.

Two days later, on August 19, for a short distance of six miles, the Tallasinius Company followed the Sweetwater, then started north across the mountains, passing through a series of red bluffs and high ridges covered in pine timber with splotches of aspen groves. The going was slow for there were no roads and no trails; other than John Colter, no one had gone before them. They were the first travelers. Zeke was no longer concerned with who was in front and who was behind the Tallasinius Company. No one was.

On the same day on the North Platte, six miles east of Fort Laramie, Lieutenant John Grattan had just turned to his troops, thinking about his wagon gun and how to better bring it to bear on a peaceful village. He watched the old man, Conquering Bear walking slowly away from the "negotiations" and Grattan's "righteous" demand to arrest High Forehead. His demand did not take into account that Conquering Bear did not have the authority, let alone the

47

inclination, to allow the arrest of a visitor to his camp. It simply wasn't done.

A nervous trooper standing in the settling dust wearing a wool tunic and suffering the heat of the day was holding his breath, sweat running down his forehead. Unfortunately, he was sighting down his government issue rifle barrel and he shot the harmless old man in the back. Eight minutes later Lieutenant Gratton was dead as were twenty-nine of his troops and the drunk interpreter. A young warrior chief just coming into his own named Red Cloud rallied his warriors and killed them all yards from the banks of the North Platte.

An hour later, Lieutenant Hugh Fleming, the officer in charge of the Fort Laramie garrison, sitting at his desk in the heat of the day, was relayed the news. He swore, thumping his desk with a bare fist, and brought the garrison to full alert. A few miles away on the banks of the North Platte four thousand Teton Lakota broke camp. It was no longer a safe place to be. The promised tribute for entering into the treaty several years before would not be forthcoming.

August 22, 1854

On August 22, after sunset, the fifth day following the Mormon cow wandering into the Oglala camp on the North Platte, Zeke took his uncle aside. They were sixteen miles north of the Sweetwater River.

"Uncle Eli," he said, "somethin' ain't right. Someone is out there. I'm guessin' we're bein' followed. If not followed, shadowed. I ain't seen nobody. But I swear they're there."

His uncle was immediately listening. "Why do ya say that? What's your thinkin'?"

Zeke looked at him. "Uncle, it's a feelin'. First, we're bein' watched. I know it. Second, I've been ridin' farther out on both sides. I see tracks. Maybe thirty, forty, fifty head of unshod horses. The number seems to be growin'. The trail disappears and I see where they double back like they're hidin' where they've been. I don't see nothin'. That's puzzlin'."

"Injuns?"

"Horses ain't shod, Uncle. Maybe we ought to double, triple the guard. Maybe everyone oughta be watchin'. I don't like this. There's no good reason for it. Somethin' ain't right."

48

Eli nodded, thinking. Finally he said, "I agree. Thirty or forty head, ya say?"

"Yes. Maybe fifty. They keep growin'. They're travelin' light. Like a war party would. I know it don't make sense but it seems they are sizin' us up. Somethin' else, Uncle Eli. There are two or three shod horses in the bunch. They could be stolen. They're there and they're together. Mostly those tracks are covered up by the others. What's botherin' me is I ain't seein' 'em with my eyes."

"How long ya think?"

"What do you mean?"

"How long since ya first noticed?"

"Ran across tracks again yesterday. Didn't think much about it. Looked like they was headin' away. Goin' north, northwest. Didn't seem like somethin' to worry about. This afternoon I saw 'em again. Came across those shod horses. They was no longer ridin' away from us but parallel, like they was shadowin'. The hair starts standin' up on the back of my neck. I tell you, Uncle Eli, I was bein' watched but I didn't find nobody. No smoke. Found their trail runnin' about five mile out on the west side. It was bein' covered. What I mean is they was ridin' single file across rock onto sod, into a creek, comin' out on an outcroppin' of rock, and off it again. I followed 'em for maybe five mile, stayin' out of sight."

Eli stared at his nephew.

"Uncle, the country flattens out five, six miles ahead. Runs through some pine, then down off the mountain, drier. It's deceptive. On the east and west ten miles from the trail is canyon country. Both sides. Lots of breaks, meadows, timber. Beyond that it flattens out again until it drops off the rim."

"Ambush?"

"Don't seem likely. We're twenty-four wagons. Every man carryin' a rifle. Seems like that would be foolish. But you never know. Crazier things happen."

"Hard ta figure."

"Yeah. Hard to figure."

"All right," his uncle said. "I'll double the guard. Get every man ta pull his rifle, fill the empty chamber, and keep her off safety. I'll make sure their rifles are handy." He smiled at Zeke. "I warned 'em that this could happen. I didn't expect it ta happen this soon. We're less than a hundred mile from where they want ta be. Fifty mile,

49

maybe. Close. We could turn around. I'll tell 'em. I expect we'll keep goin'. They got it in their heads that God wants 'em livin' down there on the river, bathin' in the hot springs. The good life."

"The good life?"

"Ya got it, boy. The good life."

CHAPTER 15
Zeke is 4.5 miles north of Alexandra

August 23, 1854
North of the Sweetwater River
Central Nebraska Territory

It was in the still of a mountain morning, the dew heavy on the drying grass. The sun had not breached the blue mountains in the east, yet the sky was bright with streaks of reds and orange. Teams were standing in their harnesses: the trace chains hooked to double trees, the column minutes away from rolling.

Up front the wagon master gave the sign to move forward, waving his right arm above his head and letting his horse move.

Alexandra Ann Wakeford had just looked down and was bending over to pick up the single rein her father had dropped. Seconds before, he'd seated himself and was in the process of picking up the ribbons wrapped around the hand brake; one slipped through his fingers. He'd looked up admiring the clear blue morning sky. Except for the high streaks of clouds in the east, there was not a cloud from horizon to horizon. It was a small moment in time, the smallest tick on her grandmother's old clock.

Without looking up at him, she'd said, "Papa, Papa, you're all fingers and no thumbs this morning." She hadn't meant anything by it, laughing even as she said it. It was just words, something to fill up the warm morning air with chatter. She reached, her fingers touching the rein. But Ol' Sam, the left lead horse, tossed his head, jerking the rein through the grass and away from her outstretched fingers.

"Me, too," she said, then looked up, smiling. At that instant she saw her father come to his feet, an arrow buried in his chest. His face was a picture of shock and disbelief, and of wonderment. So was hers. He glanced at the protruding shaft as if it amused him, then at her, his hand reaching for the hand brake to steady himself. Slowly he began to topple from the wagon box, his mouth open as if to say "I'm so sorry," or "Oh my God," or "How is this happening?" or "Where did this come from?" She watched his hand miss the brake, grabbing for the arrow buried in his chest instead.

Gravity took over and his body gained downward momentum.

51

Alexandra reached her hand out to stop him but his body rushed past her, striking the ground, rolling over on the prairie sod. The shaft bent and broke under his weight, popping like dried wood. He rolled over, staring up at her, tried to get up, tried to lift his head. But he couldn't. His chest heaved; he coughed. A line of blood formed on his lips. He blinked once, twice, as if wondering why death was taking so long, why it had come to take him so early on such a pleasant morning.

From the wagon seat her mother screamed her father's name. Alexandra glanced at her, pulling her eyes from her father to see her mother starting to climb down from the wagon seat. That didn't happen either for a horseman galloped past on the other side of the wagon. Her mother turned to the movement and caught a lance mid-abdomen. The point pierced her thin, rail-like body, striking her with such force that it ran completely through her, knocking her back into the wagon box. The dark bloodied point emerged out her back.

In the space of eight seconds, the second hand banging away one tick after another, Alexandra had reached for the errant rein, had seen her father killed, and had witnessed her mother slammed into the wagon box driven by a hard thrown spear.

Oh my God! I ought to do something.

It was a thought to which she had no response.

In the emptiness that followed she heard her mother call out her father's name, repeating it over and over again. Then: "My God, Harold! Oh my God, Harold! Harold, I'm dying! Harold?" The last words were a whisper followed by a groan and silence. Alexandra turned to her father, kneeling beside him. She wanted to do something, anything. But didn't know what.

He struggled to speak, grabbing her arm. "I'm so sorry, Lexie. So very sorry. So sorry." Then he, too, was gone. Alexandra unconsciously reached out to him, to hold him back, but like a wisp of smoke he was gone. She stared at his body: his chest still, his eyes frozen, his hands and arms limp.

Numb and bewildered, she collapsed to the sod, holding his hand, wondering what he was sorry about. He'd done nothing. It wasn't as if he'd misplaced an arrow in his chest, or traveled a thousand miles to die, or planned his death to aggravate her.

Behind her Mrs. Miller was screaming. Her husband shouted a warning. A weapon discharged. Alexandra glanced up; three riders loped past her father's wagon. She didn't see the first rider, just a movement caught on the edge of her vison. Then, to the side she saw a man walking toward her, a long bladed knife in hand, dark skinned: an Indian. He advanced, his eyes locked on her. Behind him stood a riderless horse.

His, she thought.

Up front, past the lead wagon, she saw Mr. Tallisinius stepping down from his horse as it reared. Three warriors were running at him. He fired twice, killing two. One tried to club him across the shoulders and neck. Tallasinius raised an arm in defense and shot him. She heard him cursing loudly, trying to shove another aside. He fired his pistol point blank. He turned and was struck across the head, falling to the ground, rolling. Somehow he came to his knees, firing his pistols, one then another, until they were clicking on empty. He dropped them like he would a red-hot poker. From somewhere, like magic, he produced another, laughing as he brought it to bear, firing.

Alexandra's eyes were then fixed on the approaching man, seeing the knife in his hand, the white smears of lightning zigzagging on his high cheek bones and disappearing into his black hair. He was so incredibly fearsome. She could not move. As a result she failed to do anything, mesmerized by his approach. She did not run, back up, scream, pass out, or raise an arm in defense. She waited.

It's my turn, she thought. *Please dear God! Please dear God! It's my turn. Please help me.*

She rose to her feet, her hands at her sides. There was no use.

I'm one dead girl.

Behind her Mr. Miller shouted to his wife. There were screams. Many. A weapon discharged from somewhere. Another. A solo scream punctuated the air and seemed to hold. In that moment, expecting violent death, she noted the muscles rippling in her assailant's forearms. It seemed odd.

He's going to kill me: thrust his knife into my heart, and I'm thinking about muscles?

He was almost upon her.

Don't fight it.

What do you mean don't fight?

Alexandra Ann Wakeford closed her eyes. Her assailant seized her left arm with bruising force. She cried out in alarm; her eyes flashed open and wide. Waiting, she stood holding her breath.

My heart. Stab me in the heart.

She tensed herself, expecting the knife to plunge into her body.

He smelled of sagebrush, curing grass, smoke, and something else, something he'd eaten. She couldn't place it. It surprised her, even amused her that on the brink of death she smelled sagebrush and curing grass on her slayer's clothing.

Now! Kill me! Kill me! Get it over with.

Death didn't come.

Instead he flipped her around, twisting her arm behind her back. At the same time he looped a leather cord around her wrist, a cord she wasn't even aware he possessed. Seizing the other wrist, he bound her arms behind her back, then tripped her into a disheveled heap on the sod, her face slamming into the grass. Slipping a loop around an ankle, he bound her feet together, rolling her to the edge of the wagon wheel like a sack of potatoes freshly gleaned from the garden.

Straining against the leather strings, she lifted her head to see the man test the knots that bound her feet, yanking at the leather strings. They tightened, cutting the flow of blood. They hurt. Confused and perplexed, amazed at her good fortune not to be bleeding, dying, her blood pouring onto the ground from a chest wound, she wondered why she was still alive.

Her assailant glanced about, then took off running toward the Miller's wagon. Alexandra collapsed back onto the grass, forcing herself to breathe.

Now what?

Turning her head, she craned to see her father's body, his unblinking eyes, the bloodied shirt. Above her on the wagon seat she glimpsed a tall Indian, face painted, an eagle's feather stuck in his hair behind his left ear. He returned her glance, then leaped to the ground landing deftly on his feet. She heard a muffled scream. A shout of alarm. Cursing. Someone laughed. Silence. She wondered how anyone could laugh amid this carnage.

The new menace held a wad of hair in his left hand, partially wrapped in his fingers, and a bloodied blade in his right. At first she wondered what it was; then she recognized her mother's blood matted tresses. She watched in horror and revulsion as he grabbed her father by the hair of the head and, using the long blade, circled her father's hair line, effortlessly cutting to the bone. He lifted her father's scalp, pulling it forcefully from his skull, exposing the white bone to the morning sun.

Alexandra's stomach turned.

Please dear God, make this be over! Please!

She heard rapid footfalls, heavy, labored breathing, and tortured lungs gasping for air. She turned, and to her surprise, Bethany was thrown to the ground beside her, forcing the air from her lungs. Bethany did not go quietly into the night. Instead she screamed, kicked, and lashed out with her arms and legs, and was struck solidly across the chest for her efforts. The blow drove the remaining air from her lungs. She collapsed in a heap on the grass. Alexandra stared at the same Indian who had tied her hands, watched him as he bound Beth's arms, then her ankles. Throughout the experience Bethany lay limp, prone on the grass sod, her eyes closed. Alexandra wasn't sure if she was conscious or not.

The man tested the knots, then again took off running in the direction of Miller's wagon.

"Beth? Beth?" Alexandra whispered. "Can you hear me? Wake up. Can you hear me?"

She heard a scream; it was cut short, followed by silence. Alexandra was amazed anyone was left alive who could scream. It sounded like Mrs. O'Reilly. It couldn't be.

Why not?

She thought about the O'Reilly baby.

What now? she thought. *Mrs. O'Reilly was just twenty-three. Just. Five years older than me. Gone.*

It was eerily quiet.

Bethany hadn't moved.

Why are they sparing us? For what?

Alexandra paused mid-thought, re-visualizing her mother's and father's scalps in the man's hand, blood dripping through the hair and falling slowly into the grass. Bethany's prone body lay in a heap at her feet. She studied her sister's blouse to see if she was breathing, looking for the rise and fall in her chest. She was not sure there was any. Her fingers and toes tingled for want of blood. Her thoughts went to her brother.

At least Arnold stayed home. This isn't happening to him. How lucky is that?

She remembered him telling her father: "No, I'm not going.

55

I'm not going. You're a fool."

That's what he said. That went well. If only I'd said that. No. No, I'm not going, Papa. That seemed so easy to say. No. No, I'm not going. If only, if only I'd just told Papa no like Arnold had.

In the middle of her thought a small black spot collected at the edge of her vision and then came running at her, growing, rushing, passing her as though she was standing high on the cliffs over looking the Atlantic, listening to the surf break. She could smell the New England maple, feel the brilliant colors fleeing by her, escaping. The swells were thundering against the rocks, pounding their endless madness. She passed out of consciousness, slipping mercifully into a darkness where nothing mattered.

CHAPTER 16
Zeke is 5 miles south of Alexandra

August 23, 1854
North of the Sweetwater River
Central Nebraska Territory

Alexandra Ann Wakeford was not aware of how long she lay on the unforgiving sod. In her fragile, comatose existence it could have been a minute or an hour. Unfortunately, as far as she was concerned, it was something less than forever. She awoke slowly, her emerging consciousness fighting with the desirability of unconsciousness. Blinking her eyes as though sleep walking, her feet and legs buried deep in mud, she started to move and discovered that her arms and legs were tightly bound, her movement restrained and restricted. Her memory--violent scenes of death and mayhem, red blood dripping into the sod--came rushing back. She received and felt a nudging pain in her ribs. How often and how long she suffered that indignity she had no idea. In this mental and emotional twilight, she heard someone speaking to her, indistinguishable words repeated again and again.

It was Priscilla's voice that implored her to her senses. Beside her, fourteen-year-old Bethany lay sobbing. Suddenly she was jerked upright, her feet and ankles no longer bound.

When did that happen?

She struggled to sit up, at the same time endeavoring to shake the hurt from her head. Alexandra was instantly aware of her captor standing above her, blocking out the warmth of the morning sun.

Later she remembered standing in the shadow of her father's wagon, her father's corpse at her feet, her hands securely bound behind her back, and realizing her mother's body lay inside the wagon box. She saw her father's prized horses unhitched from the double trees, their carefully oiled harnesses, collars, and engraved hames tossed aside. Several oxen were dead, their tongues cut out, their yokes bearing down on their necks. Others had been released. Dead, mutilated, naked bodies were strewn about, some hidden in tall grass.

It was oddly quiet. It was as if nature herself held her breath, horrified at what had been done, waiting for the future to transpire, wondering if that future was going to resemble the immediate past.

An Indian with a sparsely painted face, her captor, bloodied knife stuck inside a scabbard tied around his waist, grabbed her by the shoulders and propelled her to her feet. She tried to collect her thoughts. She remembered bending over to pick up the dropped rein, teasing her father, breaking camp. She remembered that they had been moving, the wheels turning. Mr. Tallasinius had waved his hand forward just as he had every morning.

"Who is that?"

Alexandra turned to Priscilla's voice. "What? What?" she asked, shaking her head to clear it.

"Over there."

"What?" Alexandra whispered, barely able to get the question out of her mouth, her cheek bearing the imprints of grass stems. "What? What did you say?" She blinked her eyes in an attempt to focus. Her captor was attending to Bethany who no longer offered resistance.

"White men. Look over there. See them?"

Alexandra heard her sister's stifled sobs as she turned to look, shaking her head, blowing to get hair out of her face. It didn't work. She still could barely see.

The three young women stood together, their hands bound behind their backs, their fingers and backs inches from the wagon box. Their captor had brought three horses, had tied their lead ropes to the front of the wagon box, and had disappeared.

No saddles. Alexandra observed.

Are they his?

Obviously. Stolen. They were ours.

What's he going to do with us?

She tried moving her hands, working her wrists. There was no give in the leather straps. She glanced at her sister and Priscilla.

We're the only ones left alive. Everyone's dead. Everyone.

Horses were milling; more than half of the victors were mounted, waiting. Others were in the process of mounting, swinging up on their horses' backs. Alexandra again glanced at the three horses. She was disoriented mentally as well as emotionally, struggling to grasp what was happening, her thoughts like used dish water rushing through her fingers, spilling onto the ground.

Everyone is leaving? Getting ready. For what? Oh my God!

58

She blinked her eyes.

We're captives. They're taking us with them. Is that good?

Good they haven't killed us. Yet. Those horses are for us.

What happened? No, not what happened? I know what happened. How did these people happen? Where did they come from?

She glanced at the horses again.

We're prisoners. Captives. Priscilla said? What? White men? What white men? Where?

Alexandra looked and saw them.

What are they doing here?

There was no answer.

Though she tried not to, Alexandra glanced at her father's body lying disheveled and immobile a few feet from the wagon box where he'd fallen, the white bone of his skull bright in the early morning sunlight.

Oh, Papa, she thought. *I'm so sorry.*

She stared across the grassy flat toward the creek.

White men and Indians? This makes no sense. None.

She studied them. A more slovenly dressed, scraggly, bearded, unkempt excuse for men she couldn't remember. They had heavy pistol belts girded about their waists. Two of the men sat their horses, cradling rifles in their arms, their hat brims pulled down shading and hiding their eyes. A third was standing holding the reins to his horse, speaking to the five or six Indians gathered around him. He carried no rifle in hand but she could see a rifle stock jutting from a scabbard tied to his saddle. Another hung in a strap from his saddle horn. The two mounted riders sat watching the activity that surrounded them, their hands close to their pistol grips, index fingers resting easily on the trigger guards of their rifles. They sat easy in the saddle, slightly hunched over. Their calculated readiness, their nonchalance while patting the stocks of their Sharps rifles reminded her of Mr. Tallasinius. And he was dead. As if to verify his death, she glanced about looking for his body and found it lying on the sod, partially hidden on the browning grass. His was the only body. There had been others. Seven or eight. The other bodies were gone.

From a distance the three white men looked formidable, a deadly force, like a rattler waiting to strike.

What were they doing among savages?

She caught one of them staring at her, a bemused expression

59

on his face. She watched as he said something to his companion. He turned and looked as well. The second, a much taller man, nodded his head in response to the comment. They were too far away, the background noise too loud for their voices to be distinguishable.

White men? Why aren't they helping us? They certainly don't appear to need or want help. Why are they here?

"What are they doing?" Priscilla said aloud, voicing Alexandra's thoughts. "Why aren't they dead like everyone else?"

"Those men?" Bethany asked. "Those men? I saw them in the wagons taking stuff. Anything they wanted. That one standing--he took Papa's rifle. See it? It's hanging from his saddle horn. They took the gold from Harry O'Reilly's strong box. I saw it."

Priscilla whispered, "They're white men . . ."

Bethany cut her off. "They're thieves, Pris. And killers. That tall one, the one in the saddle--he killed Mrs. O'Reilly. Like it was nothing. I saw it! Shot her dead."

"Oh, my God!" Priscilla whispered. "They're looking at us. What should we do?" She turned away, facing Bethany and Alexandra.

"They're coming," Bethany said. "Didn't you hear me . . . what they did? They're not coming to help us."

"What should we do?" Priscilla asked again.

"What can we do?" Alexandra whispered.

"Lexie, they're killers."

"I heard you, Beth."

"What we got here?"

The speaker leaned forward, standing in shortened stirrups, reseating himself. His legs were thick and stubby, his forearms massive. His facial features were broad, his nose flat; it appeared to have been broken. He had fat, puffy cheeks and his hair was an unruly black, some of it long: hanging over his collar, hiding his neck. His hat was resting back on his shoulders, held there by a latigo tied about his neck. He spoke to no one in particular, having a conversation with himself as though he enjoyed the sound of his own voice and liked parading it about. He stared at the three girls.

"Thought everyone was kilt dead," he said. "No one left. No one talkin'. No one rememberin' our faces. No one knowin'."

The taller man with the broad-brimmed hat did not respond immediately. Instead, from the back of his horse he studied the three

60

girls: an unsolved problem, a riddle without an answer. Leaning over the horse's shoulder, he spat a stream of tobacco juice. Behind the riders the third man was still conversing with three or four Indians. They appeared interested in what he was saying. Neither of the two riders dismounted, preferring to stay in the saddle.

The stocky man said, "Put a bullet in 'em, Crease. We gotta. Ya know it. Do it. Be quick about it."

Alexandra stared in amazement: hearing but not wanting to hear the cavalier pronouncement of their impending death. The two talked as if the girls were deaf, as if they didn't understand English. It was as if they were talking about a half empty salt shaker sitting on a plank table, and a black ant crawling on its lid about to be swatted. They spoke of their killing as if killing was an everyday casual event, a task on par with washing one's face or combing one's hair. The girls meant absolutely nothing: their life, their death inconsequential; their lives but a small difficulty represented by nothing more than the inconsequential cost of a single paper cartridge, a half ounce of lead. Alexandra was conscious of the O'Reilly dog coming from under the O'Reilly wagon box, its tail between its legs. No one paid it any attention. It turned, retreated under the wagon, then came out again.

"I'm thinkin' we better not, Shorty." The tall man finally replied, turning so he faced the man he called Shorty. "They ain't ours ta kill," he said. "I'm thinkin' we better leave 'em be. Whoever tied 'em up and left 'em here might not care fer us shootin' 'em. Their his'n."

The tall man, Crease, glanced past the second Wakeford wagon at the warriors sitting their horses, eying them. "I'm thinkin' we'd better get free of this bunch. Sooner the better. What do ya suppose's keepin' Sly? He figurin' ta get hisself adopted or somethin'?"

"Crease, these girls. . .we gots ta put a bullet in 'em. We can't be leavin' 'em here. They're trouble. I ain't likin' it. They's done seen us."

"Maybe. See them Injuns? They's a watchin' us, too."

"I don't give a damn if they are."

"Shorty, ya try and bleed these girls, you'll force me ta put a bullet in ya. I ain't wantin' ta get myself killed over three worthless girls. Hear me? They ain't of no matter."

"Crease, ya ain't thinkin'. They's done seen us." The shorter man removed his pistol from his side holster, pulling back the hammer, the click screaming loudly in Alexandra's ears.

Oh my God, she thought. *He's going to do it.*

"Shorty?" The taller man spurred his horse, placing himself between the girls and the short, fat man. "Ya idiot, I'm tellin' ya they ain't ours ta kill. Ya pull thet trigger we'll have thirty of these bucks liftin' our hair. Put thet iron away. Shorty, I swear you're gonna force me ta shoot ya right outta the saddle."

Crease had brought his rifle to bear on his squat companion and they sat eying one another like a pair of roosters.

"I don't care none fer your attitude, Crease," Shorty said. "I tell ya we gots ta shoot 'em. They's done seen our faces. If'n ya ain't got the stomach fer it I do. Now get outta the way."

"Ya half-wit. Put your iron away."

Shorty glowered at his companion holding the 1851 Navy Colt in his right hand, the hammer pulled back, preparing to dismount. He shifted his weight in the saddle.

"Whadda we got here?"

Both men turned in the saddle to see the third member of their party walking towards them,leading his horse, the reins in his right hand. He wore black boots that extended from his worn down heels to his knees. The ends of his dark, gray trousers were stuffed inside the boot pipe. Behind him the war party was taking "treasures" they'd stolen from the various wagons and packing them on their horses. Dead limp bodies were draped over the backs of horses standing together.

The newcomer let his eyes bounce from girl to girl, oblivious of the commotion stirring around him. He spat tobacco juice into the grass sod and, with the left sleeve of his faded blue shirt, wiped his lips.

"You two fixin' ta dance?" he said.

That question made no sense.

Behind him Crease and Shorty glanced at each other. "Ya talkin' ta us, Sly?" Crease asked.

"Yeah, I'm talkin' ta ya."

The girls stood waiting for the proverbial hammer to drop, Alexandra fully expecting to be shot. The decisive third vote was staring at her and there was nothing she could do, nothing any of them could do. The realization was cold but hardly unexpected. They were standing in a field of death. Everyone they knew was dead, their bodies in heaps, their eyes blank, their hair ripped from their heads, the sod soaking up their blood. Alexandra stared at the third man, a feeling welling up inside her of pure, black hatred. It was an 'how dare you even speak to me' feeling, a feeling of pure unadulterated disgust.

And he was ugly, built like a hard, green pear with thick thighs, a solid girth, and massive shoulders and neck. He looked hard, and muscular, carrying no excess weight, someone difficult if not impossible to kill. His hands were concealed by leather gloves stained by use and sweat. His clothing, except for his shirt, was dark, worn, faded. His head was covered by a felt hat pulled down around his face so as to hide his eyes and cheek bones. The wind and sun had turned him Mexican brown, though he might well have been Caucasian, a fact further established by a pale sliver of white skin revealing itself between the first and second button of his shirt. The gap was pulled apart by a heavy set of shoulders and a broad chest. Either his shirt had shrunk or he'd gained weight. Alexandra didn't know which; it didn't matter. He was so ugly.

Sly studied the girls as though judging prize pigs at a county fair, his eyes darting from one to the next, looking each girl up and down. He spat another stream of tobacco juice, glanced at the confrontational demeanor of the tall man sitting his horse, and at the pistol resting easily in Shorty's right hand. Both men seemed to be waiting on Sly.

It was the pregnant moment. Life hung in the balance.

Alexandra involuntarily backed up a half step, her retreat stopped by the wagon box. She found the visual inspection disconcerting; perhaps it was that he smelled like rotting potatoes or frozen onions left too long in the ground. If he had bathed in his lifetime it was not obvious.

What an awful, awful, man.

"We better get the hell outta here while we still can," Sly said to his companions. "These Injuns are plenty jumpy. 'Bout ta be movin'. I don't want ta be around 'em should they decide ta kill us."

"What about these women?" Shorty asked. "We can't leave 'em. They's seen us."

This is getting old. Alexandra thought.

Sly turned back to the women, staring through crazy eyes that bounced from girl to girl like a squirrel hunting nuts.

He's crazy.

"What do you want?" she blurted out. "Haven't you done enough?" She suddenly stopped speaking, the sarcasm in her voice

63

evident.

Her words focused his attention on her. After staring at her long and hard, he finally said, "I want thet blue hair ribbon and thet red watch fob hangin' on your dress."

"What? No. No, you don't," Alexandra said, trying in vain to step farther back to avoid him. There was no room. "You best be leaving," she said, "you know what's good for you."

Sly laughed. "If I know what's good fer me?" He turned to Priscilla. "I'll be wantin' thet comb stuck in your hair."

"Well, you aren't getting it," Priscilla said, "you filthy, smelly beast. You ever heard of soap? Leave us alone."

Crease laughed from the back of his saddle horse, a derisive cackle, the Sharps still cradled in his left arm. "I do believe she done told ya, Sly, 'You filthy beast.'"

For a big man, Sly was surprisingly fast. He was on Priscilla like a coyote on a gray mouse. Before she could react, he grabbed her by the shoulders, whipping her around, holding her tightly against him. With her hands bound behind her back, she could do little to avoid him. With his free hand, he deftly removed the ivory comb from her hair, depositing her on the ground like a sack of fall potatoes. Her loosened hair fell over her face, momentarily hiding it, smothering the hateful glare she threw at him.

With the girl on the ground at his feet struggling to sit up, he unbuttoned the flap on his shirt pocket and deposited the comb inside. No longer concerned with Priscilla, he eyed Alexandra standing with her back pressed hard against the wagon box. Alexandra didn't move or attempt to run. She simply stood her ground, the only act of defiance she could muster. With his right hand he grasped the watch fob, the pin that held the fob on her dress pulled taut, then jerked it, ripping the cloth. Sly looked at Alexandra, then at the fob, fingering the material.

"I'll have thet ribbon in your hair," he said.

Angry, seething with frustration, she offered no resistance to this ultimate indignation. Sly seized her upper arm and whipped her around, shoving her face against the rough canvas that covered the wagon. He grabbed her braids and unwound them, removing the ribbon which had been so carefully woven into them by Clara Wakeford not an hour before.

"Ya won't be needin' this little pretty," he said. "Pretty ain't what these bucks are about." Alexandra remained still, leaning back against the wagonbox. Finished, Sly spun her around. She stared at him, at her star-spangled ribbon in his left hand. "Mine now," he said. "All mine." He laughed.

One day I'll kill you, Mister. One day. Mark it on your calendar. I'll kill you.

That's what she wanted to say. Instead she stared at him, her eyes mere slits, her brow folded in unconcealed anger.

What do you want with a watch fob? You don't even own a watch. You can't even tell time. One day, Mister. One day.

Sly looked at her amused, glancing along the wagon bed as he folded the blue ribbon and stuffed it with the watch fob into his shirt pocket, buttoning the flap. He smiled, revealing yellowed, tobacco stained teeth. Momentarily he stared back at Alexandra, taking a deep breath, letting it out as though he had all the time in the world. Stretching his neck, he ritually popped the vertebrae, then rubbed it with his gloved hand, chuckling to himself.

"Let's get outta here, gents," he said turning to his horse. Stepping into the saddle, he pulled his bay around.

"What about these girls?" Shorty persisted.

"Leave 'em," Sly said. "They ain't ours ta kill. They sure ain't worth the risk of shootin' it out with these folk ta make 'em dead. 'Sides nobody'll see 'em. Not where they're goin'. And if they do, nobody'll believe 'em. I don't believe it and they's standin' right in front of me."

The three riders wheeled their horses about, starting south at a canter, winding their way through the disarray of wagons and bodies. Sly rode in front, the three disappearing from sight without a backwards glance.

Bethany stood beside the wagon box next to her sister. Priscilla managed to awkwardly rise to her knees, her hands bound behind her back. After a struggle, she got to her feet, glancing at the sisters with a 'can you believe that?' look on her face.

"I'm surprised they didn't kill us," Alexandra said. "That Shorty fellow sure wanted to."

Neither girl responded.

CHAPTER 17
Zeke is 7 miles north-west of Alexandra

August 23, 1854
North of the Sweetwater River
Central Nebraska Territory

Alexandra stood with her companions, waiting for the worst, expecting it: the much discussed nightmare of the western frontier had transpired in front of her; horrific stories found in dime novels no one believed. After all, it was fiction, something told to scare children into obedience. She was a protected eighteen year old, raised in an old white frame house a few miles north of Boston. All of her life she had been safe: living with an older brother, a younger sister, and two protective parents.

Death, violent, wanton destruction of another's property, thieves of that property, innocent, well-meaning peoples' blood soaking into the grass: that sort of activity hadn't been heard of in seventy-five years. It was ancient history, something read in the *Boston Herald* by her grandfather before she was born. It was not unlike what the British did in New York to that poor young man, Nathan Hale in 1776. He was twenty-one and that was seventy-eight years ago and they hung him. "You remember that boy," her grandfather had said to her once. "Don't make them like that any more. Not at all. Remember that, girl. Remember that."

The Indians who were not already mounted were catching their horses, leading them by single reins, preparing to leave. Others were still packing stolen goods on the backs of stolen horses and stolen mules who, until that morning, had pulled wagons.

A growing urgency stirred the war party. More and more took to their horses' backs. Alexandra wondered what was about to transpire. Her fearful thoughts came in rushes, in fits and starts, and in morbid observations. She glanced at her father's body. That didn't help.

I shouldn't be here, she thought. *Neither should Beth.* Alexandra tried to shake her long hair out of her eyes. *What did we do to deserve this?* Momentarily, she thought of her parents. *Neither should they. Doing God's work? Leaving our homes? Coming out here? We could be at home.* She thought of her brother, so far away, safe. *Now what? What's to become of us?* A sob built up in her chest. Her lips trembled. Her eyes teared.

Her unspoken 'now what' question was answered when a shirtless savage separated himself from the others and walked toward them. She recognized the killer who, for some reason, had spared their lives while brutally murdering everyone else. The only other survivor was the O'Reilly dog hiding under the O'Reilly wagon. No one paid him any attention.

Why? Alexandra wondered. *What's going to happen to us? I guess I should be grateful. We're alive. Who do I thank for that? Everyone's dead. Even Mr. Tallasinius. Zeke's Uncle Eli. What will happen to Zeke?* She glanced at Eli Tallasinius' body and wondered if being alive was pure happenstance or the providence of God.

I wonder where Zeke is? If he's alive.

What will he do when he finds out about me? Will he find out?

He's probably dead. Out there all alone. At least he's not here to see this. I'm glad for that.

Happenstance, she concluded. *It has to be happenstance. God wouldn't do this. He wouldn't allow this. Here we are. Right in the middle of what God wouldn't allow. Just like that poor, poor Nathan Hale.*

Alexandra watched their captor's approach. It was direct: no hesitation. Obviously, he was the winner, the conqueror. He knew it. She, the loser, the conquered. He had a doll stuck in his waistbelt. That was odd. She recognized the doll. It belonged to the Funson child.

What's he doing with that?

Their captor was dressed in leather leggings, a faded red breech cloth hanging to his knees. He also carried a large pistol stuck in the belt that secured his leggings at the waist. He carried a Hawkens rifle in his left hand. A large knife secured in a leather sheath was stuck comfortably inside the same belt holding the massive pistol. Although many of his companions carried fresh scalps, he did not. His face bore white jagged lightning streaks of paint that disappeared into a black hair line: one on each cheek. He was taller than Alexandra's five foot seven inches but not by much. He wore moccasins with red beads decorating the sides and toes. His dark brown arms were bare, sinewy. He weighed about two hundred pounds and wore his hair long, a series of three eagle feathers hanging from a knot behind his left ear.

The ease with which he walked bore testament to the strength of his arms, back, and legs. He stood straight, his eyes clear, full of purpose, confidence, and experience. He smelled of sage, the open prairie grass, horse sweat, and smoke.

Another man walked by leading a paint pony and a buckskin horse; he said something to the girls' captor, grinned and laughed. Their captor had his attention on Priscilla and did not reply to the unsolicited comment. Behind him and in front of the wagon where Mr. Tallasinius' body lay, voices were raised: loud talking, shouting back and forth, laughing. There was no rancor, no anger: good natured joking poking incongruent fun in a field of corpses. It seemed so out of place to Alexandra.

Oddly, no one had touched Mr. Tallasinius' body. Everyone else's bodies had been mutilated. The bodies of the men he'd shot, stabbed, and killed were gone, as were his pistols and his rifle. There had been six or seven bodies. Alexandra hadn't counted; they were gone.

His death cost them, she thought. *They paid. He made them pay. Pay dearly.*

Her captor grabbed Priscilla by the shoulders. With his fingers he felt her arm and shoulder muscles, then her back muscles. He nodded and said something to her. Priscilla stared at him. He opened and shut his mouth several times. Priscilla continued staring at him. He reached out, grabbed her jaw, and pulled her mouth open. For a moment he stared at her teeth as though she was a horse and he was judging her age.

"Oh, my goodness," Bethany exclaimed. "What's he doing?"

Abruptly the warrior turned his attention to Bethany. To her dismay, he seized her by the shoulders, feeling the muscles in her arms and shoulders and back, turning her around. He motioned for her to open her mouth by opening his. Bethany complied. He stared at her teeth as he had Priscilla's.

What's this all about? Alexandra thought. *What's he want with our teeth?*

When he was through examining Bethany, he performed the same inspection on Alexandra, including staring into her mouth. Though she considered resisting, she did not.

Why get myself killed? Or beaten? she thought. *Like everyone else.*

It was revolting: having the man feel the muscles in her arms, legs, shoulders, back; then stare at her teeth as if she were an animal.

What if he found something he didn't like? What would he do? I hate to think. She concluded there was no use in calling any attention to herself. *Choose your battles. This one isn't one I can win.*

"I feel like a cow at the Essex county fair," Bethany whispered. "First, those despicable men wanting to kill us; now, this one. I'm not sure what he's doing."

"Or a horse," Priscilla said. "I think he counted my every tooth. I hate to think what he would have done if he'd found a cavity."

Yes, what? Alexandra thought. *Pull it?*

Finished with this cursory physical inspection and using her left elbow to steer her, he pulled and pushed Priscilla toward a mount, then bodily lifted her onto its bare back. He didn't untie her hands. Priscilla nearly fell off the other side. Somehow she managed to get herself upright, maintaining a precarious balance. Next came Bethany, followed by Alexandra. After the girls were astride horses, he picked up the lead ropes and led them across the sod, past the wagons, and Mr. Tallasinius' body. Several times Alexandra felt herself slipping and was forced to lean to the opposite side, tightening her legs about the horse's girth to maintain her balance.

Their captor mounted his horse, swinging up on its back and started him forward, kicking its sides with his heels. As if on cue, the war party moved en masse away from the wagons, eventually forming a single column moving north at a steady walk.

They aren't in any hurry!
Why not?
No one's chasing them.

A moment later, Alexandra glanced back. Behind her sat twenty-four wagons: contents dumped in piles, unwanted clothes lying on the ground, bare bodies lying helter skelter. Down on the creek were several oxen grazing. But not one single living human being. She wondered about the O'Reilly dog, remembering it dashing under her father's wagon just before they'd left, its tail wagging nervously. For some reason, it had left the tenuous security of the O'Reilly wagon after the three white men had assaulted them, then darted back when Priscilla was thrown to the ground by the ugly fellow, Sly.

What will it eat? she thought. *No one to care for it. Poor dog.* She recalled Mr. O'Reilly sitting on a stump by his fire, talking to his wife, laughing, all the while pulling that dog's ears, sometimes scratching places it couldn't readily reach. Every evening he'd done that, feeding it scraps from his own plate, tossing him a piece of fat Mr. O'Reilly didn't want himself.

Alexandra thought about Mr. Tallasinius, his motionless body lying on its side, his eyes open, unblinking. He still had his hair: not her father, not her mother.

Why was that?

She glanced at her sister and Priscilla.

"Why us?" she asked aloud, feeling a little guilty, feeling a lot of remorse. "Everyone's dead," she said. She adjusted herself on the horse's back: moving her fingers, her hands bound behind her back, trying to stop the tingling, hoping to get the blood circulating. "Why are we alive?" Neither Priscilla nor Bethany answered. They didn't know. They didn't want to know.

The pace of the cavalcade quickened, not at a run or gallop, but a fast walk. Sometimes when the terrain was flat or downhill, a trot. It seemed as though their captors were saving their horses. It didn't take long for the ragged column of stationary wagons to drop miles behind them before disappearing from their sight altogether. Midmorning the party split; a number of men separated themselves, taking some of the captured horses, riding west. Others rode east in the direction of the rising sun and the black forests, the mountain rising high behind the pine trees. The second group took with them the vast majority of the stolen horses, but not all.

Their captor and his ten companions continued north. Among them was the man who'd scalped Alexandra's father, her mother, and two others. Their scalps hung from his belt. To Alexandra it was particularly gross. Among the scalps was that of the Griffie girl, Colleen. Her dark red hair in long braids dangled, caked in her dried blood. They brought with them nineteen shod horses taken from the wagons and several horses she'd never seen before, plus the three horses the girls rode and the unshod horses the eleven men were riding. There were twenty-five in total. One of the men, leading three horses, rode out front making a trail for the others to follow. Their captor led the horses ridden by Bethany and Priscilla. Another man led the horse ridden by Alexandra, leaving the others to mind the loose horses and keep them from straying.

After the split, the smaller group riding north moved more quickly: without stopping, without slowing. No one spoke. It seemed no one had anything more to say; the silence didn't seem to bother her

70

captors.

From time to time, Alexandra would look back, trying to fix the passing country in her memory, partially because she couldn't get Zeke out of her mind. He was back there, somewhere. She hoped he was safe. It was so hopeless, the exercise so futile; there was so much to remember, the terrain changing by the minute. Every step took her farther and farther away from everything she knew. It frightened her, left her disconcerted, and bewildered. And there was the warrior carrying Colleen Griffie's scalp, her red braids bouncing on his bare thigh, keeping rhythm with the gait of the bay horse he rode. Alexandra looked away, trying to save her sensibilities. It didn't help.

The sun fell to the horizon, then disappeared behind the western hills. Stars appeared. Soon it was dark enough that Alexandra could make out the Big Dipper. She found the North star and concluded they were traveling north. The direction remained constant.

It was late when they stopped. No fires were built: no food cooked, no water boiled. The riding horses were staked on long tether ropes. Five or six guards were selected. Others busied themselves caring for the horses. It was difficult to tell who was a guard and who was not. All seemed to serve that purpose. When they stopped, their hands were untied. The girls were placed in the middle of the camp leaving them no chance of escape. They were given water and dried venison to chew, but were never alone.

Untied, Bethany remarked, rubbing her wrists, "They must think we're really dangerous, watching our every move like chicken hawks."

"They think we'll run, try to escape," Priscilla said. "As if we could."

"I would if I could. I certainly would had I half a chance. That fellow with Colleen's scalp makes me sick," Bethany replied.

"You'd escape?" Alexandra asked.

"Yes, I would. Right now."

"Me, too. We have to," Priscilla said. "But where would we go? We're so far away from everything."

"Back," Bethany announced. "I'd go back."

"With these men chasing you?" Priscilla asked. "How far do you think you'd get?"

"I've been watching. There's eleven men. They've got to sleep sometimes. They have to blink. They can't be watching us all of the time. We have to try something. Don't we? We can't just stay here, roll over like some dog, give up without trying."

Priscilla nodded. "At our first chance."

Alexandra answered, whispering, "Yes. I agree. At the very first chance. But we must also be careful. What good does escaping do if we're dead? We need to think this through. Pris, you're right. I don't think we'd get far with everyone watching. We can't eat tree bark. We won't get far with our hands tied behind our backs. We haven't any weapons to defend ourselves, to hunt. We shouldn't talk about escaping until we can be successful. Until we have a good chance. Right now, we have no chance. Staying alive is most important. Don't you think? I really don't want to be killed if I can help it."

Priscilla said, "True. But I think that with every minute that passes we get farther away from those wagons and the road west. Farther from help. We can't wait."

"You're right, Pris. I agree," Alexandra said. "So what do we do? Right now. What do we do?"

Neither of her companions answered. They were watching the warrior with Colleen Griffie's scalp dangling from his waist belt.

CHAPTER 18
Zeke is 36 miles south of Alexandra

August 24, 1854
Forty-eight miles north of the Sweetwater River
Central Nebraska Territory

The next morning started early. It was still dark: the second day distinguished by little talking and no waiting. No attention was paid to their back trail. The men who restrained their coming and going didn't seem to be bothered at all by who might be following them. It smelled like rain and it was chilly compared with what they had experienced.

The pace remained steady. All day Alexandra, Priscilla, and Bethany were kept astride their respective horses riding bareback, their hands securely bound, their horses led. When they stopped, the girls were released from their ropes: to drink, to relieve themselves, to eat a handful of dried, bitter red berries, some chunks of dried venison, and, sometimes, buffalo meat.

By nightfall they'd traveled fifty-eight miles moving generally north. There were no stars. Rain clouds covered the skies from horizon to horizon, but no rain fell.

At first Alexandra didn't want to eat anything, but then she rethought their plight and realized she'd better eat. They'd all better eat if they were going to get through this. They were never out of sight. They were never alone.

"What do you think they are going to do with us?" Priscilla asked, keeping her voice low.

It was night and they stood together in a clearing, pine trees rising on all sides like dark sentinels pointing at the sky. Alexandra and Bethany looked at her. Alexandra didn't feel like talking, yet it was the question she had asked herself. She replied, "I don't know the answer. I think that if they were going to kill us they would have done it. They killed everyone else."

"Maybe they like our teeth," Bethany said.

Her companions stared at her. "Well," she said, "I'm just saying."

"We have to escape," Priscilla said. "Perhaps we should be leaving a trail for someone to follow."

73

"How?" Alexandra whispered. "They expect it. They keep us in the middle where they can watch us. We're never alone. Our hands are useless. It's impossible, at best extremely difficult." Alexandra looked at Priscilla. "What should we do? I mean to leave a trail?"

"I don't know," Priscilla replied. "I was just thinking. We have to try something. Doing nothing will get us nothing."

"True," Alexandra said. "This is the second day. As far as I can tell they aren't trying to cover their trail. There's already something for someone to follow. The real problem is there are three trails to follow. No one knows what happened. No one knows we're alive except those white men. They aren't going to tell anybody. You can bet on that."

Bethany looked at her sister, tears forming in her eyes, but didn't say anything.

"I'm sorry, Beth. I'm so sorry," Alexandra said.

Bethany was sniffling. "For what?" she said. "What you said is true. It's not like you caused this."

Priscilla glanced at the two sisters. "Okay," she said. "Leaving more trail to follow is impossible. Maybe useless. Besides, what would we leave even if we could leave something? We are being watched all the time. They even watch me when I . . . you know. They're watching us right now. If we could leave something, who is going to find it, whatever it is? Let's stop fooling ourselves. There isn't anyone."

Bethany sighed. "This is depressing," she said. "Really depressing."

Alexandra looked at Priscilla, nodding in agreement. She paused, considering her thoughts.

"Well," she finally said, "you might not want to hear this but I've been thinking that escape might not be what we want just yet. Right now if we did, you know, escape, we'd most likely be walking. We have no horses unless we steal them. If we could. So far there's been no opportunity to do that. Besides, where would we go? What would we eat? We have no weapons. Where are we? We don't know where we are. Not really. If we were walking or riding, how far would we get? I'm saying it might not be a good idea right now. That's what I'm saying. The only person who may know we're alive is Zeke. Given the circumstances, what good would it be if he found us?"

Alexandra glanced at her companions and answered her own question. "What I mean is really, there isn't much chance of him finding us. If he did . . . there are eleven men waiting to kill him. If he

74

isn't dead, he's as good as dead. He can't help us. That's what I'm saying."

Priscilla nodded. "It does sound hopeless," she said. "Do you think that man is going to make us his slaves? You know, slaves?"

"Slaves?" Bethany said, her voice rising.

"Well, he looked in my mouth like I was some horse and he wanted to know how old I was. That was creepy."

"I know. I know."

"Do you have any ideas?" Priscilla asked.

Following silence, Bethany stated the obvious. "Lexie's right. Right now we don't have any good choices," she said. "There is still one chance. Only one that I know of . . . right now."

Both girls stared at her, waiting.

"You know. Zeke. There's Zeke," Bethany said repeating herself. "He's our only chance. Who else is there?"

"Zeke?" Priscilla glanced at Alexandra, then spoke directly to Bethany. She said, "Forget it. If Zeke's alive, he's really no chance at all. I think he's dead. But if he isn't, if he did manage to follow us, there's nothing he could do; they'd kill him. Best he could do is get help."

Bethany was stubborn. "We don't know that he's dead. At least we're not sure. Right now he's the one, single chance we have. I know it isn't much but he's all we got."

Alexandra nodded, "I think it's worse than slim, Beth."

"I know. But who else is there? He's the only one that may be alive. He's the only one who knows where we are, or rather where we were. If someone else comes along and sees those wagons, the dead people, they won't even know we're missing. Except for Zeke."

"You're right. He's our one chance."

"Oh, my God," Priscilla responded. "Listen to yourselves. We're depending on some dead guy that can't comb his hair. And his clothes. I . . . I mean he can hardly dress himself."

"I know, I know," Alexandra said. "But Beth is right and so are you, Pris. Both of you." Alexandra stopped speaking and smiled for the first time in two days. She said, "Zeke did promise me he'd come for me. If he's alive, he probably will. If he can. Except," she paused, "I really don't want him to. He'd be killed . . . if he's not already dead."

"Wow," Priscilla said. "Now that's something to write home to mother about. If we had a mother, which we don't. Let's see if I've got

75

this right. Our hope is to be rescued by a dead man. I get it. I do. We're depending on someone who can't tie his shoes, who stares at lover girl here with gaga eyes, who promised to come for her? Listen, you two . . . in case you didn't know it, we're in trouble. Real trouble. Zeke isn't a hope. If he isn't dead, he can't find us, and he can't find us because he doesn't know where we are. We're alone. We're on our own. We're lost. To top it off, you don't want him to rescue us because he'll get killed? For crying out loud," Priscilla paused, staring at her two companions. "It doesn't matter. He's dead so he's no hope. It's stupid to think he is."

"We're traveling north," Alexandra volunteered.

"North? How do you know which way is north?" Priscilla was shaking her head. "What's wrong with you? Aren't you listening?"

Alexandra pointed to the North star. "That's the North star," she said.

Bethany looked, "What good is that going to do us, Lexie? We're still lost. Pris is right."

"Maybe nothing. But we know north. We know we're traveling north. It's a start."

"Whoopteedo," Priscilla said. "We're traveling north. As if knowing that is going to help. We've already disappeared without a trace. Nobody even knows we're gone."

"I'm just talking, Pris. I'm trying to figure this out." Alexandra paused, staring at Priscilla. "Get yourself together, Pris. You're losing it."

"I know. I know. I'm not only losing it, I've lost it. We've got to do something besides wait for a dead man to bring the Army. It's all sorts of helpful to know we're traveling north, not to mention no one, not a living soul, knows we even exist." Priscilla threw up her hands. "What difference does it make? We're lost in the middle of nowhere without so much as a prayer."

August 25, 1854

The next morning was surprisingly cool. It had rained all night. In the quasi-darkness before dawn, they were shoved on the backs of their horses. They rode north, always north. Steadily they proceeded: first along a rocky mountain rim that on their left dropped seemingly a thousand feet, defining the ends of the earth in its vast darkness; then,

76

through a valley covered in thick pine, crossing a canyon whose gaping jaws were far from inviting; and then into a dry parched country broken, disheveled, and inhospitable.

For the horses' benefit they stopped often, a kindness which indirectly benefitted the girls. The girls took advantage of every opportunity to rest that they could.

Priscilla sat on the ground, her face buried in her hands. She was sobbing, shaking, her entire body shuddering. Alexandra patted her on the shoulder as she sat beside her.

"Are you going to be all right?" she asked.

Priscilla shook her head no. "No, I'm not. I'll never be all right."

Bethany walked up to the two girls, her hands untied, rubbing her wrists.

"What's wrong?" she asked. "I mean, besides everything. What's wrong with Pris?" she asked Alexandra. "Is she all right?"

Alexandra shot her the 'don't ask,' look. "She'll be all right. Soon as she eats something, gets something in her stomach. She'll be all right then."

"Wonder where they're taking us?" Bethany asked idly, her voice dropping off, not really expecting an answer.

"No place you've ever been," Alexandra responded.

Bethany sat down on the sod on the other side of Priscilla, the grass stems extending above her shoulders. "This is really, really the worst," she commented. "I could have done without this."

Neither of her companions responded.

Priscilla coughed. "We're sunk," she said. "Did you see Colleen's red hair? I did. It really got me."

"Where?" Bethany asked, looking around at the milling horses and men.

"One of those bastards has it hanging from his belt. I saw it. Her long braids and everything. It was just more than I could handle."

"It's more than any of us can handle," Bethany mumbled.

"I know. I know. But it happened right in front of me. I thought . . . I thought I was next. That I was done for."

Bethany put her arm around Priscilla from the other side.

"Pris, maybe we should talk about something else," Alexandra said. "This isn't doing us any good."

"Right in front of me, Lexie! I could have reached out and

touched her. I mean I did. She tried to get one of them off her Papa but he was already dead. She jumped on this. . . this. . . this man and he threw off like she was a feather or something. She was getting up and he grabbed her from behind, picking her up from the ground and he. . . he cut her throat. There was blood. She was looking right at me, blood pouring down her dress. He threw her on the ground, put his knee in her back, and took her hair. Her beautiful hair. Just like that. And she was looking right at me. Her eyes blinked. I tried to touched her hand. I just knew I was next. Then that man came and got me. I was screaming. I just knew. I just knew. She was right in front of me, Lexie." Priscilla started sobbing again, tears running down her cheeks. "I saw her. I saw her. I did. Her hair, her hair . . . her beautiful hair. . ."

Bethany was sobbing with her. Alexandra turned away and watched the horses drink, some cropping grass, her mind a blank.

All is lost, she thought. *How can we ever get over this? Ever?* The images were so vivid in her mind. *How can I ever think of anything else?*

Priscilla's analysis proved correct: they disappeared into a land that rarely, if ever, gave up its dead, a land where the living vanished without a trace. Soon the fall rains would come and the "without a trace," would take on an entirely new and dire meaning.

Three days had passed since the chilling, horrific event that defined their lives, an event that ran repeatedly through their every thought, evidenced by the matted scalps of their loved ones hanging from the belts of their captors.

They rode north into the rain.

CHAPTER 19
Alexandra is 16 miles north of Zeke

August 23, 1854
North of the Sweetwater River
Central Nebraska Territory

With the sun low on the horizon, setting into the flat grassy plain on his left, Zeke rode his black horse over the gentle rise where he had left his uncle earlier that morning. He was expecting to have ten or fifteen long miles to go to catch the emigrant wagons, two or three hours in the saddle, depending on their pace. On his packhorse were two mule deer, gutted and ready for Bill and his uncle to finish skinning, cut up, and distribute. Tired, hungry, and out of sorts, Zeke certainly wasn't in the mood for patience and forbearance. All day he'd been in the saddle, moving, watching, listening, and staying out of sight. It had been a long day. If he moved right along, he'd catch the wagons by midnight. Trouble was there was no moving right along; there was only moving.

Something bothered him, a nagging, festering feeling that had pestered him from before sunrise to noon. It was the shadow riders: someone out there, ghosts that flitted in and out, there, but not there. It was something that turned him in the saddle to look back, listening, expecting . . . something. But what? It was possible, he supposed, that their trail had simply disappeared. But he lost it twice and was full of doubt.

How did I do that? It had been right there. Twice.

On the rise his horse came to a standstill, stopping so abruptly that the packhorse walked up beside him before it, too, stopped. All three were staring north into the small, narrow valley that followed the meandering creek, the center of which had been the encampment the night before. The creek, so inconsequential it didn't have a name, originated from a seep at the far northern end of the depression about a mile from where the wagons had stopped to bed down. Dark blue mountains rose on his right, climbing into silent, formidable peaks fifty miles away. Along the east side of the creek a red rock outcropping of layered shale followed tangled brush growing along the creek bottom as if someone had drawn a straight line. The land rose, then flattened

79

on the north end, disappearing into dark pine timber with random splashes of aspen.

Zeke had left the encampment early, before even a hint of false dawn. Except for a shovel full of stars sprinkled against the night sky, it had been dark. His uncle suggested that he ride north five or six miles, then circle west around the path the caravan would be traveling. He had stressed the need to conceal himself. Zeke had done that, not returning at noon, not planning on returning until late. Twice he'd come across the trail that he'd described to his uncle the evening before. He followed it, keeping out of sight and downwind. Wherever possible he'd hidden in pine trees, scrub oak, and dense brush. He found no one, saw no one. The trail he followed disappeared on rock shale and then into a creek bottom. He would have followed it but there was no time. More importantly, the trail led away from the wagons, away from his uncle. He reasoned that riders riding away would cause no trouble.

The second time he found the trail it also went nowhere, disappearing into another creek bottom, eventually coming out on the other side and disappearing again. It, too, moved away from where the wagons were traveling.

Too much of a coincidence? He thought not. *No cause for alarm. Not yet!*

In the late afternoon he killed two doe, dropping each with a single shot, cutting their throats and gutting them. He loaded the carcasses on the packhorse thinking that everything was too quiet, a factor that irritated him, leaving him uneasy. He turned north. The late afternoon breeze died to a mere breath. Ahead, four or five miles, he could see circling turkey buzzards. They weren't drifting with the wind currents. They were watching something: circling around and around, concerning themselves with something dead or soon to be dead. Probably an old buffalo bull ostracized from the herd, killed by wolves. The buzzards hadn't bothered him as much as the disappearing trails. By this time of day the wagons would be ten to fifteen miles farther north. The circling birds were much, much closer and no cause for alarm. He nudged the black forward.

Two hours later he was on the rise looking into the shallow valley. The grass was dark green, fading into brown the farther it grew away from the creek. In the middle was a broken line of twenty-four silent wagons, specters, white ghosts against a blanket of drying grass. Buzzards were roosting on the wagon hoops. Five or six coyotes were fighting over the carcass of a dead ox. They turned to look at him.

His heart went into his throat. Those wagons weren't supposed to be there: absolutely not. Yet there they were: not a soul in sight, not even a dog. He could see where the wagons had formed a column and started to roll, traveling maybe two or three hundred yards from the night's encampment. Afterwards the clarity of the column had dissolved as if struck by a hammer. Where once there was order, now the wagons sat haphazardly in multiple directions, canvas coverings flapping quietly in the evening breeze. There were no horses, no people, no signs of movement. Everything was dead still.

He looked closer and made out the corpses of a couple of horses, and several oxen lying in their harnesses, yokes still in place. Another glance revealed ten or fifteen dead animals, and dead people, bodies stripped, lying everywhere he looked.

Oh, my God! he thought. *Oh my God, my God!*

He took a breath. *Shut up. Think.*

What?

You heard me. Think.

Zeke withdrew from the rise and dismounted. Leaving his animals ground hitched, he approached the rise again, this time on his belly. Using his uncle's glass, he studied each wagon and both sides of the valley, finding nothing except buzzards and bodies.

She's down there.

I hope not. Everyone down there is dead.

Oh, shit! Oh shit! Now what? What do I do?

Maybe she's not dead. Maybe she's alive.

Maybe. Maybe not.

Retreating from the rise, his belly to the ground, he returned to his horses. The packhorse he tied to a tree hidden in a clump of buck brush. Then he mounted the black and circled to his right, giving the wagons a wide berth, keeping them on the downside of the ridge. He stopped often, studying the area, each time starting on the outside of the depression and working toward the wagons. The grass was thick and high. There had been no prairie fire in a long time, neither had the grass been grazed. Around him the grass moved in waves caught by the breeze, making it appear alive in the last rays of the setting sun.

On the far north beyond the last wagon, he found the trail of

81

unshod horses, thirty or forty head; with them were larger American horses, all shod. Fifty or sixty head of those. Most of the oxen had been cut loose, some shot. Those not dead were grazing across the creek. Seeing Zeke, the coyotes had withdrawn. Not the buzzards.

Assured that he was alone, he ventured to the northern most wagon, dreading what he would find. It was the wagon belonging to Uncle Eli that Bill drove. Bill was dead, his body lying under the wagon box, his hair gone, his white body stripped. Fifty feet away, he found his uncle. Around him there were blood stained patches, the grass flattened where bodies had lain. His uncle had taken some shots. The ground said seven. Those bodies were gone. His uncle had been shot, yet his hair remained untouched, his clothing undisturbed. His pistols were gone, his holsters empty. His money belt was gone.

That's odd. What Injun would have interest in a money belt? The pistols, I understand.

His uncle's horse was dead, an arrow buried in the chest. The ground was churned up where it had struggled. Zeke turned, glancing at the other wagons.

Lexie! Oh, Lexie. Oh, Lexie. I'm so sorry. You was all alone, so alone.

Zeke began walking from wagon to wagon. There were bodies, young and old. It was like an emigrant roll call: Smiths, Billings, Adams, Harrison, Caldwell, O'Reilly, Jones, Funson, Bishop, Coplin, Kelley, Cornwall, Sheridan, Kane, Spring, Qdora, Snyder, Nichols, Williams, Thompson, Holmes, Rieger, Anderson, Griffen, Wakeford, Carlson. Some had gathered, made a stand, a fight of it. Some had gathered, surrendered, and then killed. Except for his uncle, the bodies were stripped, their hair gone. The wagons were emptied, their contents strewn in the grass, stacked in haphazard piles around the tailgates.

No Lexie.

Again he searched, running from wagon to wagon, looking in and under every one.

No Lexie. Oh my God, what's happened to you? he thought. *No Beth, no Pris.*

He found the place where the three girls had stood next to Alexandra's father's second wagon. He saw where someone had lain on the ground. No blood was lost. He found Alexandra's father in a disheveled heap and her mother's body inside the wagon box. The sense he had was that the girls' hands were tied, perhaps their feet

82

bound; at one point, however, they stood in one place, together, waiting. He also found the tracks of a heeled boot, and three shod horses. They'd been facing the wagon where the girls stood or had lain. On foot, carrying his Volcanic rifle, Zeke followed three shod horses south away from the camp, over the rise fifty feet west from where his packhorse was tied.

The three horsemen had not bothered to cover their tracks.

White men, he thought. *Three.*

He studied the horse tracks.

Shod. Ridin' light.

Lexie about five seven, maybe a hundred thirty pounds. No. No doublin' up. Not with these boys.

No Lexie. No Beth. No Pris, he thought. *And there were no bodies. They weren't dead.*

Zeke located his packhorse, dumped the deer carcasses in the brush, then doubled back. He found himself standing near the Wakeford wagon staring at the body of Mr. Wakeford. *I ought to bury you. It'd be the right thing to do.* Turning, he glanced down the erratic line of wagons. Everywhere there were bodies needing to be buried. *I need to bury all of you. I don't have time. Can't do it.* He stared at his uncle's body. *I gotta bury you, Uncle. I gotta do that. I owe you. Maybe not,* he thought. *No, that's horseshit. I gotta do that. I do.*

Zeke remembered the O'Reilly shovel lying by the water barrel and went to get it. A thumping tail led him to the dog lying under the wagon box.

Well, I'll be damned.

Zeke held out his hand. Nothing was in it but the dog came anyway. Zeke patted him on the head. The dog whined.

Guess we're it, dog. You and me. Ain't nobody else.

By starlight, he buried his uncle under the lee of a red cliff in a grove of pine. He buried him deep to keep his uncle's body from the coyotes and the wolves. He buried no one else. Once finished, he refused to allow himself to think of the death that surrounded him. He took a breath, letting it out slowly. It was late. It was dark. Mentally he reviewed his uncle's rules: his "all is lost, you ain't makin' it" rules. The first rule had never made any sense. "Slow down." "Slow down" suddenly made crystal clear sense. "Slow down."

Second: "Think." Thinking had become an incredibly difficult chore.

He looked at his horses, listened to the dog's tail thumping, and thought about Alexandra for the ten thousandth time. "Slow down. Think."

Okay. Okay. Slow down. Think.

Mentally he made everything stop. A breeze picked up. Zeke made a mental list, taking stock. Except for the O'Reilly dog he was alone, alone with a thousand miles of nothing on all sides.

His uncle had told him repeatedly, ad nauseam, "Boy, ya get in trouble, review what ya know. Go over it. Do it more than once. Get a solid grasp on what you're up against. That's where you start."

Zeke, leaving the black and the packhorse ground hitched, walked one hundred yards north. In the night shadows the ground was difficult to see. He thought of his uncle. "Once ya got a grasp of what's goin' on, decide what ya kin do. Not what could be done but what ya kin do. Choose what ya kin handle. Do it. Simple, ain't it?"

"Lord, Uncle. This is all but impossible. There's just me and this damn dog."

The wind picked up.

There ain't nothin' I can do. It's dark. I'm tired. My horses, they're tired. Stumblin' round here in the dark with a damn dog does nobody any good.

Well?

Wait for light. I guess I have to. No choice.

Zeke took a breath. With the dog in tow he moved into the sparse timber where he'd buried his uncle and made a dry camp. He kept his horses close, his rifle closer. On uneven ground he laid in his blankets listening to the wind drift through the pine needles. In dim, diluted darkness all he could see was Alexandra's face. He reviewed their conversation again and again.

She said, "Will you come for me, Zeke? Will you?"

Those words drove him crazy, too anxious to sleep. Sleep? What was that? She was close, so very close. Maybe fifteen or twenty miles from him. Maybe closer. She'd be afraid, terrified, lying in the same darkness, staring at the same night sky. She'd be thinking of him just as he was thinking of her, wondering if he was coming. Zeke swore, turning in his blankets. He closed his eyes and saw her.

"Zeke," she said again. "Zeke? Zeke? Wake up. Will you come for me?" Tears fell from her eyes, running down her cheeks. "Zeke," she said again, "will you? Will you?"

"I ain't sleepin'."

"But will you?"

"Yes," he said aloud. "Bet on it."

"You said, 'always.'"

"I know what I said."

August 24, 1854

He awoke with a start: his fingers gripping his Volcanic rifle barrel, holding himself still, listening. In the darkness there was no sun to warm his cramped shoulders. Initially, he wondered where he was and why there were two horses staring at him, standing so close. And whose dog was that? It occurred to him that he was not in the monastery in St Louis, Missouri and he remembered the skinny Father in the black dress wondering what to do with him. Then he remembered using the O'Reilly shovel to bury his uncle deep, hiding his body from buzzards, coyotes, wolves and magpies.

Reality shoved its harsh face into his. "Wait," he cried, but it didn't wait. He rose to his feet clutching the blankets around his shoulders. He'd been dreaming of bringing three antelope for his uncle to share; no, it had been two does. He'd brought Alexandra some fresh meat, giving him an excuse to see her; any excuse would do. At first he couldn't find her, then walking on the other side of her wagon, the side closest to the creek, she'd found him.

Creek? What was she doin' there?

No one was around. Somehow they were alone.

Alone? How could that be?

Maybe they'd found each other.

But how?

Don't matter.

She was there; she'd taken him by the arm, pulled him around, a smile on her lips, laughing, his back leaning against the water barrel tied to the wagon's side.

"How was your day, Mr. Scout?" she asked. "Are we headed for all sorts of trouble?"

He'd smiled and shook his head no.

"That's good." Suddenly she'd thrown her arms around his neck; then holding her body close to his had kissed him on the lips. And her lips . . . nothing had ever tasted so good, felt so incredibly soft, warm. So desirable. Suddenly he was awake, her touch just a

85

fleeting memory.

His heart pounding, he remembered his arms around her waist, holding her close. She'd looked up into his face, smiling.

"Well, Mister Zeke," she said. "Have you decided what to do with us? Little ol' me and little ol' you? Did you think about us while you were out looking for trouble?"

He had, but now he was awake, and there was no Lexie. He didn't wait. He didn't linger. He was up: moving, rolling his blankets, wrapping and tying them behind the cantle, wrapped in his uncle's old slicker.

Damn it, kid. Don't go off half cocked. Hear me?

I hear you.

See that ya do.

Why do you keep sayin' that? I need to go. That's what I need.

This may take awhile.

I ain't got a while.

Ya still gotta eat. Ya gotta take care of yourself.

Ezekiel M. Penrose ran through a mental checklist, giving himself directions and arguments. Sometimes it was his voice, sometimes his uncle's.

See what ya kin get outta' the wagon.

I'm goin' there. I got it in mind.

See that ya have somethin' in mind. There's more than one wagon.

I ain't no thief.

Can't steal from a dead man.

They're all dead.

I said ya can't steal from the dead. Period.

It still don't feel right.

Do ya want ta stay alive?

Yes.

Well?

All right. All right.

Don't all right me. Get busy. That girl. That girl--she's out there. And you're standin' here.

She ain't that girl. She's got a name.

I know she's got a name. Get yourself a goin'.

I am a goin'.

The O'Reilly dog followed him to his uncle's wagon, lying

down by the front wheel to wait. Zeke climbed up on the seat. He sat looking down at the dog looking up at him.

You're right. What am I doin'? I ain't got no time to be lollygaggin'.

He removed the small, flat wooden box from the hidden compartment under the jockey box that his uncle had built. He counted his Uncle Eli's money and deposited it in his saddle bags, thinking he didn't know when he would return, if ever, but he may need money. Afterwards he searched the wagons, collected three cotton sacks, and goods to pack into them.

He found some salt, some navy beans, a cache of dried venison, hardtack, some rock candy, a container of ground flour, some corn meal, three tins of peaches and a butcher knife that the Snyders had hidden in a slot beneath the wagon seat, easy to hand. Mrs. Snyder's body was still in her wagon. She'd been shot through the chest. Her hair was hair gone. A bare leg showed below the hem of her dress. Zeke covered her. Her husband's body lay by the front wheel, his skull bashed in. He'd bled profusely. His eyes were open. Zeke closed them, regretting not burying the couple properly. Mrs. Snyder was a nice woman; she cared.

He discovered a sack of coffee beans and a coffee pot. The collected provisions he packed in the several bags. The bags he stored in panniers, wrapped them in canvas, and threw a diamond hitch securing them to the pack saddle. Finally, he walked wagon to wagon, looking.

Alexandra loomed large, staring at him, the hem of her blue dress flapping around her ankles. *You should bury Mrs. Snyder,* she said, *and her husband. You should bury these people. What's wrong with you? She's so nice. I liked her. She cared for you, you know?*

Lexie, he thought, excusing himself, *Lexie, I ain't got time.*

Well, take time. Not like I'm going anywhere. Besides you're stealing their stuff. That isn't right, you know.

Not like they're gonna need it. And you are goin' someplace. Right now. I gotta look for you right now. I'm gonna have to leave these folks if I'm gonna find ya.

Zeke, she said. *Zeke, please find me. You promised.*

I'm tryin'. I gotta get out of here.

He paused, staring at the wagons; he took a deep breath, letting it out slowly.

Lexie. Lexie, I'm comin'.

What are you going to do when you find me? Get yourself killed? There are thirty or forty men here.

One thing at a time.

Sometimes Alexandra's voice was drowned out by his uncle's insistence.

Slow down, his uncle said. *Think.* And then, *Get goin', you're wastin' time. Don't ya ever think of quittin'. I ain't toleratin' that. Hear me?*

I hear you.

See that ya do.

Why do you always say that? Not like I can't hear you the first time.

Damn shame, ain't it?

It is a damn shame.

Zeke stopped to breathe deeply. It was something he had to remind himself to do.

"Okay, okay," he murmured.

The saddle horse's ears twitched back and forth as Zeke spoke.

"It's not a matter of me findin' you, Lexie. It's when."

First find her, he thought. *Then figure out what to do.*

The O'Reilly dog stared up at him.

"Should I shoot you? Ain't nobody to take care of you. I ain't got time."

He ain't done nothin' wrong.

He's a pain in the ass.

Still . . . he ain't done nothin' that deserves killin'. Leave him be. If he keeps up, he'll be all right. If not, he'll be dead. Gotta take care of hisself.

"You ready, dog?"

The dog didn't respond.

"You better be."

"What should I call you? You got a name? Guess O'Reilly will have to do. You ain't got no other. Do you, O'Reilly?"

It was coming light. He was able to find the tracks of three shod horses intermingled with those of unshod horses. Those horses appeared to be led, as they maintained the same pattern constantly. Unfortunately, he didn't see them again. He concluded they must have been in the middle of other horses.

Later in the evening, he discovered where the trail split into three trails going in different directions. For a moment Zeke stared at the diverging tracks. He followed those that made their way west for six miles, then returned and followed the tracks that went east for five miles. Both trails had shod and unshod horses. Fifteen or twenty riders, he guessed. There was no way of telling if the girls were among them or not. They could have split them up, each taking a girl. He hoped not. He studied the torn earth. He'd wasted the entire day.

I don't know, he thought *Ain't no way to know. This ain't good. I'm in trouble. Sure as hell. No way of tellin'. Not without layin' my eyes on 'em. Now what?*

Zeke rode back to the split, then followed the trail north. It amounted to the flip of a coin, the roll of the dice, and a hunch. Miles later he still didn't know if he was on the right trail. Doggedly he kept at it, growing more and more frustrated.

Twenty, twenty-five horses, more or less. No distinct pattern. Tight bunch. Kept together. I don't know. Just guessin'.

All he really knew was Lexie was gone, a captive. That was bad news, except she was alive. Maybe. Maybe that was good. Three girls, their bodies not among the dead, at least they were together. Or were they? He wasn't sure. They certainly weren't with the three who rode south. All shod horses. Besides those horses did not move extra heavy: one rider to one horse. Three horses. The girls were definitely not with those riders, so they had to be with the others. No effort was being made to cover their tracks. They didn't seem to care, confident, feeling no threat from anyone.

Why would they? They were home.

On day one of tracking he realized he needed to take care of his horses and pay more attention than he did ordinarily. He let them rest periodically, making sure they ate, giving each a bait of oats not only in the morning, but at noon, and in the evening. He didn't have a lot of oats, so he measured it out. Sometimes, just for a moment, he sat down, leaning against a boulder, watching, dozing. But only for a moment.

Late afternoon he dozed off only to wake with a start, finding the O'Reilly dog lying at his feet thumping his tail. His horses were busy cropping grass. The heat of the afternoon sapped his strength. He dozed again thinking about the dog.

Damn dog.
This is gettin' me nowhere.

That packhorse has a loose shoe. Better look at it. It was Uncle Eli's voice.

What?

Ya heard me.

A loose shoe? I ain't got time for a loose shoe.

Ya ain't not got time.

Okay. Okay. Packhorse's shoe.

You're pushin' too hard.

I'm not.

At this rate they ain't gonna last. You damn well know it.

But I gotta find her.

What ya gonna do when you find her? Ya ridin' some useless horse. Hear me? What ya gonna do, then? You'll be useless. Horse will be useless. You'll be dead. What good will ya be ta that girl dead? Think, boy!

All right.

Don't all right me. Do what ya gotta.

Sure. But where is she? I'm ridin' blind.

I told ya.

I heard you.

See that ya listen.

That's what I'm doin'.

Zeke woke, the sun beating down on him. He shook his head to clear it. Standing on unsteady legs, tired, he went to look at the packhorse's shoe. The dog followed him. "Dammit," Zeke said. "Dammit, dammit, dammit."

There was a thirty-three percent chance he was following the right set of tracks. It was twice that percentage that he'd followed the wrong set of tracks. Except if there was a girl with each. There was that. He rode north with no confidence, looking for a sign that he didn't find.

August 25, 1854

The sun didn't bother coming up. Instead it hid itself behind clouds, dark and ominous. He could smell rain in the wind. He rode, keeping to the trail no one bothered to hide.

What good is this? I don't know what I'm doin'. Ridin' blind. Don't even know if I'm ridin' in the right direction. No way of tellin'. What else is there?

90

Rain began to fall: slowly at first, then steadily, then in a rush, pelting the soft earth in earnest. The weight of it bent the grass stems to the earth: covering the tracks he followed; blending the rough edges until the tracks melted and merged together; slowly erasing the sign of their passing like white chalk dust swept from a blackboard.

I'm gonna be completely blind, this keeps up.

It kept up.

Hope appeared in the mud at the edge of a nameless creek. He saw one partially dissolved print, a track protected from the rain somewhat. It was lying under the edge of a tuft of bent grass with rounded stems, leaves turned by a pressure coming from above. The ground had been stepped on, bent in a straight line by the sole of a small shoe, not something that Indians would wear.

Staring at it . . . unable to believe what his eyes were telling him, he felt angry, hollow, exasperated, and numb.

I'll be damned, he thought, touching the stems with his fingers, ever so gently, afraid they'd disappear. *I found you. One of you, anyway.*

CHAPTER 20
Alexandra is 118 miles northwest of Zeke

August 25, 1854
North of the Sweetwater River
Central Nebraska Territory

Riding in a cold, wet wind is a damn, miserable concern if ever one existed. Fingers get stiff, hardly capable of grasping the reins to a bridle, let alone the shank of a hunting knife or a pistol grip. In those circumstances, squeezing a trigger is a shaky event: tricky if eating depends on the accuracy of the shot. It is especially difficult when the shooter can't feel his index finger resting on the trigger. Discomfort is normal, natural. Zeke's back had tightened against the cold wind until his shoulders ached, sending a sharp pain down his neck. The pair of bull hide chaps he wore were lead-heavy on his legs. His shirt sleeves and leather gloves were soaked through.

His hat brim dripped steadily. Long ago it had settled down around his ears, a heavy weight on his neck. For hours he'd been riding into the wind, the rain blowing back into this face causing him to squint. Things at best were blurry. His ears were hangers for phantom icicles, their icy tops bent cold against the damp felt of his hat brim. They turned burning red in the shifting, drifting breeze. Damn cold he was, long past being soaking wet, stiff, and miserable.

This was mid-August: the shifting weather, illogical, freakish. It wasn't supposed to be this cold. Riding into the wind, it felt like deep November. Normally it was in the high eighties. At seven thousand feet, a short distance from the timberline, it was in the low forties and dropped into the high thirties: a mere forty degrees plus differential. Together with the product of gusting wind and his being wet to the core, it felt like twenty. It felt like his limbs were freezing, soon to drop off.

He continued forward. Finally, repeatedly clenching his arms against his body, he stepped down from the saddle and forced himself to move around and warm himself, thus getting the blood circulating through his arms and legs. Afterwards, he thought that might have been a mistake. The question now was whether he could get himself back on the gelding.

Maybe not, he thought.

He felt like a small boy wanting his mother. If his uncle could be believed, he might have been fifteen or maybe fourteen. By another standard, sixteen or eighteen. It was hard to tell and he didn't know for sure. What he did know was that he was miserably cold and wet, that if he was going to stay alive he'd have to do something to keep warm, to get dry. If Lexie was going to be saved, if he was going to help her, find her, he'd need to take care of himself. What he had been doing wasn't working.

From his wet, stooped shoulders to his flexing fingers he showed caution. Even in that state of misery he purposely stood back from the ridge line and stared through the pine boughs at the valley below. But for his fingers he held himself still, searching with his eyes, without moving his head. As far as he could see nothing moved. It was pure nightmare-crazy to be out in this weather. He cursed his ungodly luck, slowly shifting his weight from one foot to the other, nearly tripping as his tall boots caught in wiry blades of prairie grass. A sharp pain shot though the calloused soles of his feet. Sitting wet in his tall, soaking boots, they felt frozen cold.

Got to get movin', he thought. *Get movin' or die.*

Intermittent snowflakes drifted past his face, gently twisting and turning, only to melt when they touched the ground--if they reached the ground. Mostly he suffered from a soft, relentless rain falling from a gray sky, a sky that crowded in on him from horizon to horizon.

It was early in the year for snow but he was at a high elevation. Such things happen.

"Holy hell," he murmured, thinking his hat was lead heavy. Unconsciously he rubbed his neck feeling his cold, stub-like fingers against his wet skin. A man could live through all sorts of weather. Not this: his head wet, his shirt stuck to his shoulders, he'd die of pneumonia, or maybe the consumption or something worse. He wondered how his death would be, likely, frozen stiff or drowned. It was then he thought of Alexandra.

Removing his hat, he massaged the back of his neck, again trying to work out the stiffness. Reseating it, pulling the brim down almost to his eyes, he cursed himself. In that moment of reflection he'd taken his eyes off . . . everything.

Gettin' careless, he thought. *No argument here. If I have to move fast, if*

93

my life depends on it, I'm dead. It ain't happenin'. I can't get out of my own way.

Below him, somewhere out in the timber, there were folks that would gladly relieve him of his life, of what life he had. He was sure of that, dead sure. Finding them was a huge problem. How to rescue Lexie once he found her was another problem. He didn't know the answer. The solution seemed impossible.

Just keep goin'.
Keep goin'? Damn it. Go where?
Forward.
Just where's that?
You don't know?
Well, where is it?

A branch cracked. Both horses turned their heads to the sound. The dog rose to his feet growling. Nothing moved. Zeke sniffed at the air.

No smoke.

He looked for a telltale wisp: someone burning wet, green wood, a bending column of smoke against a gray sky, something drifting through pine. Nothing.

Lord, he thought. *I'm lookin' for smoke? What could possibly burn in this?*

Small drops of moisture beaded up on his ruddy cheeks. He'd been trailing shod and unshod horses for the better part of four days. Now this storm. There was nothing to trail: no tracks, no nothing. He looked.

What now?

The rain had weighted the once dry grass until it lay flat against the sod. The once blaring trail had disappeared: in creek bottoms full of swollen, rolling water; in the flat pelted earth; in the bent, heavy grass stems. From horizon to horizon, there was more rain. Add to that wind. Thankfully it died down from time to time. It was but a whisper for the moment. Zeke searched the valley below. There was nothing moving. Even the buffalo, the elk, the deer were holing up out of the wind and rain. Wherever Lexie was, her captors weren't moving either.

Eli once said that no trail simply disappears. "It's there. Look fer it, boy." He should have added, "If ya kin get to it soon enough," or "Unless it's rained and rained and rained," or "Unless it's covered in wet snow in August." Or both. Or all three.

94

Least there's one of you, thinking of the single track he'd found.

Who?

Don't matter. One at a time. At least there's one.

At least.

Maybe Beth. She's light. Don't weigh much. Track wasn't shoved into the ground. Barely made a mark.

Hard ta tell.

Impossible to tell.

It started raining harder. A stream of water ran off the brim of his hat. Shaking his head, he came to the intolerable realization he'd have to wait out the weather. He had no choice. But Lord, he was ready. He could go on. Delaying for a day would put him behind a day! If Lexie was moving, two days.

The driving rainfall beat relentlessly against the brim of his hat. Rat tat, tat, tat: a cacophony of loud drums. His immediate future was so bleak. It offered no fire, no warmth. Just hide and wait and eat hard tack, and jerky if he could find any dry. Worse. There was nothing to follow: not a track, not a trace, nothing.

I need to survive. Live. I gotta be careful. I gotta be real careful. No mistakes.

Yeah right! In this?

But he felt stupid, just plum, dumb ugly stupid.

No. No. I'm alive and this ain't over. What should I be doin'?

Better hurry 'cause Lexie—she's out there. Somewhere. And close.

But where?

Rainin' and there's no goin' nowhere. Not 'til this weather breaks. Not 'til I can pick up some semblance of a trail. Sooner or later somethin'll move. Got ta. Sooner or later I'll find their trail.

I need a fire. I need some shelter. Gotta get out of this damn wind and rain.

Where? This won't last long. It will warm up once this is over.

All right. Let's find some shelter.

Zeke started looking.

Just off the valley ridge one hundred and twenty yards, he found a ledge, a long crevasse, an overhang. Inside against a rock wall, it was dry. A pack rat had used the place but he was gone, leaving behind odd treasures and an old nest of dried twigs. Using those twigs, Zeke built a small fire; the light smoke drifted up over the rock into the pine needle forest, disappearing into sheets of drifting, driving rain. From underneath some deadfall, he found mostly dry wood and some fine bark. Placing the heavier wood over the small flames, he kept the fire burning using the twigs from the pack rat's nest. The fire dried the damp deadfall until it, too, burned and Zeke felt warmth begin to seep into his muscles and bones.

Under the shelter of the rock face he dried his clothing, his saddle, chaps, and blankets. The fire slowly drove the cold from his fingers and arms. Somewhere in the night he fell asleep in damp blankets lying on cold stone. Outside his makeshift shelter, rain fell; the wind let up.

August 26, 1854

At first light, walking in gentle rain, he searched for any semblance of a trail, finding nothing. He knew there'd be nothing before he looked. But he looked and got soaked in the process. Rain had covered everything, obliterating tracks. His only consolation was that the men he followed would make more.

They have to. Can't fly. Rain won't last.
But they don't need tracks ta get where they're goin'.
I do.
Could ride in a straight line. Get ahead of 'em.
But what direction are they goin'? Really goin'?
Shot in the dark. I ain't got the time.
I got all the time in the world. Lexie don't. Damn it.

Despite his need, the summer storm continued, lasting for four long, intolerable, insufferable days. Gentle streams became roaring torrents; sides of hills, slippery; muddy game trails, impassable.

He walked to the tallest outcropping of rock, climbed the tallest pine, and spent two hours searching every inch of forest and meadow looking for smoke: any movement. In minutes he was soaked again. Using his uncle's glass he searched the forest quarter by quarter, inch by inch: nothing. There wasn't a discernable whiff. Except for thirty head of elk, a small herd of buffalo, several head of deer here and there, and some mustangs, there was no movement. Except for the breeze wafting through the pine there was no sound. Everything was holed up, waiting. He wondered if the men he chased had done the same, doubted it. He assumed they knew where they were going. In the end he found himself alone sitting in a tree growing from an outcropping of rock in a pine forest that seemed to stretch on forever in all directions.

Lexie had vanished into the gloom. She was out there, wet, alone. Somewhere. Probably close. A forced captive.

How would that be?

Under the overhang, repeatedly drying out, he kept the small fire going and waited with the dog. The forced solitude, something he normally enjoyed, drove him crazy, sent him pacing, plagued by the mental image of Lexie being close yet impossibly far away.

Each day of what remained of the four-day storm, he climbed the tall bull pine, clung to the uppermost branches, tied himself to the trunk, and searched: nothing.

After the clouds lifted, he searched for a trail, riding in ever increasing circles: a mile, two miles, three, four. He found nothing but the tracks he made, not a single trail leading through the forest. Taking advantage of the rain, they'd apparently moved on, knowing that their trail was obliterated. No one would follow them even if they had been on their back trail.

Zeke worked out a plan. It was simple: get help, then continue searching until he found her. She was somewhere. She had to be. Standing on the ridge above the overhang, he stared north across the dark pine forest, listened to a hawk screaming as it hunted, its voice echoing from above. Somewhere an owl hooted.

He mounted his saddle horse and rode along the ridge for the first time. North was pine forest. It stretched forever before him. Lexie was lost to him . . . for now.

"Lexie, Lexie," he shouted, "don't give up. I'll find you . . . just not today. But I'm comin'." His voice carried several feet and fell flat. He felt silly. There was no echo bringing her name back to him. A warm breeze picked up. Zeke reined the saddle horse around, retrieved his packhorse, and headed south. He was going for help.

It was the beginning of the seventh day since he'd ridden over the rise and found the wagons, the dead, and no Alexandra, no Bethany, no Priscilla. It was August 29, 1854.

CHAPTER 21
Zeke is 118 miles southeast of Alexandra

August 25, 1854
Wind River
Central Nebraska Territory

It rained on day three in captivity. Alexandra felt limb-heavy tired. Every day, every hour, she was moving, moving, moving with little to eat. She felt tense, as if her world was suddenly and completely disintegrating around her. It was. It had. She felt numb, hollow, beaten: a shell of her former vibrant self. The image of her mother falling backwards into the wagon bed, clutching the shaft of the spear that impaled her, flickered repeatedly through her thoughts. Her father's hand reaching . . . his fingers closing on nothing, his body pitching off the wagon seat, falling, the ground catching him hard, his dying eyes pleading with her for forgiveness: these images stayed with her.

The men stopped repeatedly. Their horses drank and cropped grass. For a brief moment the bare-chested men, damp-wet robes wrapped around their shoulders, stood talking, laughing, drinking. Then they moved on.

At first she thought, *I should . . . drink*. Then she asked, *why?*

Standing alone, legs stiff, muscles sore, her hands untied, she glanced at Bethany who lifted a piece of jerked meat to her lips. Their eyes met. Bethany gnawed like a starving rat on the once bone-dried meat, chewing as if she'd never get another chance.

I need water. Who wants to drink standing in the rain?

Me. I do.

Oh, shut up. Shut up.

Hear me? I'm so thirsty.

So drink.

She glanced at the creek pelted by rain drops. Several of the horses were sipping from the stream. The water's edge was muddy, tromped by milling hooves. Others stood in the creek searching for clear water, blowing their noses, shaking their heads, their tails swishing at horse and deer flies, and mosquitoes.

But, I'll get wet.

I don't care. I have to drink.

98

She took a step toward the creek immediately aware of her captors' eyes following her.

I don't care. I need water.

No one stopped her. For a moment she stood near the edge of the muddied, swirling water and studied the stream, watched a trout darting between moss-covered rocks. She sank to her knees, then stretched out, lying in the damp grass, and sucked muddy water into her mouth.

Oh my God, she thought. *What has become of me?*

The water in her mouth felt good, dirt and all. She felt the fabric of her bodice become soaking wet. Water dribbled from her mouth as she swallowed and took another mouthful.

I don't care. I need water. What's a little wet?

It'll be my death.

Who cares? Shut up. Shut up! Stop it. Just stop it.

She swallowed and sucked more gritty water into her mouth.

Some horse probably peed in it.

I don't care.

And she didn't.

Once finished, Alexandra pushed herself to her knees, stood up, and studied the low, dark, ominous clouds that had settled down on cliffs, peaks, and ridges to the west. She wiped her forehead with her sleeve, the buttons scraping her skin. It hurt.

Oh God, please.

Rain drops began to fall harder: small droplets, long, easy, light on her skin. Minutes passed. Her shoulders were damp, then wet as she stood amid beast and men, her wet and muddy bodice clinging to her body. Soon they were riding again. The rain was falling in huge, cold drops that pelted and stung her face.

Maybe I should do something. Something to slow them down.

What? Fall off my horse?

No. They'll kill me if they think I'm an aggravation. If I'm . . . Beth, what would happen to her? What if Zeke follows me?

That fool. He will. I know he will.

No, he won't. He isn't stupid.

He is. He'll follow and they'll kill him.

Why is this happening to me? Why? Why? Oh, God in heaven, why? What did I do?

The skin of the horse she rode was warm and damp on her

legs.

I didn't do anything to deserve this.

Stop feeling sorry for yourself. Deal with it.

Oh, shut up. I must have done something.

Nothing. Nothing . . . Oh, yes I did. I did do something. I agreed to come out here. That was stupid. If I could only . . .

Well, you can't. So shut up. Think about something else.

They passed through silent, primeval forests of pine and cottonwood: parks and meadows following slow-moving creeks. Rain grew in earnest but did not slow the procession. They moved on and on and on, relentlessly riding north.

Alexandra didn't immediately feel the cold damp seep into her shoulders and back. It was August. It was warm. The longer it rained, the farther they traveled, the colder she felt. Often, more out of habit than anything else, she glanced back over her shoulder, expecting to see no one. It was a senseless and maddening effort to shift her weight around while riding on the back of a moving horse: her hands bound together, without benefit of a saddle, her fingers intertwined in the horse's mane for balance. Still, she glanced back time and again, unable to stop herself, the futility of the exercise mounting.

Had Zeke found the wagons? Of course he had. Well, maybe. Probably. If he was alive. Let's see . . . . He had left early. Three days ago.

That long?

In the evening he'd bring back fresh meat, maybe a deer. Maybe two. He always did that, too.

But we barely had started before they came, before . . .

So what?

He found the wagons. I'm sure of it. If he was alive.

He was alive.

Stop it. I don't know if he's alive. He might not be. He probably isn't.

Doesn't look like I'm going to find out. Not any time soon.

She imagined Zeke running from body to body, turning them over in a futile attempt to find her, but not finding her. Instead he'd find her father, her mother. They'd be scalped, stripped, flies beginning to blow their swollen corpses.

How awful.

Will he follow me? One boy against eleven fighters, killers, savages?

He isn't just a boy. He's eighteen.

100

She glanced back over her shoulder.

He can shoot.

I hope he doesn't. It's a fight he can't win.

No, he won't. Not if he's smart.

He's smart. They'll kill him. If he isn't already dead.

He's not. He's not. I can't imagine it.

No. He'll be like Mr. Tallasinius. He'll make them pay. Yes, he'll make them pay just like Mr. Tallasinius; then they'll kill him, leaving his body for the crows.

That's awful. Would you stop it!

She turned on the back of the walking horse and looked back, staring up at canyon walls, watching herself slip away one step after another. There was no longer any urgency: no hurry.

They feel safe.

And why not? No one is following us. What bunch would Zeke follow? If he could?

None. Rain is washing away our tracks. Everyone's.

She turned on the back of the horse, staring at the receding trees. Nothing. Each stop was brief. The horses were watered, allowed to crop grass. Sometimes one mount was exchanged for another. Then they moved on. The pace remained constant: the distance eaten up like buttered popcorn in a wooden bowl, kernels filling many mouths, disappearing, gone.

According to Alexandra's count the rain started to fall on the third day after the massacre, when her life ended and the nightmare began. Rain followed more rain. They moved along swollen creek beds, their horses walking in rushing water, their tracks disappearing in the torrent. The once waving grass was pressed to the ground. Evidence of their existence was erased from the earth like a wet rag collecting bread crumbs from the kitchen table. By noon their horse tracks were gone entirely; their very existence disappeared like cloudy breath on a frosty morning.

We're lost, she thought. *We are so lost.*

That's right. I want to be lost. I don't want Zeke to follow me. I don't want to worry. If he does, he'll be killed.

What? How's that?

Think. He'll surely follow me. Well, one of the groups. If he's alive. This rain will wash away everything. There will be no tracks. With nothing to follow he'll go back. He'll have to. He'll go for help. Help is so far away. Two, three, four

101

weeks, even a month later he will return. He won't find me. I'll be gone. I'm already gone.

She turned, looking back, nodding her head. Tears ran down her cheeks.

He'll forget me. There'll be nothing left of us. Nothing. Maybe he'll go to California. He'll go to California. Nothing keeping him here. He'll meet another girl. And they'll have babies. In California. Yes. California. Maybe Oregon. He could go to Oregon.

Her horse stumbled, regained its footing, and continued to walk. She didn't look back. Stifling a sob, she worked her fingers into the horse's mane, felt his body moving under her. Each step took her farther and farther away, dropping her into the dark abyss.

After they'd been pushed and shoved up onto the wide bare backs of horses for the umpteenth time, the girls hardly spoke to one another. Their circumstances didn't lend themselves to communication. Talking required speaking loudly. Yelling hardly seemed appropriate with dark death hanging over their fragile minds. Used to walking, they were in reasonably good physical condition but their legs were not used to riding bareback on a wide horse. Their leg muscles inevitably grew sore and stiff.

They did not stop. Once the bare-chested man who had captured them brought them wool blankets to wrap around themselves, plunder taken from her neighbors and fellow travelers. Soon the blankets were damp and wet. Once wet, their value was questionable. But it was something, even after the wet wool began to smell. The smell was the least of their problems: it ranked little compared with sore legs rubbed raw from endlessly riding; from the beast's backbone threatening to split them asunder; from gnawing hunger; from the constant wet; and, in spite of the rain, suffering from thirst.

Alexandra knew they were moving north; no one hid the fact or seemed to even care. She knew because on the first day after the rain stopped and the clouds lifted, the North star remained a constant, always in front of her, always in her face. It was a fact verified every evening after the sun sank in the west and the North star appeared again.

Rain would have stopped wagons whose owners would have wanted to avoid getting stuck, mired to the hubs in mud. Not her captors. Their measured pace held steady: riding off the mountain onto a barren, dry, broken land through the winding brilliance of Wind River Canyon; following the rushing waters of the big river; riding down the river bed, leaving no tracks.

The rain stopped as they rode out and way from it. The lost sun reappeared and the cold rain was replaced by dry heat. Their tongues grew dry, their lips chapped and cracked, sometimes bleeding. The humidity disappeared, replaced by a dry, hot endless wind. Alexandra was surrounded by red hills, sagebrush, winding game trails, the big river on her left, mountains on her right.

The girls were looked after by their captor, their caretaker, their provider, their jailer, their savior: the killer. At his hands lay the death of her parents, Priscilla's parents and siblings, their friends and acquaintances: everyone. Her parent's blood dripped from the blade he carried in his waistband. The lives of everyone with whom she'd eaten, joked, walked, talked, and, in the evenings, sang songs were gone. People with whom she remembered swatting mosquitoes and sharing a fire for so many insufferable days and nights, weeks on end: all dead. In the place of companionship was the loneliness of captivity, the fear of being killed, of suffering painful death like everyone else.

Alexandra thought about the three white men.

Men? Horrible creatures who contemplated killing us, who would have killed us but for the presence of Indians. . . Savages.

She laughed a derisive giggle. *Savages,* she thought. *What's worse? These Indians? This one now looking after us? Or those white men who would kill us because we saw them?*

There was a paradox: her intolerable captors, whose hands were heavily tainted with blood and the fact that she wasn't dead. She saw the irony: her captor preserved her life and fed her, and had killed everyone else.

Oh my God, she thought. *We're actual plunder. We're slaves. Captives.*

She thought of the Romans, their armies marching, paid by the head, enslaving entire populations, selling people into slavery, sending them back to Rome to die on the floor of the Coliseum. She thought of her grandfather, for he'd told her about Julius Caesar and Caesar Augustus.

Plunder. Property. That's us.

Alexandra studied her captor. She guessed he weighed about one hundred eighty-five pounds. He was of a slender build. Brown certainly from genetics, certainly from sun, wind, and more sun. He appeared to be impervious to the changes in temperature, to the rain, and, for a while, the snow that fell unexpectedly from the late August sky. He went shirtless, wore no head covering, wore leggings, moccasins that covered his feet to the ankles and a long loincloth that extended from his waist to his knees.

His hair was black, long and braided, tied back and out of his face with a strand of soft otter skin. Behind his left ear hung three short eagle feathers. When she'd first seen him, his face had been hidden beneath streaks of white and red paint and he was fearsome running toward her, a long knife in hand. No longer. Except for the three feathers behind his left ear, he wore no ornaments. He was tall, on the average taller than his companions. She estimated he was five eleven or maybe six feet: much taller than her five foot seven inches.

CHAPTER 22
Zeke is 140 miles southeast of Alexandra

August 27, 1854
Big Horn Basin
Central Nebraska Territory

It was morning. Alexandra had reached her wit's end long ago. The leather binding that secured her hands had loosened. She worked it repeatedly until it came completely undone. Finally the narrow leather strap fell away from her wrists, dropping off her horse's shoulder to the ground. At first she expected someone to notice; no one did. She kept her fingers entwined in the horse's mane. The feeling she had was of freedom. She was an adolescent getting away with skipping school, her hand in the proverbial cookie jar, crumbs on her lips. She had a secret.

Something should happen.

With the binding gone, she sat straighter on the horse's back, its head bobbing slightly as it walked, the lead rope slack. She waited, hesitating.

I'll get caught.

She considered slamming her horse in the sides with her heels, and racing away. It didn't matter where. The thought of leaving Bethany kept her still and silent, taking furtive glances to either side without moving her head.

Why haven't I been caught?

She watched the brown bare back of the man leading her horse.

What shall I do?

Something.

She chose nothing.

Take a chance, she thought.

No.

Yes.

She slipped off the side of her horse, her feet touching the ground. She stumbled, almost tripped herself. Stiff from riding, she could hardly walk. Somehow she kept her balance and took a step. Again nearly falling, she caught her balance and took another step. Ten

105

steps later, she was still walking beside her horse, her right hand resting on his warm skin for balance. Several times she stumbled. Yet she caught her balance, took another step, then another. Secretly, she was very pleased with herself. So far, nothing had happened. It surprised her. No one seemed to notice. Her heart was pounding. She expected something dire, maybe an arrow between her shoulder blades. Oblivious, the individual leading her horse continued on without a backwards glance. No one said anything. No one did anything. Her good fortune seemed unbelievable.

Good fortune? I'm flirting with death.

So what?

Alexandra slowed, letting her horse slide past, allowing him to go by, then stepped behind him. Fifteen minutes passed. Alexandra continued walking, keeping the bay horse's hind end in front of her, blocking out her view of the rider in front. It felt like hide and seek, with her hiding in plain sight, not stepping to the right or left. The grass and the dry sagebrush was knee high. She moved through it, each step taken with a step of defiance, knowing she'd be caught. She didn't care.

I'm not afraid, she thought. *I am not afraid. What are they going to do?*

In the heat her mind wandered. The sun felt good on the side of her face, the wind cool on her skin. Walking felt good. She began to think she might be able to slip off to the side. There was a rider fifty yards behind her preventing it; he'd see. He'd discover her. And if she did, then what? She was unsure, hesitant.

In front the lead riders turned slightly with the trail; she could see Bethany and Priscilla a hundred yards ahead. Slipping away was so impractical. She kept walking, touching the tops of the grass stems with her fingers. The line of horses seemed to lengthen. The wall of pine trees on either side was closer. The sage next to the trail was taller.

Behind her an alarm was sounded.

Now, she thought. *Now.*

Her heart fell. Faces turned. She saw two riders coming, charging toward her. She turned. So did the warrior leading her horse.

I'm caught.

Alexandra stood behind her horse, suddenly surrounded by five mounted riders staring at her. She waited, standing innocently, not moving. Her captor appeared from behind two of the outriders. One of the warriors spoke to him, laughed. Out front a hundred yards

Bethany and Priscilla's mounts had continued forward. She could see Bethany looking back at her. The laughing man reined his horse around and started up the trail, following the two girls and the captured horses, seemingly unconcerned.

Alexandra remained still, waiting, staring ahead. She could still see Bethany looking back at her. Her captor sat upon his horse staring at her without expression. Finally the trailing rider came up behind him. She stared at the ground. The captor said something which she didn't understand. No longer looking at her shoes nor staring sheepishly at the ground, she stared right at him without thinking until she couldn't stand it and had to look away.

You're such a blood thirsty savage: a bastard.

There's a word I don't dare say out loud, she thought.

I'd kill you if I could. I can't. I know that. But I would, given the chance.

The trailing rider moved on, leaving her alone with her captor. He spoke to the man who had been leading her horse. He smiled, dropping the rein and, without saying anything, nudged his mount forward, following the tail end of the moving column. Her captor picked up the single rein and handed it to her. He pointed to the trail ahead, offering a directional nod, pointing again. Alexandra started afoot, leading her horse. Her captor followed behind her fifteen yards. She dared not look back at him for fear he would change his mind.

This is progress, she thought.

Afterwards they stopped several times. He did not bind her hands, nor were they bound again. Once free, she began to cultivate one single obsessive thought: escape. It was all she could think about.

Do nothing overt, she thought. *Nothing so out of the ordinary as to draw attention. My time will come. I'll be a shadow. Someone will blink. We'll be gone. We'll escape. And soon.*

In the late evening after the stars littered the cloudless sky, they finally stopped. Reunited with her sister and Priscilla, she untied their hands. They waited for an explanation. She explained what had happened, at the same time thinking nothing had happened, really. But something had.

"Listen," she explained, whispering and looking about herself furtively, then back at her sister. "We're going to escape."

"Why whisper?" Priscilla pointed out. "No one here speaks English."

Alexandra stared at her. "I suppose you're right. But I'm

worried someone does. Maybe a word or two."

"Well, they don't speak English. You were talking about escape. What about it?"

Alexandra nodded, hesitated. "Yes," she said. "We have to escape together. We need to prepare. When we're ready, when the time's right, we go. Okay? We plan, we work our plan. We take our chance."

"That isn't much of a plan, Lexie. Is that all you've thought of?"

"Do you have something better, Pris? If you do, let's hear it."

"What? You mean better than plan, wait, run?"

"Yes."

"I don't," Bethany said, rubbing her wrists.

Priscilla grunted. "That's the problem," she said. "I don't, either. But that's no plan. It's barely even an idea."

The sisters looked at her.

"We can do this," Alexandra said. "We can. We have to."

"Who put you in charge?" Bethany inquired.

Wordlessly, Priscilla looked at the sisters, glancing from one to the other. "Yes, who?" she said.

"Father," Alexandra answered. "Our father did."

"He would. You were his favorite until I was born." Bethany laughed for the first time in days. How she did that Alexandra did not know.

"We're in this together," Priscilla said. "We'll decide together. Okay? It's a joint decision."

Bethany nodded. "I sure don't want to live like this. What are you thinking exactly? What shall we do?"

Alexandra looked at Priscilla, hesitated. Speaking slowly, she said, "I'm thinking that if we do something stupid right away like running and getting caught, our hands will be retied. Getting free will then be more difficult. Right now, for the first time, our hands are free. Hopefully they will stay that way. It's a first step. We need to be in plain sight: no threat. I say we become invisible, gain their trust. Then . . ." She stopped talking. "That's what I'm thinking. It's as far as I have gotten."

The two girls were looking at her. After the silence became intolerable, Bethany said matter of factly, "It's a start, Lexie."

"Yes, it's a small beginning," Priscilla agreed. "Gain their trust.

Prepare ourselves. Run. Any other ideas? It doesn't seem like much."

Alexandra shook her head. "No," she said, unsure of herself. "You? Do you have any?"

Priscilla replied, "Well, it's not like we can do anything right now. Not with everybody watching us like hawks."

Alexandra nodded, thinking she's sounding reasonable; be careful. "Listen," she said, "if they don't tie our hands, not again, everyone will really be watching. We'll need to be careful. They'll be expecting something. Give them nothing. I mean, nothing."

Bethany nodded. "I'm hoping someone finds us."

"That'd be nice," Alexandra agreed. "That'd be real nice."

It's not likely. Not likely at all.

"I'm losing track of time," Priscilla said. "How long's it been since . . . you know?"

"Five days," Alexandra said. "On August 25, you know, it started raining; then it rained and rained. The farther we came, the less it rained. Yesterday we went through that canyon and the rain stopped. It stayed on the other side, I guess. So five days. Today is the fifth day, I think."

CHAPTER 23
Zeke is 162 miles southeast of Alexandra

August 28, 1854
Big Horn Mountain, Head of the Tongue River
Central Nebraska Territory

Excitement is palpable. It can be felt, smelled, seen, heard. It crowds the heart, forcing it to beat faster, leaving a person caught in the swirl of it, breathless and agitated. Alexandra glanced about her. Her captors, all eleven, were "dressing up." Preening. It was not unlike the churchgoing crowd preparing for Easter Sunday except their captors weren't that normal "Sunday go to meeting" crowd she'd been used to. Their personal riding horses were painted with lightning bolts and shields and white and red hand prints on their chests and flanks. Faces were decorated: painted in whites, reds and off-blues; feathers were strategically placed; hair was brushed, combed and braided. Ordinary leather leggings and loin cloths were exchanged for a "better" more beaded, colorful variety.

Once dressed and mounted, rifles were held at the ready, barrels pointed into the morning sky, stocks resting on thighs. The several horses and riders milled about, sometimes spinning into action based on expectation and adrenaline. The chatter, laughter, and teasing was infectious.

A war party all dressed up, she thought. *Why? There doesn't appear to be any immediate danger. Nothing to attack.*

Those without rifles carried spears decorated with feathers and colored ribbons: spears carried in hands, or held across mounts, the working ends pointed down, up, or at the ready. In the east the sun had risen, framed in a light blue cloudless sky. Soon most of the eleven men were mounted, ready, and waiting impatiently.

Excitement seemed to mount until its seams began to leak and its unruly fabric nearly cracked and shattered. Minute by minute their band of captors was transformed into fierce warriors: fearsome, capable, dangerous.

"What's going on?" Bethany whispered.

"Going on . . . ?" her sister answered.

"Yeah."

"It looks like they're going into battle. Getting ready to kill someone . . ."

"Who?"

"I don't know."

From her horse's back Priscilla surveyed the orchestrated commotion, pursing her lips nervously.

Alexandra was silent, watching, expecting bad things, certain she wouldn't be disappointed.

Priscilla's misgivings finally burst. "Do you think they're . . . ?" She stopped. "Should we make a run for it? Now? While we can?"

"Just how far do you think we'd get?" Alexandra replied. "They're plenty ready for something. We wouldn't get far. Escape is just an excuse to get ourselves killed." Alexandra's voice trailed off. "Right now, running is not a good idea."

Bethany whispered, "I don't want to die."

Alexandra glanced at her sister. "They're not going to kill us, Beth. Why bring us all this way to do that? I think they have something else in mind."

"It looks like they're going to attack someone."

"Yes, but who?"

"How would I know?"

"It scares me . . . not knowing." Bethany glanced at her older sister.

"Me, too."

The warrior who'd captured and preserved them in their mortality suddenly appeared,seemingly out of nowhere. He was walking, leading a painted horse. Dressed in his finery, he approached Bethany sitting on her horse. He patted it on the shoulder and looked up at her. Alexandra watched. Today he seemed more like the frightening warrior who'd thrown her to the ground and tied her hands and feet.

Same man. Always the same man.

Looking at him, she could hardly breathe, remembering another man standing over her, staring, her father's scalp in hand, blood dripping into the curing grass. Priscilla saw Bethany start to recoil.

"Beth," she said, "don't move."

"But . . . "

Alexandra cautioned. "Stay still. Do you hear me? Don't

move."

"I hear ya, Lexie. What's he going to do?"

"I don't know. We're about to find out."

The warrior took the rein to Bethany's horse from her hands, Priscilla's also. Alexandra, seeing what he wanted, handed him hers, and sat her horse, watching him, expecting him to bind their hands. He didn't. Instead, he turned away, mounted the paint and, leading all three horses, started forward.

The procession fell in behind him: their captor out front leading the three horses that carried the three girls; followed by the others driving the captured/stolen horses, keeping them close together. At first they kept to the tree line, not venturing into the open meadows. It felt like they were hiding. Three miles later they topped a rise and the plain before them opened up on all sides. Mountains rose in the distance, their very tops white, capped in last year's unmelted snow, framed by dark forests. A mile away, sitting along a creek bed were forty to fifty lodges, tentacles of smoke rising from many campfires. Behind the lodges on the rise beyond the creek, extending to the mountains, were many horses, grazing. The procession momentarily stopped, hesitated, then started slowly, no longer keeping to the edge of the pine trees.

Oh, we're playing hide and seek.

From a distance a solitary shout rose. People began walking from the lodges to see the cause of the alarm. Seeing the riders, they immediately turned from their tasks and ran across the plain to meet them. Seconds after the shout, a trilling sound began to rise. Additional shouts of greeting spread across the plain, bringing more spectators.

Moments later, the returning warriors, dressed up, were rushed from all sides. The procession stopped dead in confusion. The trilling continued, growing louder. Dogs barked amid shrieks of joy. Fearsome men slid from their horses' backs, engulfed by smiling, laughing, eager women, and people, young and old. The hugs and cheers were like nothing Alexandra had ever heard before, not even in the Boston harbor on the 4th of July.

The return of the eleven, Alexandra thought.

In the midst of the confused celebration, the three girls sat their horses. Alexandra felt her legs being touched, slapped, sometimes struck with a stick. She looked around. Young people, boys and girls, were tapping her legs, and running away, only to return and do it again.

112

Her horse began to sidestep to avoid the onslaught, only held in place by her captor's grip on the rein.

In the middle of the milling people, their captor slid off his painted horse, holding the reins to four animals. He handed one rein to a boy ten years of age, patting him on the head, keeping the reins to the other three horses himself.

Oh, I get it. We're trophies: the spoils of war, something for everyone to see, something to admire.

A young girl, her black hair tied back, approached him from the edge of the crowd, slowly walking, then running. Their captor, the killer of emigrants, picked her up into his arms, carrying her forward. She broke into a smile, tears streaking her cheeks, her arms around his neck. It was so odd to Alexandra: such a blood thirsty, awful group, fresh from killing–a massacre—violent and savage, yet loved and adored by these children.

How could this be? I wonder where his wife is? Are we his gift to her? Slave girls? The girl is probably his daughter, the boy obviously his son. I wonder if there are others.

The killer of emigrants started walking, holding the young girl in his arms, the boy walking beside him leading one of the horses. A keening sound arose on Alexandra's left, growing louder and louder, followed by tears and cries of lament. As quickly as it arose, the persons emitting the cries were engulfed by those around them. It had an odd feel to it: an understanding of loss; a sorrow; a pride; an acceptance framed by denial, accompanied by fear and remorse. Others appeared, clearly glad that the sorrow wasn't theirs, that their men had their arms around them, that they were there walking with them.

"Lexie . . . what's wrong with . . .? That kid keeps hitting me with a stick."

"Don't do anything."

"I'm not. But I am going to take it from him and beat him with it."

"What's the . . ?"

"I think someone important didn't come home."

"This is home?"

"I think so. Yes."

"That lady over there. She is really upset."

"Don't point. I think she's discovered that her man is dead, that he's not coming home."

"Me too . . . I'd be upset. Hard to feel sorry though. What do you think . . .?"

"I don't know. I'm hoping she doesn't take it out on us."

The horses they rode were led through the lodges. Another girl joined their captor. A little older, perhaps thirteen or fourteen, she walked with him, chattering incessantly. She looked over her shoulder at Alexandra, Bethany, then Priscilla. She smiled. The killer listened., nodded. He handed the small girl, the one in his arms, a blue and red doll, pulling it from his waistband. She examined it, laughing, excited, wanting down. In response to her sudden wiggling, he set her feet on the ground.

Beth, clearly agitated, said, "Lexie. Lexie, did you see that? He gave her that Funson girl's doll. Oh my God. She's dead. I saw . . ."

"Beth . . . get hold of yourself. We don't want them looking at us."

The killer handed the boy a folding knife. For the older girl, he produced a red dyed wool blanket that Alexandra recognized. It had belonged to the O'Reilly woman. At the moment she couldn't think of her name and really didn't want to think about her. The older girl was clearly appreciative: all smiles, clutching the red blanket in her arms, running her hands across the fabric.

They're his, Alexandra concluded, noting the similarities: high cheek bones, same skin coloration, the set of the eyes, the gait with which they walked.

Clearly his daughter for she is too young to be his wife.

"Lexie?" Priscilla said, her voice a whisper. "That's my father's. That pocket knife. That, that was my father's," Priscilla said softly, almost in tears. "That bastard," she whispered. "I'll kill him. I swear I will."

"Pris, keep it togethr. Get hold of yourself."

The ten year old boy was talking to his father, engaging him in an animated conversation, waving the pocket knife, working the longer blade back and forth.

The procession--three girls, four horses, the killer, three young people--had separated themselves from the others and walked through the lodges.

Alexandra whispered to Priscilla, "Pris, don't do anything. Don't say anything. Hear me?"

"It was my father's." Her voice was hard, angry.

"I know. I know. It was. Not any more. They won. Remember? We lost. Your father's dead." Alexandra paused, glancing at Priscilla. "Everybody's dead . . . Pris . . . except us." She could see that Priscilla was beside herself. "We have to keep it that way."

"But, Lexie, Lexie," she said, "no, please, no. I can't stand it. I'm going to kill him. That bastard. I'm going to kill him. He had to pull that knife right out of papa's pocket. He's a murdering thief. I'm going to kill him."

She started sobbing, her hands covering her face and eyes. The killer turned to the commotion, seeing Priscilla choking back sobs. He said something to her, then he spoke to the boy who held his "new" folding knife in his left hand. The boy nodded and took off running, disappearing amid the lodges. The little girl standing at the man's side watched Priscilla futilely trying to wipe tears from her face. They kept on running down her cheeks onto her blouse.

It's about a knife? Alexandra thought. *Just a knife.* She longed to put her arm around Priscilla, pull her closer to comfort her. She wanted to say, *Is it just a knife?*

No. No, not that. I'm wrong. It's all about loss. Her father, her mother. It's about . . . it's about dying. Being dead.

I'm so full of it. What do I know?

Priscilla seemed to be melting on the broad back of the bay horse she rode. Alexandra glanced behind her at the many people yet walking into the village, the returning warriors, their greeters.

I can't believe it. It's all wrong. They're so happy. So many smiles. Look at us. Look at Pris. So frightened, so angry. What are we going to do?

Oh shut up. Please just shut up. You're insane.

She glanced at her sister and again at Priscilla. What she saw was a mountain of darkness, distrust, anguish. She felt the fear emanating from their beings: fear that death was imminent, that at any moment someone would leap out and stab them.

If it happens . . . when it happens . . . no one will be surprised. No one will know. No one will remember. And these . . . these savages will go on smiling, waiting like they did for a warrior's return. And this man's such a savage--a killer--and he's home. I wish I could kill him, too. I do.

Oh, shut up. Shut up. Do you hear me? I said shut up. Stop feeling sorry. Do something.

Like what? Kill him? Like I could.

115

Oh, shut up. Just shut up.

Alexandra glanced at Priscilla, watching her shoulders shake in grief.

Someone should die. It should be the killer.

Stop it.

Around them the August morning was shaping up warm, cloudless. Insects were buzzing. A wafting breeze shifted from the east. The eleven o'clock sun had marched steadily up the sky almost reaching its zenith.

The horses that carried the girls stopped when the entourage stopped. They were standing in front of a large lodge that sat on a flat, grassy bench ten or twelve yards east of a clear running stream. Foot traffic, in and out, had tromped the grass flat around it. To one side was a yellow fire encircled by large white rocks collected from the nearby stream. Next to it was a stack of dry limbs and branches broken into useable lengths.

The killer motioned for them to dismount. They did and he, the child with the Funson doll, and the girl with the blanket, busied themselves, chattering back and forth, smiling, laughing. Bethany, Priscilla, and Alexandra stood alone on the edge of another people's universe, Priscilla stood sniffing, fighting a runny nose, red eyes, and sobs that welled up inside her. The sisters were silent, waiting.

The three captives waited. They had no place to be, nowhere to go. The only safe place they knew, they'd left months ago. Here everything was so different: so new, so threatening, so unexpected, so dangerous. They held their collective breath, waiting for unwanted attention, wanting to disappear into the very grass that lay trampled under their feet. Tired, exhausted, traumatized, worn thin, they were ready to be quiet, patient, to go unnoticed. No one spoke, each fearing to call attention to themselves, each leery of the grief, heartache, and, perhaps, separation that attention would bring upon them.

Alexandra glanced at Priscilla whose hands covered her mouth, her cheeks streaked with tears. She was seconds away from another massive, terminal melt down.

Hang in there, girl, she thought, glancing at Beth.

Now what?

Their captor handed the reins of the horses to the boy who'd reappeared. He led the horses away, pulling their reins taut, talking to them, urging them to move forward. They finally did but not as fast as the boy wanted. The killer glanced in Alexandra's direction and said something to her; she stared at him, hardly breathing, completely in the dark.

What does he want?

He repeated himself. The littlest girl, Funson doll in hand, came to her, seizing Alexandra's hand with small fingers, looking up at her through large brown eyes as she pulled at her hand. Alexandra glanced at the killer, then followed the six year old who led her to the opening in the east side of the lodge. Pointing, the girl held the covering back, waiting, staring at her. Alexandra looked at the opening, glancing at the little girl.

What does she want? What is she saying? I'll bet she wants me to go inside. Should I?

The six year old, still holding Alexandra's hand, dropped it, disappearing through the opening only to turn and look out at her, beckoning her to follow.

"Beth, Pris, come with me. She wants us to go inside."

Tentatively, Alexandra followed the small child, stepping inside, allowing herself to be directed to her right.

The interior was larger than Alexandra expected. Outside it hadn't looked this large. It was conical shaped, a tipi, given shape by lodge poles rising above her. It was a large circle. Bethany and Priscilla had followed her. All three stood inside the entry. Rib-like lodge pole pines jutted upwards, meeting at a tight opening high off the ground. Buffalo skins formed double paneled walls. A cold ash fire circle dominated the center; black coals were dead, their edges gray-white. A taut leather strap extended down from the top of the lodge and was tied to a stake driven into the earth in the middle of the circle slightly to the side, out of the fire circle. Its purpose seemed to be to hold the tipi down, tying it to the ground. Except for the center fire ring the lodge floor was covered in cured skins. Alexandra glanced at the venting flaps above her head, seeing a small piece of the noon sun.

Why would they need a leather rope tying down a heavy tent? It's not as if it would float away.

The girl, the Funson doll in one hand, pointed to a place where multiple cured skins were stacked. Alexandra nodded and sat down. Her sister followed suit. Alexandra looked up at Priscilla. She hadn't stopped crying and was an emotional wreck: her eyes puffy, her cheeks stained with tears, her lips trembling uncontrollably Alexandra

117

remembered her crying when she saw Colleen's scalp dangling from a warrior's belt; she thought of Bethany's involuntary tears. But not she.

No not I. *I haven't. Crying is due*, she thought. *We all ought to be crying.*

"Pris, Pris, sit down here," Alexandra whispered. "Here, come sit by me."

Priscilla complied, Alexandra pulling her in, hugging her. The singular act of kindness caused Priscilla to cry more, the emotional dam breaking. Alexandra rubbed her shoulders and whispered in her ear. Words didn't help.

How could they?

Alexandra glanced at the little girl clutching the doll; her dark eyes followed Alexandra's every move, watched Priscilla's sobbing, Alexandra rubbing her back. The girl spoke. Alexandra smiled at her, wondering what she said. The girl smiled, walked around the fire circle, then stepped outside.

Bethany was massaging her left leg and glancing curiously around the inside of the lodge.

"Boy," she said aloud, "that kid smacked me. Did you see that? He whacked me with a stick, then ran like I was going to beat him. I would have." Examining her leg, she continued. "I think he bruised it. What was that all about? Do you think they're going to keep doing that? I certainly hope not."

From outside the lodge they heard a low keening, a cacophony of sound rise and fall on balance. It was an odd combination of laughter and joyous celebration amidst cries of sorrow and remorse.

"Listen to that. I guess we're lucky we're still alive," Alexandra observed.

"You call this luck?" Bethany replied. "What are they going to do to us? That's what I want to know. I'm hoping . . . I'm hoping we make it through this day alive, in one piece. Sounds like a lot of unhappy people. What's with that boy whacking me with a stick? The little savage. I'm going to whack him back. That's what I'm going to do."

The six year old girl reappeared, climbing through the opening, the doll in her right hand, strips of dried meat in the other.

She asked if we were hungry. Must have.

Holding the doll under her arm, she distributed a piece of jerked venison to each of the girls, patting Priscilla on the hand as she did.

"Thank you," Alexandra said.

The girl looked at her, hesitating.

From the left of the entry way she brought them water in a leather container, handing it first to Bethany who looked at it, hesitating, surprised. Alexandra wondered if Bethany would drink, whether she was even thirsty, and was amused when she did.

Taking a deep breath, Alexandra closed her eyes; she had her arms around Priscilla, patting her shoulders. When she opened her eyes, the girl was standing in front of her holding the water container. Alexandra took it. Dark round eyes following her every move. "Thank you," she said.

The girl mimicked her words, again patting Priscilla on the shoulder as Alexandra took a swallow. Alexandra handed the container back; the little girl stood looking at her, then at Priscilla.

"Pris, she's offering you some water. Do you want a drink? Better take it."

Priscilla sat up, looking from the girl to the water container.

"Thank you," she said taking the proffered container. She took a swallow, wiping her lips with her sleeve. "Thank you," Priscilla said again and handed the container back.

The girl mimicked the words, saying "thank you." She smiled, patted Priscilla on the shoulder three times, and took the container to where she'd gotten it, setting it down by the entryway.

Alexandra leaned back, lying on the skins, and closed her eyes. She listened to the breeze slap the skins against the lodge poles.

Oh God, she prayed, *make this all go away.*

CHAPTER 24
Zeke is 132 miles south of Alexandra north of the Sweetwater

August 29, 1854
Big Horn Mountains-Head of the Tongue River
Central Nebraska Territory

The prisoners stayed inside. In the evening the man Alexandra called the killer brought a tiny woman to the lodge. Tiny, small, petite: she was under five feet in height, slender. She smiled and stood patiently, a woman with every hair in place, her doe skin dress clean and neat, fitting her small frame, a narrow belt encircling her waist. Long fringe decorated the bottom of her sleeves and dangled from the bottom of her skirts. Beads in intricate, expanding patterns decorated her blouse. Her feet were adorned in small beaded moccasins.

The two sat down on the skins, the killer seating himself first. Once the man made himself comfortable, he pointed to the woman and said something they didn't understand. The three young women stared at him, collectively hesitating, their worst fears etched on their faces.

The woman spoke. She said simply, "He say listen my words."

Bethany responded, excited. "You speak English? Oh my God, my God! You speak English! What a relief."

"Beth!"

"Don't Beth me, Lexie. We can get our questions answered. That's what we want. That's what I want."

The small woman nodded. She said, "English. I speak. This one wants, Me talk what his words say."

"Okay," Bethany said, looking from the passive face of the man to the intricate features of the woman. "We have some questions. I mean what's he going to do with us? Why are we here?"

"Beth!"

"Lexie, we need to know why we are here. What does he want with us?"

The woman looked at Beth. "You . . ." she paused. "You, how you say it, taken big fight." The small woman nodded, then turned and spoke to her companion. Following their conversation, she turned her attention to the girls. "First, number one. This one. My sister husband.

120

This one."

She paused as if thinking. "I think you talk slow. No understand too much. This one, me," she smiled, "This one," she pointed to their captor, "Name. Walking Eagle. He called after father. Father great medicine talker, singer. You know this one? This one in fight take many scalps, count much coup. Brave. Some say shirt wearer someday. Understand this? One in front. Much respect. Many people come this one, talk, plan. You understand this?"

Bethany spoke, her voice soft, like a whisper. She asked, "And you? Who are you?"

"I am, how you say . . . Small Bird, I think this? No speak English too much. I am name of not so big bird."

"Small Bird?" Bethany asked.

"No. I am called what called."

"Little Bird?"

"No. I not remember how said. What I called."

"Blackbird?"

"Not this one."

"Snowbird?" Bethany asked.

"No. No important. This one Walking Eagle. He husband." The small woman's voice trailed off as if deep in thought. She glanced at Walking Eagle, then at Bethany.

"He's your husband?" Bethany asked.

"No," she said. "Sister husband."

Alexandra thought this fact must be important; the small woman had mentioned it twice. "Where's your sister?" she asked.

"No sister."

"No sister?"

The small woman hesitated. "Sister gone. You know this? Gone."

"Gone? You mean dead?"

"Yes. Dead."

Alexandra hesitated. *What do I say to that?* she thought. She said, "I'm sorry."

"What this sorry?"

"Sad. I'm saddened for your loss. Sad for you."

"You are?"

"Yes. I just lost my mother, my father." Alexandra glanced at Walking Eagle. *This bastard killed them.* She hesitated, then looked back at the small woman.

"This is true?" she asked.

"Yes."

"Sister die. White man sickness."

Bethany leaned forward speaking quietly, breaking into Alexandra's conversation. "Why are we here?" she whispered. "What's going to happen to us?"

"Small Dove. I called Small Dove."

"Small Dove? All right. Small Dove," Bethany paused. "do you understand my question? What is going to happen to us? Why are we here? Why didn't he kill us with all of the rest. He could have. He didn't."

"Beth," Alexandra said. "Slow down. We don't want to get ourselves killed. Be quiet. Understand me. No more questions like that."

"What do you mean? I want to know." Bethany turned her attention back to the small woman who was looking at her intently.

Small Dove hesitated, nodding slowly then speaking slowly. "You now Oglala. Belong Walking Eagle's lodge. Here. You learn Walking Eagle lodge." Small Dove looked at the three girls to see if they understood. "Take up. Bring down. Walk with. You learn this." She stopped speaking, looking from one girl to the next. "Woman," she said. "What do. Learn. Understand this? This one save lives. Belong his lodge."

Bethany looked at the diminutive woman. "What do you mean what women do? Small Dove, are we slaves? I know we're prisoners. But are we slaves?"

"What this?"

"Does he own us? Like he owns a horse?"

The small woman looked at Bethany without understanding.

"No," she said slowly. "Not horse. No need. Has horse. Many. You taken from rolling lodge by Walking Eagle. Count many coup. Much brave. Captive. Live his lodge."

"So we are prisoners. What are we supposed to do?"

Small Dove looked at the impetuous fourteen year old girl. "Do work," Small Dove paused. "Lodge. This one." Small Dove looked around the lodge, moving her hand, pointing. "You do this one. Make stand up. Take down. Live this place."

"I don't understand." Priscilla interrupted her. "I don't

understand," she said. "Whose lodge is this?"

"My sister."

"And she's dead?"

Small Dove nodded.

"Whose is it now?"

"Walking Eagle. This one." Small Dove pointed at her companion.

Priscilla nodded and asked, "Small Dove? What are we supposed to do? Work? Is that what he wants? He wants us to work?"

"Yes."

"For always?"

"No understand."

"Okay. What exactly are we supposed to do?"

"Sister. My sister. What she do," Small Dove said, nodding.

"We're taking her place?"

"Place? What mean?"

"We're . . . me, Lexie, Bethany are taking her place . . . because she's dead?"

Small Dove paused, hesitated, blinking her eyes, then said, "No. place. You not sister. You do work. I learn it for you. You learn words of people. You learn. Understand this one? Learn words of Oglala, Teton Lakota."

Alexandra nodded, interrupted. "You want us to learn to speak your language."

"This one," Small Dove said. "It better."

Bethany softly asked, "How long before he lets us go?"

"How long? What this one?"

"How long are we his prisoners? How long do we have to live here before he lets us go?"

"No prisoners. For always. Live here, this lodge. I think this. You say it. You like. It good."

Bethany looked at her sister. "Lexie," she whispered, "did she say 'always'?"

"Yes, Beth, she said 'always.'"

"Oh, my," Bethany said, her right hand covering her mouth. "That's a long time. Do you think she understood my question?"

"Yes. She understood."

For the first day and the first night, the three girls stayed in the lodge of Walking Eagle. The opening looked out on the eastern sky and the bald granite escarpments of the Big Horn Mountains. All of the lodges of the Oglala faced that direction. The little one slept next to her chatty sister. The little girl was called Morning Flower. Her sister, She Who Smiles, was pretty with intricate features and a sunny disposition, certainly not retiring, but full of energy and laughter. The boy slept closest to the door on the west side. He was called Whip the Bear. According to Small Dove, one day he too would be known as Walking Eagle: the name given his father, his grandfather and his great grandfather. But not yet. It was a name that must be earned.

The inside of the lodge wasn't crowded even though seven people slept within its confines: the three girls together, Walking Eagle next to his son close to the entryway, his weapons close to hand and east of where the three girls slept.

All of this Small Dove explained to them. It did not make sense to them but that was the way it was from the beginning. Those first days in the lodge of Walking Eagle were not restful; sleep was a stranger sitting outside the door. It was a shadow that did not visit. When it was needed and wanted, it was gone. Some say it walked along the creek called after the red berries of August, turning its back on the lodge of Walking Eagle, avoiding the captives. Some say it was wading in the cold, swirling water.

That first night as they lay amid the skins of their benefactor, they listened to the wind play with the smoke flaps, sometimes forcefully flapping the heavy buffalo skins against the poles that carried the weight and gave the lodge form and function. Any sound seemed loud and full of torment, promising evil.

"Lexie? Are you asleep?" It was a whisper. "Lexie?" Bethany asked again, not waiting for a reply.

Alexandra sighed softly. "Yes," she said. "I'm awake. Who can sleep?"

"What do you think is going to happen to us? Really, I mean?"

"I don't know," Alexandra replied. "I don't think they do. Whatever it is, it isn't good."

"I'm thinking we'll find out soon enough."

"I suppose you're right."

"Maybe," Bethany whispered. "Did you hear her? She said 'always.' Did you hear that?"

"I heard her."

"Lexie?"

"What?"

"'Always' is a really long, long time."

"Yes, it is, Beth. Try and get some sleep."

"I'm not sleepy. I'm scared."

"Me, too. At least we have a lot of time."

"Ha, ha. Very funny."

In the morning before first light, when all was quiet and false dawn was a shadow in the east, Alexandra was shaken awake by Small Dove.

"Come," she said. "Wake up. Okay? Need wood for fire. Show you. For cook. For food," Small Dove explained.

"Cook? Cook what?"

Small Dove smiled. "Learn this. Okay, good? Understand. First word." She pointed at a stick lying on the ground. She said, 'cha aletka' and waited. "Cha aletka. You say."

Alexandra repeated the word, staring in the dim light at the small woman. She said it again; it sounded like chahn-ah-lay-dkah. She repeated the sounds again, looked at Small Dove and asked, "What does it mean again?"

"Tree. Limb. Wood. You know the 'branch' tree. You need for fire."

Alexandra repeated the phrase, "Cha aletka."

This is going to be all sorts of difficult, she thought.

Alexandra woke the other two girls and they made six trips up the creek into the aspen groves, then into the pine timber forest, bringing back armloads of wood. Alexandra repeated the words "Cha aletka" again and again.

"What are you doing?" Bethany asked her.

"Learning. Trying, anyway."

"What's it mean?"

"Tree branch. Stick, I think. Maybe it means firewood."

"Oh." Bethany looked at her sister over her armload of wood. "That sounds hard. How long do you think it will take?"

"Forever if we don't get started."

"Don't you think you're smart enough? I do. I just don't think I'm going to need it. Someone will come for us. Maybe Zeke. Maybe he'll come."

"I hope you're right, Beth. I hope he comes tomorrow."

"You don't. You don't think he's coming. You think we're going to die. So you don't want him to come for us."

"Beth, he doesn't know where we are so he can't come. And even if he did he'd be killed. So you're right. I hope he doesn't come."

"But you wish he would."

"Yeah, I wish he would and hope he doesn't." Alexandra looked at her sister. "We aren't going to die. I can tell you that. I will not let it happen. As soon as we can, we're walking out of here. That's what's going to happen."

"Did you hear Small Dove say we are moving tomorrow?"

"Yes."

"Why?"

"They found buffalo."

"Buffalo?"

"Yes. Do you know how to say that in Oglala?"

"Buffalo?"

"Yes."

"How?"

"Tatanka."

"Tatanka. Wow. How many words do you know now?"

"Thirteen."

"Do you know how to say 'where's the nearest white man?'"

"No. I don't. But I know which way is south. I know that's the way we want to go. South. You need to get with it. You need to help and try not to get us killed."

"I didn't get us killed."

"You're right. You didn't but you could have gotten us killed, running off at the mouth like that. You don't jab the wolf in the ribs standing in his den. Know what I mean?"

"Okay, Lexie, okay. I'll help. That's what you want, isn't it? You want me to help."

"Beth, I wish you would. And you are. I'm not saying you aren't. Really, I'm not. We just need to prepare. We need to be ready so when the opportunity comes, we can take it. We need to learn how to stay alive. That's what we need to do."

"All right. All right. Jeez, Lexie."

Bethany looked at her sister. She asked, "What do you think that means? To us, I mean?"

126

"It means tomorrow we're following the buffalo."

"What did she really say? Do you know? I mean, really?"

"She said, 'Tatanka kici ahakab.' I think that is what she said. It was something like that. It means 'I follow the buffalo,' I think."

"That's amazing. How do you remember that, those sounds?"

"I say it over and over again, ten thousand times. I asked her to say it to me. I listened. It's so hard to hear. You should try."

Priscilla dropped an armful of wood at her feet, glancing at the sisters. "What's going on?" she asked suspiciously.

"We're about to move," Bethany answered.

"What does that mean . . . move?"

"They're looking for buffalo. That's what it means," Bethany answered Priscilla. "It also means nobody will find us. We move and it's more difficult. If it's not impossible already. Right, Lexie? No one knows where we are or where to look." She glanced at her sister, waiting for her response. It came.

"Beth, believe me, no one knows where to look right now. Following buffalo will not make any difference at all. What makes a difference is food. Small Dove said for us to fill those leather sacks. She called them something. Parfleches, I think."

"They are hunting buffalo so we can fill those bags?"

"I asked her, 'fill them with what? Buffalo?' She said she'd show me. She said we need to fill them with dried meat from deer, elk, buffalo, with something called pemmican, and with dried berries."

"We're just slaves no matter what Small Dove says."

"I know. We all know that. What I don't know is where we are. We need to know that in order to go where we can get help."

"We have to stay alive until we can get help. Right, Lexie?"

"Help? No. There isn't going to be any help. We have to escape. We have to know where we are so we can go someplace safe. Otherwise, what's the point?."

Alexandra looked at her sister. "What I'm saying is if we don't gather food we will have nothing to eat. So we need to gather food, store it, and then escape. Rescue? That isn't going to happen. We need to prepare ourselves. On top of that, winter is coming. We need clothes, coats, food, three horses. We can't run in the middle of a snow storm so we have to work hard now. If we take off right now we're dead. We'll have nothing to eat, nothing to keep us warm and dry. What's worse we don't know where to go other than south. So we need to prepare, put together the necessary things we'll need. We have to work like no one is coming," she paused, "because nobody is. It's up to us."

"Well, Lexie," Priscilla said, "I think this Walking Eagle is punishing us for being white. I think he holds us responsible for his wife dying. That's what I think. That's why we're alive. It's sort of torture. That's what it is."

"Lots of women get sick and die, Pris."

"Wow," Bethany exclaimed, "and I thought he just needed us to work. So he's punishing us, too?"

"I think it's more than that. He could have gotten another woman from here. There are plenty of them. He didn't. Instead he got three white girls to replace his wife. He thinks the white men killed his wife. That's why we're here. He's punishing us. That's what I think."

"His son and daughters are nice," Bethany said.

"Yes, they're nice and we're their replacement moms. That's what we are. He's an angry man. And he's somehow holding us responsible."

"Why do you think that?"

"From what the Dove woman said."

Bethany stared at Priscilla. "Do you think he'll hurt us?" she asked.

"He already has. Where have you been?"

"Okay, you two. What you're saying makes it even more important to prepare our escape as quickly as possible. Let's work as hard as we can, get ready, actually be ready. Listen, I think we have a problem. More than just what you're talking about. Winter's coming. If we get snowed in before we're ready we're going to be in real trouble. We'll be stuck until spring comes."

Priscilla nodded. "I think we agree, Lexie. I don't want to be punished for the rest of my life. And I certainly don't want to be here. So, what do we need to do?"

Alexandra looked from Bethany to Priscilla. "Okay. We need food. We need three horses. It would be nice to have four: one to carry our food, bedding, extra clothing. The closer we get to winter we'll need warmer clothes. We need weapons. We have to be careful. Really careful. That's what we need. We need to get all of these things without anyone suspecting or seeing us. We have to hide these things in plain sight.

128

Bethany looked at Alexandra. "Let's talk about what you don't want to talk about. What about Zeke? What about being rescued?"

"Forget it. Beth, it won't happen. Like I told you. Nobody knows where we are. Not a soul. They're dead. Zeke, too. Even if Zeke's alive and he found us, they'd kill him. So forget him. He isn't coming and if he did there's nothing he could do for us. We are on our own. So please. I don't want to hear his name again. Ever. We're on our own. No one is coming."

Bethany stared at Alexandra. She said, "I wish what you said wasn't true."

"Well, it is," Alexandra said.

Priscilla didn't say anything.

CHAPTER 25
Alexandra is 267 miles west of Zeke in the Big Horn Mountains

September 5, 1854
South Central Nebraska Territory
Fort Laramie

Zeke and the O'Reilly dog forded the North Platte river below the spot where the Sweetwater dumped into it. Keeping the big river on his left, Zeke found Fort Laramie at its confluence with the Laramie River. The Platte ran high and muddy, full from extended rain. A local cloudburst had turned it a yellow hue but the high water was caused by rain much farther away.

Zeke needed supplies to augment what he had, as well as more oats to feed the black and his packhorse. He needed conversation. He needed some idea of what to do, who could help him. He needed information. Most of all he needed hope. Zeke had never searched for a particular someone before, someone helpless, someone lost in a vast, unforgiving land. Other than the three riders he'd trailed for a short distance toward the Sweetwater River south, he was the only one living or dead who knew anything about Alexandra, her sister, Bethany, and Priscilla. The rainstorm hadn't reached that far south. Their tracks were there, etched in the earth, though more than a week old. His was a singular bit of information that only he knew. What had befallen the hapless emigrants, his uncle, and the three missing girls was news.

It was his duty to tell someone. He needed help. He needed to get going and quickly. Time was wasting; daylight was burning. The girls were gone.

Zeke reached Fort Laramie September 9, 1854, the seventeenth day following the massacre north of the Sweetwater. Fort Laramie wasn't the size of St. Louis or Independence, but it was busy. Wagons moved in and out. The U.S. army maintained a garrison of troopers. There were trappers, Cheyenne, Hunkpapas, mountain men, and bums and everything in between. Long ago, it had been known as Fort William, then Fort John, and had existed since the 1830s for the protection and convenience of trappers and pilgrims. Same place, different names.

Riding down the only street, he saw wagons full of emigrants, horsemen, and soldiers in blue tunics, wearing pants with a light-colored yellow stripe up the leg. He saw more soldiers than he had ever seen in one place. That caused him to wonder what was happening that required so many men, so many guns, so much anxious energy. Dust hung heavy in the street. It had the makings of a hot September day.

Securing the bay with a wrap hung loosely around the hitching post, the packhorse's lead attached to the back of his saddle, he stopped at the Sheriff's office. He was first on his list of first things. Given the serious nature of his message it was the place to start. The O'Reilly dog sat on the boardwalk, his tongue lolling out of his mouth, watching him as he grabbed the doorknob and turned it.

The marshal, a middle-aged man with a pot gut and a drooping mustache, sat behind a scarred desk that looked like it had been raked by the rowels of several spurs. A rifle rack half full, sporting one Hawkens and two Sharps rifles, hung on a solid log wall behind him. A saddle was thrown in the corner, the cinch lying haphazardly out onto the floor. Two boxes of paper cartridges sat on a dusty shelf: one opened, the other not. A second man was making a vain attempt at building a fire in a Franklin stove. He wasn't winning; the coffee pot sat cold on the top burner, waiting. The man swore, shaking his hand vigorously, but did not look up from his task. Zeke liked coffee but not that much. Still, his mouth watered thinking about it. It had been a while.

The marshal, his gunbelt partially hidden by his protruding stomach, looked up when Zeke stepped inside pulling the door closed behind him. The office smelled of cigarette smoke and burnt coffee grounds, unwashed men, and horse sweat. There were no curtains on the windows facing the street. In the back were three jail cells but no current residents and no windows. Zeke felt the eyes of the seated man resting on him. The other fellow kept his attention on the stove, periodically grumbling, the blue tipped wooden matches failing to light one right after another.

Zeke removed his hat and nodded a greeting at the sheriff.

"Help you?" the man behind the desk asked.

He seemed pleasant. Still Zeke was nervous, not liking that "alone" feeling, wishing his uncle was there to back him up. Not that he needed help, he told himself. He could hold his own, carry his weight. That wasn't the problem. It was just that this "alone" wasn't his favorite feeling and he'd gotten a fair dose of "alone" lately. It was being "alone" and on his own that pressed down upon him, weighing heavily on mind and spirit.

"Yes, sir. I need to report a killin'. Several killin's."

"Ohhh?" The marshal sat up in his chair. "Who's dead?" he asked.

"Everybody, sir. Everybody's dead."

The tall lanky man trying to build a fire stopped what he was doing and stared at Zeke, suddenly interested in what he had to say.

"Dead? Like in killed?

"Yes, sir. Dead like in killed."

"I suppose you better tell me your story. You see this killin'?"

"Yes, sir. I mean, no, sir. I didn't see no killin'. I just came back and everybody was dead."

The marshal paused. He said, "Let's start with who you are."

"Name's Zeke, sir. I ride with my Uncle Eli."

"Eli the wagon master? Tallasinius?"

"Yes, sir. He's dead, too, sir. You know him?"

"Most everyone knows or has heard of your uncle."

Zeke didn't respond to the statement.

"When was this?" the marshal asked.

"It's been two weeks, sir."

"You say you didn't see this killin'?"

"No, sir. I didn't."

"Well, how do you know? You ain't tellin' me a helluva lot."

"I looked at the ground, sir. It was all right there. Besides, they was all layin' there dead. All of 'em. Not like I could miss seein' 'em."

The marshal stood, continuing to size up Zeke, pulling a pipe from his pocket, popping the bowl in his left hand. "Start at the beginning," he said. "You're confusing me."

"Yes, sir. I didn't mean to confuse you." Zeke took a deep breath and began. "Sir, before we took off on our own we was a day and half behind the Wilcox Company and in front of Johnson Company about the same distance. I'd gone to hunt fresh meat. Do some scoutin'. Left early mornin'. Came back in the evenin' with two doe dressed and cleaned. When I got back the wagons was where I'd left 'em except everyone was dead."

"Everyone?"

132

"There was three girls. I didn't find their bodies."

"Know who done it?"

"Injuns, sir."

"Injuns?"

"Yes, sir. And I figure three white men."

"Three white men? With the Injuns? That's serious charges. How do you know?"

"They was there. I followed 'em here."

From outside there came a row: an angry dog barking, growling, a yelp in pain. Someone swore. A weapon of some caliber discharged. The dog started shrieking, howling in pain as though he'd been drop-kicked into the next county and shot for his trouble.

"Excuse me," Zeke said to the marshal and stepped to the door, grabbing the handle, yanking the door open.

Outside a weapon discharged again. The dog renewed his shrieks and pained howling, then began a low, menacing growling. Zeke stepped out into the bright light of day. In front of him the O'Reilly dog was crouched on the boardwalk in front of the hitching rail, the black horse staring down at him, pulling at his reins. The packhorse was pulling at the black. The dog was facing a man with a .36 caliber Navy pistol in hand, deliberately bringing it to bear on the dog's head. The fellow was a study in concentration, not taking his eyes off the dog even after the door flew open and Zeke filled the doorway.

The marshal had seen it before: the young man turning toward the door, his right hand brushing the leather loop off the hammer of his side arm, hardly noticeable, reaching for the door knob, the left hand seizing the butt of another pistol hidden behind his gunbelt in the small of his back. Yet there it was. He heard it before. The clicking of the hammer being pulled back, locking, was unmistakable. Whether the sound emanated from the pistol on his thigh or the one hidden in the small of the man's back was harder to discern.

It was both.

Zeke immediately addressed the situation. He said, "You drop a hammer on that dog and they'll be throwin' dirt in your face 'fore the sun sets. Your choice. Make it quick. I ain't got all day."

"That son of a bitch bit me. He's a dead one. I'm gonna kill him. He's mine."

"You kicked him and you obviously can't hit a door with a

133

rock, you standin' in the doorway, it bein' right in front of you. You done had two shots and ain't hit the ground. Lucky for you. Otherwise you'd be dead."

The shooter stopped short, holding himself still, sensing danger. He turned his head slightly toward Zeke.

"How do ya know I kicked him?"

"He barked."

"He's in the middle of the walk."

"Best you reconsider."

"Who the hell do ya think ya are?"

"I'm the one who's gonna ventilate your worthless hide should you shoot my dog. That's who I am."

"Ya and who else?"

"There ain't nobody else."

The marshal's voice broke up the conversation. "Eddie," he said, "you ought to reconsider. Best you put that iron away, you know what's good for you."

Maybe the marshal's voice was one of reason. Maybe not. But the barrel of a Navy Colt pointed at his abdomen did give Eddie some pause. What he saw was the young man's right hand on the grip of a pistol he hadn't pulled from the thigh holster and the left hand holding another Colt without a tremor, the hammer pulled back and locked.

"Easy, dog," Zeke said softly. "Easy."

The dog whined.

"He hurt your dog, boy? He hurt?" the marshal asked. "Eddie? Put it away."

Eddie seated the hammer softly.

The marshal said, "Boy, let it go."

"I ain't no boy."

"I can see that."

"Eddie, back away."

"Not with him . . . ."

"Eddie, back away."

"Marshal . . . "

"Eddie."

"All right. Okay. I'm puttin' it away."

"See that you do. Slowly."

Zeke hadn't moved.

"Now, Eddie."

Eddie Harmons had been close to shaking hands with the grim reaper before. Maybe not this close. Suspecting it, knowing it, he said, "All right, Marshal, I'm backin' up. I'm puttin' it away. I'm leavin'. Ya better get that . . ."

"Don't do anythin' stupid," the marshal interrupted. "Now, boy . . . Let him go. Hear me? Let him go."

"I ain't no boy."

Zeke's right hand moved away from the pistol butt. Not far. His left hand, however, did not waver. The O'Reilly dog was standing; he sniffed at Zeke's pants leg, his tongue lolling out the side of his mouth. It was growing September hot in Fort Laramie.

"Over a dog?" the marshal said.

"The dog didn't do nothin'," Zeke replied, still watching Eddie. "Mindin' his own business. Not hurtin' a soul."

"Best you come inside. Mighty quick pullin' that iron, don't you think? You coulda killed a man over a dog."

"Didn't have no time to be askin' permission and I ain't got but one dog."

Zeke was watching the would be "dog killer" walk backwards down the boardwalk. He hadn't taken his eyes off Zeke. Stepping off the boardwalk, he worked his thumb and index finger in the form of a pistol, pointing it at Zeke, letting the thumb go forward, a smile etched on his face.

"Why not now, killer? Pull it and go to shootin'." But Eddie was off the boardwalk into the street, moving away.

"Eddie, get the hell out of here," the marshal said. "Now, come inside, kid. Finish your story. Where'd this massacre take place? Best you get off the street. Eddie ain't worth shootin'. Did you say a two week's ride north?"

Zeke turned, glancing at the marshal.

"No. Six days from here. It took me six days to get here."

"Survivors?" The marshal followed his deputy inside, looking back to see if the kid was following him. "Was there any survivors?"

Zeke glanced at the dog, rubbing his head, then down the street before following the marshal inside. He said, "Not countin' me, there are three girls missin'. That'd be Alexandra, and her sister Bethany and a girl named Priscilla. I couldn't find their bodies. They ain't dead far as I know."

"Three girls? How old?"

"Fourteen, seventeen, eighteen."

The law officer took a deep breath, glanced at his deputy. "What can we do, Richie?"

"Nothin'. Too far. We ain't got no authority up there. That's Army only. We ain't even supposed to be up there."

Richie glanced at Zeke. "You're talkin' that Sweetwater country, ain't you? This side of the Wind River Mountains?"

Zeke nodded.

"It's impossible, anyways. Time we get there it'll be close to three, four weeks. They're already to hell and gone. If there was a trail, it wouldn't be readable. Time and weather will see to that."

Zeke nodded his head in agreement. "There ain't no trail," he said. "It rained, even snowed a bit, if you can believe it. Lost it." He thought about telling them he wasn't even sure who he was following at the last: didn't want to mention the band dividing, riding in three directions. He didn't. He couldn't. It was already bad enough.

"There you go, boy," the marshal said. "No trail. We get there, assumin' we could get some help, there ain't nowhere to go. Time we get there, there ain't nothin' to do except bury bones. Those girls are gone no tellin' where. Besides, it's Army only up there."

Or in which direction.

The marshal looked at Zeke. "There you have it, boy. Nothin' I can do. It'd be a wild goose chase. I can't raise no army. 'Sides, I ain't got no authority in that country and I ain't got it in me to kill every Injun there is. Some folks would sure as hell like to. Nothin' I can do." He paused, staring at Zeke. "Ain't what you expected, is it? What did you expect?"

"I don't know, sir. I figure I'm supposed to tell someone. I told you. You bein' the Marshal."

"Easy on the kid, Buck. He's just reportin' a massacre."

"Richie, I know. I know. What he's doin' I sure as hell know. But I'm not the Sheriff. I'm the Town Marshal. Besides there are ten thousand square miles betwixt here and there. The Sweetwater is about two hundred miles from here. Crawlin' with Injuns. He ain't said it but he's expectin' me to ride out there and find the women. That's just crazy."

"Buck, he's just reportin'. Cut him a little slack. Loosen up a bit."

"All right, Richie. All right. I hear ya." The portly marshal

136

turned to stare at Zeke. "Now look, boy, I appreciate you comin' ta talk with me but this is Army business. They're here to protect the citizens from the Injuns. You take yourself right over to the fort and tell it to the general or that Colonel, whoever it is they gots over there. He's some worthless sonofabitch but he's there. Got all those soldier boys kilt. That's what he did. Sawdust for brains. You tell him. Understand me? I can't do a damn thing for ya. It's in his hands, not mine. He's done started hisself a Injun war all by hisself. Ain't needin' no help."

Zeke nodded, glancing at the man called Richie, then back at the marshal, hesitating, trying to decide how to leave.

"One other thing, boy. Best you stay away from that Eddie. He ain't too smart. Liable to shoot you in the back. Stay away from him. Hear me? I don't want nobody gettin' kilt on the account of you and that damn dog. Not in my town."

"I hear you, Marshal. Go to the colonel. Stay away from the dog shooter. Don't cause no trouble in your town." Zeke paused. "Thank you, both," Zeke said, and quickly stepped outside where he could breathe. And breathe he did, thanking God for clean air, wondering what the hell that was all about.

The officer in charge of the Fort Laramie garrison was a man named Lt. Hugh Fleming. The marshal didn't like him much and it didn't look to Zeke like he'd get to see him. The adjutant, a master sergeant Leodegar Schnyder, seemed to be in charge and talkative so Zeke introduced himself.

"What do you want?" he asked Zeke, leaning his arms on a desk, his tunic open, a five day beard on his face. "The Lieutenant hasn't got time."

"I'm come to report a massacre. Don't suppose he could make time, do you? I think he needs to know what I got to say. The marshal in town sent me. Said that Injuns would be you folk's business."

"Not another one."

"Another one?"

"Massacre." The master sergeant sat down and leaned back in his chair. "You aren't from around here, are you?"

Zeke shook his head. "No, I ain't," he said.

"Well not three weeks ago, August 19, Lieutenant Gatton took twenty-nine of our troops eight miles east of here to arrest an Injun named High Forehead for the offense of killing a Mormon milk cow."

"A milk cow?"

"A milk cow. Seems that High Forehead killed and ate him. High Forehead didn't take to being arrested for killing a cow. While they were standing around talking one of them trigger-happy troopers shot the old man, Conquering Bear in the back. Kilt him dead. Well, mostly dead. Died later from what I hear. What did they expect? The entire detachment was dead in minutes. The whole detachment and Lieutenant Gatton, rest his miserable soul. They were standing in the middle of five thousand Oglala, Hunkpapa, and Brule Injuns camped thereabouts waiting for their allotments. Allotments they never got, by the way. What'd they expect? Sawdust and horseshit for brains."

"I just rode in here from up north. I didn't see no five thousand Injuns."

"That's because they left after the killing of those soldiers. Gone. Moving north. You passed them. Sure as hell surly bunch."

"Over a cow?"

"Over a cow. That's why the Lieutenant is busy as hell. Another massacre, you say?"

"Yes, twenty-four wagons, all the emigrants except for three girls and me. Up on the Sweetwater."

"Must have run into those Injuns leaving here. There were a lot of them. That'd sorta explain it."

"Could be. There was three white men with 'em. I trailed 'em mostly to here. Wasn't much of a trail. Old. Did the best I could. Looked to me like they came this direction."

"I'll see if the Lieutenant will speak with you. Don't be expecting him to do anything, what with losing twenty-nine troopers and his first officer. No replacements. We don't have enough men to defend this place. Plain and simple."

"Thank you."

"For what? I haven't done anything yet."

First Lieutenant Hugh Fleming was seated when Zeke came through the door. He remained seated.

"A massacre?" he said without offering Zeke a seat or allowing him to introduce himself.

"Yes, sir."

"Sweetwater?"

"Up in the Wind Rivers."

138

"Nothing I can do about it. Give the sergeant the particulars. We'll investigate soon as we can. It won't be soon. Anything else?"

"They took three girls captive."

"Tell Sergeant Schnyder. That all?"

"No, sir. I mean, yes."

"The Sergeant Major will show you out."

It was a short conversation.

The O'Reilly dog, waiting outside the adjutant's office, was all tail and tongue when Zeke reappeared. He was the only one happy.

CHAPTER 26
Alexandra is 267 miles north of Zeke in the Big Horn Mountains

September 5, 1854
Fort Laramie
South Central Nebraska Territory

Saloons, God bless them. They are everywhere, in every settlement, and not by chance. Sometimes they are the settlement. Most are housed in a nondescript square or rectangular building where folks are brought together not so much for a drink but for the society that results from having a drink. For travelers they are a pause in a journey to somewhere else. For locals they are a destination: somewhere to hole up on a regular basis for a few precious minutes; to be provided an opportunity to get out of the relentless sun, the ceaseless wind; to take shelter from an unforgiving, hostile land. They are a place to dry off or out, to be entertained by a sweet voice, to forget, if only for a few hours, the difficulties and dangers accompanying the activity of simply sucking in and breathing out in an inhospitable, unforgiving country side.

For most, they are the proverbial 'watering hole', a place to let the day's cares evaporate in thin mountain air, to hear how old 'Steam Boat' still hadn't been 'rid' by some two-bit cowhand from west of the Pecos. They are a place of commiseration: to feel sorry for "ol Buster Billings getting hisself near tromped to death, escaping with just a broken leg and a busted arm," a place to offer sympathy. To the man, they were glad to hear he'd only be "stove up" a year; it could have been two. "Good gravy, Aunt Martha, he coulda been dead, that lucky so'n'so." Most importantly was the cold, yet certain, unspoken conclusion: the realization that it could have been one of them. Thank God it wasn't. That's saloons. That's what saloons are for and why they are important and why there are so many of them west of the Missouri River.

Zeke had been in saloons; the first time he was nine. His Uncle Eli liked to set up his 'guidin' folks west' shop there, conduct his traveling business in the back room, or at a corner table with his back against a wall where he could see everyone coming and going. Pilgrims came to see him, to find out when he was leaving Independence and,

140

before that, St. Louis, and more important, where he was going that year. They looked him up to get an understanding of what they'd need and if they were to go with him. What would it cost for him to guide them, their wagons, and their life's possessions to Sutter's Mill, Auburn, California, or the Oregon Territory to see the preacher Marcus Whitman? Except he was dead along with his wife, Narcissa, killed by Indians. They knew that. No matter.

If the emigrants were fortunate and Tallasinius was going where they wanted to go, they wanted to know what the possibilities were of reaching the green rolling hills of San Francisco alive. He'd say, "nine outta ten." The travelers would stare at him for a moment, finally nodding their heads, looking knowingly at one another. It wasn't them that was going to die. It was someone else. Those were damn good odds when it wasn't you dying. That so-and-so, he was just trying to scare them. Well, winners don't scare easily. They were all winners.

"When we leavin'?" they'd ask. In response Eli would say, "Soon as I get some of your gold coin . . . not a minute sooner."

Young Zeke never stayed long in a saloon; he didn't like men staring at him like he was a nasty cockroach, like he didn't belong because he'd barely learned to walk, everyone thinking it was "no place fer a child." That first time he was hungry and his uncle had brought him there to feed him.

The second time, he'd gone to see his uncle to get instructions on what Eli wanted him to do. In his young life his uncle had all the answers: the hows, whens, and wheres. Having someone who knew things like that was a comfort to the boy. Besides, his Uncle Eli was better than the priest who had no time for him at all.

That "first time" was in St. Louis, Missouri, ten minutes after Eli Tallasinius had "rescued" his nephew from the grips of the Catholic Church. The "second" time was two weeks later. Back then, it was early April; he was hungry. The long room was dark--not so dark that he couldn't see--but dark. Men were playing cards at some of the tables while others were standing at the bar talking. He remembered thinking how elegant the bar was with the dark bottles behind it and the long picture of an almost naked girl above. His Uncle Eli sat at the corner table, a bottle and several glasses in front of him, talking to two men, emigrants determined to go west. After they'd left, Uncle Eli looked at him and told him to sit himself down. So he did, sitting in a chair too large for him, in a smoky room too dark, his belly growling from being too hungry. In that first time Zeke ate boiled beans and his Uncle Eli's partially eaten steak. It was a little tough, probably bull buffalo meat, but it was good because young Zeke was a saddle horse running on empty using the last few blades of curing prairie grass to get by.

"This place, boy," Uncle Eli began, waving his hand about, "is the emporium of news. If ya want ta know somethin', just walk in, find yourself a table, preferably in a corner where your back's against the wall. A table where ya kin see everythin' and everybody. Order yourself a drink, some beans, a steak with a piece of corn bread, perhaps some apple pie, if it's the season fer it. Sip and chew, but not fast. Figure on takin' all mornin' ta get yourself around a single drink and a nice slab of fresh buffalo steak. Just sit and listen. At the end of the day ya'll have learned more than ya kin imagine. It's right handy, boy, ta know these little tricks. It'll help ya get by."

Eli had looked at Zeke.

"Remember that, boy," he said. "A saloon is the library of every contemporary ill-conceived rumor imaginable. Know what that word "contemporary" means?"

"No, sir," Zeke said. He didn't know what 'ill-conceived' meant either but he didn't say so.

"It's every bit of new gossip that kin pass through those portals and cross the lips of men ready ta talk. It's a place ta go when ya need ta know what's goin' on."

"What's a portal?"

"The door."

"Oh," the boy said, not sure why that was important or exactly what he could possibly want to know that would bring him to a saloon, where solitary men stared at him, their faces telling him that he didn't belong, that he wasn't wanted. Besides, the place smelled like rotten apple juice, like soured barley kept too long in a fifty-five gallon drum, and old moldy men who used soap once a year, the last time being eight months past.

"Another thing, boy."

Zeke looked at his uncle, waiting.

"Don't go into a saloon with the loop hangin' over the hammer of your shootin' iron. Don't do it. Never know when ya'll need ta get ta it. That's one of those 'nevers' ya shouldn't oughta forget. Gents, capable men, have lost their lives fer less. Zeke, if ya remember anythin' I tell ya, remember that. It's a life saver."

Once the harried, worried, and now discouraged Zeke arrived in this dusty collection of buildings called Ft. Laramie, he had gone to speak with the marshal, then to the livery. He had his horses grained, fed some timothy hay, and rubbed down. Afterwards, he had their shoes looked at by the smith. Uncle Eli had said ad nauseam, "take care of your horse. First and foremost: take care of your horse." So he did. Second, he went to the Carlyle General to order supplies: coffee beans, bacon, salt, flour, cartridges, beans, jerky, hard tack, a new shirt and a slicker that didn't leak so much. He also had his left boot repaired, the heel replaced, and new soles sewed on.

Lastly, after he'd had the conversation with the local marshal, he spoke with the U.S. army adjutant, a worn out master sergeant who hadn't shaved in a couple of days and who stared at him through red, bloodshot eyes. He didn't smell very sweet either but he liked to talk.

After the first two frustrating, fruitless and condescending conversations he found himself in a quandary, certainly augmented by his standing in the middle of the street in a one street, one horse town, in the middle of nowhere: Nebraska Territory. His youthful brow was worn down; three lost girls were depending on him and only God knew where they were. Furtively, he looked up and down the roadway feeling especially ignorant. He needed to know what to do: what was going on, especially up north where men and women disappeared, never to be heard from again. Being eighteen was bad enough. Being eighteen and stupid was worse.

Uncle Eli had said that folks disappeared but Zeke had never seen people just vanish like smoke drifting through pine needles. He'd thought his uncle was just talking. At the time disappearing seemed to be an improbable, remote idea. Everyone was someplace. Lexie was someplace. His self-appointed, yet simple task was to discover where. On this Tuesday afternoon he needed to know where to look for three white girls: especially one wearing a billowing blue skirt, with eyes that sparkled, who was always smiling, and who needed his help.

She could be dead.

Yes, but he refused to think of her in those terms. Alexandra's death was inconceivable so he shook the thought from his mind: pushing it away, keeping it at bay, refusing to accept the possibility. Zeke looked for "an emporium of contemporary knowledge" and located three saloons. He selected the one with the most horses tied to the hitching rail. It was the closest. Still, he glanced at the closed door with some apprehension before mounting the worn boardwalk. He'd already been turned down and around twice.

Before pushing the door open he glanced at O'Reilly, listened to his thumping tail pounding the boardwalk.

"Better stay here, dog," he said. "No use you gettin' yourself stomped on. Stay outta the way. Hear?"

The dog stared up at him, his long tail thumping away in a syncopated rhythm.

"I reckon not."

Turning his attention to the door, he remembered the leather loop that held his pistol in the holster, sliding it off the hammer as inconspicuously as possible. He patted the Navy Colt he'd tucked behind his belt buckle, the walnut grip easy to his left hand.

Odd, he thought. Uncle Eli's voice was ringing in his ears, his words hard, if not impossible, to forget. Zeke took comfort in that and stepped through the doorway, pushing the door open before him.

It was dark inside, dimly-lit. The windows in the room provided just enough natural light sufficient to see. The bar itself was a series of three planks held together by cross pieces; the planks rested on top of two empty water barrels. The surface had been sanded and was smooth to the touch, certainly not level. It looked like dark pine. The room was rectangular, longer than it was wide. In front of him on his right were tables and chairs, men seated playing cards, drinking, talking, and laughing. More importantly they paid him no attention. The heavy plank bar on his left extended halfway down the length of the room. It was just as he remembered except the bars in St. Louis and Independence were of dark, polished wood, gleaming in dim light. This bar didn't gleam; it made do.

He remembered the second time he stepped inside the Diamond in St. Louis to find his uncle, to tell him what he'd said and done, following his instructions. He remembered searching the room for his Uncle Eli. He'd found him in a corner, his back against the wall. Hurriedly, feeling anxious, Zeke had scurried across the room, not wanting to be stopped, stepped on, or interfered with. In short, left alone.

Out of nowhere someone had slapped him behind the ears.

144

He'd been knocked to the floor by the sheer force of the blow, so hard that stars snapped off in his head like fourth of July sparklers. The floor was hard and he struck it hard, not having time to brace himself, the wind knocked from his lungs. After his senses cleared, he found he was lying on the hardwood floor. His uncle towered over him, speaking to the man who had struck him.

"That's my boy," he said. "Ya best be pickin' him off the floor, dustin' him off."

"Tell that whelp ta get out of the way. He's takin' up space intended fer a drinkin' man."

"And you're breathin' air belongin' ta real men. Mighty presumptuous on your part."

Knowing he'd been insulted, the stranger didn't hesitate to reach for his Navy Colt. Right in front of Zeke, his uncle stepped into the stranger, his hand coming down hard, full of iron and steel. The pistol bounced off the man's skull; the sound of it could be heard across the street, or so it seemed to Zeke. The man's pistol went flying and suddenly the stranger was on the floor beside Zeke, though he wasn't moving. Zeke scrambled to get out of the way.

"Ya all right, boy?" his uncle asked.

"Yes, sir," the boy replied.

"Get up. Get that colt and hand it ta the barkeep, then check ta see if this fellow's got hisself a hideaway."

Zeke got up, shaking the fog out of his head, and picked up the man's pistol, handing it to the man behind the bar. He glanced at his uncle a little bewildered.

"See if he has a hideaway, Zeke. See if he's packin' more than one."

Zeke discovered a long knife and another pistol. He remembered it being on the small side.

"Give 'em ta the barkeep, boy."

Zeke did as he was told. When he turned back to his uncle, he watched Eli stomp on both of the stranger's hands with the heel of his hobnailed boot. His uncle looked at Zeke, then back to the prone, unconscious figure with the buggered-up hands. "A little trick I learned," he explained. "Now this gent will be a little slow pullin'. Them hands will need ta heal some. He might hesitate 'fore he slaps a boy around."

"Yes, sir," he said, looking at the swelling hands, the broken

145

fingers.

His uncle was looking at him. "Well, boy, bet you're a bit hungry. Come. Sit at my table yonder and tell me what's goin' on. There's some left over steak and beans. Get after 'em before your Ma comes along and throws 'em out ta the chickens."

"My mother?"

"Yeah, I know. She's dead. But ya never know. Hard ta be too careful."

It surprised Zeke how these "lessons" stayed with him. The fellow behind the pine plank bar, slightly overweight and wearing a dingy white shirt without a collar, his sleeves rolled up, was watching him, waiting.

"Beer," Zeke said, studying the room before he brought his attention back to the bartender. A dark, semi-stained glass was placed in front of him, filled to the brim, foam leaking over the top and running down the side. It looked pretty nasty to Zeke; it was not something he really wanted.

I should have asked for black coffee.

"Two bits," the bartender said.

Two bits, Zeke thought, wondering if he was being over charged. Zeke handed him a ten-dollar gold piece and received the change. "Do you have any vittles? Somethin' handy to eat?"

"Buffalo steak. Pot of navy beans. Cornbread, several hours fresh. My woman baked the cornbread in the skillet this morning. First thing."

"I'll have a bowl of beans and some of that cornbread, and a steak. 'Preciate it."

"Two bits."

Is everythin' two bits?

Zeke paid the man twenty five cents and looked for a table. He found one to his liking in the corner, empty but for a worn deck of cards sitting in the middle of it and two kitchen chairs with tall backs and scarred seats.

Perfect, he thought. *Right where I'd find Uncle Eli, bless his soul.* Suddenly Zeke found himself missing his uncle.

Gently he set the mug of beer down on the table top, then seated himself, his back against the wall. Before doing so, he loosened the Navy Colt in his holster and adjusted the one he'd stuck behind his belt buckle, wondering what he could learn in this place.

Uncle Eli sure liked 'em.

The saloon wasn't crowded. Without counting he estimated fifteen or sixteen men. The bartender was pouring a whiskey for a short, stubby man leaning on the bar talking, a smile on his lips, a few front teeth missing. Directly behind the bartender was a mirror. On either side were rows of mostly dark bottles, some clear. There was a momentary disturbance three tables away. Voices were raised but trailed off without amounting to anything. It was a commotion that Uncle Eli called a "fart followed by a giggle," nothing to worry about. What caused this particular "fart followed by a giggle" Zeke couldn't tell.

A matronly woman, wearing a white blouse and long dark-gray skirts, her dark hair wrapped up in a tight bun, brought him a large bowl of beans. Ham chunks floated amid the beans; three squares of cornbread, butter, some honeycomb and a slab of well-done buffalo steak dominated a tin plate. She smiled and he thanked her. He lifted the foggy glass to his lips, tasted the dark, almost black beer and grimaced, shaking his head. Why people drank the stuff, he'd never figured out.

The woman had turned to leave. "Ma'am," he said, "would you folks have some black coffee you could spare? I sure could use some to brighten my day."

The woman stopped and looked at Zeke. "I do, young man" she said. "I certainly do. I'll bring you some."

"Thank you kindly," Zeke replied, looking at the beer.

Uncle, he thought, *it'll take me all day to get myself around one sip let alone the whole mug of beer. It'll be a month of Mondays. If I was goin' to. And I ain't. That stuff'll gag a maggot. I hate maggots. I surely do. I'll take coffee any mornin', any day.*

Zeke wondered what his uncle saw in the dark, bitter liquid that compelled him to keep ordering it, time and again. The cornbread, butter and honey, beans and ham and thick buffalo steak were another matter. He could take his time but with fork and knife in hand there was no call for hasty decisions. What the woman set in front of him was all but gone in twenty-five minutes and he hadn't heard "one damn thing" worth remembering. Halfway through the steak Zeke slowed down, but he was hungry and the smell of fried meat overwhelmed his nose and taste buds; he found no reason to allow his meat to get cold while he listened to "unimportant" chatter.

The woman brought him a tin cup filled with dark black coffee, some dregs swimming around in it. He thanked her but did not touch it.

An hour later, beer still in his glass, the dinner plates clean, the coffee cup half empty, he'd learned what he already knew. A Mormon pilgrim's milk cow had escaped from her lead rope and wandered into a Lakota encampment. Seeing the old milk cow, they naturally killed, butchered, and ate her. It wasn't even an issue of taste. The milk cow had already walked a thousand miles and was incredibly skinny, a bag of bones.

It seems that after the loss, the prior owner of the dead and eaten cow wanted all "redskins" in the world arrested. The Miniconjou Indian, High Forehead, who hadn't found the old cow particularly appetizing, didn't want to be arrested. That was the problem the local Lieutenant was dealing with. Apparently not too well. Ironically, the problem had never been his to begin with. According to a statute, the cow problem belonged to the Indian Agent who conveniently wasn't "in town." Folks figured the Lieutenant was about to start a shooting war over a worthless cow. Twenty-nine dead. Zeke knew the story.

There was mention of the Wilcox and Johnson companies. They'd stayed in the settlement several days: resting, repairing wagons, taking on supplies, getting their bearings for the next haul across the big mountains. The Tallasinius company had rolled right on through, heading for the Sweetwater. Eli wasn't one to let the dust settle. Margaret Jonas had given birth and the new father was celebrating by getting very drunk and buying folks black South Carolina cigars.

Most of the talk was about a probable Indian war and a not so probable war back east over black folk and whether a state could withdraw from the Union "if they damn well pleased." The question was just how tied to the union were they? Indians were a different matter. Someone had found a settler dead in front of his burned out cabin. He'd been scalped. He hadn't been long dead. The man who found him buried him right there where he'd fallen: in the doorway. Indians were an Army problem. Wasn't the Army there to protect the wagons and the emigrants moving through? Everyone seemed to be in agreement on that subject except the Army.

"What the hell was they doin' anyways?"

"Crazy bunch of bastards. Gettin' all those soldier boys kilt like that."

"What'd they expect?"

"Ya don't toss a full grow'd griz a rock dog and expect the rock dog ta live through it. That's pure craziness. Only an idiot would do somethin' like that."

Those were the comments that Zeke remembered.

Sitting in the chair, listening, Zeke saw something he never expected to see. It was a simple splash of color that knocked the air from his lungs. It was as if he'd been tossed from the back of a green mustang and landed squarely on his shoulders. In the mass of card playing, beer drinking humanity Zeke caught sight of a red watch fob and a blue ribbon with hand embroidered white stars hanging from an unbuttoned shirt pocket. For a moment he stopped breathing.

He gagged and set his coffee cup down, spilling coffee on the table. His eyes watered. He blinked, unable to see clearly. He wanted to say something but there were no words; he couldn't speak. Odd how a red watch fob and a star spangled piece of blue silk ribbon affected him but there Zeke was staring at those items in a forced silence. He considered the probability of finding a blue silk ribbon folded over, tied with darker blue thread, laced with embroidered stars in a man's shirt pocket–and not in Lexie's hair. What were the chances? The odds? And a red watch fob? Yet there the man sat at a card table in a faded blue shirt: double pockets, two rows of black buttons, sleeves worn out at the elbows and neatly patched.

The card shuffling stranger could only have gotten those items directly from Lexie.

There it was.

Zeke took a deep breath. The thought settled heavy and cold on his heart, an unbearable weight. In a moment of singular clarity he realized this man was the last to see Lexie alive, the last to speak with her, and lastly, he had forcibly removed those innocuous items from her person. She would not have given them up voluntarily: not the watch fob; Zeke had given it to her, and his grandfather to him; not the star-spangled ribbon her mother had given to her. Anger settled on his chest, heavy, feeling like a five-pound lead weight. He told himself to breathe; he would have, too, except right then he didn't give "a damn" about breathing.

"You ain't drank your beer. Somethin' wrong with it? Somethin' wrong with you? You don't look too good."

Zeke tore his attention away from the faded blue shirt pocket to the bartender standing in front of the table looking at him.

"You pay for that coffee?"

Zeke shook his head.

The bartender smiled. "On the house. What's wrong with you? You look a bit peaked. Steak a bit raw?"

"I . . . I . . . I'm fine, thank you. Don't know if there's somethin' wrong with the beer. I just don't like it. Never have. Got nothin' against the beer, mind you."

"Why's you order somethin' you ain't gonna drink?"

"All sorts of stupid, ain't it?"

The bartender laughed. "Sure is," he said.

Zeke breathed out, letting the air escape between his teeth, thinking before he answered the "what's wrong with you" question.

"I ordered so's I could sit and listen," he said. Zeke pulled himself together. "Did you know," Zeke said, "beer was invented in Egypt by the Pharaohs? Least that's what my Uncle Eli told me." Zeke looked at the bartender, forcing himself to relax, his mind on the blue ribbon. The words he spoke sounded lame to Zeke.

"Didn't know that. What you listenin' for?"

"News. Uncle Eli said this was the place to find out what's goin' on."

"Who's your Uncle?"

"Eli Tallasinius."

"The wagon master? Went through here ten, fifteen days ago."

"I know. I was with him. He's dead. And most everybody with him."

"What?" the bartender said, incredulous. "Nothin' could kill Eli."

Zeke's eyes met those of the bartender, then strayed to the shirt pocket across the room. He watched the ribbon move as the card player shifted in his chair, dealing a new hand. The man laughed, dealing a round of cards, flipping the cards one after another, sliding them across the table.

Without an invitation the bartender sat down at Zeke's table.

"When did this happen? He was just here. I spoke to Eli myself."

"Two weeks ago. All killed dead except maybe a girl, her sister and a friend. I didn't find their bodies. I'm fixin' to go look for 'em."

"Who done this?"

"Injuns—a bunch of 'em."

"Brule? Hunkapapa? Oglala? Cheyenne? Who? Injuns ain't just Injuns."

"I don't know. They rode unshod horses. Scalped the dead, looted the wagons, took three horses, and left the oxen. I don't know what kind they might be. They was Injuns."

"You tell the law?"

Zeke nodded. "I did. First thing. Marshal said it was none of his damn business. Six days ride north is too far. No authority up there; that's what he said. What a helluva note. You know? Three girls needin' a little help and that fellow don't so much as leave his chair."

"How about the Army? Did you let 'em know?"

"Yes. That's another fellow. He said he'd have a look soon as he could. Said some fool emigrant farmer lost a cow, the Injuns ate it, and he has to deal with it before a shootin' war starts over nothin'. Sounded pretty busy. Said it would be a week or ten days before he could even think about it. If, then. No men to spare. Didn't know what he could do even if he had the men. Said that six days ridin' north was to hell and gone. I didn't think it's that far. Sweetwater ain't that far. Six days."

Two travelers came in and sat at the table next to Zeke on his left. The bartender glanced at them and then back at the bar. He spoke to the men. "Be with you fellows in a second," he said.

"No hurry," the tall one wearing a gray shirt responded. Taking his broad-brimmed hat off, he laid it on the table and ran his fingers through his long, brown hair.

"Where were you," the bartender asked Zeke, "when this all happened?"

"Where was I when?"

"When the emigrants were attacked by them Injuns."

"What Injuns?" The tall traveler interrupted, reseating his hat.

Zeke answered, turning slightly to his left. "Injuns attacked my uncle and the party he was leadin'. West of here. North of the Sweetwater. I was huntin', scoutin'. That's what I did for my uncle." Zeke paused. "Got back in the evening around sundown and everyone's dead exceptin' three girls." He glanced over at the man with the pocket holding the watch fob, then back at the bartender. "I trailed 'em 'til I lost 'em. Four days' rain wiped out the trail. I came here.

Thought I should tell someone. Get some help if I could. They was attacked; killed in the early mornin' 'bout two weeks ago."

"How many?"

"How many what?"

"Injuns. How many in the party?"

"Hard to tell. I trailed maybe forty, maybe as many as sixty, unshod horses. Not all was bein' rid. The same ones that'd been shadowin' us for several days. Add to that about sixty, seventy shod horses, those taken from the wagons. As I told you. they took all the draft horses and saddle horses except for three they killed. Didn't take any of the oxen. Turned 'em loose. Butchered, ate one. Took the mules. It was hard to know exactly. I'd guess maybe forty; sixty on the outside. I followed 'em. Movin' fast. Headin' north. Separated into three groups. I followed the group headin' north."

The tall man sitting next to him, listening, said, "Injun." Maybe it was a question; maybe it wasn't.

The room had grown quiet. Everyone had turned their attention to Zeke, even the man in the blue faded shirt, his hands holding five cards, his index finger tapping the last card without looking at it. He, too, was staring at Zeke with dark eyes, a somber face. His hand went to his shirt pocket. He stuffed the contents inside and buttoned it.

"That's who did the killin'. Scalped the dead. Looted the wagons."

"How long you trail 'em?"

"North four days. 'Til I got to the Red Butte country. Rained three, four days. Lost all sign. Tracks disappeared in the grass. Leastwise, I couldn't follow 'em. There was nothin' to follow."

"You a tracker?" The dark man sitting at the next table asked.

"I do the best I can. I get by. 'Bout all I can say."

"Cut him a little slack, Bailey," the bartender said. "He tracked them for four days movin' fast. Add ta that rainin' hard. That ain't bad. That was some gully washer. It's a wonder there was anythin' ta track after the first day. I'd have trouble doin' that and I'm fair at readin' sign.

"What you doin' here?" the bartender asked Zeke.

"Gettin' supplies. Notifyin' the sheriff, the army. Thought I could get some help. Ran a little low on vittles. It's been the better part of two weeks now. Without huntin', I was runnin' a little low."

152

The bartender asked, "How many white folks died?"

Zeke took his time answering, thinking about the dead. "About fifty adults. With kids, young folk--twice that. Maybe more. I never counted." Then he hesitated, staring across the room at the man with the watch fob and blue-starred ribbon, his eyes locking on him.

"Ask that feller," he said, "the one wearin' that blue shirt sittin' right there. He was there. He and two others was with them Injuns when they attacked. When they killed all those folks."

Why Zeke said that he'd never know. In retrospect, he regretted it for he could have settled the matter privately. He just opened his mouth. He was so angry the words tumbled onto the floor like glass marbles. The bartender turned to see where he was pointing.

The room full of men were already anxious, heavy in silence listening to his words. Suddenly death was waiting on the second hand, tick, tick, ticking away. It came in a rush. Tick. Tick.

One.

Men, every one in the saloon, turned to look at the card player sitting at the card table, ostensibly looking at a handful of cards: jacks and three ladies. The weight of Zeke's words, what they meant, settled uneasily like heavy dust after a wild wind storm. Those were words a man didn't say unless he was itching for a shooting. A white man simply didn't ride with the red man, not ever, especially not to kill other white men.

Two.

"How you know that?" the bartender asked, suddenly suspicious.

Three.

"His shirt pocket. There's a red watch fob and a piece of blue silk ribbon. The blue ribbon has white stars embroidered on it. The red watch fob was mine. I gave it to a girl; she was the daughter of one of them dead emigrants. She had 'em the mornin' I left, always carried 'em. That blue ribbon . . . she wore it in her hair. Her mother gave it to her; embroidered those white stars on it for her eighteenth birthday. He took 'em. I couldn't find her body 'cause she's alive. He was there. Ain't no other way he'd come across that watch fob and that embroidered ribbon. That's how I know. And that's how he knows."

Four.

In that dark room there was just time for a breath of air, then nothing at all. Everyone in the room was staring. Their gaze rested on

153

the card player, Sly, like he was a cockroach hurrying, scurrying across the sawdust-covered floor, vermin about to be stomped out of his misery.

His uncle had explained trouble to Zeke when he was much younger. Ironically, it was in a saloon over a glass of beer and three cups of black, bitter coffee. It was April in Independence, Missouri. It was a long speech. What his uncle said was: "Boy, sometimes, on an occasion, a man will find hisself standing looking at trouble, an angry, festering sort of trouble. Now, don't get me wrong. A man doesn't want ta be lookin' fer it. It's not like he goes out of his way. Though sometimes, he foolishly does. Somehow it'll find him and there it is. And there he is.

"There'll be no chances. No choices. No place ta run. No way ta leave it behind. He'll blink and trouble will be all over him, ripping the flesh from his bones. Glance away and the priest is saying those last few lying words over his still warm body; and there'll be the sexton standing patiently. . . waiting . . . leaning on his shovel . . . thinking of his tomorrows 'cause he has 'em.

"Boy," he said, "it's not one of those things that a man would find at a birthday remembrance or a weddin' party, though he could, I suppose. But when trouble finds him, and it will, in that instant the very fabric of his existence is flayed raw and laid bare. Time stands still and minutes stretch themselves into unbelievable hours. And when he finds hisself lookin' trouble dead in the eye the stuff he's made of will either stick together or melt, crumble ta the earth. There won't be no "never mind" and there sure as hell ain't gonna be no "tomorrow." There'll be just you and trouble. And you're gonna have ta deal with it."

In that quiet, silent moment in a dark saloon in Independence, Missouri, his Uncle Eli had looked at Zeke, smiled, and said, "Ya pay attention, boy. Ya'll find what I'm tellin' ya is the God's truth. There will be no doubt 'bout that. None at all."

For Zeke that first time came in Fort Laramie, Nebraska territory. He found trouble sitting at a table across from him, dealing five card stud with a deck of fifty-one, wearing a patched, faded, blue shirt, with a blue ribbon and red watch fob attached to the left breast pocket.

Five.

The card player rose to his feet as if the Creator himself had

154

sent for him and he was bound and determined to run like hell in the other direction. But he wasn't running. Instead, he came to his feet in an angry rush, scattering men, poker chips, and fifty-one face cards everywhere. He was staring right at Zeke, a malicious scowl wrinkling up his face, pursing his lips in anger, his sole intent to kill. He had that look of having been caught, his hand sneaking another square of fudge from his mother's cabinet jar, exposed as a no good "so'n so" without any redeeming grace.

"You're a damn liar," he said and reached for his pistol butt, his thumb pulling back the hammer, the clicks loud.

Zeke saw him, heard him, but he didn't expect what happened. Not like this. Not without some warning. Even a block headed long eared mule gave some warning before kicking a man into the next county. Usually. It hadn't dawned on Zeke that he should keep his mouth shut, that words, even true words, would bring trouble running right at him. That thought was overshadowed and lost the moment he saw Alexandra's blue hair ribbon and his red watch fob hanging from another man's pocket.

Sly's Navy Colt was coming up over the table top, filling Sly's hand. The dark realization of what his Uncle Eli had described slapped Zeke a stinging blow across the face.

In front of Zeke, the bartender was diving, throwing himself away from the table where Zeke sat. Zeke was buried in amazement. He'd just finished saying "that man was there." The unspoken conclusion was not only obvious but correct, for the card player had his red watch fob and Alexandra's blue silk ribbon with embroidered white stars. It was self evident, a truth. It never occurred to Zeke that the card player would object to his telling the truth. But there it was.

Later, in the telling, the barkeep had it right. "Zeke was just a damn fool kid that didn't know no better. He surely should have."

The percussion of the Navy Colt being fired filled the room instantly; a slug ripped the table top in front of Zeke, throwing splinters of wood at his chest. Sometimes a Navy Colt discharging in a closed room will shatter the glass in the windows. It is deafening, so loud that it'll addle the mind, and shake the gold fillings from a man's teeth. Zeke was past being addled. The weapon discharging had done that. In one fluid motion Zeke was on his feet, his own Navy Colt clearing the holster, the hammer pulled back. The card player's second shot flung a lump of lead so close to Zeke's neck that it burned his skin, leaving a red mark. Zeke never flinched, never hesitated; his index finger squeezed the trigger as he returned fire. In that room full of celebratory cigar smoke he only saw the top button on the fellow's shirt, and the glare of a sliver of white skin showing on his stomach. He felt the pistols in his hands buck, once, twice, three times. He was walking toward his assailant doing what his Uncle Eli said needed to be done.

"Shoot without hurryin', shoot 'til "whatever's botherin' ya is dead. Then reload as quick as possible 'cause whoever ya think is dead might not be."

In front of him the man possessing Zeke's watch fob seemed to stumble, falling backwards, trying to maintain his balance and failing. A small red dot appeared on his forehead; his Navy Colt was flung backwards, two .36 caliber slugs from an 1851 Navy slamming into his chest, shoving him back across a table top, then onto the floor. Zeke walked toward him, a pistol in either hand, hammers back and locked; but they were no longer needed for his adversary was no longer alive. Amidst the acrid smoke, Zeke reached down, unbuttoned the pocket, and retrieved the red watch fob tied to the blue silk ribbon from the dead man's shirt pocket. Around him men were picking themselves up. To Zeke's surprise, he also found Bethany's silver pin and Priscilla's ivory comb.

They was all alive, Zeke thought. *This man was there; he was there; he'd seen Lexie. Oh my God, what have I done? I've shot the man with answers. He knew. He knew. He'd seen her. The last one to see her. He'd seen Pris. He'd seen Beth. What have I done? What have I done?*

"Where are they?" he asked aloud, his voice but a whisper. He nudged the corpse with his boot. "What did you do to 'em? Tell me."

But the dead man just stared at the ceiling through blank unseeing eyes, blood leaking onto the floor from the exit wound in the back of his head. Zeke stared at him, willing him to speak. But dead men never do. Around him men were getting up, finding their hats, checking to see if they were shot, if they were still alive. Reassured, they stared at him and at the dead man at his feet. He could feel their eyes, their questions unanswered.

He heard a voice say, "Ol' Sly deserved killin' ridin' with Injuns. Damn fool."

Zeke stared at the corpse. He said, "There was two others with him. They rode with this fellow. I followed 'em here."

156

"That'd be Crease and Shorty," a thin, angular man said.

Another voice added, "Yeah, they rode in maybe ten days ago. Crease didn't stay long. Neither did Shorty."

Zeke looked at the speaker and speaking matter of factly said, "I'll bet one had a broken shoe on his horse's left front foot. The other's horse has a deformed frog. A third had no shoe on the left hind foot. Favored it a bit. Needed a shoe."

A burly man wearing worn denim pants and a plaid shirt with a single row of dark buttons, undone at the top, and a worn gunbelt cinched about his middle, strode into the saloon. His hat was pushed back on his forehead exposing unnaturally white skin. He glanced at Sly's body as if it were a curiosity at a freak show; then, once ascertaining that it was dead, ceased to be concerned about its presence in the middle of the room. It was easy to recognize the marshal, remembering the conversation he had with him when he first arrived in town: the marshal sitting at his desk, bareheaded and balding, cranky, with a cold coffee cup at hand. The town marshal had expressed interest, but not enough to set his coffee cup down, cold or not, or get up out of his chair. But he'd listened, for whatever listening was worth.

The marshal looked at the dead body laying askew on the floor, then at Zeke.

"You do this, boy?"

Zeke nodded.

"Thought I told you to walk easy. You go to the Colonel like I told you? Surprised to find you here. I told you nothin' can be done; there's nothin' nobody can do; you ain't findin' them girls. You deaf? There ain't nothin' you or any other livin' person can do. Why's this feller layin' dead on the floor?"

"To answer your questions: yes, I spoke with the Lieutenant like you told me to. I ain't askin' for nobody to do nothin'. I ain't deaf and that feller's dead 'cause I shot him."

"You smart mouthin' me, boy?"

"No, sir, I ain't."

"Leave him be. Marshal. The kid had no choice. None a'tall. The dead feller pulled and started this shootin' ruckus hisself. Me and the kid were sittin' at a table having ourselves a conversation. The kid here was havin' a beer, mindin' his own business. The kid pulled after that fellow was already shootin'. Near got himself kilt. It was self

157

defense from the get go. Nothin' the kid did. That dead fellow just went crazy."

"That may be but I want you out of town, boy. I don't want no more trouble. No how. None. Hear me?"

"Ben, the kid didn't do nothin'."

"I don't care. I want him gone."

"Well, start carin'. The boy didn't do nothin' and you ain't throwin' him out of town for somethin' he ain't did. What the hell's wrong with you?"

"Butt out, Charley. I want . . . you know what I want. He's trouble. I want him gone."

"Ben, this is Tallasinius' boy. He's that short kid that followed him around all the time. Tallasinius is dead. He's just a boy lookin' for some girls. There ain't nothin' wrong with that. And it pretty much describes all of us, come to think of it."

"I said. . ."

"I know what you said, Ben, but this is Eli's boy. This ain't nothin' to be arguin' about. Right now there are three girls out there somewheres needin' help. We gotta figure what to do before they disappear permanently."

"They already have," the marshal said. "Dispersed."

Charley stared at the town marshal who was still looking at Sly's body.

"Know who this boy kilt, Charley? This dead fellow, he gots a name?"

The barkeep answered him. "Yeah, he's got a name. Goes by Sly. Came here about ten days back, or it might have been two weeks ago with a couple of roughnecks: Shorty and Crease. That Crease, he's a mean one. All three rode in together. The kid says they were with the Injuns when they overrun Eli Tallasinius and them emigrants. Maybe fifty adults dead. More, you count the youngin's. That right, kid?" The bartender asked.

"Yes, sir."

"Where'd they go?" the marshal asked.

Zeke was about to answer but Charley beat him to it. "You mean the Injuns? Or those two that rode with Sly? 'Cause only Sly hung around. The others left soon as they got here."

"Where'd they go?"

"You mean Crease? Dakotas. He was ridin' for the Dakotas."

158

"Dakotas? What for?"

"Buffalo. That's what Sly said. Said it right there playin' cards. Said they heard there was buffalo up there. Them Injuns, they rode north. Two weeks ago near as the kid can figure."

Sly's leg was jerking and twitching. The marshal glanced at him, then at Zeke. "I told you, boy, two weeks is like two years. There ain't no followin' them Injuns. Nobody knows where they are. They's just gone; them girls with 'em. They could be anywhere. What'd that army general told ya?"

Zeke nodded.

The marshal repeated his question. "What'd he tell you?"

"That he ain't got any men, that he don't have the time, that he's busy. Somethin' about a cow bein' killed and eaten by some Injuns camped about a mile or two from here."

"It was eight mile and me, either. I ain't gots no men. Nobody round here can be runnin' and gunnin' after the entire Injun nation. This here is an army problem." The marshal turned to Charley. "They're gone, Charley. It's been ten-fifteen days, two weeks, and a four-day gully washer. Time we get ourselves together, it will be another ten or fifteen days. It'll be a month before we can turn around. They ain't standin' still. They're goin' farther north or sideways. Lookin' for buffalo theyselves most likely. There ain't no findin' 'em."

The marshal glanced at Zeke. "That right, ain't it, boy? Been two weeks?"

Zeke nodded.

The marshal turned to the bartender and said, "See what I'm tellin' you, Charley. Ten or fifteen days. There ain't no trail to follow even if you was fool enough to follow it. No tellin' where or which way they went. Time we get to Tallasinius' wagons, it'd be near a month old. There'll be nothin' left. There's nowheres to go. It's not like I don't want to track them thievin' bastards down and kill 'em all but it ain't gonna happen. I told this boy to take it to the army. It's his only chance and it's no chance. And they can't do nothin'. Them girls, if they ain't dead, they're just as gone. They ain't no more. Hear me? If they ain't dead, they might as well be."

Charley was nodding in agreement. He turned to Zeke. "Ben's right, kid. It'd be a goose chase. You said it yourself. Rain washed out what's left of a trail. If we'd left a week ago, we'd still be ridin' dark. No trail. No direction. No army. Nothin' but grass, mountains and

Injuns, north of here. No use. Them girls," Charlie paused, "they're gone. No knowin' where. Chargin' out there you'll get yourself killed. What's makin' it worse, in another week or two them Injuns'll be splittin' up, fixin' on winterin' somewheres on some creek in some valley. No tellin'. No way of knowin'. Them girls, they're as dead to you as if the Injuns had kilt 'em and took their hair."

Charley stared at Zeke, pausing, then surveyed the disheveled room: watching the chairs being picked up, tables being uprighted, cards being collected and reassembled into short decks, such as they were.

The tall, skinny man who had been sitting at the table next to him said, "Kid . . . no matter how bad you want to, there's nothin' you can do. Nothin' nobody can do. The chances of you findin' them girls even if you had the whole United States Army ain't likely. There's a million square miles of country out there. When those Injun boys want to hide, they simply disappear. You'll be trackin' a wisp of smoke in a howlin' wind. Damn shame what it is."

Charley picked up a chair and set it on its legs, pushing it under a table. He glanced at the man who had finished speaking. "Wanna beer, Bailey?"

"Naw, Charley, I'll be havin' a shot of rye. I ain't drinkin' beer, a dead man layin' right there in the middle of your floor. Three ladies gone. Know what I mean? Am I smellin' your woman burnin' some fresh steak? I'm a bit on the famished side."

CHAPTER 27
Alexandra is 268 miles from Zeke on the Big Horn Mountains at the head of the Tongue River

September 5, 1854
Fort Laramie
South Central Nebraska Territory

Zeke walked out of the saloon having found out more than he wanted to know, nothing that helped him, and feeling hollow inside. In the parlor he left a dead man, his blood leaking out onto the sawdust-covered floor. He didn't know what to think or feel. Standing on the short forty foot boardwalk he felt so dejected he could hardly spit. A gust of wind pulled at his hat brim. Squinting, he looked north down the dusty street, watching the stout breeze kicking up dust.

Somewhere in the tens of thousands of square miles that was Indian Territory was his Lexie. Standing on the edge of the street, his boots covered in dust, he imagined her standing on a rise, or perhaps sitting on a flat rock, hopefully out of the wind. She was saying, "Zeke, please. Please come for me. I don't know what's happening. It's bad. Please hurry. There's not much time. I don't know what is going to happen to me. Are you coming? Please?"

And like the love sick fool he was . . . he answered, "Always, Lexie, always" and remembered her walking away from him, tears falling from her eyes.

Everybody tells me I ain't got a chance in hell of finding you. Lexie. Not a chance. They say you're good as dead. That I'll just get myself killed tryin'. They say there ain't no use. You ain't no more, you're someone else's woman, that I wouldn't want you no more. That part ain't true, Lexie. It just ain't true.

Zeke's heart died as he stood on the edge of that dusty street, bleeding blood red over a promise he had no possibility of keeping. He fingered the watch fob in his pocket, pulled it out, stared at it. He smelled it, remembering the last time he'd seen her, her back turned as she went to help her mother clean up the dishes, to get ready for tomorrow. Her tomorrow didn't come--not in the way she had wanted it to.

Dejected, he walked down the boardwalk across the dusty, potholed street and ended up at the livery. He sat on the top rail of the corral fence and watched his two horses. He sat there for the better part of an hour trying to come to grips with what he could do: what he should do knowing what he knew. Certainly he could go back to Independence or to California or Oregon. Any one of those directions was reasonable. He thought of the three girls . . . somewhere out there in an Indian encampment.

He slapped his hat against the top rail. Dust flew.

Who the hell do they think they are? he thought. *Tellin' me I can't? I've tracked folks. Just need a trail. There's only so many places she can be. It's not like she's been removed from the planet. She's somewhere. I can get to where she is. I ain't givin' up just 'cause somebody says it's impossible. I ain't. Why should I?*

'Cause you'll get killed.

So what?

He took a breath and glanced north over his shoulder. There she was again: Lexie standing, the wind whipping her blue skirts around her legs, goose bumps running up her arms, her enemies walking all around her.

I'm her only hope. I can get this done. I got chances. I got plenty. But if I don't get off this fence, I ain't got none. I just gotta get off this pole fence and go to work. Get out there. This ain't nothin'.

"What's wrong with you, boy? You look like a starvin' badger: your face all pinched up, nothin' to eat except your own leg."

Zeke turned, looking down from his seat on the top rail, and discovered the liveryman. Not knowing how to lie, he said, "About five, six days ride north of here, a girl, her sister and a friend was taken by the Brule or maybe the Cheyenne or Oglala Injuns. Somebody. They're alive. I ain't found their bodies. Injuns killed everyone--my uncle, everybody—exceptin' those girls. They're gone. I need to find 'em. I don't know where they are. I can't get no one to help. They tell me those girls are as good as dead. Nothin' no one can do and if I try, I'll just get myself killed."

The liveryman man nodded his head and spat tobacco juice on the ground at his feet. A puff of dust blew up. "That's a hell of a story, kid," he said. "A real sad one." He paused, looked across his corral at the four o'clock sun. "The girl? One of the three missing? You took a fancy to her?"

Zeke nodded.

"Bad luck for you."

162

"Yes, bad luck for me."

O'Reilly whined, changing his position on the shade of the pole corral fence.

"Your mutt?"

Zeke nodded.

"Ugly dog."

"Yes, sure is."

"Name?"

"O'Reilly."

The liveryman leaned his rail-like body against the fence poles, his head lost under the large brim of his hat. He stared at the horses standing in the corral that he had yet to feed and water. He said, "Tell you what, boy. Don't know if it'll help you none. You look down the road. Far north as you can see. Kind of on a knoll stands a mostly dead cottonwood. Might be all dead. I ain't been out there in a while. See it? It's the only one."

Zeke nodded. He said, "Yeah, I see. What about it?"

"On the other side of that tree maybe a half mile is a dugout. Built right into the side of a hill. Sorta hard to see but it's there. A feller named Emile somethin' or other, lives there. Off and on. Don't know his last name. Not sure. Injuns call him Bad Horse, most likely 'cause of that damn mule of his. You'll find him sittin' out front, most likely on top of an empty whiskey barrel." The liveryman chuckled. "Top's knocked out. So are the bung holes. Most likely he'll be sharpening one of them long knives of his. That's 'bout all he does. You might ask him how to find a white woman stolen away by the Injuns. If anybody knows, he knows. I reckon he's more Injun than an Injun. But," he paused and looked at Zeke knowingly, "don't you trust him. If the truth hit him in the ass, he wouldn't know what it was. Hear me? He knows Lakota but he ain't knowin' the truth. He's a lyin' thievin' bastard. Understand what I'm sayin'?"

"Yes. Ask him but don't believe a word he says." Zeke wondered what good it'd do to ask a question if the answer was going to be a lie.

The liveryman smiled. "That's it, kid," he said. "Ties that old bull frog up right nice. Puts a bow on him, know what I mean? He's a worthless, ornery cuss, Ol' Emile. My opinion, he shoulda never been born, but he knows Injun. I hear tell part of him is Injun. Don't know which part."

163

CHAPTER 28
Alexandra is 260 miles north of Zeke in the Big Horn Mountains

September 6, 1854
Fort Laramie
South Central Nebraska Territory

Zeke lay on a ticky straw bed on the second floor of the Madson-Lowery Livery with a worn out wool blanket draped about his bare shoulders. He lay, lost amidst worn out saddles, sundry saddle blankets, curing timothy hay, old straw and a decade of collected dust. He spent most of the time awake. Sometimes he sat in the dark, listening to a south wind whistling around the eves. He tried to sleep but sleep didn't come. Lying back on the blanket, he listened to his heart beat and to the dry rafters squeak and moan in the wind.

In the moonlight he watched a gray barn mouse run across the plank floor, stopping to inspect a kernel of oats, gnaw it, and, dissatisfied, drop it and pick up another. Pausing, it glanced around, sniffing, its nose sampling the various smells. Sensing danger, it dashed across the floor to a pile of burlap sacks, disappearing under a corner, not venturing out.

Sleep was impossible.

In the morning, without bothering to eat, Zeke walked beyond the barn and gazed northwest down the winding road that led to the North Platte River crossing, the Sweetwater, and the Continental Divide. It disappeared into the distance--a mere thread, a thin line of dry wagon tracks vanishing in the rise of hills beyond his sight. In the distance were the skeletal remains of a leafless cottonwood whose brittle, spartan limbs reached into the red morning sky. The stark image of the leafless cottonwood tree engendered little hope and provided no encouragement. Still it was there and didn't seem far.

Zeke decided to visit this man Emile, if that was his name. Thinking it best to save his horses, he chose not to ride. It didn't look far so he walked toward the tree. Walking gave Zeke the opportunity to sort out his thoughts, which he did, reviewing them over and over.

Midmorning he reached the cottonwood finding it much bigger and farther away than he'd imagined. Staring up at the leafless limbs, he wished he'd ridden. Walking had been a mistake.

164

Two miles beyond the tree, then another five hundred yards, he located the dugout described by the liveryman. It sat in the side of a hill carved back into the red earth; the roof was made of split cottonwood poles, covered with a thick layer of prairie sod. Grass grew tall on the roof. It had been there awhile. In the spring rains it turned green, then yellow when the rains disappeared.

O'Reilly was growling.

In front of the dwelling, sitting on a whiskey barrel, was what appeared to be an old man. His singular recognizable characteristic was a wild disarray of white hair that hung in his face and over his collar. His eyes were sunk back into his head. Eating appeared to be a pastime rather than a necessity. He was stoop shouldered and bowlegged and wore patched pants and a dirty shirt in need of buttons and a soaking of hot, soapy water. No socks covered his ankles; worn and tattered moccasins adorned his feet. To his left, hanging on an ax scarred stump was a felt hat, the dark oily brim pulled down by use. The composite result was the "old man" looked old, felt old, and smelled old. Zeke thought that if the old fellow fell there was a distinct possibility he might not get up. Zeke stared at him as though he was some mythical creature, one he'd never seen nor heard of. But there was something odd about him.

This is a mistake, he thought. *This feller can't even help himself.*

The white-haired man eyed Zeke like a vulture eyeing the rump of a two week dead buffalo cow. Neither spoke, the silence dragging out. It was the man who broke the stillness, his voice a startling, incongruent oddity. It was starkly clear, strong, and buoyant. The man's skin normally covered by his hat was that of a younger man. It stood in stark contrast to his weatherbeaten and wrinkled cheeks, neck, and hands. Dark circular birthmarks covered them. It was as if two different people were occupying the same body.

"You!" the man said. "You. Get the hell outta here. Don't like the way you're lookin'. I don't like ya a'tall. Go on, get, 'fore I jerk your heart right outta your chest. Feed it ta my damn dog. Ya hear me?"

A big black dog was sitting behind him and to the left, growling, baring yellow teeth, wearing a matted coat as if it were a blanket. He moved his head as if to get up, then apparently changed his mind. Everything appeared wrong. Nothing was what it was.

O'Reilly had dogged Zeke's every step from the edge of town. He was suddenly nowhere to be found.

165

What is this? Zeke thought. *The old man bares his teeth and his dog growls? Except this fellow don't appear to have any teeth. Dog probably don't either. What a pair! And the liveryman thinks he could help me? It's this man that needs help.*

The voice brought Zeke to his senses. He replied, "Sorry. Really, I'm sorry. I know'd better. I am really, really sorry. Don't mean to stare. How are you?" The question was insane.

The ragged man stared at Zeke from under dark hooded eyebrows, long and white like his hair, unconcerned with the proper manners of a more gentle society. "Well?" he said. "Ya ain't movin' and I done told ya ta get 'fore I cut your throat, sick my dog on ya."

Zeke ignored the old fellow's threat. He said, "I was told that you might be able to me, that you might have some thoughts that could prove useful. That's why I'm here. I'd like to ask a question or two about Injuns."

"Injuns? Exactly why do ya expect I'd help ya? Ya makin' fun? I told ya, I ain't likin' ya. I'm fixin' ta cut ya up, feed your carcass ta my dog. So get. Hear me? I said get 'fore I stands up."

"Excuse me. The man at the livery told me that you'd know how I'd find three white girls stolen by Injuns. I walked out here hopin' you could tell me, maybe, where I should start."

The man hardly blinked. He just stared.

"Ya walked?"

I wonder how old he is really? White hair. Looks old but his eyebrows are not the same color exactly, sorta white, kinda gray. But his skin? Young lookin'. Tight around the eyes. No wrinkles on his forehead. Damn.

"Yes. It's important to me."

Taking one long draw of his blade across the whetstone, the white-haired man paused. He stared at Zeke until Zeke felt uneasy. "Well, Sonny," he said. "What the hell would ya want ta do a fool thing like thet fer? How long they been gone?"

"Couple of weeks. Goin' on three."

"Where?"

"Where what?"

The old man stared at Zeke as if he was a piss ant. "Where was they taken, ya nincompoop ninnie? What the hell we talkin' about here?"

"Above the Sweetwater, over on the Wind River."

"Sweetwater?"

166

"Yes, north of there."

"Two weeks? They're ta hell and gone. You're a day late, two bits too little. And ain't got a clue on what you're doin'."

"I've been told that. Repeatedly, in fact."

If you only knew. Gone in three different directions, too. Tell him.

No. What difference would it make? He can't even stand up on his own.

Won't make no difference. Better get the hell out of here while I can.

The old man with the clear voice and clear, supple skin stared at Zeke. Finally, he said, "They's gone. Be hard ta find. There's plenty of women, boy. They's all over the place. Foolish ya riskin' your top notch fer no woman. Doin' that'd make ya plumb dumb stupid."

The black dog was growling again. The old man turned to look at him. He said, "Shut up, ya miserable dog. Who asked you?" He turned back to Zeke and in the same voice said, "Get the hell out of here, boy 'fore I split ya from one end ta the other. Damn dog's hungry. Can't ya see thet? Sides, ya ain't got a lick of sense lookin' fer a girl long gone."

Zeke nodded, said, "The girl--I promised her. Gave my word. The Lakota took her. Killed everybody 'ceptin' me. Took her sister and her friend. They'd of killed me 'ceptin' I wasn't there. Lost their trail in the rain. I'm all she's got. No choice."

"Kilt everbody? Woman and child?"

"Yes."

"Don't sound right."

"Well, it's the way I found 'em. Everyone dead. Scalped. Nobody alive. Couldn't find the bodies of the three girls." He added, "There was three white men involved."

"White men?"

"Yes."

"Don't sound right."

The wadded up, crumpled up, not so old, old man continued to stare at Zeke, slowly nodding his head. He said, "Thet ten, fifteen day ago rain? Thet four-five day rain?"

"Yes." Zeke said.

"How old them girls?"

"Eighteen, seventeen, and fourteen."

"Those be young women. Ya say the Lakota took 'em? Thet right?"

"Sioux. It was Injuns and three whites."

"Not Cheyenne?"

Zeke nodded. "I was told Teton Lakota, maybe Brule, Hunkapapa, Oglala. That's what Charley at the bar said. I don't know the difference."

"Ya don't know shit. Don't really know who took them girls? You're guessin'."

"No, I don't. I know I trailed 'em four days north of the Sweetwater. I know that."

"Where was ya again?"

Zeke told him.

"Charley'd be right. He would. Seen some Arapaho up there once. Been a while. Cheyenne. Mostly Oglala."

The old man hadn't moved. Closing his eyes he stretched, cracked his neck, and after a moment spoke as if he was handing down judgment.

"Wives. They took 'em fer wives. Probably not Lakota, killin' all those folks. It don't sound like 'em. Could be, though."

Zeke didn't respond. The breeze shifted, drifting into his face. There was a smell of dead, rotting meat, of a sour slop pail full to the brim, swill percolating in the sun. Zeke gagged, covered it with a cough, as though he'd swallowed a mosquito or a deer fly.

"Sound of it . . . it'd be one man. Lookin' fer a wife, maybe two. A prestige thing. Expensive. Livin' in the same lodge. It's the way of it. One man lookin' fer a cheap wife. One he ain't gotta pay fer. No dowry. Ain't gotta give up no horses." The white-haired man paused, felt the edge of the blade with his thumb. "Even if ya find 'em ya won't like what ya find. Better ta figure they're gone; go about your business. Sure's hell. You'd have ta be damn lucky ta find 'em. Those folks move around all the time. Don't stay in one place long."

The old man looked up from his knife. "Know'd a man had three wives. Stole 'em from the Crow. Big job, thet. Women fightin', raisin' hell. Poor bastard never knowin' what ta do. Told him he was crazy, oughta get rid of them. Said he thought so. Not so lucky thet one. Got himself drilled killin' Crow in the spring." The old man laughed, staring out over the horizon, north. "Maybe he gots himself killed a purpose," he said.

"Better to be lucky than good," Zeke replied. The wind shifted again. Zeke took a breath, gagged.

"What?" the sitting man asked.

168

Zeke swallowed. "Somethin' my uncle said."

The old man grunted, then took another swipe of his blade across the whetstone, the grinding sound of the rasp hanging in the air. His dog rose, sat back on his haunches, and scratched himself vigorously.

"So how do I find 'em? Can you tell me?"

Why am I askin' him?

The old man smiled, his yellow teeth flashing. A deer fly lit on his hand; he smacked it, crushing its body against his other hand and blowing it off. "Ain't no tellin'," he said.

"I gotta try," Zeke replied. "No choice." He turned to go. "Thanks for your time."

"Ya ain't listenin', boy. Time ya find her she's another man's woman. All of 'em. They ain't gots no choice. They's gotta survive. Them Injuns'll adopt 'em. Thet's it. If ya finds 'em they won't go with ya. Not a chance. Seen it myself."

You don't know Lexie.

The disheveled man stared at Zeke for what seemed a long time, his gaze steady. Zeke found it disconcerting. Finally he spoke.

"Think that's somethin' ya kin handle, boy? Your woman's linkin' up with Injun? Most folk can't. Ya can't, then ya oughta go home, boy. She'd be better off ya never find her. Those people she's with--they'll take her in, accept her, make her one of them. She'll turn Injun. Sure's hell. Her people'll shun her like she's got some sickness. Won't talk ta her. Walk across the street ta avoid her. They'll be thinkin' she shoulda kilt herself rather than let some buck touch her. I seen it."

"I promised," Zeke said as if the entire conversation could be reduced to two words.

The man looked at the boy. "Go home, boy," he said. "Forget her. Find ya some other woman. There's 'nough of 'em. Ya ain't even got ta be choosy."

"I can't. I gotta find 'em. I gotta find her."

The man nodded. "'Cause ya made some fool promise?"

"That's right."

"You're dull. A half wit. Dead in the head." The old man paused, examining his blade, looking it over as if he'd never seen it before. Finally he looked from the blade to Zeke. He spoke, starting slowly.

"Ain't easy. You'll have ta go out there among the people: trade with 'em, talk with 'em, listen to 'em, hunt with 'em. Find out what they know, what they're hidin'. Everywheres ya go, one village ta the next ya ask, identify thet woman you're lookin' fer as your'n. Chances ar' someone'll know her. Maybe you'll find her, if she's out there, if she ain't dead. Everyone knows everybody. Most related someways. Ya might find her. Maybe never. Gotta be friendly. Gotta understand 'em. Gotta be so they ain't afeared of ya. They's can't be afeared. Ya can't either. They'll know it right off."

The old man took another swipe on the whetstone, stared at his blade again, turning it in the sunlight. He looked up at Zeke. "Boy, ya oughta go home. You'll get yourself kilt. Ya won't be likin' this woman of yourn havin' an Injun baby on one hip, another on a cradle board hangin' from her shoulders. Ta get her you'll have ta kill her man. She won't be carin' fer that. Even if ya do find her, ya can't be bringin' her back. Can't take her ta her own people. Them bastards'll be tossin' her, treatin' her like some dirty, mangy dog. Findin' her'll be the worst thing ya kin do. Go home. Best ta leave her be. She's gone."

Zeke looked at the old man and shook his head slowly, thinking.

"I don't see it. Baby or no. Another man or no. If she broke her arm, I ain't throwin' her out as bein' no good no more. That ain't right. So, I can't. I ain't givin' up on her. I told her I was comin'. That's what I'm doin' one way or t'other."

"Can't or won't? Damn fool, that's what ya are." The old man stared at the blade again, took another swipe on the grindstone, fingering the edge, Seemingly satisfied, he glanced at Zeke. "Better catch my mule. If you're able. I figure ya ain't able. Figure you're as worthless as the third tit on a boar hog. Ya walked here? Damn fool."

"Mule? What do you need a mule for?"

"To carry me, ya ignoramus. What do ya think a mule's for?"

"I . . ." Zeke stopped talking.

"That's what I thought. You're too damn dumb ta know a mule. Better than a damn horse. Far better. 'Sides Injuns don't like 'em. Won't eat 'em. Don't steal 'em less'n there ain't nothin' else."

Zeke stared at the old man, trying to keep upwind without being obvious. Downwind he couldn't breathe. The breeze kept shifting and Zeke kept moving. There was nothing else he could do.

"Sorry," he said, "I shouldn't have bothered you none. That

170

fellow at the livery said you'd know how to find someone if they was stolen by Injuns."

"Ya mean Lowery?"

"Don't know his name."

"What do ya know?"

The breeze shifted again, the smell . . . He'd had enough. "Sorry," Zeke stammered. "Didn't mean to bother you none." Zeke took a step backwards. It was, to his thinking, "half past time to leave."

"I said catch up my damn mule. Gonna go with ya. Hear me? I'm speakin' English. We'll be needin' trade: iron pots, trinkets, blankets, liquor, and knives 'n such. Tradin' will give us a reason fer bein' there. Keep us from gettin' kilt. We'll look around; see what we kin see. Tellin' ya boy, ya ain't gonna like what ya find."

"I don't need nobody to go with me."

"Yeah? Let's see. Ya don't know a damn thing 'bout Injuns. Not these ones. Don't know what makes 'em tick. Don't know why they do what they do. Can't speak no Injun. Ya can't say, 'Ya seen a white girl runnin' loose?' You'll just get yourself kilt. Won't know why you're dyin'. There you'll be dead as hell and thet so-called woman of yourn, she'll be out there in some lodge somewheres wonderin' where the hell ya are. She'll be raisin' a pack of red wolves, her younguns fixin' ta grow up and scalp decent white people, murderin' 'em in their sleep. Thet 'bout the size of it?"

Zeke stopped himself from saying anything in reply. He was thinking.

If I'm dead . . .that's true. There ain't nobody else.

Make up your mind.

Now what? How do I respond to the ugly truth?

Well, say somethin'.

"Where's your mule?" Zeke asked.

Ya gutless wonder! Why the sudden change? Careful. Don't trust him. Jeez, he smells somethin' awful.

"He's out there somewheres. I ain't seen him lately. I ain't seen him since Christmas. I ain't seen him before last fall. He could be dead 'fer all I know. Can't remember what I did with thet sontabitch. Ya find him."

Zeke hesitated.

This is a lie. He knows. Why lie?

What am I doin'? What shall I do? He's right. I don't know Injuns.

171

Uncle Eli says: 'don't trust nobody. Pick 'em with care. Ya never know.' I surely don't. Be careful. This fellow . . . he ain't likin' me. And I ain't likin' him.

That'd be all right. That livery stable man said if anybody knows how to find 'em, he knows. More Injun than an Injun.

Maybe he ain't as bad as he appears.

No. He's worse.

Just how bad is he?

Don't trust him. Whatever ya do. Don't.

"All right," Zeke finally said. "I'll see if I can find your mule. Do you have any other livestock I'm lookin' for?"

"Got a damn horse somewheres."

"Don't tell me you don't know where?"

"You're a smart sack of horseshit, ain't you? Ya play smart with me one more time and I'm gonna kick the shit right outta ya. Take it right outta your hide. Thet too damn complicated fer a worthless piece a shit ta get yourself around?"

"I understand," Zeke said becoming irritated. "Where do you suggest I start lookin'?"

Am I crazy? How can I stand bein' near this fellow?

"Suit yourself. I'll be restin' here ta see if ya kin get out of your own way. That's what I'm a waitin' for. Now get 'fore I change my mind."

"It'll be a time 'fore I get back. I walked here savin' my horse."

"Stupid. Plumb dumb stupid. Never walk when ya kin ride. Wal' get to it, boy. Ya already burned up a half a day jawin' with me. How the hell ya expect ta find them girls?"

Zeke was about to say something but thought better of it. The odd fellow with gray-white hair and the skin of a ten year old would just light into him. He didn't need that.

Where's O'Reilly? That damn dog.

Zeke walked back to town not sure he shouldn't grab his horses, saddle up, head north, and keep on riding. Except he was standing in the dark, his eyes wide open, seeing nothing. The smelly old man was right. He didn't know. It seemed wrong. What choice did he have?

And I promised, he thought. *I ain't got no choice. Shit.*

That old man must never bathe. Never. And I didn't tell him everythin'. Don't start now.

172

Lowery was sitting in his makeshift office watching him as he entered the livery stable.

"Gotta get my horses," Zeke said to him.

"You know where they are."

"Gots myself an impossible chore. That old fellow wants me to find and catch up his mule and some other horse. Said he didn't know where they were."

"That shouldn't be too hard seein' how he brought 'em here early last fall. Asked me to care for 'em. Never came back."

"They're here?"

"Standin' out there in the hoss corral burnin' timothy hay. Worthless sonstabitches. All they do is eat and dump hoss biscuits." Lowery looked at Zeke, nodded. "Smells, don't he?"

"Somethin' awful. Like sin." Zeke paused. "I don't figure it. His animals: he acted like he don't know they're here. He says they're somewhere runnin' loose. I figured they was runnin' from him. Smells so bad."

Lowery laughed. "Oh, that stinker knows. Emile, that 'ol man, he's the one that's runnin' loose. Be all sorts of obliged if you'd take 'em. Cut down on my feed bill. Never intends to pay me. They ain't worth what they're eatin'. Can't sell 'em. Nobody wants 'em. I've been thinkin' about turnin' 'em loose. Lettin' 'em walk. Prob'ly wouldn't go.

"Looks old, don't he? Nothin' about him is what it seems. Keep that in mind. He looks like he's a hundred years old. Maybe he's forty.

"See his mule?" Lowery smiled. "He'll tell you I stole him. The bastard. There's one thing in your favor, as sour as that fellow is, as bad as he smells, he knows Injun. Spent his life livin' with 'em. He's at least half Injun hisself."

"That's helpful. Seein' how I don't know anythin'."

"Give you a word of warnin'. Don't take an eye off him. He'll steal you blind."

"Says he talks Injun."

"He can. Crow. Sioux. Some Cheyenne. Blackfoot. And he can sign. But he won't hesitate to lie, cheat, kill you, and leave you for dead if it'll make him two bits and get him to the next hill, the next lodge, the next handout. Remember what I said. He'll steal you blind and leave you for dead. Don't ever let him get the drop on you. Ever."

"Sneak up on me? Ain't likely. He smells so gawd awful bad

it'd be hard for him to sneak up on anyone. I'd smell him comin' the day before."

"Careful, the old fart might take a bath and you'd be in trouble."

Zeke smiled. "I'll keep him in front of me," Zeke replied. "He's done told me what he thinks of me."

"Bet that ain't much."

"No. It ain't. He thinks I'm plumb stupid for lookin'. Says it's over for them girls. Says they're as good as dead."

Lowery looked at Zeke, hesitating. "Don't mean to be throwin' water on your fire, but he may be tellin' you the truth, boy. I've seen a goodly number of white women taken by the Injun, what with emigrants goin' through here all the time. Wonder it don't happen more than it does. Lived with 'em a spell myself when I was younger. Liked 'em. Thought they was good people. It ain't good what comes of white women. Some just give up. Die. There ain't no goin' back.

"The old man's right about that. He'd know. If you find this gal, she'll no longer be fit for polite society. Here, there, they'll be ostracized, excluded, abandoned, and kicked out by both Injuns and their own. It will be like they got somethin' awful, somethin' there ain't no cure for. Nobody will understand what it is that they went through. They'll just stare at 'em and shake their heads. Far as white folk are concerned your gal is dead. All of 'em are. She's worse off than dead 'cause she ain't dead. She'll want to be. Everybody will figure some buck had his hands all over her and figure she should kill herself. Nothin' worse."

Lowery nodded. "Knew a woman that lived down the road a piece. Nice lookin'. Stolen by the Cheyenne when she was a girl— musta been thirteen or fourteen when that happened. The Army rescued her, brought her here. After four months it got so bad she stole a horse and went back to the Injun. Couldn't live nowheres else. No one wanted her."

The liveryman stared straight at Zeke. "You're buckin' a helluva hard wind, boy," he said. "What you should do is leave here yourself; never come back. Just leave. You'll be better off. She'll be better off. Sorry for havin' to tell you. It's just the way it is. It's a long, long road goin' one direction. It ain't pretty."

"What you're sayin' is I ain't got no chance, that I'm runnin uphill into a stiff head wind. I get it. I do."

"In so many words. That's it."

Zeke stood in the livery stable barn and stared at the liveryman, his heart so heavy he could hardly move. He didn't doubt the truth of the matter but he remembered Lexie. Finding her behind her father's wagon. He remembered her arms around his neck, the soapy smell of her skin. She'd said, "What are you going to do about us, Zeke? Did you figure that out?"

Standing in the livery barn, his face grim, he could feel her slender body so close to his, her breath on his skin, the way she felt with his arms around her slender waist. She'd asked, "Will you come for me, Zeke?"

"Always," he'd answered. "Always."

All he could do was nod when the liveryman asked him what he wanted to do. His voice was gone, his throat aching. When he didn't say anything the liveryman simply nodded, helped him catch his horses, helped him catch the old man's mule. Afterwards he found a sway backed gelding and bridled him, too. It sure looked bad–a poor excuse for horse flesh. Zeke left the livery stable leading three animals and headed west down the winding road, leaving the hostler standing in the shade of the barn, staring after him.

CHAPTER 29
Zeke is 268 miles south of Alexandra at Fort Laramie

September 7, 1854
Top of Big Horn Mountains, head of Tongue River
Central Nebraska Territory

"Lexie? Lexie, are you asleep?" It was a Bethany whisper. Everyone around them was sleeping.

"No. But I'd like to be."

"Sorry."

"Nothing to be sorry over."

"Did you notice how many of those poles there are in this lodge?" Bethany asked.

"Twenty-two."

"You counted?"

"Yes."

"Have you asked yourself how we are going to get them down?"

"I have."

"Would you two be quiet?" Priscilla said. "I'm trying to sleep."

"Sorry, Pris," Bethany said. "I'm trying to figure out what we need to do. How we get this tent down and what we do with it. And after that how do we get it back up?"

"Tomorrow you'll know. Small Dove will tell you, sort of," Priscilla said, "considering how she talks."

"It looks impossible. It is impossible." Bethany turned under her buffalo robe. "Lexie, are you okay? You seem worried. We've got to talk. Know what I mean?"

"We are talking and, yes, I am worried sick. I'm anxious. We have to get out of here, you know. And soon. Real soon."

Bethany said, "Yes, I know. That little woman, that Small Dove? She said 'always.' Remember?"

"I remember," Alexandra replied. "'Always' just means until we can get out of here. We have to figure this out. What to do? And we have to figure it out soon. We just need a few things to go our way."

"Yes. You are right. Good night, then," Bethany said.

"Good night, Beth."

She'd wished her sister 'good night" but Alexandra didn't sleep. Instead she lay awake wondering what had gotten into Bethany. Suddenly she was so nice, so responsible.

Alexandra was awake when Walking Eagle came inside. She listened to him undress, then lay his unstrung bow and his quiver of arrows beside the wall. Always he placed his heavy knife and his Walker pistol inside the opening. The pistol was kept under the beaver pelt he used for a pillow; both were at hand as he left the lodge. He brought with him the smell of sage and pine and something else she couldn't define: perhaps lavender or mint. Something pungent.

She listened until he took the deep breaths of sleep. Above her head the wind played with the smoke flaps. She turned onto her side, her face toward the lodge opening, and finally drifted off to sleep.

The next morning Small Dove brought the three girls to her lodge. Under her supervision they helped take it down. She reminded them over and over of the logical progression involved. Every item had its order, its need. The lodge poles, for example, were used for building the travois. Each item was packed so as to make it available when raising the lodge. Other women helped. Soon only four poles remained perpendicular to the ground. Afterwards all seven women dismantled the lodge of Walking Eagle. They were a merry bunch, giggling at things Alexandra did not understand. Small Dove reminded them repeatedly of the logical progression, ending with packing everything on the travois in such a manner as to be unloaded in order of need. Walking Eagle's lodge contained a lot of things to be packed. By noon they were finished and the journey north began.

The winding trail taken by the men, the women, the old, the infirm, the children, and their horses crawled like a snake: winding, turning, twisting. Riders far ahead led the way. Others, unseen, brought up the rear. To the right and left were flank riders. Scouts beyond those riding point looked for "tatonka," the buffalo. According to Small Dove this animal tatonka gave life to everything. It was hard to imagine any single one thing upon which all life depended.

Alexandra, Bethany, and Priscilla walked, each leading a horse pulling a travois. Morning Flower rode, as did She Who Smiles. Feather Woman had three horses pulling travoises ridden by the son of Walking Eagle and two other young people Alexandra didn't know.

From time to time they exchanged places with the aged and infirm when they could no longer walk. Feather Woman rode one of her horses while Alexandra walked alongside leading two. No one saw Walking Eagle.

And so ended the second day of travel.

By the end of the third day, they were proceeding off the mountain following long narrow loops: game trails that switched back and forth moving steadily down the grade. From high up on the escarpment, Alexandra could see the smoky-hazy plains below as well as the loops of horses pulling travoises. On the plains below, Goose Creek wandered north away from the big mountain, twisting and turning amid rolling hills. Grass grew as far as Alexandra could see. Miles later camp was pitched along the creek bed, offering plenty of firewood and water. The temperature was noticeably different from that on the mountain. It felt warm, hot—the way summer was supposed to feel.

Sitting, her bare feet planted in loose dirt along the creek bottom, tired, worn thin, and exhausted, Priscilla looked at her two companions, the six travoises, and the horses standing in the hot afternoon sun. She who Smiles and Morning Flower had gathered with the three women. She was tired.

"Well," she said, "Let's put it up here. If we can. If we can remember how we took it down." She took a breath and let it out slowly. "I'm wondering why are we doing this?" she said, collapsing back in the dry dirt. Morning Flower, holding the Funson doll, fixed her round brown eyes on her.

An equally tired and exhausted Bethany remarked. "Couldn't be too hard. Little Indian girls do it."

"Oh, sure! Except we aren't little Indian girls. No trouble, though. Couldn't be hard considering we don't know what we're doing. And these two don't speak English. The little one is useless. Too small to be of any help. She doesn't even count."

Bethany took a breath and smiled. "Well, let's get the poles loose and lay them out where we can use them. Here? Are we going to put it up here?"

She Who Smiles said something, a long string of syllables that made absolutely no sense to the girls. They looked at her, no one saying anything, no one doing anything.

"Not here, Beth," Alexandra interrupted. "I'll bet she's saying 'not here.'"

"Why not? What's wrong with here? It's not far to pack water. There's firewood. Besides, I can't take another step. Look at Pris. She's had it. We've had it."

"I don't know. Floods, maybe. One thunderstorm and we'll need a canoe."

"Oh, yeah. Never thought of that. How did you think of it?"

"I didn't. I'm just guessing."

Priscilla sat up and looked at what the other women were doing. Everyone was another twenty, twenty-five feet away from the stream. "Lexie is right. We're too close and I'm too tired."

"And not high enough."

"And not high enough." Priscilla repeated Bethany's words. "Bethany? Bethany, why are we doing this? Why are we?"

"So we have a place to sleep."

"That's horseshit, Beth."

"Pris!"

"It is. That's exactly what it is. Who needs this? Those bastards killed my sister, my mama, my papa. And what am I doing? Leading their horses! Putting up their lodges! It's horseshit."

"Okay. What do you want to do, Pris?"

"Kill them. Kill them all. That's what I want to do." She looked at Morning Flower standing before her, listening. "Except you. I don't want to kill you."

"Nice. Real nice," Bethany said, smiling. "Wait until I get a good night's rest to kill everybody, will you? And something to eat. You really shouldn't talk like that. These two didn't do anything to any of us. I'm glad they don't understand a word you're saying."

Alexandra shivered, clutching her arms around her, listening. She was cold in spite of the warm breeze blowing off the valley floor.

"What?" Priscilla said. "Beth doesn't want to kill on an empty stomach? I sure do. I really do."

Alexandra interrupted. "Pris, please. Not so loud. Someone might hear you."

"They might hear me but they don't understand a word I'm saying. Stupid people."

The sisters stared at Priscilla.

"Jeez," Bethany said to her. "What's got into you? I sure don't

179

want to kill anyone."

"Nothing. I just want to kill them for what they did. It's what they deserve. And I don't want to play house with them. I don't. It's wrong to even ask."

Alexandra stared at her. "Okay, Pris. Okay. What's your point? Do you have one? The fact is if you work, you eat. If you work, you sleep in a bed. If not, just sit there and pout. Being angry does no good. We need to escape."

"Yeah, we need to escape. Exactly what are we doing about that? Nothing. We are doing nothing. We just talk."

"What do you want to do?"

"I told you what I want to do."

"Well, you can't."

Bethany smiled at Priscilla. "Unless you want to commit suicide. You can do that. That'd be killing someone."

Priscilla stared at Bethany, her brow wrinkled, her eyes mere slits, her lower lip quivering.

She Who Smiles said something to Alexandra, pointing to the ground above the creek bottom and away from the creek. She repeated herself.

"Okay," Alexandra said. "I think this one thinks we should build the lodge up there." She turned and looked at Priscilla. Morning Flower was sitting in the dirt beside her, playing with the Funson doll, chattering as if Priscilla was listening. She held the doll up and smiled at Priscilla.

"Do you want to kill her, too?" Alexandra asked.

"Oh, shut up. Leave me alone. I said I didn't."

"I can do that," Alexandra said. She turned and looked to the business at hand.

Everyone is tired, she thought. *We're all losing a grip on ourselves.*

A flat piece of earth was finally selected; rocks were pulled out, divots replaced, ridges smoothed. The big rocks were tossed to the outside of the circle or stacked in the middle for later use in constructing the interior fire circle. Brush was cleared and stacked to the side.

"What about this ant hill?" Bethany said. "We don't want to put this tent on an ant hill, do we? I mean I sure don't. What about the ants?"

Alexandra dropped a rock outside the proposed circle and looked at the offending ants. "I don't know," she said and picked up another rock.

"We'd better find out," Bethany said. "That's what I think." No one stopped to address her question.

Five sturdy lodge poles about twenty feet long were selected, their slender tops laid next to each other. Bethany tied the tops of the poles together using square knots, half hitches, and a long, braided leather rope, longer than the longest pole.

Standing up, Bethany looked at her work. "Is that right? Did I do it right," she asked. "That's the way that short woman did it." She Who Smiles examined her work, retied some of the knots, and tightened up the wraps that would hold the poles together at the top.

"Think that will hold?" Bethany asked her. She Who Smiles only stared. "Me, too," Bethany said. "What do you think, Lexie? I don't know. Should we ask that woman--Small Dove?"

Your friend there seems to know." Alexandra looked at the knots and shook her head. "No. What you two have done is better than I can do, I'll tell you that." She smiled at She Who Smiles and patted her on the shoulder. "Shall we stand them up?" she asked.

She's the same age as Beth, she thought. *An inch shorter.*

Priscilla was sitting on a flat rock. She hadn't moved. Morning Flower was sitting beside her, playing with her doll. Priscilla stared at her. Morning Flower smiled, patting her on the knee, handing her the doll.

"No, thank you," Priscilla said. "I'm too old for dolls."

Morning Flower smiled at her, again.

"Would you stop doing that? I can't stand it. I already like you."

Bethany and Alexandra grabbed the five poles tied together at their tops and, with She Who Smiles' help, stood them up as one, perpendicular to the ground. One by one the bottoms were spread out until they stood at the edge of the proposed circle. Thus the first four were seated, tops bound together and standing in the afternoon sun on the edge of Goose Creek. The remaining eighteen poles were quickly set up, leaning each individually against the top where the tops of the first three poles were tied together. Thus, they formed a circle. The three girls stepped back to view what they'd created. She Who Smiles said something in Oglala and smiled brightly.

"Hope that holds up, too," Bethany said aloud. "If that's what you said. We tied it with a thousand knots and every which way to Sunday. So it should. Hate for it to come down in the middle of the night with me in it."

"Me, too," Alexandra agreed. "That wouldn't be good."

"What about those ants?"

"What about them?"

"I hate them and they're big red piss ants. If they got hold of you, you'd really squeal."

"There are piss ants everywhere."

She Who Smiles was pulling the cured buffalo hides from the travois.

"We'd better help her," Alexandra said.

"I know but what about those ants?"

Alexandra began helping She Who Smiles. "I don't know," she said.

She Who Smiles had led one of the horses pulling a loaded travois to the far side of the circle. She'd started dragging the hides out, leaving them around the edge of the established circled. The buffalo skins were stitched together using wooden stakes. Then the covering was pulled up and wrapped around the circular structure created by the twenty-two lodge poles. They'd gotten that far when Small Dove arrived. She walked along the outside of the circle created by the lodge poles. She nodded approvingly at what they'd done, glancing at Priscilla sitting idle with Morning Flower.

"Good, good," Small Dove said.

The sisters smiled at Small Dove because she smiled. "I was worried about the poles being wide enough," Alexandra said to her. "It looks like they might be. Are they?"

"Okay, okay," Small Dove said. "Good. Hang tatonka skins. Outside. Then inside. Is good."

"Say please," Bethany said. "It's the magic word."

"What this 'please'? Magic?"

"You ask please, it makes things happen. It's the polite thing to say if you want people to help you."

The small woman, with the aid of She Who Smiles, Alexandra, and Bethany, drew the final upper wrap tight and fastened the buffalo hides together where they met. Twenty-one tanned hides were used. They had a light caramel color where smoke had stained them over time. Inside the lodge, using a large rock, Alexandra drove a stake deep into the earth. The leather strap that extended from the tops of the poles was cinched down and tied to the stake.

"What's this for?" Bethany asked, looking up at the smoke hole, worrying about her knots.

"Wind," Small Dove said. "No blow down."

"Wind? Never thought of that. Makes sense. Tie it to the earth so it doesn't move."

Last, a lining was attached inside the lodge around the entire structure at a height of six feet from the floor. A fire ring was constructed in the middle using rock from the creek bed. The floor was covered in brain cured pelts. They were nearly done. It had taken two hours. The other women noticed and came to see, offering their critique through Small Dove: the top of the lodge poles could have been tied tighter; the inside layer of skins, higher; the inside fire ring constructed of bigger rocks; the circle itself wider.

"Oh, well," Bethany said. "Ask about those ants."

Two light poles were attached to the smoke hole flaps, their ends used for controlling the flaps, allowing for draw adjustment and additional ventilation depending on wind, smoke conditions, heat, and the need to breathe. They were done. With Small Dove they went to help the others, starting with Feather Woman's lodge.

Priscilla remained on the flat rock, Morning Flower buzzing around her, waving the Funson doll about in the air, chattering. Bethany followed her sister, glancing at Priscilla as she followed after her. "Hey wait, Lexie. Do you think Pris's right? Why are we doing this? I mean, really."

"I don't know, Beth," Alexandra answered.

"Cannot live . . . related no one," Small Dove responded.

Bethany stared at her. She glanced at her sister and shrugged her shoulders, then proceeded to locate and arrange the lodge poles for Feather Woman's lodge. The women noticed Bethany and She Who Smiles working together, tying the longer lodge poles together.

"Small Dove? Small Dove?" Bethany questioned. "What do you mean "cannot live without being related to no one?" I am related to nobody. Not here anyway. Except Lexie. I'm related to her."

"Cannot live no relatives. No family. No good. Bad thing."

"I don't understand."

"Old: wise, knowledge, no strength, no food, no stick to burn.

Need help. No relatives: no good, die."

Bethany looked at the small woman and said nothing, getting ready to lift the four poles up. Small Dove looked at Bethany, touching her arm.

"Family. Family everything. Must care for old ones. Family. Important. Die no family. Not this way with you?"

Bethany glanced at her sister's receding figure, at Priscilla with her slouched shoulders, at She Who Smiles walking toward the lodge they'd constructed for their use. "I guess so," she said.

All told, on that day they assisted with the raising of five structures, each made exactly the same as the one before: different sizes, same shape.

And the women noticed who worked and who sat.

CHAPTER 30
Alexandra is 28 miles from Zeke on Upper Goose Creek

September 28, 1854
Big Horn Mountains
Central Nebraska Territory

An unlucky fool could get lost on the Big Horn. John Colter crossed her in 1807 and eventually found himself standing looking down on "Old Faithful," one hundred miles west. Its sudden eruption belching steam and hot water no doubt scared the hell out of him. He wasn't lost but would have been hard pressed to explain where he was and was hard pressed to explain what he'd seen. No one believed him.

Emile Villon crossed the Big Horn in late September 1854; he'd crossed her many times before 1854, for his mother was Oglala, his father French. In a matriarchal society he went where she went. As a boy and a young man he lived on the mountain. The significant difference was that in 1854 he was followed by a "damn kid" looking for a lost girl. Before 1854 and while yet a young man, he lived on the mountain during the summer; he brought down his first buck as it drank water from a spring where the Tongue River was a mere trickle fed by melting snow. In the winter his mother knew better; no one stayed on the mountain in winter. No one.

On the fifteenth of September 1854, Emile Villon left Fort Laramie. He approached the mountain from the south, coming off the Divide, then following the Sweetwater. Riding with the kid in tow, he followed the Popo Agie, Wind River, passing through Wind River Canyon. In the canyon, where he could, he rode beside the river. Most of the time he kept his horse in the river itself, riding right down the middle. There is no other way. Out of the canyon he kept to the east side of the river, riding forty miles before turning east, heading up Tensleep Canyon. It was a ten-day ride from Fort Laramie. The Oglala called the place Tensleep for that reason.

Once within the walls of the canyon, Emile Villon followed the creek to the top of the Horn. Emile ended his journey three days later on the east slope of the Big Horn, camping on Clear Creek. Clear Creek is ten miles west of the Crazy Woman, Central Nebraska Territory, and sixty miles north of Tensleep, an easy three day's ride.

185

Emile was born during the winter of 1807 on Clear Creek. It was his home.

There are large groves of aspen growing high up on the sides of the mountain. In its valleys the Tongue flows north, seeking a way out of the mountains. These groves witnessed Villon's mother's father's father, as a mere boy–a teenager, hunt and kill his first white tail, drop his first elk, and seek his 'life' dream in sweat lodges built by his father's father's father. It is an old place where old spirits live. It is said that in the evening if a man is quiet, if he listens, he can hear the restless ones walking on the edge of the wind, breathing the pine needle song, rattling through the aspen leaves, leaving no tracks to follow. The mountain is old, very old. It has witnessed many things. Most will never be told for they are long forgotten.

CHAPTER 31
Zeke is 30 miles east of Alexandra on Clear Creek

October 7, 1854
Goose Creek
Central Nebraska Territory

The wind played with her tresses, blowing strands of brown hair across her face and in front of her eyes, tickling her neck and cheeks. Alexandra didn't bother brushing the hair away. She couldn't; her arms were full of firewood.

The wind never stops blowing, she thought. *Not ever. How long has it been? I've lost track again.*

No. No. It's been six weeks, I think. I haven't lost my mind altogether.

Above her, on the rocky hillsides and in the meadows the long grass was turning yellow and brown. In some places it was a deep brown but growing lighter as it dried in the dry, ceaseless wind. It seemed that way everywhere.

Everywhere? Where in 'everywhere' am I?

Off the mountain it was fall. She could smell it. No frost. Not yet. It was in the wind, in the grass as it cured on the stem, in the leaves rattling in the cottonwood trees, in the breeze whistling through the pines, and in the very air she breathed. Soon the first frost would color the aspen, chokecherry, and cottonwood yellow, the skunk and currant brush, red. It was not far off.

Alexandra understood no one was coming to rescue her. It made perfect logical sense, for no one knew she was gone, lost.

But no one? Not ever?

Those thoughts were hard, hopeless, steeped in futility, so she took a deep breath, held it in her lungs, letting it out slowly. Fall, though late, preceded winter. Winter was coming no matter what she did or tried to do.

Winter? Winter? Do I still have time? Time enough to get out of here, leave this all behind?

Maybe Bethany is right. Perhaps, someone would come; the cool days of fall wouldn't stop a traveler. But winter?

How much time do I have? Winter? Fall is already here.

In winter, snow fell, filling the pine forests, burying the wolves' dens, sending the bear into their caves to sleep; no one would come. Not in winter. Winter? Soon the snow would fall and men would hover around their Franklin Stoves, cozy in their long underwear and their warm homes. Once in a while they'd go out to tend their horses, care for a winter-born calf, maybe hunt for fresh meat like her father had. That seemed a long, long, long time ago when they'd lived along the rocky coasts north of Boston. The wind blew in from the blustery Atlantic, cold and damp. unlike this place, where her lips were chapped, bleeding, and sore.

Not like here. In this gawd awful place.

Three days before, the lodges were pitched on Goose Creek. The lodge poles were set, the buffalo hides draped about them and stretched. Large rocks were placed on the bottom ends to keep the skins from riding up the poles in the wind. Now, it was another creek somewhere north of where they'd been. It was their third move. Time was running out. There were no calendars, no days to mark off, no ticking clocks. But she could feel it. Winter was indeed coming. Fall was there already.

It shouldn't be this warm.

The creek water felt incredibly cold. Yet she waded, the rocks sharp under her feet, her toes numb.

It has been six weeks, maybe a few days more: six, maybe. Certainly not two months—well, probably not two months—since father and mother were killed.

She wasn't sure. She'd lost track. Her time stick worked if she used it. She wasn't sure that she used it righteously: not every day. Time passed. It kept slipping away. She made notches: seven notches for a week, twenty-eight for a month. It was now sixteen days past twenty-eight; those were the days after she'd started keeping track, each day one notch. Days missed? Not many. Hopefully, not many. Her feet were numb. Her psyche was numb.

The people around her, those walking through shrinking daylight hours, spent little time watching her, their curiosity diminished, their time now spent preparing for winter, for the cold that would come. Hides were tanned, food stored, meat dried, and late berries dried and ground into a flour. There was too much work and not enough time to work, and no extra time to watch Alexandra. She was a shadow, a morning person carrying firewood, skinning a deer, cutting up venison, someone trying to survive like everyone else. No one had time.

188

We're old news, Alexandra thought. *Good. Escape is easier.*

Escape? All we talk about is escape. Escape to where? Where are we? How will we live if . . . no, when . . . it's when, we escape? What will we eat? No weapons. No way to defend ourselves. To hunt.

We're in such trouble. Especially if we go right now. But we have to. We must. If not now, when? It has to be soon. Really soon.

Stop it. We've been in trouble for a long time now. This is doable. We'll steal weapons. Something to hunt with. That'd be a rifle. Powder. Lead. We have to escape!

If we're caught . . ?

Don't think about that. It's the last of September. No, probably more likely October. A month and a half. It could be. It has frosted higher up. Way up. The brush is turning.

Oh my God. No one knows where we are. We're not even missed. Not a living soul knows except us.

Stop it. That's not important. We have food.

Not enough.

It will do. It has to. We've got clothing.

Nothing warm. And horses? How do we get horses? We can't just walk out and bridle one. And once we're ready, what do we do?

Go south.

South? Miss a trail and we're lost.

We're already lost.

Alexandra turned and studied the mountain and the cold, blue sky above it.

We'd better hurry, she thought. *Is it already so late? It's time. Past time. Still, if we take their food what will they eat? The boy. The little girl, her sister.*

Stop it. It doesn't matter.

It matters.

No, it doesn't. They can get more. We can't.

Her mind went to Whips The Bear; she imagined him without food to eat, a boy of ten summers. She thought about the little girl with big brown eyes: both children starving, both sitting in the lodge shivering, without coats for winter. Freezing.

I don't even like him. I don't. He's not my problem. None of this is my problem. We'd better go now. If we're going to.

No ifs. We're going to. But can we?

Yes. Yes. We can. We have to. We can't wait. No more.

189

She mused about how she, Bethany, Priscilla, and She Who Smiles had set up Walking Eagle's lodge for the third time: erecting the lodge poles, pulling the buffalo skins tightly around them, weighting the bottom edges down with large stones. She glanced up the creek, then down. Her feet were numb. All along the creek were lodges-- maybe forty or fifty. She hadn't counted. What did it matter? They were all around her.

She'd tried counting just people and stopped before she'd finished. No one stood still.

We may be old news but we're never alone, always watched. I'm paranoid.

No, I'm not. We'd better leave. Go. Soon.

Horses. We need horses.

I've been over this.

Okay. Horses? How do we do that?

Alexandra forcefully dropped her armload of wood on the lee side of the lodge, sending sticks flying.

Stop it.

Shaking her head, angrily pursing her cracked lips, she began collecting and stacking sticks one after another, breaking them into short lengths to make them fire manageable. She placed them within easy reach of the exterior fire ring. It wasn't necessary to stack the firewood but she did it. Other women did it that way: not all, but some. Before she finished, Priscilla joined her with her armload of firewood. Priscilla wasn't nearly as fastidious with where she dropped the wood she'd collected or how it was stacked. Both took a drink of water, afterwards wiping their lips on their sleeves.

Meadow larks were singing. So were some killdeer. She thought it ironic. It felt so late, yet the birds were still here. It had to be October at least.

Don't think about it.

"We'll need more," Priscilla said, glancing at the growing stack, and as an afterthought, added, "He'll be here soon. He always shows up about now."

Wonder what's gotten into her. Normally she doesn't help a lot, let alone see the need for more.

"Don't remind me," Alexandra said. "He'll bring another deer." She paused, the breeze tugging at her skirts. "I know we need it but I wish he'd slow down. What do you think it will be like when there's buffalo? They're much bigger."

190

"He wants us to fill all those bags. That's what everyone else is doing," Priscilla replied, staring at the drying racks. "We still have a few empties left. That's good. Maybe eight or ten. I guess it's good."

Alexandra glanced at her before replying. "I wonder how much he thinks he needs."

What's going on?

"All of them. Enough for winter. There are seven of us now. Personally, I don't think there's nearly enough. Not if everyone eats. Can you imagine eating dried meat--I mean, all winter? Just the thought of it. We'll need more skins to keep warm because there are more of us. There aren't enough. Did you see what it takes to make a skin useable? I mean that's work. Scraping the inside, rubbing it with brains. Over and over. I guess he needs it because we need it. When it snows . . . it's going to be awful cold. You know, living in a tent. I don't think a fire will be enough to keep this place warm." Priscilla looked at Alexandra. "Won't matter. Not if we escape."

"Or someone comes," Bethany interjected.

Both women turned to see Bethany carrying more firewood in her arms.

"Or both," Priscilla said.

Alexandra said, "I have been thinking about it. Like all of the time. Tell me it doesn't matter if we take their food."

"It doesn't matter. He killed my father and my mother. My sister. Do you think I care if they all starve? I mean, really!" Priscilla replied. "Do you think I care?"

"The little girl didn't kill anyone. Neither did the little boy. They're just children."

Bethany dropped her load of wood. "Lexie, would you stop it? It's us or them. Right, Pris?"

"Right."

"Well, it matters to me. I'm sorry. I just don't want the little ones to suffer. I know I shouldn't care. Anyway, we need more food," Alexandra said.

"There's those berries. Some of the women have gathered those bitter little berries. Like months ago," Bethany replied.

"Have you tasted them?"

"Yes. They're bitter, bitter. Sharp," Priscilla said, shaking her head.

"What are we doing?" Bethany said.

191

"We're talking about food and eating. Especially during the winter," Priscilla said.

"We won't be here," Bethany said, dismissing their concerns.

"I know. I know but we need to eat and we'll be somewhere. And it will be winter."

Priscilla said, "So we're talking about how much we'll need. We can hunt."

Alexandra glanced at Priscilla. "What we should talk about is when. When are we leaving? Planning the exact details. I personally think it should be real soon. Fall is here. Winter is coming. If we don't leave soon, we won't be able to. We'll be stuck."

"Let's leave, then," Priscilla said. "Now. Tonight. We need food to take with us. How much I don't know. We only have ourselves to think about."

"Not just ourselves," Alexandra said.

"Lexie, stop it. It is foolish to worry about the boy and the two girls." Priscilla looked at Bethany.

Bethany explained. "She thinks if we take their food they'll starve. I say it's not our concern. They'll get along. And it doesn't matter if they don't. Right, Pris?"

Alexandra responded. "I just don't want to hurt them. They didn't do anything."

"Neither did we, Lexie," Priscilla said, "and here we are. We don't have any choice. If we don't run for it, then someone has to come for us. That'd solve this problem, too."

"That isn't going to happen," Alexandra said.

"I know. I know. But it could." Bethany looked at her sister. "Well, we could get lucky," she said. "It could happen."

"It doesn't matter, Beth. We go, we stay—either way we need to eat. It would make me feel better if there was plenty of food for everyone, especially the little ones. That's what I'm saying. At the end of the day, we need more food. More dried meat and a lot of dried chokecherries, a lot of dried buffalo berries. There aren't any more berries to pick, not now. We'd need them to make pemmican. For us. If we're going to."

"Okay, all right. I get it. We need more." Priscilla shook her head. "And we need to get out of here real soon. Do you like those little red berries, Lexie? I think they're awful. So bitter. I hate to think we're going to live on them."

Glancing at Bethany, she said, "We could get lucky. That'd be really nice." She looked at Alexandra, paused, and said, "Speaking of nice, I don't think you should forget your fellow, Lexie. Your fellow is still missing. We don't know he's dead. Right? I mean there is a possibility. It's slim, I know."

Alexandra nodded and said, "If we're lucky, Pris. Although I don't think it has anything to do with luck. I doubt anyone knows we're alive. We've seen no one and we've been . . . ? How long has it been since . . . almost two months? There has been no one. Realistically, no one is coming."

Priscilla took a deep breath. "What do those women do with those dried berries? They have pits. Big ones. It'd be like eating gravel. What good are they . . . for winter, I mean? I mean, what good are they? If we had them how would we eat them?"

"They grind it up pit and all," Alexandra replied.

"Lexie, you're just saying that, right? Pit and all? Together?" Bethany was incredulous.

"No, I'm not. That's what Feather Woman is doing. She ground dried berries all yesterday. And the day before. She showed me how . . . or tried to. We need one of those flat rocks. She let me taste them. I guess they're edible. If you're starving."

"We might be."

Bethany started stacking the firewood. She was joined by her two companions. When they were finished Bethany broke one of the dried branches, stomping on it with her left foot, and stacked the parts in the growing pile. She picked up another branch, broke it, picked up the pieces, holding them in her hands as she saw Walking Eagle stop in front of their lodge.

"He's here," Bethany whispered.

They turned to see Walking Eagle push a doe's carcass from the back of his mount, dropping it to the ground. The three women looked at him, then at the deer carcass. No one moved. Without a word he wheeled the bay around and left at a trot.

It was Alexandra who broke the silence. "Let's get started," she said.

"What's the hurry?" Priscilla said softly. "I'm having real trouble doing anything. Why should we help any more? He's the savage. I don't like being his slave. That's what we are."

"You know what the hurry is."

193

Alexandra glanced at her. "I'm tired of it too, Pris." She looked at Bethany, then Priscilla. "Look, why do anything? Just keep thinking that, but if we're not rescued . . .?" She paused. Both were now staring at her. "Or rescued right away, what will we eat? How will we keep warm? How will we stay alive? If that man . . . if he is willing to hunt, at least we have meat to dry and later something to eat! His food will allow us to escape and I want to get out of here. I keep thinking we haven't seen one white person in two months. Not one. We really really are on our own. No one is coming. The reality is when we escape, we've got to eat. What's worse is where will we go? We don't know where we are."

Pausing, she took a breath and continued. "Think about it. Except for maybe Zeke, no one knows we're alive. And he's a big, big 'if'. No one is looking for us. No one. If we work, if we're smart, maybe we'll escape but we'll need to eat. If we prepare food we'll have something to take with us. If, God forbid, we're stuck here and with winter coming, we'll need food to survive until we can leave. We're running out of time. Don't you see? We have no time. Get it?"

"I know. I know. And you're right. Still . . ." Bethany began slowly, hesitating, "Zeke, if he's alive, won't forget us. I mean, come on, will he? He won't. I know he won't."

"You're right, Beth. We didn't see him killed. But, logically what are the chances? Right now, we don't know where we are. If he is alive he won't know either. Chances are really good he's dead. Remember he was out there all alone. There were so many that attacked us. What chance did he have? Anyway, even if he got here they'd just kill him. I simply don't know if he's alive. Maybe he's already forgotten us. If I were him that's what I would do. I really don't want to talk about him again. It makes me so sad. . . This is the last time, okay?

"Look, even if he isn't dead, what do you suggest we do? We have to do something. We're in the middle of nowhere. We've nothing to eat unless we prepare it. We have nothing to keep us warm unless we make it. We belong to a man who doesn't speak English and we don't speak what he speaks. He can't even tell us what he wants us to do. And frankly, I don't want to know."

"She's right, Pris," Bethany said. "Much as I hate it. We have to figure out how to stay alive until we escape. We have to face the fact that no one will come for us. Our only chance is to run. And we'd

194

better do it soon or we'll be stuck here for a long, long time."

Priscilla nodded, but remained unconvinced. Denial was in her eyes, in the way she stood, listening; she was an unbeliever and angry.

It so exasperated Alexandra. She took a deep breath. "All right, Pris," she said, "for the last time, please listen to me. No one is going to find us. That's it. We're on our own. Escape is our only option. We have to prepare for it. Now. First, we have to decide how much we need and when. I think it's now. It hasn't snowed yet. That's a miracle. But it's going to. And soon. When it does and if we're still here, it'll be too late. We'll be stuck here until spring. It might be too late already."

"All right, Lexie, what do we do that we aren't doing?" Priscilla replied.

"We have so much to do. Food to pack, a gun to steal, everything. Right now. Everything."

"So, when? When do we go?" Bethany asked.

"Within the week. Tomorrow. The next day. As soon as possible."

Priscilla glanced at Alexandra. "Someone could still come, Lexie," she said. "Beth is right about one thing. We have to hope. I'd just die if I didn't believe that somehow we will get out of here. I won't be able to get through the next day if I don't. Maybe someone will come. It's a hope. I have to hope."

Alexandra nodded. "Maybe, but I can't think that way. I think escape is our only option. It is something we will do."

She stared at the two girls who were unwilling to give up their hope.

"Okay. Okay, you two. Are you listening? It's been almost two months. We haven't seen anyone. No one has seen us. No one knows we're gone." Alexandra paused. "See? It's up to us. We have to do it. It's our only chance. We are our only chance. So help me with this meat. One way or the other, we're going to need it."

"Jeez, Lexie," Bethany said. "I was just saying."

"Well stop 'just saying' and help me."

Together they pulled the deer carcass into the clearing off to the side of the lodge and began cutting and pulling the skin away from the muscle, careful to keep the meat clean and untainted. No one spoke for the longest time. Finally Bethany broke the self imposed silence.

"You're a real knot head, Lexie. A knot head, hear me?. Zeke will come for us. If not him, then somebody will."

"Beth," Alexandra said, staring at her sister, shaking her head, "sure, Beth, sure. He's coming. If you want to believe that. Believe it. I don't. As far as I'm concerned, he's dead. Dead like everyone else.

Get this: even if he were alive he's not coming. Maybe not because he's dead but because if he were alive he'd be in Sacramento or Oregon or St. Louis. He's at least that smart. He's gone. Hear me? I don't want to hear his name again. Get it through your head. We're alone. We're on our own. If we make it, it's because we make it." Alexandra grunted, tugging at the doe skin. She looked at her sister. "There isn't anyone except us, Beth. We're it. Got it?"

Bethany smiled weakly. "Ahh, shit, huh," she said.

Priscilla and Alexandra stared at her, surprised.

Alexandra nodded. "Yes, Beth. Ahh, Shit. That's what it is."

Bethany took a deep breath. She said, "What do you think Walking Eagle is going to do with us? What did he want us for really? He could have killed us but here we are. He didn't. That's something. He could have gotten another woman, one of these women right here, to cook. He doesn't need us to cook."

"He didn't kill us. That is something," Priscilla repeated, reluctantly. "It is something. The question is what? The answer is nothing if we get out of here soon. If not . . ." Her voice trailed off.

Alexandra smiled through tight lips. "Look, we're captives. We're work animals. "We take care of his stuff, his lodge, his things. We are his things. At the end of the day there's no one to save us from him; there's no one to help us. I know you don't want to hear this but right now whatever he wants he gets. There's nothing to stop him. So we have to get out of here. Soon."

Bethany was insistent. She said, "So far he hasn't wanted anything from us other than cooking for him . . . And you know, packing and hauling things, drying meat. What else is there?"

Priscilla pursed her lips. "I am guessing that will change," she said. "He's a bastard, he's a killer, and he's a man."

Bethany continued. "And we bring water. Getting water, and firewood, and picking berries." Bethany paused. "Everyone here--all the women, they do that. It's nothing different. We know he had a wife and she died. Apparently from smallpox or measles. Something like that. Small Dove said as much."

196

"What she said, Beth, was that her sister had spots on her and she died. That sounds like smallpox or measles or chicken pox. You know how she talks. It isn't clear."

"So what are you saying, Pris?"

Priscilla straightened up, stretching, then rubbing her back. She looked from the carcass to Bethany. "I am thinking he is going to want us to do . . . you know, what wives do. Nobody has said it but I think when he gets around to it–he's a man–he won't be asking. That's the only reason he'd keep white women or any woman for that matter. Probably why we're alive. I'm thinking it is the only real reason. This way when he wants what he wants, he won't have to ask. That's what I'm saying. That's what I'm thinking our purpose is."

Both girls were staring at Priscilla. She continued. "Small Dove said we replaced his wife. Three for one."

"Well, I'm too young to be a wife! I can tell you that," Beth said, her voice rising. "What should we do? When he asks, I mean. If he asks. What should we do?"

"What choice do we have?" Priscilla responded. "I mean really, what choice do we have? We could kill ourselves. Do you want to do that? Personally, I think I'll kill him. That's what I want to do. The bastard."

Bethany started sobbing softly as she pulled the hide off the flanks of the deer. "No," she mumbled. "No, I don't."

Alexandra whispered, "Beth, stop it. Don't let anyone see you crying. We don't know what's going to happen. Except we are going to escape. We know that."

"I'm sorry, really sorry," Bethany said quietly. She wiped her eyes with the back of her hand. "I'm really sorry." Tears ran down her cheeks anyway.

CHAPTER 32
Zeke is 30 miles east of Alexandra on Clear Creek

October 21, 1854
Goose Creek
Central Nebraska Territory

"He's coming. He's bringing Small Dove again," Priscilla observed. "I imagine he wants to say something again. I get so tired of this."

Her companions turned to look. Walking Eagle was coming toward them with Small Dove walking slightly behind him. She was carrying a stack of tanned deer skin in her arms. It looked like clothing. Small Dove smiled and greeted Feather Woman as she walked past her lodge, stopping in front of the girls who had been working on a deer carcass. Walking Eagle glanced at the partially dressed deer, its hide pulled back exposing muscle and a pile of entrails. He turned to Small Dove, waited for her to catch up to him, then said something in the language of the Teton Lakota. Whatever it was he said took a lot of words.

The girls waited, watching Small Dove, waiting for her to explain, but he kept talking and talking. Small Dove interrupted him, asked a question, nodded, and then turned her attention to the girls.

"Walking Eagle, want you know what he thinking. He want you learn, talk language People quick. Hurry. It good." She smiled and continued. "He like work. He like you learn Walking Eagle lodge. Woman job. He pleased."

Alexandra nodded slightly.

"What does he want now?" Priscilla asked.

"He bring you clothes. Want use dress of people. No white man. Not good. Deer skin. Good. Oglala. Understand this? Yes?"

Priscilla looked at Small Dove. "He wants us to change our clothes? Is that what he wants?"

"Yes. You said."

"Those clothes?"

"Yes," Small Dove said and proceeded to hand each girl tanned doe skin clothing, soft to the touch. They were light-brown and much heavier than what they were wearing. "He want this. You wear it.

Yes?"

"Right now?" Priscilla questioned.

Small Dove nodded. "Now," she said. "He want now. Yes." Small Dove nodded again. "The way you say it."

Alexandra interrupted. "Okay, he wants us to wear these clothes."

Small Dove smiled. "He give you. You give him. Want white man dress. You understand this one? Trade."

"Trade?" Priscilla said, her distrust leaking out. "Give up our clothes?"

Walking Eagle waited, giving the girls an opportunity to respond to Small Dove. Then he spoke to her. She replied. He nodded, turned, and walked away, disappearing behind the lodge of Feather Woman.

Bethany stared at Small Dove. "What's going on?" she asked. "What's wrong with our clothes?"

Priscilla, protesting, asked, "He wants our clothes? That's what he wants? Am I correct? Why? Why does he want our clothes?"

"I bet he doesn't want us to stand out. He doesn't want us to be seen. Am I right?" Bethany asked Small Dove.

Before the woman could answer, Alexandra voiced her opinion.

"You're right, Beth," she said. "Everytime someone's here, everytime someone's passing through we're sent packing. He hides us."

Without regard to the woman standing in their midst, the girls continued their discussion of this new request. It was a dilemma they hadn't anticipated.

"What should we do?" Alexandra asked the girls standing beside her.

"I don't know," Priscilla said. "Something's going on. Maybe we're being adopted and he's dressing us up. Remember him looking in our mouths, like he was counting teeth? Like he was trying to see how old we were? Remember that? I think he wanted to make sure we could eat. The idiot." Priscilla glanced at Small Dove, then back at Alexandra and Bethany. "Don't ask her why; she doesn't know. What should we do?"

Bethany responded. "Maybe this change of clothes is marriage. Maybe that's the way it's done here. Do you think?"

"No, that isn't the way it's done. They probably just live

199

together. You know: in sin. They don't have preachers," Priscilla replied.

"No. That isn't it. This is ridiculous." Alexandra shook her head, then turned and started walking away.

"Where are you going?" Bethany asked.

"To change my clothes."

"Now? Right now? Are we going to do what he said? Shouldn't we talk about it, first?"

"If not now, when? Isn't that what she said he wanted?" Alexandra replied.

"I don't know if I want to. I like my dress," Bethany said. "What about our underclothes? Do Indian women have underclothes? Our pantaloons, petticoats, chemises? Pris, what do you think?"

"I don't know. I don't think so. I haven't seen any."

"Well, I am not going to take mine off," Bethany stated. "Lexie, do they?"

"Do they what?" Alexandra replied.

"You know . . . wear underclothes? Are they all naked under their dresses?" Bethany asked.

Priscilla interrrupted. "Well, I'm not taking my underclothing off. I'm wearing my chemise until it wears out. I'm going to keep wearing it until we escape. Or we're rescued. My pantaloons, too. I am not going to be naked under this . . . I don't care how good it feels or what Indian women wear. I am not going to do that. There is a limit. I've reached it."

The two girls followed Alexandra to the lodge, carrying their "new" clothes in their arms. Once inside Alexandra pulled the entrance covering shut and proceeded to examine the doe skin dress and the other paraphernalia. Bethany watched her.

"Are you going to change your clothes just because he wants you to? Just because he said so?"

Alexandra turned to look at her. "Pick your fights, Beth. This one isn't worth it to me. Do what you think you should."

Bethany looked at the leather article Alexandra was holding up for inspection. "What are those things for?"

"They're leggings. They go on your legs."

"My legs?"

"Yes," Alexandra replied.

Beth looked at the leggings more closely. "But how do they

work? What holds them up?"

Alexandra patiently explained. "You tie that leather strap like a garter; tie it just below the kneecap. They go from the kneecap to their shoes."

"Look," Priscilla said, "she even gave us moccasins."

"No socks? Don't they wear socks? I've never seen anyone wearing socks," Bethany said.

"I'm keeping mine on," Priscilla replied. "My feet will get cold without them."

"Me, too." Beth studied her pile of clothing. "What about winter? When it's cold. Do you think they wear something different when it gets cold?"

"Winter? We're not going to be here come winter," Priscilla blurted out, rather loudly.

"Shhh, don't talk so loud. Someone might hear," Alexandra said, quickly.

"Just the same, I'm saving my socks. I need them. Especially when it gets cold." Bethany glanced at her companions. "I'm keeping my shoes, too," she whispered. "I need my shoes."

Priscilla removed her dress and slipped into the doe skin garment. "Look at this," she said. "Now here's a fashion statement. How do you like it?"

"I like your pantaloons peeking out over the top of your leggings," Beth said, smiling.

Alexandra weighed in. She said, "It looks weird. It is weird. That's what it is."

"How about the bottom of my chemise? Do you like it peeking out, too?" Priscilla asked.

Neither girl replied. Bethany was busy putting on the doeskin dress.

"This dress needs a belt."

Alexandra looked at her. "I'll bet that's what that leather tie thing is for. To tie around your waist like a belt."

Looking at Priscilla, Bethany said, "This skin is soft and clean. It's heavy, though. What kind of skin is it, I wonder?"

"Does it matter?" Priscilla replied.

"It's doe skin. That's what Small Dove said," Alexandra replied.

"Did she?"

"Yes, she did."

"This dress isn't long enough," Priscilla complained. "It only goes past the knees. It is sort of like a long shirt. The way it hangs."

"Do you think that's why they have those leggings? Because the dress isn't long enough?" Beth asked.

"I doubt Indian women think about it. I think this is a two deer skin dress. One hide for the front, another for the back. They're cut, sewed and stitched with sinew at the top to hold them together." Priscilla paused. "Have I done this right? How does it look?" she said.

Bethany looked at her. "It looks terrible."

"Why don't we ask Small Dove. She'll know," Alexandra suggested.

"Is she still here?"

"I think so. Probably."

Bethany agreed. "Good idea. She can tell us."

Bethany opened the flap and peered out through the lodge opening and discovered Small Dove standing, waiting, keeping the dogs away from the deer carcass. Bethany beckoned her, waited while Small Dove covered up the meat, then held the flap open for her to enter the lodge. Once she was inside, Bethany closed the covering, tying it shut.

"Is this right?" Priscilla said to Small Dove. She had removed her cotton broadcloth dress and replaced it with the doeskin, keeping her pantaloons on. "I'm keeping my underclothes," she announced.

"Is this how it is supposed to fit?" She looked at Small Dove. "Is it?" she asked.

Bethany joined in. "I think it needs a belt. Do you have a belt? You know, to keep the waist together. I want a waist."

Small Dove nodded, looking at the girls. "Two," she said. "Two dresses."

"I see that. What about this one?" Beth asked.

"Good. You like?"

Priscilla had turned her attention to the second dress. It was made of finely tanned deerskin. Someone had not spared any effort in its creation. Priscilla inspected it carefully, running her fingers over the bead work on the back and front. Taking off the first dress, she tried on the second. It was heavier, yet soft, smooth to the touch. It extended from the shoulders to midway between the knee and ankle. The sleeves reached nearly to the wrist and were tied at intervals on the under side. Priscilla noted the ample openings about the armpits, probably for the convenience of nursing mothers. Both sides of the dress were sewn from the armpits to the bottom of the dress.

On the second dress, fringe hung from the bottom of the skirt and from the sleeves. There were no seams. It was finely decorated at the shoulders and arms with porcupine quills, beads, and shells. A little love-charm was fastened to the shoulder of the dress just above the left breast. The first dress was plain and functional. The second was not.

"You like?" Small Dove said. "My mother's. Given by her mother. This," Small Dove touched the love-charm, "given my mother. Cast spell over lover. She young. Much good luck."

"Small Dove, why are you giving it away? To us? You can't. It was your mother's." Alexandra was alarmed.

"My mother gone. Better dress."

"But. . ."

Small Dove looked at Priscilla. "You like?"

"Sure. It's beautiful."

"No for work. This one for work. This one for special. Buffalo dance."

Alexandra interrupted. "But, Small Dove, it should be for you to give to your daughter."

"I make. Give daughter with love button. Cast love spell," Small Dove replied.

Looking at Bethany, Small Dove pointed to the cotton dress at her feet. Small Dove said, "Me take."

Bethany stared at her before answering, then said, "Okay. But just a minute, Small Dove. Understand I'm keeping my pantaloons, and the rest. You don't get my underclothes."

"All," she replied. "All. No need. This better. No white man's. Understand this?"

Alexandra glanced at her sister. *All?* she thought. *My pantaloons, my shoes, socks, too? That isn't happening.*

Bethany looked at Alexandra. "What are you going to do, Lexie?" she asked.

"I'm not giving her mine."

"Me, either," Bethany said.

"Okay," Priscilla said. "Looks like the Wakeford girls are prudes on the prairie. I'm keeping my drawers, too, seeing that it is so fashionable these days on the western frontier." She looked at Small Dove. "You don't get my dress, either." She slipped out of the second doe skin dress and put her cotton dress back on. "I like my dress. I'm keeping it."

Bethany picked up her blue cotton dress and handed it to Small Dove, saying, "This is all you get. I'm keeping my underclothes as well."

Small Dove smiled, accepting the cotton dress.

Over wasn't over and done wasn't done. Three days later while washing themselves and their remaining "white man" clothes in the cold waters of Goose Creek, Alexandra's dress and those remaining undergarments disappeared. The thief was not apprehended, although the girls looked. Priscilla still had her cotton dress. At the time of the theft, she had been wearing it.

CHAPTER 33
Alexandra is 30 miles west of Zeke on Goose Creek

October 21, 1854
Clear Creek
Central Nebraska Territory

Emile Villon sat on the flat surface of a granite rock overlooking Clear Creek, listening. It had been a good day trading on Clear Creek. Just being home felt good. It always did. Since leaving Laramie, he thought about killing the kid. No one would know. No one would care. People disappeared all of the time. The fruits of killing him were obvious. He'd inherit another fully loaded pack animal, packs filled with more trade than he'd ever owned plus the kid's personals: a black gelding, the Navy Colts, saddle, a pack saddle, and an unending supply of money, or so it seemed. It was all good.

It was his conclusive determination that the kid was an idiot. There was no other explanation for his chasing captive teenage girls among the Teton Lakota. Once in a while the army came across a white woman wandering in and out of an Indian camp. They made a big deal out of the rescue, of freeing them from the savages. It seemed, however, that these women always went back to the people who had captured them. Killing the kid would be easy: shove a blade between his ribs, turn it hard, then put a round betwixt and between his eyes. Sitting on a rock on the banks of Clear Creek, baking in the fall sun, he decided he'd use the knife. *Damn kid deserved it fer bein' stupid.*

But he didn't kill him. There were multiple opportunities but they slipped by like a drifting thunder cloud. "Next time," he kept thinking. "I'll do it next time." Next time never arrived. He asked himself why and determined it was the kid's pistols. It seemed the kid's fingers were always brushing against a walnut butt. Or the light wasn't right. Light and fingers made him edgy, over careful. It wasn't just that, either.

Zeke had four or five of those Navy Colts. Emile hadn't seen them all but every day the kid "played" with them. The kid fired several rounds through two of them, never kept a hammer on an empty cylinder: twelve shots, two pistols. In the evening he practiced and practiced ad nauseam: not firing them but getting to them, bringing them to bear, sometimes dry firing on empty cylinders. Click, click, click. Afterwards the kid would reload, wiping each pistol clean of dust and burnt power. Every day. It drove Emile crazy. And there was that knife: big, heavy, sharp, accessible. The knife wasn't as bothersome as the pistols, especially up close. Still . . .

Emile rethought his decision a dozen times and decided the best way was to let someone else kill the kid. All he had to do was watch and wait. Having re-decided, Emile started counting his yet to be earned profits and decided that his singular problem wasn't killing the kid; it was packing the hides he'd get from trading the kid's goods. A good problem: he'd trade for another horse and he'd use the kid's once he was dead.

It was a very good problem to have. Someone else could kill the kid. He'd have little risk and he wouldn't have to trade for another horse. He could feel the uncollected coins in his pockets jingling. This was a good day.

Emile's second trade of the first day was with Standing Bear's woman: a cured doe skin for two yards of red cotton cloth. He could have gotten a better deal but Standing Bear was his cousin and he was right there watching. Out of curiosity he asked the woman in Oglala, "Ya see three white girls, eighteen, twenty winters maybe? They'd be new. Not seen before."

She looked at Standing Bear and he answered Emile's question.

"There are three white girls with Walking Eagle's band."

"Where?"

"Upper Goose Creek," Standing Bear said. "Half a day's ride west. You know where. You've been there."

"Half a day's ride. How do ya know?"

Standing Bear smiled. "I talked to my uncle yesterday. He knows Walking Eagle. They are moving north following the buffalo. There are many buffalo north of the Greasy Grass. They go. We go. We are leaving tomorrow. Maybe this afternoon. The last hunt of the year."

"Today? Ya may leave today?"

The Indian nodded. "Why do you want to know?" Standing Bear asked.

Emile pointed at Zeke. "He wants ta know," he said. "One of them girls is his woman. He wants her back."

"You need to hurry."

"Hurry?"

"They are moving to the Greasy Grass."

Emile nodded. "North? Today?" he asked.

"Walking Eagle left yesterday. The girls was with him."

Emile did not mention his discovery to Zeke.

The next people with whom Emile conversed didn't know about any white girls.

At noon Zeke asked him if he'd inquired about the girls, if he'd learned anything.

"I asked, but no, kid," he lied. "I ain't learned a damn thing. Nobody seems ta know nothin'. Except one feller thinks he heard of some white girls travelin' with an Injun named Broken Nose. They be headed east ta the Belle Fourche. He ain't sure 'cause he ain't seen no girls. Expect that's a dead end," Emile Villon lied, except for the part about it being a "dead end". That was the truth. A disappointed Zeke nodded, then went to take care of his horses while Emile traded with his next visitors.

Emile's next visitors had seen the girls. The short woman, the one who liked red beads, explained, "They're with Walking Eagle. Live in his lodge. They follow the buffalo. I believe they went north. I think they have already gone. If he wants to catch them, he needs to hurry."

"Oh, yes," said another. "White women. Three. Livin' in the lodge of Walking Eagle. They belong to him. They follow the buffalo. We are getting ready to go, too. You should go. There will be lots of trade: many people and many buffalo hides."

Emile said he might. He'd think on it. "They left yesterday, ya think?"

"Two days ago. They left from Goose Creek. You know Goose Creek?"

"I do."

"They left two days ago following the buffalo north of Greasy Grass."

"Have you asked?" Zeke inquired again.

"I have."

"And what did they say?"

"Nothin'."

"Nothin'? These people seem to know you. They call you by one name."

"They know me. I was born here. My ma--she lived here herself. They're my people, these ones."

"Emile, for some reason, I'm gettin' the impression you ain't askin' about Lexie and Beth."

"I'm askin'. Be patient," Emile said. "Slow down. Wait."

"Wait? For what?"

"Fer someone who knows. So far nobody knows. Get me? Patience, kid. Someone will know and they'll tell me."

"Not if you ain't askin."

"I'm askin'."

In the morning of the second day Emile spoke to visitors, women interested in cloth and red beads. In Oglala they asked him, "Who is the young man?"

Emile answered in Oglala for they understood nothing else.

"He is lookin' fer his woman. Taken in the south by hunters fer buffalo."

"In the south? This year? He looks angry."

"Yes. Taken after Conquering Bear was killed on the Platte." Emile glanced at Zeke. "He does look a bit peaked. Woke up thet way."

"Over the cow?"

"Yes, over the cow. Not long ago," Villon replied.

"No one hunts buffalo in the south. No buffalo south."

"It was a war party. Maybe thirty or forty days ago."

"Oh, a war party. There were several. After Conquering Bear was killed, many warriors killed the Gatton and his long knife soldiers. They all died."

"Yes. After the old cow was butchered and eaten. After Gatton," said one of the women.

"The people left the place called Fort Laramie. No one stayed. There was shooting. There were more soldiers coming. The white man with the blankets and cows did not come."

"Yes," Villon said.

"Maybe the Oglala. Maybe Walking Eagle has his woman. Could be they were seeking war. The young men were hard for the shirt wearers to control. Wanted to drive the whites from the land of the Teton Lakota."

"Yes, maybe. Whoever it was took this one's woman and two

other girls," Villon said.

"Three? They belong to this one?"

Emile nodded. "Yes," he said.

The woman looked at her companions, then, calling Emile by name in Oglala said, "Bad Horse, that would be Walking Eagle. They followed the Buffalo from Goose Creek. They are going north; maybe they will hunt on Greasy Grass. He has three white women. I think they are his wives. Did they belong to this white boy?"

"He thinks so."

"There will be trouble, I think. This one is young to have so many wives. Does he have many horses? He is wealthy?"

"Wealthy? A little." Emile paused. "Ya think there will be trouble?"

"Yes, Walking Eagle has them for wives. They belong to him; he thinks this way. Now they follow the buffalo. Tomorrow we are also leaving to hunt buffalo. Tomorrow. I think he will have to fight with Walking Eagle for his wives. Three are too many, I think. Maybe they can share." She laughed, as did her companions. "This one," she said, pointing at Zeke, "he might not live long when Walking Eagle finds this out."

"One is too many," Villon grumbled.

"Two is too many." The women laughed.

Resuming to their inspection the woman asked, "How much?" She pointed to the bolt of red cotton cloth.

"One elk skin? Tanned with brain of the buffalo. Soft," Villon replied.

"Too much. How much of the red cloth do I get for tanned elk skin?"

"Enough fer two dresses. A good price. Not too much."

"And how many of the beads? The red ones. I will need enough cloth for two dresses, and many beads. Elk skins are valuable."

Emile smiled.

Yes, they are, he thought.

After the women left and before he bargained with another customer, Emile spoke with Zeke. He said, "I spoke ta some women."

"Did they know about the girls?"

"One knew about three white women. Said they belonged ta Walking Eagle. They're his wives. I told ya that's what's goin' on."

"Where are they?. Did she tell you where?"

209

"Said they went east maybe ten days or a week ago. Headed east. That's what she said. Maybe goin' ta the Belle Fourche River country, huntin' buffalo," she said. "Said there was a lot of buffalo on the Belle Fourche."

"You know that country?"

"I do. She is right about plenty of buff." Emile studied Zeke.

"How far?"

"Oh, I don't know. Maybe seventy-five or hundred mile. A two or three day ride."

"A week to ten days ago? They would be there, now."

"True. I told ya we would find 'em. Folks know. If they're huntin' buff they'll be there a while. No hurry. Takes time ta kill, skin, and dry the meat. They'll be fillin' their parfleches fer winter. That's what they'll be doin'. She said they was up on Goose Creek before they started after the buff. Goose Creek--I'd say thet was maybe thirty mile west of here. Said she saw 'em passin' through goin' east, maybe a week, ten days ago. They's come down offa the mountain lookin' fer buff. That's what they do."

"We'd better hurry. A hundred mile might take us two or three days with two pack animals: that mule of yours and that horse. We'll be through with October before we know it. We ain't time. Winter's comin'."

Villon nodded. "You're right," he said smiling to himself. "After they hunts the buff they'll be lookin' fer a place ta hole up fer winter."

Zeke looked at Emile, wondering what he was missing. Something wasn't right for he was never this agreeable.

Zeke was restless, egged on by the thought that Lexie was out there. Not far away. She could be a mile from where he was sitting. That was close, real close--reach out and touch close.

"We need to go," he said to Emile Villon. "We can't stay here no longer. I'm thinkin' we ride west to Goose Creek. Pick up their trail. Follow it. If the trail goes east, we go east. A trail, something on the ground, would prevent any mistake, reduce our chances of being wrong. That's what I'm thinkin'."

What Emile Villon thought wasn't what he said. What he thought was:

Go? Go? Ya . . . worthless, useless pile of used horse biscuits, ya sack of

210

turds, I gots money ta collect here. Hides ta get. Go? To Goose Creek? We ain't goin' there. Does he know? Naw. He don't know shit. He's guessin'.

What he said was: "Goose Creek? What I'm told is thet Walking Eagle went east, thet he has those girls. They're followin' the buff. Another man said he heard about them women bein' east ta the Belle Fourche with Broken Nose. East," he said. "Ya wanna go east not west. We kin pick up a trail here. Don't have ta go a day's ride outta our way."

Zeke thought for a moment. The words were logical. They made sense. "All right," Zeke said. "I expect it's the thing to do. Did you hear anythin' else? Anythin' at all?"

Emile Villon was rubbing his chin, thinking.

Stupid kid. I gotta get rid of this little jackass. He don't know shit. 'Sides he's gettin' in the way of me makin' money. Takin' it right outta my pockets. But I gots him now. Good fer me. I'll see what I kin do ta run hisself off a cliff. Kill him.

Emile Villon smiled to himself.

It's all about separatin' a fool from his money. That's what it is. And I'm the right man. Stupid. Stupid kid. He ain't gonna know'd why he gots up in the mornin' I gets through with him.

"Naw," he said, clearing his head. "I ain't heard nothin'. Just thet fellow and those women said they thought they was east of here. Belle Fourche. That's what they said."

"Okay," Zeke paused, hesitating. "You don't think they'd be lyin' to you? They pullin' your leg?"

"Naw, they're tellin' it how they sees it." Emile Villon stood up. "All right," he said to Zeke, "pack 'er up, and we'll be gettin' soon as you're ready."

Let this old woman do the work seein' how he's wantin' ta chase them skirts. How'd I saddle myself with this jackass? Best a luck ta me. Best a luck.

"And no, they ain't pullin' my leg none. Them white women, they ain't in these parts. If they was we'd know'd it. I figure they's east. Best guess: Belle Fourche. That's what the people, they ar' sayin'."

"All right. We'll go east." Zeke said it out loud but found it worrisome.

On a hunch, turning, staring, he said to Emile. "You sure?" he asked. "A side trip of two weeks is a side trip of a month just gettin' back to where we started. I ain't got a month. I got no time for lollygaggin'. Winter will be here before we know it. I ain't got a month."

211

Emile looked at Zeke. "I'm sure, boy. Anyways, that's what they're a sayin'. What do ya want ta do? Ain't makin' no difference ta me."

"East. I guess it's east."

CHAPTER 34
Zeke is 290 miles east of Alexandra on Clear Creek

October 28, 1854
Greasy Grass Creek
Central Nebraska Territory

One week later at first light camp was struck; lodges came down like a cold wind dropping off the pine-covered ridges of the Horn. The activity was furious as if hurrying was a requirement of being awake, the very order of the day, as if something somewhere was getting away, escaping. An hour and a half later the journey north began. And Goose Creek became a memory.

It was overcast, gray clouds extending from horizon to horizon. Small Dove said the "hurrying" was about the "tatonka," the buffalo. Once they started moving there were no stops--no loitering, no pausing to appreciate the new day or the crisp fall breeze that followed them. Their passage continued late into the evening, a forced march for three days. Excitement, however, was high. They were tired, yet there were no weary feet. At the end of the third day, the lodges were pitched on the edge of Greasy Grass Creek in and out of the cottonwood trees.

Above the flood plain that followed along the meandering creek bed the grass was stiff and brown. There was a raw, cold quality to the breeze. The song of the meadow lark was gone. There was no redwing blackbird, no fluttering dove. The piercing cry of the killdeer was no longer heard. Remaining were the magpie, snow bird, camp robbers, and sparrow.

"Tomorrow, tatonka," Small Dove told the girls. "Tomorrow, big hunt. Last hunt. No more hunt before snow and time when buffalo cow drops calf. Long time. Hunt. Big celebration." She looked at Priscilla nodding, with a smile. "Wear dress. Big celebration. Yes. You like."

This is it, Alexandra thought. *It's now or never.*

While gathering wood for the fires, Alexandra spoke with Priscilla. She said, "Tomorrow there will be a lot of confusion. There will be horses available. Everyone will have one for the hunt. While everyone is working, when everyone is doing something--that will be

213

the time. It may be our only time. So be ready."

Bethany joined the two, listening.

"Where will we go?" she asked.

There's the true question.

"I've thought about it," Alexandra said. "I think we have to go back the way we came. I don't see any other choice. Even then, we could easily get lost. We'll have to avoid everyone. At first our tracks will be hidden in everyone else's comings and goings. We'll have to be careful and avoid being seen."

"It's getting colder. It will be cold on the mountain. Really cold," Priscilla commented. "Before we left Goose Creek there was snow high up. Did you see it? It stayed. That isn't good for us."

"Yes. You're right. It isn't ideal. Do you see any other way? I'm completely open. We'll get in and out of the mountain quickly. It's our only choice."

Priscilla looked at Bethany, then at Alexandra.

"I don't," she said. "But if another storm comes while we're on the mountain, it'll kill us. We'll freeze to death. That's all I'm saying. Pointing out the obvious. I don't think we have a choice either. Not if we're going to escape. It's now or never. You know what I'm saying? Now or never."

Alexandra nodded. "I agree with you and I think it's now. I'll have the food ready. I'll put the parfleches aside. As many as I can get."

Bethany interjected, "Weapons. Come tomorrow they'll be using most of them. We'll have to be careful. I think I know where there will be a rifle. And horses. We'll all have to work at getting horses."

"At least with the hunt there will be more horses available. Everybody, every lodge will have two or three. If each of us has one, we'll be ready," Priscilla said.

"I think the best time will be just after the kill. Or the day after tomorrow when everyone is recovering and sleeping late. That's what I'm thinking."

"Okay," Priscilla said, "the earlier the better." She glanced at Bethany. "Are you set?"

Bethany nodded. "I'm set," she said. "I've also located three pistols. They're loaded. I think, anyway. I know where they're kept."

"We already have the parfleches available," Alexandra said.

"Four, full . . . hopefully that will be enough. It's what we have. It probably doesn't matter because I don't think we can carry more than four. We're limited in what we can take. At the very last we can grab three buffalo robes from the lodge. I'll get them ready. Will that be enough, do you think? Three? I hope so," Alexandra said. "Beth, remember some flint to start a fire. Remember that."

"Yes, I have that already. I have it in the little bag I carry." Bethany smiled. "Okay, Lexie. I'm ready. As ready as I'll be."

"Me, too," Alexandra said. "As ready as I'll be."

Priscilla took a deep breath. "Okay," she said, nodding her head.

CHAPTER 35
Alexandra is 146 miles west by northwest of Zeke on the Greasy Grass

October 27, 1854
Belle Fourche River
North Central Nebraska Territory

Rifle percussions echoed and re-echoed across the rolling hills. One wallop didn't have time to die before another followed, each adding to the cacophony of explosions that filled the air, each bouncing off the hills again and again and again. Emile Villon sat atop his mule, listening. He cleared his throat, grumbling.

"Fifty-six Sharp," he said, nodding knowingly at Zeke. "Fifty-six Sharp. Hear me, boy? That's what that'd be. It be them buff they're a shootin'. Tell ya that. Hide hunters. Sound of boys gettin' rich. And there'll be plenty. See fer yourself. Ain't no end to 'em."

Emile watched Zeke riding ahead of him. He grumbled to himself, thinking as he followed the kid.

What am I doin' playin' nursemaid ta this here kid? I oughta be tradin', collectin' hides, getttin' rich. Gotta kill this kid 'fore he gets me kilt. 'Fore I'm dead broke. What am I waitin' fer? Damn me.

He glanced up at the overcast sky and took a deep breath of cold fall air. *"Gettin' late. Must be late October. Elk comin' down outta the mountain. Aspen turnin' yellow. If'n I kin kill this kid, I kin do some tradin' 'fore the first snow.*

The mule's ears twitched back.

Emile shook his head. *First snow? That'll be soon. Gotta think about winterin'. Where? Not thet damn Fort Laramie. Don't want ta do thet again. Livin' in thet hole. Not goin' thet far south. Maybe I'll stay on Clear Creek doin' some tradin'. Gotta get rid of this damn kid. What's holdin' me?*

Emile thought about the question and didn't immediately provide an answer.

It's those damn pistols. Pistols and thet knife, he admitted. *Thet and he's young.*

Young? That's no excuse! I've known plenty of folk with lots of pistols. Has ta be somethin' else. What's wrong with me?

Thet kid never seems ta sleep. Always listenin'. Every evenin', every mornin', he checks them loads. Shoots and shoots. Every night he's sharpenin' thet blade, drawin' it across the whetstone

I do thet.

I'm losin' my mind.

There was another thing Emile Villon noted: the kid never left a chamber open, not on the Navys, not on the Volcano.

Damn rifle. And he should, damn well should. Everyone leaves a chamber empty. Most everybody. Hammer could pop off a round on accident. Misfire. They do thet. Not this damn kid. Right now thet Volcano has one restin' in the chamber. Sure as hell. Thet boy's fixin' ta be hard ta kill. How'd a boy get a Volcano? Ain't natural. It ain't.

Be careful. Real careful. Thet barkeep said thet kid drew and shot thet fellow Sly. Sly had his Colt out and already tried ta kill the kid once or twice. Folks said the kid shot him twice--no four times. Was it four times? Thet Sly bein' dead on his feet. Right there. Yes. Hard ta kill. I gotta get him dead ta rights.

Emile's hand brushed the grip of the Walker Colt hanging off the shoulder of his saddle. He stared at it, momentarily wrinkling his brow.

Damn heavy: four and a half pounds. Thet's what it is. At least.

He imagined pulling it, holding it with both hands, bracing himself, and firing, shooting the kid in the back: killing him.

Damn Walker'd misfire. Sure as hell. It'd happened. So many times. Can't count it. The kid would hear thet hammer.

Damn right, he would.

I'd be dead. Stone cold dead. Gotta be careful.

What the hell's wrong with me? I ain't never this careful. Never.

Out in front of Emile, Zeke walked his horse up to the rise. Zeke kept as low as he could in the saddle, guarding against skylining himself. Slipping to the ground, he crawled up to the top of the rise and looked east across the rolling hills to the blue mountains sitting squat on the distant horizon. Buffalo dotted the hills like fleas on a dog's belly. They moved steadily away from the constant percussion of rifles. It felt as if the entire hillside was alive, a dark black-brown mass moving steadily away. He'd seen buffalo, but never so many. The shooting didn't seem to bother them. It bothered Zeke.

"It's them little things," Emile mumbled to himself. "Little things." He watched Zeke, noted how the kid kept himself low, never skylined himself, never moved fast, dismounting and approaching the edge of the hill as if he was going to find a thousand warriors waiting for him to make one little mistake.

217

"Trouble is this kid don't make mistakes. How the hell am I gonna kill a kid like that? Where'd he learn thet belly crawl?" he muttered. "Someone taught him good. What'd I get myself into here? Ah, just shoot the bastard. He bleeds. His heart stops stone cold like everyone else's. He dies. Yeah, but so do I. I bleed."

"What?" The kid was standing up, having worked himself back from the edge of the cliff.

"Nothin'," Emile said. "Now, there's a herd of buff! I hear them boys ar' gettin' three dollar a hide. That's what I hear. A shooter kin knock down maybe two fifty a day. All he gots ta do is shoot. A good skinner kin pull the hide off a buff in five minutes. If'n he ain't lazy. If'n he works it. That's what I hear. A good shooter, a couple of skinners. That'd be a hell of a lot of money. Hear me, boy? A man could get himself a stake huntin' buff." Emile looked at Zeke. "Wanna get some of thet buffalo money, boy?"

Zeke shook his head no.

"No? Ya crazy? Shootin' buff. What's easier than thet? Not like they's goin' anywheres. Thet'd be more money than ya ever seed."

Emile was staring at Zeke, wondering what the kid would say.

"I don't want to," Zeke said. "Seems a waste. Killin' for the hide and nothin' else. Don't seem right."

"Buff tongue, thet'd be damn good eatin'. Bet ya ain't never et buff tongue. Have it sittin' in your mouth meltin' like candy. Have ya, boy?"

Zeke didn't reply, stepping into the saddle smoothly, then guiding his horse off the hillside, mindful of keeping low. He rode past Emile, letting him talk to his back.

Emile raised his voice. "Ya rather waste your time lookin' fer thet woman. That's it, ain't it? You're a damn fool, boy, lookin' thet kind a money straight in the eye fer a set a skirts."

Zeke nodded. "I'm a damn fool."

"Ya ain't gonna find her. It's been what, damn near two and a half months? Ya ain't found nothin'. I say let's get some of these buff. Get ourselves a stake. Ya do the shootin'. I'll pull the hide right off 'em. We'll make ourselves a killin'. No use ya chasin' thet woman. She's dead ta ya."

"That fellow you spoke to said she came in this direction; she's around here somewheres."

"Broken Nose?" Emile paused, "Thet's what he said all right."

"We close?"

"Close ta what?"

"That tradin' post?"

"Five or ten mile. It be sittin' down there on thet Belle Fourche Creek."

"That's close. Maybe we can learn somethin' there. She could be there."

"Maybe," Emile said.

"Well, I ain't killin' no buffalo. I ain't killin' no more than I can eat."

"Suit yourself, boy."

I will, Zeke thought. *I will*. He imagined Lexie; she could be really close. Close enough to talk to, to hold in his arms. A heavy pain rose in his throat, making it hard to breathe. He kept moving, determined to ride away from it, if he could. Behind him Emile had turned away, the breeze at his back. He sat staring at the buffalo.

The Sharps rifles were banging away, punctuating the late morning like hammers pounding steel. They were getting close to the camp. Zeke absently loosened the leather latch, pushing it off the hammer of his Navy Colt, thinking that a camp was one thing and a saloon another. *Still*. He pushed the leather latch away from the hammer, moving it out of the way. It wasn't an overt act, hardly noticeable, certainly not threatening; nevertheless, being watchful was the order of the day.

O'Reilly had dropped farther and farther behind until Zeke couldn't see him. He'd disappeared.

They found the hunters, several skinners, four freight wagons, and stacks of green hides plagued by a host of magpies and a storm of flies a mile and a half east. The camp sat in a ravine, occupying a shallow depression in a hillside. A seep spring provided water; skunk brush and scrub oak furnished additional cover. A short distance from the camp three hunters were shooting buffalo from a natural blind. Close to three hundred carcasses littered the hillside waiting for skinners to descend on them with sharpened steel blades.

After Villon and Zeke found the camp, the shooting diminished, then came to a stop altogether. Hunters and skinners drifted in to see the visitors, get a drink of water, some fresh fried buffalo tongue, and the latest gossip. They'd been there seven weeks. Between the several wagons dried hides were stacked up waiting to be loaded and hauled away.

The afternoon was left to the skinners as well as to the vultures, crows, ravens, magpies and a slinking coyote. The latter never went hungry. They were joined by wolves. Ordinarily the camp was busy. The skinners pulled the hides free, leaving the carcasses to rot in the hot afternoon sun. As soon as the green hides were detached, they were stretched and staked out on the prairie to shrink and dry hard in the sun. Visitors were welcome. Mostly there weren't any. But when there were visitors, work stopped; men gathered around the campfire to drink black coffee and chew on venison and fresh buffalo steak. They listened and talked into the late evening.

"Naw," Emile Villon said to a skinner and several hunters, a piece of tongue in hand, "ya ain't gonna get the kid ta do no shootin'. I tried. Reckon he could kill hisself five hundred buff 'fore noon, if'n he gets hisself started. Damn good shot. Kilt hisself a man in Fort Laramie. Fella up and starts shootin' and the kid puts four rounds in his head. Just like that."

Zeke stood on the edge of the campfire, listening, hungry, his stomach growling in protest. He shook his head, uneasy, leaning in the shade against a freight wagon box. Emile saw him.

"What's wrong wid ya, kid? Somethin' wrong wid your head? I'm tellin' it like it is."

"I ain't killed nobody like that."

"Don't go turnin' red turnip on me, boy."

Red turnip? What's that?

Villon turned his attention back to the four hunters who were listening, and continued. "He's got hisself interested in some gal, three gals, truth be told. Stole by the Injun up there on the Sweetwater. Been lookin' fer 'em. Ain't had much luck."

"Ain't had no luck," Zeke commented, "None at all."

Villon added, "Heard she might be over here on the Belle Fourche. Havin' ourselves a look-see."

"A girl? Injuns gots her?" A rangy hunter, dressed head to toe in old buckskin, raised himself on his arm, resting his torso against a saddle. "How'd thet happen? Recent, you say? On the Sweetwater? That's a ways from here."

"Injuns took her. Kilt everybody. The kid's tryin' ta find her. She's out here somewheres. Been lookin'. Ain't thet right, kid?"

"That's right," Zeke said. "Three gals. Oglala got 'em. Took 'em late August."

The lean hunter studied Zeke, nodding, speaking low and slow, clearly not given to much speaking. "Might as well give up on 'em, kid. Heard that once they's gone they's gone. You're on a fool's errand. Get yourself kilt for nothin'. They's takes 'em--you ain't wantin' 'em back. Thet's the way of it."

"Maybe," Zeke responded. "Maybe not. You boys seen any white women out here? Livin' with the Injuns?"

"Saw some down south around Fort Laramie. Damnedest thing. Soldier boys were gonna rescue this one woman, save her from the Injuns. She done disappeared 'fore they got her rescued." The hunter sat up. "They don't want to get rescued once they've lived with the red men. That's the way of it. Don't know rightly how to figure it."

"You know thet story 'bout that woman up there on the Crazy Woman. You heard thet, ain't you? Named after her."

"Everybody's heard thet story, Joe, ya hayseed. Everybody."

"Just the same, she was a white woman. Sure as hell. Saw her people kilt. Scalped right in front of her. She went plumb crazy. That's what folks say. Injuns wouldn't touch her. Sometimes they'd leave things fer her to eat. She's dead, I suspect. That's what I heard. Heard she done starved herself to death," Joe said.

Another hunter, wearing buckskin for a shirt, nodded in agreement. "I seed a white girl or two livin' with the Injun. Seed 'em myself. Never said nothin' to me a'tall."

"Three, ya say?" The question came from a skinner, a large portly man with a protruding belly. He sat on a pack saddle holding a tin plate, eating some bread sopped in grease, looking at a slice of buffalo tongue on a fork.

Zeke hadn't sat down. He found himself staring at the speaker, arms folded across his chest, feeling uneasy, as though he'd forgotten something, something important, and he wasn't sure what.

He remembered standing in a saloon with his uncle, listening to a series of conversations, waiting for his uncle to decide what he was going to do. Men were standing by, some leaning against the bar: talking, drinking from a common bottle of yellow rotgut, taking a sip, passing the bottle. Oddly, his uncle had not touched the corn liquor. Three times the bottle had circulated; three times Eli had waved it off. Two bottles were emptied.

In the mass of humanity, amid chatter and banter, he saw Eli, his hand brushing nonexistent lint from his shirt and his trousers. In the shadows, leaning against the bar, Eli's fingers had also pushed back the leather loop that secured his pistol in the holster. Zeke saw the loop drooping past the trigger guard as Eli's hands came to rest on his hips, thumbs in his pockets, his eyes following the bottle. It slipped as if on cue and fell, shattering on the floor. A fellow laughed, jumped aside to get away from the splash. Someone swore. For a moment there was silence.

To Zeke's surprise, his uncle was suddenly standing in front of him, his left hand pushing him back into the crowd, his right hand wrapped around the butt of his Navy Colt. Where there had been men laughing and sharing a drink, suddenly the same men were swinging, cursing, and pulling weapons. Shots were fired. Zeke found himself out on the street, his uncle smiling at him.

"Hell, of a thing, that corn squeezin', ain't it?" Just that quickly they were walking down the board walk, Uncle Eli's hand on his shoulder, guiding him. Behind them, men were boiling out of the saloon door where they'd just been, the fight pouring onto the street. "They figure it's pure gold and it ain't theirs. Get a might upset if'n it gets spilt. The damnedest thing."

Zeke nodded at the skinner who'd just asked the question, thinking about his uncle. His left hand brushed at his shirt; his hands were now resting on his gunbelt, his fingers inches away from the butt of his Navy Colt. From the fire he could smell the black coffee boiling in the kettle. He wanted a cup, but he waited.

"Where was this, you say?" the hunter asked Villon.

"South. Up on the Sweetwater. Five, six day ride from Laramie."

The hunter glanced at one of the skinners lying back. He was a big man, wearing a tied down pistol, a rifle at hand, a skinner's knife stuck in his belt. He was leaning against a pack saddle and chewing on a baking powder biscuit. He wasn't tall, more wide and heavy.

Villon continued. "Injuns got 'em. Took her and two others. Headin' north."

Zeke studied the skinner, something he didn't normally feel inclined to do.

"Ain't that where you was a while back, Shorty? Up in that Sweetwater country?" the hunter asked. The question was innocent

222

enough. But the name: *Shorty*.

Zeke cleared his throat. "Shorty? Your name's Shorty?" he said, no longer leaning against the freight wagon box, his gaze on the biscuit-eating skinner. "You pards with a fellow name a Sly? Another fellow, Crease? That you?"

Zeke's heart was beating to a slow rhythm of thud, thud, thud. His hands and arms felt heavy, relaxed.

Shorty was staring at him from over his belly, the biscuit crumbs laying below the pockets on his blood-stained plaid cotton shirt. Shorty didn't answer right away, waiting, perhaps too long, the mere passing of time casting a shadow of guilt over his face and shoulders. He pulled himself upright until he was sitting, looking at Zeke, not taking his eyes off of him, not liking the fact that he was sitting down.

"Don't reckon I know'd them folks," he said, pulling the brim of his hat down over his eyes.

For an extended moment no one spoke, the only sound being the breeze rustling through the flat green leaves of the scrub oak, the skunk and buck brush.

Emile Villon stretched and popped his neck. He looked at Zeke. "Boy, ain't thet fellow Sly the man ya shot dead there in Laramie? Ain't thet his name?"

"That's his name."

Zeke continued speaking, staring at Shorty. "He your pard?" Zeke asked again. "You and him, that other fellow, Crease, be the so'n'sos that led them Injuns to the Tallasinius wagons? That you?"

Shorty didn't answer.

Wordlessly, Emile Villon stood up and moved away from Zeke, an overt action, the reason for which was patently clear. Then the slow talking hunter wearing the sow belly hat moved left of Shorty, away from the cook fire.

"I ain't got no pard," the skinner said. "Ain't me. Ya gots the wrong man."

"Ain't you?"

"No, it ain't."

The short, round man with thick legs came to his feet, dropping the biscuit, brushing crumbs off his shirt, the crumbs falling to the dry sod.

"Got somethin' else ta say ta me, kid?" he asked.

223

"Yeah, was you up there on the Sweetwater last of August?"

Shorty again didn't reply immediately. "What if I was?" he said.

"If you was, you was with Sly and Crease. And you know what happened to my woman."

"And what if I was?" Shorty said again.

"Then you're a dead man."

"I ain't dead yet."

"You just don't know it," Zeke said, his voice low, measured. He took a step farther away from the wagon box, his hands resting on his hip above his holster. "I've done seen the dead you left behind."

Shorty was standing among the tack and saddles, motionless, a smirk on his face, staring at Zeke. The half-eaten biscuit was at his feet. The red piss ants had already found it.

The conversation was dead. The only sound was the popping crackle of the fire. Seconds passed. A lone magpie squawked, complaining from the branches of a scrub oak. The sound of black coffee simmering in the tall, suet-covered pot could be heard.

"Ya better be eatin' them words, boy," the skinner said. "I ain't feelin' righteous. Ya runnin' off the mouth thet way."

"Truth is what it is."

"What's thet suppose ta mean?" Shorty asked.

"Means you got a lot of innocent folks killed: my uncle, men, women, and children. I can't make it clearer except to say the wagon you're ridin' ain't goin' no further. This is it for you. Do you want me to draw a picture? Paint the important parts red?"

Everyone moved at once: hunters, skinners, Villon. One fellow dove for cover amid saddles and packs. Finding it inadequate, he rolled to his feet and ran behind a wagon. Shorty reached for the skinner's blade stuck in his waistband, something Zeke didn't expect. It was a casual, offhanded grab which covered and hid his other hand streaking for the pistol grip jutting from the oil stained holster secured high on Shorty's waist.

Shorty's fingers wrapped around the butt, jerking his pistol.

Without hesitation, Zeke pulled his Navy Colt from its holster, thumbing the hammer back, simultaneously squeezing the trigger. Shorty took the shot dead center in his chest, at the same time firing. He missed. Not by much. His second shot misfired. It didn't matter for his heart had stopped beating. Shorty fell backwards, dropping his skinning knife, grabbing his chest. Zeke wasn't where Shorty thought he'd be. Zeke's second shot caught the skinner above the right eye. Shorty's knife fell to the earth, landing, hilt first, at his feet.

In less time than it took to pour a cup of black coffee, Zeke was standing over the skinner, his lips drawn tight across his teeth, both pistols cocked. All Shorty could do was blink, thinking he'd told Crease they should have shot those damn girls. It was his last blink, his last thought. Zeke's third shot landed right between Shorty's eyes. Shorty's body jerked from the impact. Zeke stared at him, waiting.

Seconds later, Emile Villon stood beside him. He spat a stream of tobacco juice that landed on Shorty's contorted face, without saying a word, very much aware of the pistols in Zeke's hands. Mentally he made a note, thinking Zeke had three live chambers in one pistol and six in the other.

Damn kid! He's plenty quick, he thought. *I sure as hell gotta get shuck of him 'fore he gets trigger happy with me and has done shot me dead.*

Villon glanced at Shorty's body, noting that he took one in the chest, one above the eye, and one between the eyes.

That's good shootin'. No hesitatin'. With a Navy. Beat that. I better shoots him while he's sleepin'. Better use two irons like the kid. One misfire and I'm dead.

Only I ain't gots two. I gots ta get two. He ain't gots two, he's got five. Five?

No, four.

I only gots two hands. I needs two. The kid is gonna be hard ta kill. This Shorty, he can't do it. And he was plenty fast. Tricky, too.

Club him over the head, ya fool.

How the hell am I gonna get behind him ta do no clubbin'? He ain't normal. I gotta be damn quick. Damn it. What's I gots myself into?"

A damn kid, too. Just a damn kid.

CHAPTER 36
Zeke is 136 miles east by southeast of Alexandra on Belle
Fourche Creek

October 29, 1854
Thirty-six miles north of the Greasy Grass
Central Nebraska Territory

The men started on horseback; the women and early teens followed afoot. The women with little babies carried them on their backs snugly attached to cradle boards. The older men, those with gray hair and bent, broken bodies, and the young women stayed behind with the very small children. Guards were left to watch over them. Out front the cavalcade of horses broke into a trot leaving the women walking behind them. No effort was made by the women to keep up with the horsemen. The morning sun was still below the horizon but it wouldn't be for long. A quarter of a mile east of camp was a ridge line; the riders disappeared over it leaving the women walking in the predawn quiet. There wasn't much talk. Ten minutes later the women reached the ridge line and the horsemen were visible again: a long line of riders moving down the long slope at a trot.

Nothing in the New England Bostonian world where they'd grown up as adolescents and early teenagers prepared the girls for what they saw as they walked over that rise. In front of them was a black, steadily moving mass, a dark blanket stretching as far as they could see. Imagine the unimaginable. Picture a carpet comprising innumerable two thousand pound beasts stretching as far as a person could see and beyond. Millions of bison were moving steadily, traveling east in countless numbers, a breathing, unstoppable tide of flesh, bone, horn and hide. The very earth trembled as they moved forward and away.

"Tatonka," Small Dove whispered, excitedly.

Alexandra glanced at her. "Tatonka," she repeated. "Tatonka."

Below them more than a mile's distance, the riders merged with the moving line of buffalo, disappearing from sight over the next rise.

"Should we go down there?" Alexandra said.

"No," Small Dove answered. "Will run over us. Stay here. Wait. Safe here."

226

Coming out of the depression, the riders seemed to merge into the dark mass that surrounded them. Alexandra watched as a large animal fell to its knees and rolled onto its side. A rider raised his arms in triumph. It seemed so easy, so ethereal. Not for long. On down the line a tormented bull buffalo stopped and flipped about with great speed, agility, and enormous physicality. A clearing opened up around him. Suddenly it charged a lone horse and its rider. The rider avoided the sudden rush, his horse smartly stepping to the side, moving around, leaving the bull standing in the open. Its head up, it pawed the earth, throwing dirt and grass behind it.

To the side, four animals were dead, lying on their sides. The advancing tide had left them behind, dark forms lying on the yellow-brown carpet of prairie grass. A clucking sound erupted from the women watching. "Not always this way," Small Dove said to Alexandra. "Tatonka not start run. Maybe tatonka run."

The bodies of six animals were now lying on the sod, the mass drifting by as though nothing had happened to diminish their numbers. One wounded animal bellowed rage and defiance. Tail in the air, it burst out into the open, its woolly head up, its eyes on the closest rider. Alexandra watched as the rider kicked his mount in the sides, beating it to move. For some cause, the horse reared instead of running. The old bull was there planting its massive head in the horse's chest, thrusting upward. The horse was tossed high, came down, rolled, the rider clinging to its back, a feather floating on the wind. Alarm rose from the group of women watching.

A shaft of light exploded through the clouds, illuminating the rider flying in the air separated from his horse: the horse falling, the raging bull bellowing. Another rider galloped by, sending an arrow deep into the animal's chest just behind the front leg. It meant nothing. The bull did not stop; he charged the fallen, struggling horse, the rider had disappeared on the other side in his plunging descent. The horse rolled. Help arrived, if there is such a thing as help from a raging, mortally stricken, twenty-five hundred pound bull buffalo fighting for its life and using every ounce of adrenaline that it could muster. An effort was made to draw it away from the downed rider who, thrown to the sod, was struggling to get to his feet. The massive beast turned to the hazing rider. Suddenly it switched ends again and discovered the downed rider hobbling toward his stricken horse. The buffalo charged.

There is nothing in this world that can stop such a

combination. Riders on both sides of the animal tried. Arrows were shot into the beast but it was moving quickly. From out of the dust another rider raced to the hobbling hunter, picked him up, and carried him a few feet before his grip slipped and was lost entirely. The rider fell again, obscured by the dust and milling horsemen. The bull made it to the fallen horse, to the other side of the horse, and three steps, four, before crumpling to the earth, bellowing. Its heavy, labored breathing threw up gusts of dust. It died there on the prairie just east of the Greasy Grass, down the ridge four hundred yards from the shocked and stunned spectators.

The bellow of the dying creature sent the surrounding herd serging forward in panic. They plunged right and left, away, galloping up the rise. Others lagging behind were shot. They were not immediately dead, but dying—a most dangerous combination. Riders followed at a dead run. In the aftermath, twenty-three carcasses littered the slope and ravine. One rider's horse had broken its leg stepping in a hole left by a long gone badger, throwing the rider over its head. The horse stood head down, unable to walk, unable to move. The rider picked himself up, walking slowly back to the beleaguered animal. Alexandra watched, knowing there was no hope for it, only mercy and a swift death.

We need horses, three horses, she thought, *and now there's one less.* Shading her eyes, she glanced at the sun inching its way slowly above the horizon. *By noon, we should be gone. We'd better hurry.*

Half an hour of turmoil had passed and the women joyfully started toward the killing field, skinning knives in hand, with light hearts. Some, however, walked with fear and trepidation, expecting the worst, for they'd witnessed the charging bull, the injured rider. Before the women lay the business of cutting throats, bleeding, skinning, gutting, cutting away, and using every piece of meat and bone from horn to hock.

The mood turned somber as they identified the injured rider lying on his back, not moving, waiting for help. There were also shouts of glee as the women identified which animal belonged to whom by the marking on the arrow or arrows that killed it.

The girls walked together, the rising sun in their faces, looking for the specific arrows that identified Walking Eagle's kill. Separating, they moved from animal to animal, finding three kills: younger animals, cows whose meat would be more tender than the larger bulls. They cut the throats of the slain animals so they might bleed and the meat be saved. It was difficult working the blade through thick hair and hide, seeking the arteries in the throat.

In the midst of the killing field several women gathered around the downed hunter. Alexandra approached the gathering group of women to see who it was. She could feel their indecision. She saw Small Dove leaning over the broken man. She felt the pain suffered by the small woman. Alexandra moved closer. It was the same warrior, that very warrior, who had stood over her father. His horse was dead. Someone had shot it. An arrow was buried in its chest, a mercy killing: it had been gored, its stomach muscles ripped open, its guts hanging out.

Alexandra stared at the warrior, remembering him pulling the scalp, peeling it from her father's head, her mother's already hanging on his belt. She glanced at his left leg. It was broken: the big bone. He wasn't moving. He wasn't going anywhere, not with that leg.

If this could happen to anyone, I'd wish it happened to you, she thought, conscious of his pallid face, his rapid breathing, sweat beading up on his forehead, his lower lip pulled tight across his mouth. He was in such pain. *Good. Very good.*

Small Dove stood beside her shaking, distressed, obviously not knowing what to do.

"It's him." It was English. For some reason the sound of her mother tongue shocked her. Alexandra glanced to her left and found Bethany standing beside her.

"Yes," was all she could say in response. "It's him."

Bethany was silent for a moment. She touched Alexandra's elbow. "Lexie," she said, "let's go. We've got work to do. We've got to hurry. We can't be standing here. You know."

"Yes." Alexandra said and turned to leave, but hesitated. "Beth, it's Small Dove. Just a moment."

"No, Lexie. We have to go. Now, Lexie. We have things we have to do." The two girls had walked a few steps through the crowd of women. Bethany whispered, "Lexie, we can take three horses. Load them with meat. Go back to the creek. Everyone will be busy. They'll never see us leaving. It's ideal. It's now, Lexie. Just like you planned. We can't be standing around."

"You're right," Alexandra said, "but it's Small Dove. I don't think it's her husband. I'll be just a moment. She's. . . she's been kind to me. She needs help. I'll tell her what to do. That's all. I'm not going to do it. I can't. I couldn't."

"Lexie," Bethany whispered again, "we don't have time. You can't help."

"I won't. I'll be just a second. Wait for me. Please? I won't be long."

"Lexie, my God, have you lost your mind? We've got to go now."

"Stay here. I'll be just a moment."

Alexandra turned and wound her way back through the crowd, slipping through the milling people. When she reached Small Dove she put her hand on her back.

"Small Dove," she whispered, "you need to get help. Listen to me. You need to get a travois to carry him back to his lodge. Get a travois. Get him out of here."

Alexandra glanced down at the pain-contorted face of the wounded man, beads of sweat standing on his brow. "Do you know this one?" she asked Small Dove. "Is he your husband?" She asked the question hoping he was not, thinking that Small Dove didn't deserve such a 'blessing.'

Small Dove shook her head. "No. This one Uncle. Four little ones. A baby. My grandmother, he takes care her. What will they do?" she said, not expecting an answer.

Sniffing, holding back tears, Small Dove knelt beside the wounded man. Taking his hand, she said something to him that Alexandra didn't understand. She didn't want to understand. She refused to look at him again Not any more. She was glad for his pain, not giving a thought to those who depended on him for necessities. All she remembered was his bloodied hands, his awful face, his knife, the way he'd looked at her on the ground, her hands and feet bound.

Hate is a wondrous, driving, all-consuming emotion. Everything it touches is darkened by its festering need, painted by the same muddy brush. It leaves a black, rotting heart slowly eating itself, a soul awash in dripping, gangrenous poison that ultimately and inevitably destroys itself. It consumes raw anything that is kind or benevolent, wilting and destroying any possibility of forgiveness or tenderness, of living beyond the need for retribution, vengeance, and the compelling need to right the wrong. Forgiveness and healing are pushed aside by the need, the demand for vengeance.

The scales of righteousness must be balanced: a right for a wrong, a wrong for a right, a forced exchange of my pain for yours. It is punishment. Understanding never lives in the same lodge as hatred. It is unrelenting. It leaves nothing in its wake that is redeemable except the fleeting feeling that to some degree an evil has made right, something somehow balanced, that 'payback' has been extracted even if in a small, inconsequential way. It's a need. It was Alexandra's need. It was Bethany's need.

"Lexie?" her sister said. Alexandra glanced at Bethany, surprised that she was back by her side.

"I'm coming, Beth." Her left hand patted Small Dove on the back. "Get a travois," she said. "That's what you need to do."

"He never walk," Small Dove said. "No more. Never ride horse. Look. Look leg. Little ones starve. Wife. Son, daughter. My grandmother. Very bad."

Alexandra straightened up, her voice rose, exasperated. She turned to leave, her soul divided by a need to be kind to Small Dove and a demand to destroy the object of Small Dove's concern.

"Small Dove, just set it, splint it. Keep him off it. In six months he'll be fine. It's just broken. He's not dead. I've got to go. Small Dove, get a travois and carry him back to his lodge where you can take care of him. That's what you ought to do. I've got to go. I can't help you. Your uncle is a very, very bad man."

Alexandra immediately covered her mouth shocked by what she'd said. Hurriedly, she followed Bethany, hurrying to get away, her face a mask of contradiction, somber, filled with the urgent thought "I have to get out of here now."

I don't care if she is my friend.

Friend? She's not my friend.

She is. She helped me. Without her I couldn't have made it this far, for this long.

"Where's the first one, the closest kill?" Alexandra asked her sister.

"It's over here. I already have two horses. We need one more."

"Where's Pris?"

"She's over there doing what we ought to be doing. We've got to hurry." Bethany pointed.

Alexandra nodded. "Let's help her," she said, "and let's look for the third horse. It doesn't matter who it belongs to. If you can find

231

a fourth, do it."

"Okay."

"Where is she again?"

Bethany pointed. "Down there," she said.

"Oh, I see her."

It sounded like "hokeydey." What was said or what was meant is of little consequence. Both girls turned to see who was yelling at them. They saw Small Dove running towards them, holding her dress high to keep from tripping and falling, enabling her to run faster. She stopped in front of the two girls, breathless, staring up at Alexandra, her eyes desperate, her face a mask of contortions.

"Is so?" she said, breathing hard. "Is so?"

"Is what so?" Bethany asked.

"What she say," she eplied, pointing at Alexandra.

"What did I say?" Alexandra asked.

"You fix? Yes."

"Fix what? What did you say, Lexie?" Bethany asked.

"Nothing."

"You must have said something."

"I told her to set it, splint it, and keep him off it. That's what I said."

"You fix." Small Dove said again. "Okay. Yes."

"I'm not a doctor, Small Dove. I've never . . ."

Small Dove interrupted. "You fix."

"Small Dove, I've never set a broken leg. Never. Ever. I've never even tried."

Besides . . .I don't like this man. I hate him. Really, really, hate him. I wouldn't pour water over his head if he was roasting in hell, if he was on burning on fire. I wouldn't do it.

Well, maybe I would if the water was really hot, scalding hot.

"Lexie, you're not."

"I'm not, Beth."

I'd rather tear his heart out and feed it to the dogs.

Small Dove was staring at Alexandra. "What need?" she asked. Small Dove grabbed her hand. She was filled with hope and expectation, driven by desperation.

Small Dove was on the edge of shrieking. "What need? What you say? Magic word? What magic word?"

232

Bethany sighed and answered her. "Please," she said. "You say, please. Please is the magic word."

Small Dove turned to Alexandra. "Please," she said, her voice barely a whisper, her brown eyes large, hopeful, desperate. "Please," she said again.

Alexandra, staring at her, whispered, "Jesus, help me."

"No, Lexie, this isn't a Jesus thing. It's another 'Ahh shit.' You shouldn't involve Jesus. Not in this one."

"Bethany! Please . . ."

"Please what?"

"Nothing. Nothing. You're right. 'Ahh shit.' That is clearly what it is."

The mere thought of touching the man's leg turned her stomach, twisting it in knots. Right now hanging in this man's lodge were the scalps of her father and mother and Colleen Griffie.

And I'm supposed to touch him. Repair his leg.'Ahh shit doesn't even begin to cover this.

Alexandra looked at Small Dove. "Look," she said, "I've never set a man's leg. Ever. Besides, it might not work." *Frankly, I hope it doesn't.* "I don't know. Do you understand? I have no idea."

Small Dove stared at her, waiting, not speaking.

"Please," she whispered again.

Dread washed over Alexandra. Also significant quantities of loathing and hatred, together with a longing to aid Small Dove, a desire to repay her for the kindness that she'd so often extended. But Alexandra didn't want to fix the man; she really, really didn't want to.

I can't live as if I have no relatives. What's that mean anyway?

"Okay, Small Dove, all right." Alexandra found herself saying. "You'll need four sticks as long as your uncle's leg is long. About this size." She held up her hand, index finger and thumb making a circle. "They must be very straight. Hard. So they won't break. And you'll need six or ten pieces of leather straps. You know, strings about this long." She held her hands up measuring a little over two and a half feet. "That's what you need." Alexandra paused. "Small Dove . . . after all I do, it might not work. I don't know. Do you understand? It might not work."

"Okay. Good. I get. You fix."

"All right. Come and get me when you have those things. I have work to do."

Alexandra looked at her very disappointed sister, then turned and walked away leaving Bethany and Small Dove standing in the knee high, sometimes waist high, grass.

I've had enough, she thought. *I can't do this. How can I? Who am I kidding?*

She looked over the field of dead buffalo, at women bending over carcasses, horses pulling travois waiting to be loaded with meat. She spied Priscilla and started walking toward her.

It won't work. They'll kill me. If only I'd kept my mouth shut. I can't even touch him. And we surely don't have the time. Not today of all days.

Twenty minutes later the three girls had the hide pulled back from the body of the first buffalo cow and were proceeding to open up its belly to extract the intestines, heart, liver, and kidneys. Walking Eagle arrived with yet another horse pulling an empty travois. He held the reins and waited, watching the girls work but did not offer to help.,

What good are you? Alexandra thought, then she saw the horse. *Oh, that's three. Thank you. Thank you. Now, we're really ready.* The sun was half way up the morning sky. *I must really hurry. I have an hour. Maybe two.*

In the midst of this activity Small Dove came running, reaching her, out of breath from sprinting across the killing fields.

"Sticks," she said. "You fix. Now. Please. Please."

Alexandra looked at her companions, then bent down and wordlessly wiped the blood from her hands on the prairie grass. "Well," she said, "I'd appreciate it if you two would come with me. I am going to need your help: someone to talk to, someone I can communicate with. I can't do this alone."

"As if we have time," whispered Priscilla. "I hope you know what you're doing."

"So do I."

"Sis, this better work," Bethany said. "That's all I have to say. That and you must be crazy."

In the midst of this conversation Walking Eagle said something which clearly agitated Small Dove for she lit into him. He responded. Whatever he said really agitated her. She started in on him a second time, voicing her displeasure. After she finished her thoughts, she looked at Alexandra. "We go," she said. "We go now."

The three girls followed Small Dove, walking behind her, followed reluctantly by Walking Eagle. There remained a crowd gathered around the wounded man. It split apart as they arrived, allowing Small Dove to pass, closing behind Walking Eagle.

I guess we're important, Alexandra thought, looking down at the man and his bent leg lying on the sod a few feet away from his dead horse and a dead bull buffalo. Someone had cut the buffalo's throat, leaving it to bleed. A travois had arrived to carry the broken-legged rider back to his lodge on Greasy Grass Creek. No one had attempted to move him. Everyone was waiting. To Alexandra it felt warm in spite of the cool October day. The air felt like a wet blanket. There was no talking among the spectators.

"What are you going to do, Lexie?" Bethany asked. "He isn't going to like you touching that leg. Look at it. It's bent backwards. He's practically lying on it. It's gross. Do you think you can really fix it? You know, it's different from fixing a chicken with a broken wing. Remember that? That one never flew anyway. But it didn't matter."

Alexandra nodded. "Yes, I know this time it matters."

Alexandra glanced at Small Dove and said, "Listen, Small Dove, to fix the leg, we're going to have to move him. Understand? It's going to really hurt. There isn't any way around it. You'll have to hold him down while we straighten the leg out. Understand? You must hold him down to keep him from moving. He isn't going to like it. I'll straighten it out. You have to hold him down or I won't be able to do that. That's the first part. Small Dove? Okay? Do you understand? That's only the first part. Afterwards, it's going to get difficult."

Small Dove said something to Walking Eagle who again spent considerable time replying. Neither was pleased. Small Dove responded to him in a slightly more hostile voice. Alexandra glanced at her sister. After the conversation, Walking Eagle knelt with the man's head between his knees, pressing his shoulders to the ground with both of his hands. Two additional men seized the wounded man's arms, pressing them into the sod. Another held his good leg. Small Dove literally sat on his chest.

I guess he isn't going anywhere. Alexandra thought. *I wonder if he can breathe with Small Dove sitting on him like that.*

"Should she do that Lexie?" Bethany asked. "Do you think that's necessary?"

"Is this going to work, Lexie?" Priscilla said. "I mean. This is crazy."

"I don't know if it's going to work. Do you have any other ideas?"

235

"No, I don't. But I just don't know. Maybe it'd be better . . ." Priscilla stopped talking, staring at Alexandra.

"To shoot him like a horse?" Alexandra said.

"That's one way," Priscilla said.

"Yes, it is."

Alexandra bent down and took hold of the awkwardly bent leg by the ankle. "Here goes," she said and without hesitation pulled the offending leg straight. The warrior squirmed, his breath hissed out, emptying his lungs. His body went limp. The leg was straight as well as floppy, appearing to be longer than the unbroken one.

Alexandra took a breath of air, *That's something. Can't believe I did that.*

"Are you going to leave his pant leg on him?" Bethany asked.

Priscilla looked at her. "Good question," she said. "How would we get it off?"

The warrior suddenly sucked in his breath, his white knuckled fingers clenched into fists. The men holding his arms and leg did not release him.

Ahh shit, Alexandra thought. *That's truly what this is. Ah, shit.* "I don't know," she said. "Should we leave it on? I guess we could cut it off."

"We could cut it where it's stitched," Bethany said.

"The sinew you mean? Cut the sinew?"

"Yes."

"What this?" Small Dove interrupted.

Alexandra looked at her. "We're trying to figure out how to get his pant leg off so we can see his leg. We're trying not to hurt him."

She glanced at the small Indian woman. She hadn't moved.

"Stand away," she said.

Small Dove got to her feet. The girls moved, standing back. Other women took their places, cutting the belt that kept the wounded man's pant leg up, pulling it off his leg without any thought to the wounded man's comfort. The four men holding him to the ground were hard pressed to keep him from moving. It wasn't easy.

"Oh, wow," Priscilla said to Alexandra. "That's one way."

"Yes," Bethany murmured. "That is one way. Just jerk them off, I guess." She glanced at her sister. "It won't hurt long that way."

"Okay, okay," Alexandra said. "Let's get this over with. Small Dove, I'm going to feel the bone in his leg. I will determine what the break is like. I need to know this to fix the bone."

Small Dove did not respond. She said something to the men holding the afflicted hunter. Walking Eagle nodded.

Kneeling, Alexandra worked her hands up and down the man's thigh twice, oblivious of the wounded man straining against those that held him.

Finished, she said to Small Dove, "Okay, it's broken in only one place. I'm going to pull the leg straight, then push the bones together. You need to hold him really, really still. Small Dove, tell them what I'm going to do. Tell him to ready himself. Tell your friends. Tell them everything I told you."

Small Dove translated, then turned her attention to Alexandra. "It said, like you say it. You fix."

"It is really going to hurt."

"You fix. No hurt. He no move. Do it."

"Beth, get on this side. Pris, you on the other. Hold his upper thigh while I push the bones together." Alexandra said, then took hold of the ankle with both hands, pulling the stricken leg straight, then immediately pushing the bones toward each other until they slid together. She felt the bone with her fingers. It seemed united. The stricken warrior didn't move. He couldn't.

He must have passed out. Maybe he had no choice. Maybe he couldn't move if he wanted to. He didn't cry out. That's amazing. She stopped herself. *Are you kidding me? He's a murdering savage. He should suffer, the bastard!*

"Good. That's good." Alexandra looked up. "Now, we're going to pick his leg up about an inch. Keeping it straight, we'll slide one of those sticks under it. I'll check again to see if the bone is together. Understand? We must lift at the same time keeping it straight. I'll lift the foot, holding the lower leg. Pris, you lift the thigh. Beth, you slide the stick under his leg once we have it raised. We'll do this slowly. Keep it together. Just an inch. We'll use four splints: one on each side, one behind, one on top. Okay? Do you understand? Any questions?"

Both girls nodded, then lifted when Alexandra gave the signal.

The man did not move, forced to remain perfectly still. Splints were placed on each side, with the one on top directly opposite the one on the bottom. Leather strips were tied around each staff to keep them from moving. Ten times this was done: each strip tight but not enough to restrict the flow of blood, tight enough to keep it from moving.

Finished, Alexandra rose to her feet. "All right, Small Dove.

This is important. He can't use that leg. He cannot walk on it. He cannot put any weight on it. He cannot do anything until the bone knits. Nothing at all for six months. Six months. If he does, the bone will not grow together. It's just the way it is. Six months. The moon six times. If he stays off it and if it is together, he'll be able to walk again. That's it. You better tell him. Six months. Hear me? Six months. Not a day less. Leave the splints on his leg. Do not remove them. If you do what I'm telling you it will work; if not, he will not walk again. Not on that leg. Not ever. Understand?"

Small Dove nodded and rose from her uncle's chest. The three men released his arms and shoulders, standing erect. She spoke to the stricken man. The travois was brought up and the warrior was lifted onto the buffalo skin by many hands, laying him between the two poles. He didn't look comfortable, his face pallid.

Good, Alexandra thought. *I'm sorry, but I hope it hurts really really bad.*

"Come on, Lexie," Bethany said, "remember? We're in a hurry. It's noon."

Alexandra and Priscilla followed her. *More importantly,* Alexandra thought, *we have the third horse . . . maybe a fourth.*

"I don't know how you did that," Priscilla said to her.

"How did you?" Bethany enjoined. "Especially after what he did to mother."

"I don't know." She stopped, looking at her companions. "I wouldn't have, except for Small Dove. I can tell you that. I don't know if it will work. He might be a cripple forever."

"Good," Bethany said. "Hope he never walks again."

"Me, too," Priscilla said.

The smell of death was everywhere. Working diligently they loaded the three horses pulling travoises with fresh meat. The horses were skittish, bothered by the smell.

Theirs was a simple plan: use the horses, take the meat back to the creek, unload it for drying on the racks, use the same three horses to escape, get another if they could, load all four with the needed supplies, then amid all of the fervor and the hubbub surrounding a great hunt, disappear. They'd leave the village one after another, ostensibly to get another load of buffalo meat, and disappear never to return. With everyone busy it would be hours before anyone knew they were gone. They'd head south keeping to the timber where they could, where it was available, to cover their escape. They planned on using the contours of the land to stay hidden, the streams to wash out their tracks. No fires, no smoke. Travel at night, if possible; move quickly to cover distance, a lot of it.

Bethany started for the creek first, leading her horse pulling its loaded travois. Minutes later she was followed by Priscilla. Lastly, a few minutes later, Alexandra followed. Not wanting to arouse any suspicions, they decided not to return to the creek together, although they could have. Alexandra squinted at the overhead October sun. It was a little after noon. It was time. It was now. She glanced around and took her first step. This was it. Relief seemed to lift a weight from her shoulders.

Finally, she thought.

Alexandra made the ridge and came across Priscilla sitting on the ground, bent over herself. She was holding the reins to her horse, crying, sobbing hysterically. Alexandra hurried to her.

"What's wrong?" Alexandra asked, kneeling beside her, dropping the rein to her horse.

"I've done it. I've really done it."

"Done what?"

"My ankle. I've broken it."

"Your ankle?" Alexandra breathed out the unspoken question, disliking it.

Can this be happening?

"Broken?" Alexandra looked at the offending ankle hidden beneath Priscilla's leggings. "Let me see, Pris."

Priscilla leaned back, bracing herself with her arms, letting Alexandra work the legging up her calf, rrevealing her moccasin, her old sock, and her ankle red and puffy.

"It's swollen. You sure have a big knot. Can you move it? Will it accept your weight?"

"I don't know. It hurts really bad. I mean it hurts, Lexie. It's broken. I know it. It hurts so badly."

"How did this happen? What did you do?"

"I stepped wrong on that rock." Priscilla pointed. "That one. I stepped on it and it moved. I tried to catch myself. I fell on it trying to keep from hurting myself. And then the stupid horse stepped on me. I can't stand it. Can anything else possibly go wrong? Anything? I can't move, Lexie. I can't. It hurts. Look what I've done," Priscilla looked up at Alexandra, "to us." Tears were leaking from her eyes.

"Lexie, listen. You and Beth, you're going to have to go without me. That's all there is to it. You can't wait. Not anymore. I mean it. This is it. You've got to go. This may be your last chance. Take this horse."

"As if I'm going to do that."

"What do you mean? You have to. You have no choice."

"It's okay, Pris. We'll see how it is in the morning. It could be better by then. You never know. Your ankle's probably not . . ."

Priscilla interrupted her. "No, Lexie. Listen to me. You never listen to me. You have to go now. You can't wait. If it's broken, it'll be months before I can use it properly. If not, it will still be weeks before I can use it. You have to go now."

"Pris, if you can't stand, if you can't walk, if you can't ride, we're not leaving you. We'll see how it is tomorrow."

"It's not going to be any better tomorrow, Lexie. It's broken, I tell you. My God, it hurts awfully bad."

"I believe you. Tell me, is the pain sharp or dull, aching? What's it like?"

"It's dull right now but I'm not moving it." Priscilla started crying. "I'm so sorry, Lexie," she sobbed. "I'm so sorry. You've got to leave without me. Please go." Tears ran down her cheeks.

"Don't be ridiculous. We're not going without you. Period. Besides, it's probably just a sprain. A bad one. It's swollen. It's hard to tell. Maybe we'll be lucky. Tomorrow we'll know."

"Lucky? Lucky? Lexie, listen to me, you can't wait. Do you hear me? You can't."

"Pris, not without you. Hear me? Not without you. We'll wait. We'll see if you can put weight on it. I'll fix you a crutch. We'll leave just like we planned. Just not today. This little thing isn't going to stop us. Postpone maybe, but not stop."

"This little thing? Really? Look at my ankle. Are you blind?" Priscilla glanced at Alexandra, grabbing her hand. "Stop it, Lexie. Stop it. Listen to me. Please. You have no choice. Understand. You and Beth have to go now."

"Pris, this time you listen to me. Not without you. Do you understand me? What I am going to do is look at the ankle, then get you back to the lodge. Somehow. As soon as I get you situated, I'm

240

going to make you a crutch. Okay?" Alexandra paused, looking at Priscilla. She said, "Besides, you don't have to be able to walk. Hear me? You can still ride. I'll put you on a horse myself. All you have to do is sit. We're not leaving you. And that's that. It'll just take more time. A few more hours. Maybe tomorrow. We'll work on leaving tomorrow."

"We haven't any time, Lexie." Tears were everywhere on Priscilla's face. "I feel so cold," she said, her voice a whisper. "So useless. What are we going to do ?"

"Whatever we have to," Alexandra said.

A horseman suddenly blocked out the sun. The two girls looked up, startled. Walking Eagle threw his leg over his mount and slid to the ground. Handing the single rein and the Hawkens rifle to Alexandra, he knelt beside Priscilla.

What's he doing?

He examined her ankle, gently touching it. Priscilla tried to move; he looked at her, shook his head, then turned his attention to Alexandra. He said something and smiled. Both girls stared at him, not knowing what he said.

Effortlessly, he scooped Priscilla up, holding her in his arms as if she were a small child. Steadying herself, she grabbed hold of him, her arms around his neck, her face grimacing as if she expected pain, surprised when it didn't come. He said something to Alexandra and when she didn't move, stepped around her to his horse and set Priscilla on the horse's back as if she were but a single feather loosened from a goose down pillow.

Alexandra grabbed Priscilla's good leg, her hand on her thigh supporting her. "Are you okay?"

"I think so. He's, he's really strong."

"He is that," she said. "Your ankle?"

"If I don't move it, it doesn't hurt." Tears were running down her cheeks again.

Alexandra nodded her head, "Yes, Sweet Lady, I can see it isn't bothering you at all."

"It's not."

"I know. I can tell."

Walking Eagle spoke. Both girls turned and looked at him.

He took the rein and rifle from Alexandra, pointed at the lodges, then started walking toward them, leading his hunting pony with Priscilla aboard holding onto its mane. Alexandra followed, lagging behind leading the two horses pulling the meat laden travois.

Walking Eagle was getting farther ahead. Priscilla looked back at Alexandra leading the horses. She shrugged her shoulders. Alexandra didn't try to keep up. She watched Priscilla moving slowly with the plodding of the horse.

Oh boy, Alexandra thought. *Oh boy. What now? We're really in trouble. As if we weren't already.*

It was quiet. Really quiet. So quiet Alexandra could hear her heart beating in her chest. It was disconcerting. Thump. Thump. Thump. Thump. Awakened, she lay awake, listening. Thump. Thump. Something was so wrong. Something oppressive. From across the lodge floor, she could hear Morning Flower turning in her sleep, her hands no doubt clutching the Funson doll.

Alexandra touched Priscilla's hand. Priscilla was awake, her wounded ankle resting out from under the blanket on a stack of skins. The cool air felt good on her skin.

"What?" she whispered.

"I don't know. Something's wrong. I can feel it. It's so quiet."

Pulling the buffalo robe away from her body, Alexandra crawled on her hands and knees to the other side of the fire circle, undid the ties that held the flap in place, and peered outside. Her eyes were met with a curtain of gray and white, cold, swirling flakes falling out of a morning sky. Everywhere: snow. Five, six inches. More coming down.

"Oh, no," she said to herself and started to cry, covering her mouth to keep her sob from being heard. "Oh, no." She sat back and retied the opening shut.

A disconsolate Alexandra crawled back past the cold fire circle and buried herself under the heavy buffalo robe. Soon she'd have to get up and start a fire. But not yet. What good would it do?

"What's wrong?" Priscilla whispered. "What's wrong? Are you all right?"

"Nothing," Alexandra sobbed.

"Nothing? What do you mean nothing?"

"It snowed, Pris. It's snowing. There's a lot of it. It's everywhere. It's everywhere, Pris." A sob caught in her throat.

In the dark confines of the lodge, the smoke hole closed,

242

Priscilla was quiet a moment, holding her tongue. Finally she whispered aloud, "Ahh shit?"

"Yes, truly."

CHAPTER 37
Alexandra is 123 miles west by northwest of Zeke
on Greasy Grass Creek

October 31, 1854
Belle Fourche River-Wells Brothers Trading Post
Central Nebraska Territory

One-horse towns aren't much to write home to mother about: a half dozen saloons and a general store, sometimes a barber shop that serves as a dentist's office. (It's a scary proposition: a barber holding a pair of rusty pliers staring into a man's mouth.) But small towns are everywhere: built on river crossings, trail heads, end of the line railroads, and for no reason at all other than folks needed a town, a place to gather.

Often they arise when some enterprising soul decides to build a one room log cabin and trades for skins and furs out the front door, or where some creative lad pours water into a thirty-five gallon wooden barrel full of dried corn seed. Several weeks later, in the heat of the afternoon, he drains the golden liquid off the bottom, perhaps applying some heat, then storing the percolated yeast infected water in earthen jars behind the cook stove. If he's any good, folks stop at his establishment, play a few hands of five card draw, and wash the trail dust away, smacking their lips, wondering why they voluntarily submit themselves to such incredible hardship.

Such was Wells Brothers on the upper head waters of the Belle Fourche River before it was a river, when it was a mere stream fed by melting snow and an occasional thunderstorm. It sat in the Bear Lodge Mountains in Nebraska Territory before Wyoming, before Montana, before roads. In 1854 Nebraska Territory's western boundary was the Continental Divide sitting in the tops of the Rocky Mountains while its eastern boundary was the Missouri River. North, it reached to the Canadian border, and south, to Kansas. Wells Brothers, and, eventually, just Brothers, consisted of a half dozen saloons and a general store sitting off the creek, sheltered by a red rock ridge. Its main and only street followed a game trail bending along the creek until it disappeared. On a weekday, or any day for that matter, it held a population of eighteen souls, more or less--sometimes less, hardly ever more.

Needing to get some wheat flour, some corn meal, more trinkets to trade, and to unload furs collected, Emile Villon thought they ought to stop their immediate search for the lost girls and restock. Emile considered that the money acquired from the sale of collected furs would be kept by him and only partially accounted for. Besides, he'd need money to buy supplies as soon as he killed the kid. In the meantime, he thought Zeke would give it to him without even thinking about it: stupid is as stupid does.

For Emile Villon, it was the business; for Zeke, the search.

When Villon suggested stopping at Brothers, Zeke merely nodded, remembering that the Teton Lakota and especially the Oglala and the Hunkpapa wintered on the Belle Fourche River. So it was possible that someone saw the girls. After all, their captors were Oglala. Chances were good that maybe one or more of the traders working out of Brothers would have heard of them and maybe had even seen them. He was hopeful.

Emile Villon never gave that subject a thought for he'd already declared the three girls dead and wasn't looking for them. If they weren't dead, who would want them? He didn't, so no one would.

In front of the trading post, Zeke stood among the stacks of hides and watched the trader, a fellow named Charles Harpster, examine Villon's buffalo hides one by one. Emile was talking, shifting his weight from one foot to the other, watching the trader's dog slink among the stacks. Harpster commented on the weather, mules, horses, the amount of rain water that hadn't fallen, the late fall and whether he expected a hard winter. In his conversation he noted recent thunderstorms, hail that beat the yellow leaves out of the cottonwood trees, the Lakota that had been seen around the trading post.

Eventually Harpster finished his inspection, studied Emile, and suggested a price for the hides. Emile suggested another price more favorable to him. Neither man paid Zeke any mind. The dog had disappeared behind the outhouse. He was barking at something; Zeke didn't know what. He wondered where O'Reilly was hiding. He hadn't seen him.

Emile Villon and Harpster walked toward the trading post talking about whether two dollars a buffalo hide was a reasonable price and considering whether the hide was cured, tanned, green or dried. They disappeared inside. Zeke looked east toward the red, juniper-covered hills, the creek bottom that followed the edge of the hills running behind the trading post. He took a breath and thought about the money that Emile and the trader were dickering over. Some of it was his. He patted the walnut grip to the Navy Colt he'd stuck behind his belt buckle. The trader's dog came running past him, barking, disappearing on the other side of the trading post. Zeke removed the leather loop from the hammer, then loosened the pistol in the holster. He glanced at the doorway, listening to the dog barking, then started toward the open door.

Inside, the trader was standing behind a cluttered counter bargaining with Emile Villon. Emile glanced at Zeke, then back at Harpster. "All right," he said, "I agree. Pay me in gold coin, two dollars and ten cents a hide."

The trader brought out a metal box, opened the lid and began to count out gold coins. It totaled one hundred fifty-five dollars. Emile greedily began to gather the gold coins.

"Leave the money on the counter, Emile," Zeke said.

"What?"

"Leave the money on the counter."

"What for?"

"Count out sixty-seven dollars, the amount I advanced in Laramie. Count it and push it aside."

EmileVillon turned angrily, whipping his head about, finding Zeke standing in the shadows. Immediately wary, he took some comfort in seeing that Zeke had not drawn his Navy Colt, that he held nothing in his hands. Still . . . . this was a new, unexpected development. The alarm in his head was going off, ringing like crazy. Care was warranted.

This damn kid. He is messin' everythin' up.

Turning to the stack of gold coins, Emile stared at the collection, then grudgingly counted out the sixty-seven dollars, pushing it to the side. He glanced at Zeke. "Now what?" he asked, feeling the gold slipping through his fingers.

"Give the trader the list."

Emile hesitated, then reached into his pocket and pulled a list from his pocket, and handed it to the trader.

"I'd say ya ain't trusting me."

"There ain't no use in trusting you at all. Count out fifty to pay for the things on the list. Leave it on the counter."

"Look, there's no need ta . . . "

"There's every need, Emile."

Emile Villon began counting out fifty dollars, grumbling to himself. The trader was staring at Zeke, his expression full of wonderment for the kid was telling the older man what to do . . . and the older man was doing it. Emile finished, then glanced at Zeke. He was about to say something but Zeke interrupted him.

"Divide the remainder in half. Two equal piles. Take your half. Leave mine on the counter."

Looking at the trader, Zeke asked, "Can you fill the list?"

The trader picked up the list, ran down it, then nodded.

"Please do so. There's fifty to pay for it. You need more, tell me."

Zeke looked back at Emile Villon. "All right," he said, "you got that divided equally, yours and mine?"

Emile Villon nodded.

"Which is your stack of money? The one on your left?"

"Yes."

"Good. You take the pile of coins on your right. I'll take your stack."

"What? What ar' ya sayin'?"

"I ain't sayin' nothin'."

Emile Villon hesitated, staring at Zeke.

"The two piles--they're equal, ain't they?" Zeke asked.

Emile Villon was silent, his face clouded with anger but he didn't move. A look of being caught flashed in his eyes. In that instant he simply did not know what to do. His shoulders were rigid as he turned back to the stack of gold coins. He breathed out holding himself steady as if he were negotiating a patch of quicksand. Stoically, he began picking up the gold coins in the pile on his right, placing each coin in the leather sack he carried in the loop around his neck.

"All right, then," Zeke said, "I'll take that equal pile on your left. Equal is equal, ain't it? Ain't no difference in equal is there?"

Emile Villon was conscious of Zeke's hand resting on his pistol butt, his index finger tapping the walnut grip. He nodded as if in agreement, forcing himself to breathe in and out, knowing something had changed and not knowing what, not clearly. He definitely did not like it. He finished putting his coins in the pouch, then turned, glancing at the saloon side of the trading post, pausing. He said, "I'm fixin' ta have myself a drink, a large one. That's where I'll be," he announced and started walking toward the south portion of the trading post.

Zeke glanced at the trader. "How long to fill the order?" he asked.

"An hour."

"Good, I'll be back to settle up."

"All right," the trader said.

"I asked if that fifty will cover it."

Harpster studied the list, then nodded. "More than enough."

"I'll be needin' some paper cartridges and some lead balls for a Navy Colt. Got some?"

"I do."

"Ten, eleven boxes. 36 caliber?"

The trader nodded.

"Good."

"One other thing. Injuns? They been around? I'm lookin' for some white women. Captives. Three of 'em. In their late teens, early twenties."

The trader nodded. "I've seen some white women. Not recently. Heard of some," he paused. "Come ta think of it, I have," he said

"You have what?"

"Seen a white woman. One. Not long ago."

Zeke was staring at him. He'd stopped breathing.

"Six weeks back. Maybe seven. Saw a white woman. Waitin' outside fer awhile. Down by the creek. Never came inside. Didn't see her up close. She never said nothin' ta me."

"What was she wearin'?"

"Doe skin dress. Leggings. Moccasins. Normal stuff they all wear. Had light brown hair. Almost blond. Long. Like I said, she never got close. Stayin' down near the creek until that bunch left."

"Was there others?"

"Not that I saw. Wasn't my business."

Zeke nodded, thinking. "Which way did they go?"

"North. I'd say. But they could've gone in any direction once they left."

"Do you know which band?"

"They was Oglala. That ain't sayin' nothin'. There's a lot of Oglala, Hunkpapa, Brule. Odd, you know. Them Injun women don't wear nothin' in their hair. Just men.'"

"This white woman? The one you saw? Her hair long? Have anythin' in it?"

"No, nothin' I could see. Long hair, braided. She was standin' afar off. Didn't get a good look at her." Harpster stared at Zeke. "Why ya askin'?"

"I'm lookin' for her."

"How long?"

"Two months. Injuns took her and two others up on the Sweetwater."

Harper shook his head. "Two months? Ain't my business but it ain't gonna do no good you keep lookin'. Ain't gonna find her. I've seen 'em before. Seen 'em right where you're standin'. They turn into Injuns. They get it in their heads there's no goin' back. Just livin' 'til they die. Poor bastards. That's what I'd say."

Zeke nodded. "That's what I'm told."

"You goin' ahead anyways?"

Zeke nodded again.

"I'd look north if I was you. Been awhile. When I saw 'em the whole band was a movin'. Followin' the buff. They was movin' north."

"Do you know where? Which direction, exactly?"

Harpster shook his head. "Like I say, north. Followin' the buff. Them buff they go pretty much anywheres. I don't know where they end up."

"Anythin' else you can tell me?"

"No. Like I say she was down there on the creek standin' alone. Looked ta be holdin' the reins of their hosses, waitin'." The trader hesitated. "Look," he said. "It was probably her buck up here buyin' what he needed, leavin' her ta hold their hosses. You're ridin' down river. Ain't no good you chasin' after what ain't no longer there. There just ain't."

Zeke nodded. "Thanks, Mister. Thanks for the conversation. I'll be back to get those supplies in a hour or so."

Zeke turned and walked to the open door. He stopped. "One other thing," he said. "They would be ridin' with a fellow name of Walking Eagle. He took 'em this last August. They are with him."

"Walking Eagle? That's another thing altogether. Walking Eagle, last I heard, was over on Goose Creek. Don't see him around here much."

"Goose Creek? You sure? Not here?"

"Goose Creek. He likes ta summer on the Horn. Come fall he comes down on Goose Creek. Just before winter he goes a little north for buffalo. Fills up his parfleches. Sometimes he winters up there on the Judith River, sometimes the Missouri Breaks. Was a time he'd come over here, winter on the Belle Fourche. I ain't seen his people lately. Been years."

"Right now, you figure he's on Goose Creek?"

"Can't say exactly. But if you're lookin' for Walking Eagle that's where ta start. Goose Creek. Listen, boy, it'll take a few minutes me gettin' these things together."

"Appreciate it."

"You're welcome," the trader said starting to turn away.

"Take your time, friend," Zeke said. "I'm aimin' to see what's goin' on in your drinkin' establishment. Get myself around some fresh steak, some beans, if you got 'em. Smells like some fresh baked bread, maybe some corn bread, butter. Maybe I'll have some of that before I hit the saddle."

"Help yourself," the trader said. "Gots plenty."

CHAPTER 38
Alexandra is 123 miles west by northwest from Zeke on the Greasy Grass

October 31, 1854
Wells Trading Post, Belle Fourche River
Central Nebraska Territory

Zeke left the trader, walking toward the kitchen and the makeshift bar, picking his way through the tables and chairs. Suddenly he found himself sprawled on the floor, feeling the grit on the palms of his hands, grit carried inside on the soles of a hundred hob nailed boots. He turned, looking up at the face of the fellow who had tripped him, catching the smile, the "got you but damn good" grin. Someone at another table laughed. Zeke came to his feet, brushing the grit off his hips, shirt, and pants. He looked at the man over whose boot he'd tripped, holding his eyes, anger coming to a slow boil inside.

"Now that was all sorts of rude," Zeke said slowly, rubbing his hands together. "Floppin' those big, flat duck feet out there where some unsuspectin' soul can trip all over 'em. Your mother musta been some quacker."

Zeke didn't know why he added that remark about the man's mother being a duck. He'd never met her, never said "hello, how you been?" Nothing like that. Those words just came tumbling out before he could stop them. Truth was he wanted to grab the fellow and slap him silly.

Someone laughed. Someone said, "A duck, Rudy, you're a flat foot duck. And so is your ma." A loud guffaw filled the room, hung there with the cigar and cigarette smoke, falling flat on the sawdust-covered floor. Rudy's face turned red.

Tripping the "boy" may have been an accident. Maybe not. Being laughed at wasn't what he'd bargained for, certainly not from a "yonker" that hadn't ever taken a straight razor to his face. Rudy rose to his feet, pushing the table away, leaning on it as he did. He turned toward Zeke, furious. The table tilted; beverages slid, fell to the floor. Someone swore.

What Rudy had in mind was anyone's guess but Zeke had a fairly good idea it wasn't shaking hands. Nor did he think the man

251

intended to join him in drinking that awful, just-run-off-your-boot-beer that this two-bits for a bowl of beans outfit served on festive and non-festive occasions.

Zeke did what his uncle taught him to do, which was the only thing he could do. He closed the distance fast, reaching Rudy as he pulled, his Navy pistol clearing his side holster. The double click of the hammer echoed in the room. Men dived for cover.

Zeke's left hand grabbed the pistol, pushing it down and away, pointing it to Rudy's left, across his body where it discharged into the floor. Zeke, turning his body into Rudy, pulling himself around, slugged him in the nose, felt it crunch against the knuckles of his right fist. He slugged him again, blood splattering and spraying. In that instant of time, Rudy's body turned, his eyes watered and Zeke twisted the pistol against Rudy's hand; the bones popped, broke. Zeke jerked the weapon from Rudy and brought the butt down on Rudy's head with a thump that fell flat in the room, sounding like knuckles testing a ripe watermelon. Rudy's eyes rolled back into his head and he crumpled onto the floor with Zeke standing over his inert body.

Whoa, he thought, *I sure as hell didn't mean for this to happen. I'll be damned.*

The silence was broken by someone muttering, "Good God in heaven. Ya done kilt him." That epithet was followed by a cacophony of sound as the room picked itself up. Tables and chairs were righted; cards, chips and Bull Durham sacks were picked up from the floor.

"Naw, he ain't dead," someone said.

Another crowed, "Least I didn't spill nothin'".

Another said, "Geez, Rudy, what'd you all have in mind? You fool. Actin' like that."

Zeke's eyes came to rest on a man sitting in a chair beside an upturned table. It was the table that Rudy had pushed away as he came to his feet. An empty beer mug, its handle broken, rolled on the floor in front of him and came to a stop.

"What'air ya gonna do with Rudy's pistol? Ya aimin' ta steal it right here in front of God and everybody?"

Zeke eyes rested on the speaker, an older man dressed in a buckskin shirt and ragged denim pants. He wore high-topped moccasins with intricate bead work across the top of the moccasin and up the sides. Silver buttons and latigo strips of leather bound the tops of the moccasins about his calves.

"I ain't no thief, mister," Zeke replied. "But I ain't fixin' on givin' it back! That fellow comes to his senses, he just might open her up: shoot me full of holes. I don't think much of that idea."

"Ain't likely, ya bustin' his gun hand. Rudy--he might shoot ya with his off hand but it'd be plum accident."

At least he ain't dead, Zeke thought.

"Ya might consider leavin' it with the barkeep."

I might.

"What about him? This fellow layin' on the floor?"

"Leave him be. Let sleepin' dogs sleep. He ain't botherin' nobody lyin' there."

Zeke smiled and said, "Well, I'm fixin' to order me a steak and some beans. Maybe somethin' to wash it down." Zeke turned, looking for Emile, finding him leaning against the bar staring at him. Zeke motioned for him to come to the table.

After he arrived, Zeke asked, "You et, Emile?"

"No, I ain't," Emile said. "Ain't had a chance."

"I suggest we get ourselves around some steak and such. I want to leave soon as the trader has the list you gave him. He told me Walking Eagle is sittin' on Goose Creek or he's headin' north. I want to be on Goose Creek in the next couple of days. To see what I can see, maybe get some information on where this Walking Eagle's headin'. I can't be lollygaggin'. Winter's comin' and we ain't got much time to figure it."

Emile nodded but the expression on his face belied being pleased. On the floor, the fellow with the duck feet groaned but didn't move. Zeke called the bartender over and ordered steak and the fixings.

"You want some?" he asked Emile. "How 'bout you?" he asked the older man.

Emile nodded and replied, "I reckon I could stand some vittles."

"Me, too," the old fellow replied. "If ya buyin' I'm eatin'."

Rudy was snoring. All three glanced down at him.

"Well," Zeke said, "let's get the cook fryin' some steak, scramblin' some eggs, and boilin' some black coffee."

One hour later, Zeke left for Goose Creek, backtracking across the grassy hills of Central Nebraska Territory with Emile Villon leading the way. It took three days to get to the Crazy Woman, riding west from the Belle Fourche River.

CHAPTER 39
Zeke is 123 miles east by southeast of Alexandra on the Belle Fourche River

November 1, 1854
Greasy Grass Creek
Central Nebraska Territory

The first snow didn't last.

During the night the gray clouds that had brought the snow disappeared over the now white hills on the east. Stars decorated the night sky, dimmed by a bright moon. Orion hung low on the western horizon, faint, but still visible. It was clear, cold, silent. Lying warm beneath the heavy buffalo robes, listening to the quiet, Alexandra could hear her heart beat, hear the deep sleep breathing of Priscilla who left her injured foot outside of the heavy robes, Bethany next to her.

Trails of smoke drifted steadily from the smoke holes of two dozen lodges, rising high in the late fall sky. Later, just before sunrise, a warm breeze rose, rattling what remained of yellow cottonwood leaves that hung resolutely on stark branches. It blew in from the south, melting the snow into the brown grass, leaving the yellow stems waving stiffly in the breeze, warming faces, feet and hearts.

The drying racks were weighed down with buffalo meat cut into narrow strips, draped in rows and rows. The cooking fires were burning; bellies were gorged with fresh tongue and rump roast. Of the buffalo, every piece, every sinew was cut, separated, and used. Thankfully, no flies buzzed the racks, laying their eggs in the drying meat. The first snow killed them. Magpie and crow hung around squawking, protesting, trying to steal small offerings should the concentration of the young girls guarding the racks momentarily lapse.

The opportunity to quietly disappear in the midmorning confusion fled with the damp, melting snow and the drying meat. In camp a spontaneous celebration erupted, multiplying the crowd, sending the dogs into a tizzy, the children running playing the stick game. The once available horses were gone, released to graze upon the ridges west and east of the creek. The small window of opportunity to escape had evaporated in the thin air of Central Nebraska Territory.

Once available weapons were tucked away in their hiding places. Only fresh buffalo meat remained in abundance. Of that there was plenty.

The sounds of song and dance continued into the early evening, all awash in the glow of a successful hunt and parfleches that were bulging with winter storage. With the cacophony of sound, motion and triumph, there was the sore, extended pain and healing of the broken leg and the severe ankle sprain. Priscilla stayed inside massaging her malady. The opportunity died.

Most of Walking Eagle's band of Oglala stayed on Greasy Grass Creek, a creek known to white men as the Little Big Horn, moving their lodges to take advantage of windbreaks, availability of wood, of winter game. Others spread like spooked prairie chickens, traveling to winter on a dozen different creeks in a dozen different directions, hopefully out of the wind, away from the soon to be drifting snow. They looked for a place with plenty of firewood, plenty of deer and antelope to hunt, maybe even an old bull buffalo who had separated from the massive herds, driven away from the cows by younger, stouter bulls. It had always been so.

CHAPTER 40
Zeke is 46 miles south of Alexandra on Goose Creek

November 3 , 1854
Greasy Grass Creek
Central Nebraska Territory

Except for the arrival and changing of seasons announced at the whim of capricious winds and the moving, shifting clouds, there was no accurate reckoning of time. The girls were caught in the vortex of captivity. Days blended into days. None of the days were distinguishable from any other. Generally speaking, one day followed another with the same people engaged in the same activities, in the same place, with the same problems to resolve. Each day demanded more wood to burn, more food to prepare, a doe to butcher, and cleaning, always cleaning to be done.

In time calculated and noted by white men who walked the dusty streets of New York City or Albany, wearing importance like it was a sharp wool coat, keeping pocket watches in their vests that chimed on the hour, a week had passed. For the girls, the calculation of the days of a week was suspect. It could have been six days, seven days, eight days, or even ten. The gentle grind of each day melted into the next.

There was a rhythm and that rhythm pushed the edges of time and had nothing to do with watches or calendars. There was no accurate method available for keeping track: no writing instruments, no paper. And no real need to do so. Each day was lost in the next day. The minutes slipped by and time passed like a ghost in the evening shadows. It didn't matter and yet it did. A bruised, swollen ankle and the need for horses kept the girls grounded and diminished their flight risk substantially. Ankles take time to heal; healing has its own biological clock, one that ignores calendars and the steady changing of seasons. Whatever time it needed, it needed; it demanded. It received what it demanded.

Alexandra carved a notch in the shaft of a broken spear. She carved the notch every morning except on days when she didn't carve the notch until after the sun was halfway up the sky. She'd find herself sitting by the fire circle; wood had been gathered, food cooked, and

257

her knife and broken shaft were in hand. She'd struggle to remember if she'd already carved the notch that day, perhaps earlier, or if she hadn't. As a result, she sometimes carved twice. Sometimes not at all. With or without carving, the day passed, stretching into the next and the one after that. All of this weighed heavily on the shoulders of these girls . . . caught in an ancient society, time out of mind.

Often Small Dove came to visit the girls with Walking Eagle. They developed a commuication ritual: first Small Dove spoke with Walking Eagle, then, after she received instructions from him, she translated what he said into a broken English. This time she said, "He want you and you," pointing at Priscilla and Bethany. "Pack parfleches. He want this one." She pointed at Alexandra.

Bethany grabbed Alexandra's arm, hesitating, suddenly on guard.

"What does he want me to do?" Alexandra asked.

"He no say. He want you. He show you. He talk."

Small Dove spoke again with Walking Eagle and then turned to Alexandra. "He want now."

"All right," Alexandra said. "Are you coming with me? I will need to know what it is that he wants. I don't understand your language, not yet."

Again Small Dove spoke with Walking Eagle, then explained his words to Alexandra. "No," she said. "I no go. He show you. He say. He want that."

"He wants me to go with him? But not you? You're not to come with us?"

"Yes."

"Now?"

"Yes."

Alexandra wiped her skinning knife, tucked it into her waistbelt and glanced at Walking Eagle.

"Lexie?" Bethany said, apprehension rising in her voice. "I don't know. . . What do you think he wants? Aren't you worried? I am."

Alexandra glanced at her sister. "I don't know," she said quietly. "Stay here. I'll be all right. Don't follow me. I think he wants you to pack and store the dried buffalo meat. Stay close though. Okay?"

"Okay," Bethany said.

Walking Eagle turned and walked toward the lodge. Alexandra hesitated, glanced at her sister, then followed. Small Dove remained behind with Priscilla and Bethany, talking in her herky-jerky fashion about storing meat in parfleches, making pemmican, and what to do with chokecherries amd buffalo berries in their season. Bethany asked questions.

Alexandra followed Walking Eagle, a little apprehensive, wondering where they were going and what he wanted. She felt relatively safe; people were all around her. The camp was alive with activity. Even so, she prepared herself to stop if she felt any danger. Her safety was relative and she knew it. Alexandra did not want to leave Bethany and Priscilla's sight.

She noted that he was tall--maybe five foot nine or ten--walking with a certain grace she hadn't noticed. She noted the way the muscles of his back rippled as he moved. These thoughts ran through her mind tinged with fear. Mostly she remembered what he was capable of, having seen with her own eyes the death of her friends and acquaintances. To her surprise they didn't go far, walking only to the entrance of the lodge. Walking Eagle stopped and motioned her inside.

What's he want?

She hesitated, glanced back at her sister. They were gathered around Small Dove. She caught Bethany looking at her, smiled as if to say everything is okay, then stooped to go inside. Walking Eagle followed after her, shutting the covering of the lodge entrance behind them, tying it closed. Alexandra, stood in the middle of the lodge floor by the side of the fire stones, waiting. Her nose tickled from the acidic smell of dead ashes that had accumulated. She turned toward him, watching as he moved around her in the shadows cast by the sunlight shining through the open smoke hole above her head. She rubbed her nose, wanting to sneeze, stifling the urge.

The man sat down on a layer of buffalo rugs and looked up at her, patting the skins beside him. She did not move, staring at him. He patted the buffalo robe again.

He wants me to sit down? she thought.

From outside she could hear her sister laugh and dogs barking.

Why am I so afraid of you? Why not? After all you've done? And keeping us here against our will. All right. All right I'll sit down.

She sat cross-legged, arranging her dress about her legs and knees and looked at him, waiting.

259

What now? More language lessons, perhaps. We've never done this before. Maybe he wants to see what I've learned. Sort of a test.

But why? I don't think so. I've done this every day with Small Dove. No. This must be something different.

He tugged twice at the hem of her dress, holding the doe skin between his finger and thumb, then releasing it. Alexandra repeated the word for dress aloud. She gave him the word for buffalo robe, then elk robe, and blanket and patted it with her fingers. He nodded, said something to her in Oglala, pulling at the bottom edge of her dress again. She gave him the word for dress, repeating herself, beginning to be suspicious.

Walking Eagle nodded and pulled at her dress, exposing a small part of her ankle. Alexandra didn't move. She stared at him. Again he pulled the hem of her dress.

Oh, no, she thought, not taking her eyes from his.

He nodded, waiting.

"I'll bet you're not asking me if I remember the word for foot?" she said in English, knowing he didn't understand a word she spoke.

In response he nodded.

Walking Eagle tugged at the bottom edge of her dress again, exposing more skin on her ankle. She looked at him and thought "ahh shit." He nodded. Alexandra's mind froze. Above her head, sunlight filtered though the smoke hole; the buffalo skins flapped against the lodge poles. She could hear the voices of Small Dove and Priscilla. Priscilla had asked what Walking Eagle wanted with Lexie. She said she didn't know. Bethany said, "I'm worried. He's never been alone with her before. Do you think she's all right?"

The small woman said she didn't know. Somewhere a camp dog was barking incessantly. More than likely he'd chased a squirrel up a tree and had it cornered. Someone yelled an unintelligible string of sounds followed by abrupt laughter. Alexandra heard horses running, then quiet. It was as if the world was listening, watching, waiting.

She heard Bethany's voice from a mere thirty feet away. "Shouldn't we get more firewood before all the wood close to us is gone? That way we won't have to carry it so far. How's your ankle, Pris? Can you help gather wood? I don't want you to if it hurts."

"It's a little sore but I can help," Priscilla responded. "You're right. We should. Maybe we should do it right away. I don't know how

260

much walking my ankle will take, though." She paused, looking at the lodge. "I wonder if Lexie is okay. Should we wait for her?"

Walking Eagle once again reached to tug at her dress but Alexandra grabbed his wrist, looking at his impassive face, his dark eyes, his secret thoughts hidden in the shadows of the lodge and another language. The sound of her breathing was lost in the flapping of the skins against the lodge poles; a trail of smoke from a dying fire ascended through the smoke hole. Alexandra nodded understanding, holding herself very still, tears unavoidably leaking from her eyes. She released her hold on his wrist, staring at him, not moving when he tugged on her dress again.

CHAPTER 41
Zeke is 46 miles south of Alexandra on Goose Creek

November 3, 1854
Greasy Grass Creek
Central Nebraska Territory

Bethany and Priscilla found her on the edge of Greasy Grass Creek sitting on a flat stone worn smooth by hundreds of years of rushing snow water. Her arms were wrapped around her legs as she listened to the gurgling stream. Her eyes were puffy, her cheeks red. Upon hearing her companions, she did not say anything and did not turn to the two girls. Instead, she continued staring at the running water like a stricken animal.

They'd been looking for her. When they returned with more firewood she hadn't been where they expected her to be. In the late afternoon, Walking Eagle had brought them a young, fat doe to butcher. After they'd finished skinning the doe, they sliced the muscle into long slender strips, hanging them to dry. So much meat. They looked for Alexandra. Not finding her, they looked for more firewood, going farther than they had thought they would: first up the creek with the other women to where it turned, then downstream a quarter of a mile. All told, it had taken several hours. They had expected to find her as they went about their tasks but didn't. They'd made two trips, stopping to watch the young boys racing their ponies in some sort of game that resembled tag.

"You all right?" Bethany asked her sister. "Where have you been? We've been looking for you."

Alexandra didn't answer.

"You don't look all right," Bethany said. "You've been crying. Why? Did. . . did he hit you?"

"No. I'm all right. A little sore. And tired. I'm really tired. I've just had all I can take. I just want to go home. And I can't. I have no home."

"You're tired?" Bethany repeated. "You're sore. You've had it." She paused. "Aren't we all?" She paused, staring at her sister. "Oh my God!" she said. "He, he . . . he did, didn't he?"

262

Alexandra didn't answer. Bethany's hand went to her mouth. "Oh my God, my God!"

She sat down on the stone beside her sister. "Oh, Lexie. What can we do?" Her arms went around Alexandra's shoulders, hugging her. Alexandra leaned into the embrace without a word: wanting it. Priscilla sat on the other side of her and wordlessly began tossing small flat stones into the rushing waters.

"I guess I'm not all right," Alexandra sobbed. "I didn't know what to do."

"We should kill him," Priscilla said. "I told you. We should kill him in his sleep. He's got to sleep. The bastard."

"And then we'd be killed, or separated, or . . ." Alexandra's voice trailed off. "Without him, we starve to death. Without him, we have no place to stay. It's winter. We'd freeze to death. Without him, we don't live five minutes, that's what. We're dead without him." She wiped her nose on her sleeve and rested her head on her knees.

"We trade our bodies to live," Bethany said. "Maybe that's living," she paused, "maybe it's not."

Priscilla stared at the water and threw another stone that splashed in still water and sent ever widening concentric circles rippling. "Is it really worth it?" she asked. "We should kill him."

Bethany said, "Is it really living, I mean, really?"

"Oh, just listen to yourselves." Alexandra started crying, sobbing, tears running down her ruddy cheeks. She buried her face in her hands.

I expected so much more, so much. Why am I even here? What'd I ever do? I don't deserve this. What did I ever do?

Bethany put her arms around her sister. "Lexie, I'm sorry," she said. "It's just . . . remember that woman? We were in Fort Laramie. Remember how everyone looked at her?" Bethany said. "I don't remember her name. She'd been captured just like us. She lived with them for three or four years. One of them made her his wife. Maybe he forced her; maybe she just gave in.

"She had two children, a boy and a girl. Remember? They didn't say it out loud but some of the women were asking themselves why she didn't kill herself. I heard them say they'd kill themselves rather than let a heathen lay a hand on them. I remember that's what one lady asked her. Nobody would talk to her. Everybody looked at her like she was an animal or something. She told mother that she would have been better off not to have been rescued.

"That's exactly what's happening to us. That's what people are going to say. We won't be able to go anywhere without people saying it. No one will talk to us. That woman couldn't keep her children because they were half-breeds. Can you imagine how they'd be treated? She told mother she'd left them with their father. She never saw them again. Not ever. Poor thing."

Priscilla threw another rock. She said, "I heard she went back to her kids. That's what I heard."

Bethany sighed.

"Well, he's had his way with me," Alexandra said. "And I figure he's going to again and again. He really enjoyed doing what he did. I can't stop it. A baby will follow. I can't stop that either." She paused, staring wistfully down the creek. "If only we'd left a week ago."

"Well, we didn't," Priscilla said. "It's my fault."

"Nobody's fault," Alexandra whispered. "No blame. If it wasn't your ankle, it would have been something else."

Bethany said, "Mother and Father wanting to come out here. That's somebody's fault. They knew better. And they're dead. And we're lost."

"Beth, don't say that."

"It's true."

"I know. I know."

Priscilla interrupted, saying, "We'll all be expecting. That's what happens you know. Sleeping with a man. We're all sleeping in the same tent with the same man. We have nowhere to run. We can't escape. We're trapped."

Bethany grunted in acknowledgment. She stared at her sister. "What happened, Lexie? Did he knock you down?"

"No. No," Alexandra said. "It was while you were packing the parfleches. I was with him. I made a mistake. I was alone. I didn't think he would do anything like that. Not in broad daylight. Not with everybody around. I thought I was safe." Alexandra paused. "I really don't want to talk about it."

"We were packing the . . . ?" Bethany asked incredulously. "You mean we were right there?"

"What was I supposed to do?" Alexandra asked.

Bethany's hand covered her mouth. "Supposed to do?" she

asked. "Are you kidding?"

"Beth," Priscilla said, "Lexie didn't have a choice. What are you going to do when he reaches for you? Say no, thank you very much. I'd rather have a cup of coffee?"

"I think I'll die. That's what. I'll just die."

"No, you won't," Priscilla said. "You can't die. We have to live. All of us have to live. Something will happen. Someone will come for us. We will be rescued or we'll rescue ourselves. We have to believe it."

"Is that living?" Bethany asked. "What if we do have babies?"

Priscilla looked at Bethany. She said, "You mean when, don't you?"

Bethany was shaking her head.

"Listen, listen, you two." Alexandra had turned around. "I'm not killing myself. I want to live."

Priscilla nodded. "We all want to live, Lexie," she said.

"Then let's talk about living. Let's talk about staying alive. I don't want to hear about dying."

"All right, Lexie. All right. I was just saying. So what do we do?" Bethany asked.

"I don't like this conversation," Alexandra answered. "I don't like it at all."

"We stay away from him!" Priscilla exclaimed. "That's what. And we stay together as much as we can. If we are not alone we'll be safer."

"Good idea. Impractical because we're living in the same lodge."

Bethany threw a larger rock into the creek, splashing water, causing the concentric circles to ebb to the sides and downstream. She smiled at Alexandra. "Ok, Lexie, we'll just stay away from him. We'll keep him dizzy looking for us. And we'll escape. Escaping is the most important thing."

"My ankle is better." Priscilla said matter of factly. "There's nothing keeping us from leaving except opportunity."

"Yeah," Alexandra said her voice full of dejection. "Except we have no horses, no guns."

"But I know where they are," Bethany interjected. "Should I get weapons now? It's getting the horses that will take some doing. We can't wait," Bethany said.

"We'll get horses. Somehow. We'll get them," Priscilla replied.

"How? Without someone seeing us? We missed the opportunity with the hunt. All those horses standing around," Alexandra said.

"I said I was sorry."

"It's not your fault, Pris," Bethany said. "Lexie's not blaming you. I'm not blaming you. Just drop it. We have to move on. Look for the next opportunity."

"It's not today," Alexandra said. "I don't see how."

"I know. I know. It's horses. That's the problem. Should we just walk?" Bethany said.

"No. We can't make it afoot," Alexandra replied.

"Securing weapons will be more difficult now than it was a week ago. They've hidden them again. They're not out in the open. At least the snow is gone," Priscilla added.

"Won't be for long," Alexandra answered.

Bethany began again, brightly. "Let's relocate the weapons: what we're going to steal. When the time comes we'll take them."

"I don't think it will work," Alexandra said.

"Why not?" Bethany asked.

"We need them now. As soon as we get horses," Priscilla said, "we can leave."

Bethany nodded. "It'd be better if we steal them when we're ready," she said. "Not before. It has to be at the same time. That's safest. They won't be looking for what's not missing. We need to wait to get a rifle until the last moment. We have our knives. No one says anything about that." Bethany was pleased with herself.

Priscilla pulled her skinning knife and threw it at a log that was lodged partially in the stream. It landed hilt first scarring the water soaked wood.

"We'd better practice. A lot," she said. "A knife isn't as good as a gun but it's something."

"What do you mean? Practice what?"

"I don't know. Throwing it, I guess. We have to do something."

CHAPTER 42
Alexandra is 46 miles north of Zeke on Greasy Grass Creek

November 4, 1854
Goose Creek
Central Nebraska Territory

Leaving Belle Fourche Creek, Zeke had tried to hurry; he wanted to hurry. He had looked for short cuts, not finding them. Instead, impetuous decisions, forced by the need to get to Goose Creek, pushed and shoved him, caused him to backtrack, moving back and forth around mountains, hills, valleys, and canyons, unable to travel in the straight, quick line he desired. In the end, the long way would have been quicker. Sometimes it felt like he'd seen the same creek a dozen times though he hadn't. It just seemed that way.

They reached and crossed the Middle Fork, Red Fork, and North Fork of the Powder River, then the South Fork, Mid Fork and North Fork of the Crazy Woman. Finally, they reached Clear Creek and some streams that Emile didn't know the names of or even if they had names. In the late afternoon of the third day, they made Little Goose Creek and slowly followed it northwest to Goose Creek.

Goose Creek flows north by northwest out of the northern foothills of the Big Horn Mountains. It is joined by the Little Goose and becomes bigger. The waters of the combined streams, in turn, drop into the Tongue River just a few wandering miles from where Goose Creek begins.

Zeke didn't know what he expected to find. Not exactly. He hoped he'd find Alexandra, not knowing what he'd do if he did find her, doubting that the man who'd stolen her would let her go without some disagreement. So he hoped, knowing the sand was running out of the hourglass, that winter was coming toward him in giant steps. In the morning, hoar frost was heavy, the edges of Goose Creek were a line of ice crystals, his breath and the breath of the Black were white clouds.

Alexandra wasn't there.

He told himself over and over to be patient but he wasn't. He stewed in restlessness and impatience. The evening they arrived the breeze was cold and sharp, the gray clouds low on the mountain. In that dark, inhospitable climate, he watched, searched, and waited, finding nothing to his liking. He guessed that what he'd come for in such a hurry had moved north. And for all of his "wanting" he didn't know enough Lakota language to ask. He had to wait for someone else to ask and he was pretty sure Emile Villon wasn't asking. Emile didn't give a damn.

In the morning a cold wind continued to blow gray clouds off the mountain. Zeke could hardly stand still: the cold wind so sharp and cutting. Thankfully, by midmorning it died down and Emile Villon started trading. Zeke was suffering in this mental and emotional tumult but Emile wasn't. He was in his element, trading bright blue and equally bright red cotton cloth for buffalo skins. Buffalo hides, the Oglala had; brilliantly colored cotton cloth they did not. As further incentive, if the cloth didn't carry the transaction, there were glass beads of red, yellow, bright green, and orange: beads and cloth for doe skin, beads for elk skin, beads for buffalo hides, some tanned and cured, some not.

In this depressing set of doldrums, Zeke found himself leaning against the alligatored trunk of a stark, leafless cottonwood, listening, absently watching his unsaddled horse crop dried grass, when he spotted a cotton dress. His reaction was strange; Zeke literally had to instruct himself to breathe, something he'd never before had to do. The dress was a faded light blue with a small string of white ribbon and lace at the very bottom just above the hem. He remembered Lexie's mother chatting with her while she sewed the sleeves to the bodice and attached ties for the bow. The dress had no hoops and hung straight from the hips, covering her petticoats. The flowing skirt allowed her to walk, even run, without it riding up. "Comfortable" is how Alexandra had described it. "And pretty" she had added, turning completely around so he could see the dress, her smile, and her flashing eyes. How pleasant she was. It'd been so long. Three months.

The young woman wearing Alexandra's dress was standing with the other Oglala women who, by contrast, wore tanned doe and elk skin dresses, and beaded leggings tied about the calves of their legs. They wore moccasins: the soles made of buffalo bull hide, the tops of them made from the softer skin and sewn together with sinew. The blue cotton dress set her apart. She spoke with the other women, laughing, listening to Emile Villon discuss trading beads for tanned rabbit skin, his mouth going and going, laughing when no deal was made. The dress fit the Indian girl surprisingly well, though she wasn't as tall as Lexie. The bottom hem of the skirt dragged lightly on the sod. When Lexie had worn it, the hem broke against the top of her black leather shoes, just below the ankles, where two rows of eye hooks started disappearing under the skirt.

Leaning against the tree trunk in the soft morning light diffused by the midmorning covering of gray clouds, Zeke stared at the young woman in shock, taken aback. He couldn't help himself. Without thinking, he pushed himself upright and walked straight toward the dress and the young woman wearing it. His direct, straightforward movement immediately made him the center of attention. He wasn't thinking about propriety. The woman was wearing Lexies's dress and he needed to know where she got it.

"Where did you get your dress?" he asked as he approached.

The young woman did not understand a word he said.

Zeke didn't stop to think. He kept on coming.

"The dress?" he asked. "Where did you get it? Where's the girl you got it from?"

The young woman hesitated. Zeke's advance frightened her. She started to back up. Zeke didn't stop. She turned to run, tripped, fell, and rolled trying to escape. Automatically, Zeke reached out his hand to help her up. Help wasn't what she thought he was offering. She tried to escape, thinking he meant to harm her. She screamed. Zeke stopped abruptly. She scrambled to her feet and ran. The crowd closed in around her, stopping Zeke, protecting one of their own.

The scream brought a young Lakota warrior, Spotted Weasel, running to his wife's defense. He charged the younger Zeke, a single, white man in a sea of Oglala. The stationary Zeke saw him. At the last second, he stepped aside and shoved Spotted Weasel, using his weight and direction against him. His attacker fell helter-skelter to the ground, rolling, coming to his feet embarrassed, as gracefully as a three legged dog chasing two rabbits.

Spotted Weasel pulled his knife, much more leery than he had been, equally determined to kill the white boy. After all, he'd attacked his wife. He had no choice, pride being what it is. The crowd separated and Zeke stared at the advancing man and the flashing blade, moving back and forth like a snake's tongue.

What have I done? he asked himself.

269

From out of nowhere Emile Villon appeared, placing himself between the two combatants. The surprised and astonished Zeke could not have been more grateful. He said to Emile, "I asked the girl where she got the dress. It's Lexie's. I just wanted to know where she got the dress. I don't want to kill this guy. I don't want to be killed by him. Not over a dress. I just want to know where she got it."

Emile glanced at Zeke. "What dress?"

Spotted Weasel had advanced five steps.

Zeke located the girl in the crowd. He pointed. "That's her. That's Lexie's dress. Her mother made it. I just want to know where she got it. I'm thinkin' she knows where Lexie is. She might know."

Emile Villon looked at the girl wearing the cotton dress. He glanced at Zeke, then at Spotted Weasel and the knife in Spotted Weasel's hand.

Emile Villon recognized opportunity. It was right in front of him in a sea of Oglala. He said to Spotted Weasel in his language, taking his time, pointing at the girl wearing Alexandra's dress, "He wants your woman. How much? How many horses? How many buffalo robes? He likes her very much."

Anger immediately clouded Spotted Weasel's face. He told Emile Villon to get out of the way and started advancing toward the two men. Emile stepped aside, looking at Zeke.

"What did you tell him?" Zeke demanded.

"I asked him where the woman got the dress."

"What's wrong with him, then? He looks like he swallowed a bull frog whole."

"He says it's too late. He's gonna feed your heart ta the camp dogs."

"What? No. Tell him I only want to know where she got the dress. Nothin' else. Tell him it belonged to someone I know. I seek her. Tell him that. I don't want to fight with him."

Emile wanted to smile but he didn't. His good fortune was being handed to him. The kid was dead.

Emile turned to Spotted Weasel and in Oglala said, "He wants your woman. He asks how much? How many horses?"

"Get out of the way," Spotted Weasel said in response.

"Gladly," Emile said, "but beware, this one is treacherous. He carries hidden weapons. He will give ya five horses fer your woman." He glanced at Zeke. "No, six. He says he'll give ya six horses fer the

270

woman."

"Get out of the way, old fat one."

Emile Villon moved farther out of the way. He said to Zeke, "He said he is goin' ta kill ya. His woman is worth ten horses and she's not for sale. He says ya have no courage, thet ya ar' a weaklin' and an old woman. Besides ya bein' a coward, he doesn't think much of ya."

Spotted Weasel had courage. Zeke gave him that. Without hesitation he came right at Zeke, intent on killing him, knife out in front, flipping back and forth, creating a deadly shield. He was a formidable sight.

Zeke couldn't help but think that if he got himself killed Lexie would have no one. She'd be lost. He started to back up. Spotted Weasel took the slow retreat as a sign of weakness and came on without hesitation, thinking the white boy a coward. He said something to Zeke. Zeke didn't understand a word.

"Look," Zeke replied, "I really don't want to fight with you. I only wanted to know where your woman got the dress. I asked her about the dress. She slipped and fell. I didn't push her. Her fallin' was an accident. I tried to help her up."

Spotted Weasel moved forward, advancing, crouching low, taking one step at a time, his eyes on Zeke, his knife at the ready. He parried the blade, moving it back and forth in front of him, readying himself for what he knew would be a fatal lunge.

Zeke had never fought a man who used a knife before and it was unnerving watching it flick back and forth.

This isn't gonna to end good. I'm gonna to have to shoot this fellow.

His hand touched the walnut grip on his Navy Colt, pushing the thong off the hammer. Then what? There were so many of them. It was obvious that Emile wasn't going to be any help.

Another voice broke the building tension. It was the voice of a tall warrior standing to Zeke's left, his arms folded across his chest as though he were sitting in judgment of prize hogs at a county fair, midsummer.

Zeke didn't dare to even glance at the speaker, his concentration on Spotted Weasel.

It's either get stabbed or shoot him, he thought. *Better him than me.*

The tall one spoke to Spotted Weasel in Oglala. "The old, fat one, Bad Horse, lies. This white man wants to know where your woman got the dress she's wearing. He never said he wanted to

271

purchase her. He never offered horses. He looks for his woman. It was her dress before it belonged to your woman. That's what he said. You are being made a fool of. Bad Horse is tricking you. The white man carries two short guns against your blade. Who do you think is going to win this fight?"

What's he sayin'?

Emile Villon immediately interjected, his voice high pitched, obviously angry. He glanced at Zeke. In Oglala he said, "I'm not lyin'. I speak the truth. This white one wants your woman. He offered six horses. How kin ya pass up this trade?"

"The truth is not in Bad Horse. The young white—he asks about the dress. He said nothing about buying your woman."

"The dress? I got it from Walking Eagle. Why does he want to know this?"

The tall warrior pointed at Zeke. "He says the woman who wore the dress belonged to him. He seeks her."

"He doesn't want my woman?"

"No. He looks for his woman. Bad Horse lies."

Spotted Weasel nodded. "Walking Eagle took her after Gratton's fight. She belongs to Walking Eagle. She is his woman."

Emile Villon nodded and replied in Oglala. "We go," he said.

But the tall warrior his arms still folded, said to Villon, "Why you lie, Bad Horse?"

Emile Villon smiled without answering the question, then turned to Zeke and said, "We should go. Spotted Weasel is lettin' ya go. He decided not ta kill ya. He says you're young and stupid and there's no honor in it. Let's get out of here before he changes his mind."

"What about the dress? I want to know where his woman got the dress."

"They ain't tellin' ya, kid. They're sayin' your woman belongs ta a man named Walking Eagle. They're sayin' they ain't tellin' ya nothin'. Like I told ya, she's someone else's woman. Ya ain't gettin' her."

"No." Zeke turned to the tall man who was staring at him.

"You speak English?" he asked. "I'm glad that you do. I want to know where the woman got the dress. I want to know what this man said," pointing at Spotted Weasel, "about her." He pointed at Emile Villon. "And I want to know what he said and where the white woman is. That's all I want to know."

272

"You should leave," the tall man said. "You should leave. Spotted Weasel not talk about dress. Dress not your business. White woman belong to Walking Eagle. She far away."

"Where?"

"North. You should leave."

"North?"

The man nodded.

"Not east?"

"Not east."

"Is this that woman's husband?"

The man nodded.

"Tell him I want to know where the white woman is. The one that used to wear the dress his wife now wears."

"You should leave, I think."

Villon was walking away, leading his mule and the two packhorses. He did not look back.

"I want to know where he got the dress," Zeke said. "That is all I want to know."

The tall one did not answer his question.

Zeke, frustrated, turned to Spotted Weasel. "Where did you get the dress?" he asked in English. "That's all I want to know. I just want to know about the dress."

Spotted Weasel looked at the tall one. "What did he say?"

The tall one replied in the language of the Oglala. "I told you, he wants to know where you got the dress. That's what he wants. Nothing else."

"Tell him to leave."

"I have. He wants to know where the white woman is."

Spotted Weasel raised his knife for the second time, staring at Zeke with an angry glare. "I will take his heart," he said. "I will kill him."

Zeke saw the knife. "Tell him I do not want his life or his wife. I want mine. She was mine before she was stolen from her father. I aim to have her. She's mine. I come for her."

The tall one smiled, shook his head, and repeated the words to Spotted Weasel.

Spotted Weasel stared at Zeke. "He doesn't pull his knife. He's a coward. What's wrong with him? Doesn't he listen?"

The tall one glanced at Zeke, then he said to Spotted Weasel,

273

"He is standing in front of you. He makes no effort to run. He carries two pistols and a blade. I don't think he's a coward. I think he wants his woman. I think this trouble is because Bad Horse lies. You heard what the old fat one said. There is no truth in it. Bad Horse said this one wants your woman. He does not. Spotted Weasel, fighting over a woman is not a good thing. Not with a man carrying two pistols. This isn't a good day to die. Not over a woman that belongs to neither of you."

Spotted Weasel laughed. "Tell him the woman he seeks is with Walking Eagle on the Greasy Grass. She is not here."

The tall warrior looked at Zeke. "He said woman you seek north of here on Greasy Grass."

Zeke pulled his knife from the scabbard. Spotted Weasel jumped back in surprise. But Zeke made no effort to advance. Instead he handed the knife butt first to the tall warrior.

"Give it to this man. A gift from me to him. Thank him. Tell him that killin' him would be difficult and I do not want to kill a brave man over a woman."

The tall one nodded. "I say to him your words. You walk lightly. Walking Eagle strong man," he said. "Maybe another woman."

"I do not doubt that he is strong but she's my woman and I aim to have her."

"You crazy. I think this. Bad Horse make up big story."

"Bad Horse? What did he say?"

"He said you want woman of Spotted Weasel."

"What's your name? How are you called?"

"I Hanska Kangee. Means Tall Crow."

"Hanska Kangee? Tall Crow?"

"Yes."

"You've been helpful. I owe you for this kindness. I will not forget."

Zeke turned and picked up the reins to the black horse, led him to his saddle, and saddled him. After he mounted, he looked at Hanska Kangee, nodded, touched the brim of his hat, reined the black around, and rode after Villon at a canter.

I sure lucked out. How am I goin' to get to the Greasy Grass when I don't know where it is? That Villon sure turned out to be what he is. Bet he's been lyin' all the time. Damn near got me killed. What am I gonna' to do with him?

Emile Villon, riding his mule and leading the two packhorses, had already made the ridge overlooking the encampment and the small valley that sheltered Goose Creek. His mule kept walking, never slowing down. Bad Horse Villon never looked back to see if Zeke and his "damn" dog were following him. He hoped they weren't and knew they were.

CHAPTER 43
Alexandra is 48 miles north of Zeke on the Greasy Grass

November 4, 1854
Upper Goose Creek
Central Nebraska Territory

Winter came to the Big Horn on little cat feet. There was no roar of winddriven snow: no weather drums beating against the ridges and canyon walls, no sudden thunderous immersion of the land in ice and snow. Instead it arrived as a thin, innocuous gray line of clouds on the far western horizon. It was small, insignificant, and, in the beginning, hardly visible. It came gently, moving across the Absarokas, covering the pine forests and the gray peaks of the Yellowstone with a light dusting of white. For a moment the gray clouds appeared to retreat.

In spite of its innocuous beginnings, the wind brought the first big storm. By midmorning the thin line of dark gray had steadily grown. Sometimes a winter's beginning takes days, drifting slowly eastward teasing the brown land with a few flakes; but not this time.

In the morning, after the wind died, the land was still, quiet. By noon, however, falling flakes appeared here and there. An hour later a sharp breeze came up, almost as an afterthought. It brought with it swirling flakes. Those flakes began drifting, filling canvasses, filtering down into the prairie grass until the grass was obscured. By mid afternoon the sifting, drifting accumulation of freezing cold was everywhere, visibility limited to only a few yards. The so-called accumulation didn't stop accumulating for days. Winter had arrived.

The fingers recognized the arrival of winter first, then the toes. The pain and stiffness becomes unbearable and numbness settles in. The cold had the inhabitants hunting for coats and gloves, stamping their feet to get the blood circulating, the heart pounding. They rubbed their fingers and hands vigorously but to no avail. Soon they were staring into the gray, cursing what they knew was coming, what they knew was already there. After an hour, then two, they resigned themselves, went inside, banked the fires, huddled around potbellied stoves, and kept warm. They waited: sometimes for a few hours, sometimes for weeks and months, sometimes until the spring thaw

276

brought deliverance and the fresh pungent smell of decaying humus.

Animals suffered the most. Inevitably, they drifted before the wind, humping their backs against the cold, beaten by the unending blast of ice and snow. They huddled as bitter cold was driven painfully into bone and sinew. They sought refuge in ravine and canyon, seeking to avoid the ceaseless wind. In the silence of the night, they looked for a blade of dried grass, finding it on windswept ridges or buried in snow. Once, they had sipped fresh water, drinking from running streams. In the cold, frozen winter, they ate snow and more snow; there was nothing else. Everywhere everything was frozen over and deadly.

Inevitably, the weak, the weary, the sick, and the aged die, their bodies eaten by the wolf, the coyote, the turkey buzzard, magpie and crow. Inevitably.

Men stare out their cabin windows, through the openings in their dugout walls. They huddle in their lodges, seeing darkly through crusted over peepholes, waiting for the green edge of spring to appear over the icy ridges of the Horn. It takes so long, even longer living in a lodge made of buffalo hides.

CHAPTER 44
Alexandra is 49 miles north of Zeke on the Greasy Grass

November 4, 1854
Upper Goose Creek
Central Nebraska Territory

Zeke followed Emile Villon at a quick, distance-eating trot, moving south off the creek then over the eastern ridge. He had to. Villon wasn't waiting to receive what both he and Zeke knew he deserved. That expectation certainly wasn't a pat on the back and a 'hardy how the hell are ya?' Ten thousand feet of mountain lay in front of him, gray clouds blotting out the tops of the massive escarpment. Hidden in the afternoon gray was the sun. By the time Zeke caught up with Villon, snow flurries danced around him, periodically making visibility impractical, sometimes impossible. The longer he followed Villon the less visibility he enjoyed.

Zeke didn't say to him what he wanted to say. He kept it in letting the anger build and fester like a canker sore.

"Where we goin'?" Zeke finally asked. O'Reilly was right on his horse's heels.

"Where? Up there, down off the next ridge where the creek comes off the mountain, there's a cabin, a dugout. We kin hole up over there a couple days 'til this thing blows over."

Do you think it will? That's what he thought. But "all right," is what he said. "Better find it soon or we'll be findin' nothin' a'tall."

"Keep up," Villon said. "Ya better, ya know'd what's good fer ya. This blow is fixin' ta be a real sumbitch."

I have a pretty good idea what's good for me. And what's good for me ain't so good for you. You damn near got me killed. Why'd you do such an unholy thing?

They made the cabin half an hour later, just before darkness began to set in. Toward the end they rode blind amid swirling snow flurries. The old looking., fat man, Bad Horse, found it, knowing where it sat along the side of the mountain. Cabin? It wasn't much to look at. In the blowing, driving snow it was even less. The front was log; the ill-fitting door stood ajar, hanging on cracked leather hinges. The windows were square holes axe-cut in old logs, the opening nailed shut, covered loosely with split pine. In many places the chinking had fallen out, leaving long open gaps between the barkless logs. The back side of the cabin was literally the mountain. The roof was composed of five inch thick pine poles laid close together, covered in thick sod. The floor was pounded dirt, a hard pack composite of granite and rock. Once they dismounted and were inside they still had to hurry. Emile started a fire in a rock fireplace using flint and dry sticks from a pack rat's nest, a rat who, looking for a better home, had simply left, leaving behind his collected treasures and a pile of decaying trash.

While Villon busied himself with fire, Zeke turned the horses loose in a horse corral, also built, in part, up against the mountain. Fortunately for the horses it was out of the sharp wind. There was no feed, however, and night was coming fast. As much as Zeke disliked the idea, they'd have to wait until tomorrow to eat when he could see. Right then, he couldn't see to find grass and water for them: a task complicated by the snow obliterating everything. At least they were out of the wind. He closed the pole gate, swinging it on the hub of an old wagon wheel.

A wagon wheel hub? Clear up here? Where did that come from?

For a moment he stood leaning against the rail fence, braced against the swirling snow. Squinting, he looked up at the gray clouds which hid the pine-covered mountain. Visibility was less than twenty feet.

The cabin was a hundred yards off a creek bed and running water. Stands of cottonwood, mixed with aspen and pine followed its meandering off the slopes of the Horn. There were plenty of trees, and thus, a ggod supply of firewood. Something to burn mattered right then. Otherwise it was going to be one cold, cold night.

Zeke turned his back to the wind and picked up Villon's saddle and one pack and carried them inside, depositing them on the floor against the back wall. The old man had the fire burning, throwing heat, at the same time pulling frigid air through the gaps between the logs where the chinking had fallen out, and around the edges of the ill fitting door.

Zeke glanced about. *Not much,* he thought.

"Better than nothin'," Emile commented, as if reading his thoughts, working fresh wood into the flames.

"It'll do, I suppose," Zeke said, looking around again. "With a little work we might keep the outside out and the inside in."

He smiled at Villon's back, thinking that a day of reckoning was coming, that he was going to force it.

No, it's here. I'm wrong. That day's here and gone. I can't believe what he did. Out and out lied. Tried to get me killed.

"Work on the door," Zeke said aloud. "I'll get my saddle, the other packs, then if I can get some mud outta the creek, we'll plug the chinkin' best we can. If I can find some grass to mix with it, it'll hold together better. Some of the chinkin' fell out but didn't fall far. We can reuse 'em Lessin' some fool uses 'em for firewood. Hear me? Don't do that. I'll be back."

Zeke looked at Villon. "That was horseshit what you did. Don't think I don't know it. Damn near got me killed." Zeke wiped his mouth on his sleeve. "Fix the door. I suggest you do as you're told. You don't, I'm gonna drop you where you stand. I ain't got time for this horseshit. I ain't got time for ya."

Outside, the wind was howling, sounding like a dozen starving wolves. Zeke stopped speaking, looking directly at Villon, then restarted in measured tones. "Because of you it turns out that all I've done for the last three or four weeks has been a waste of time and I didn't have none to waste. No tellin' what's happened to Lexie 'cause of you. I'm holdin' you on this one. I got a mind to kill you. Save on what grub we got. Hear me?"

Emile Villon stared at him, not moving, watching, his eyes following his, visibly relieved when Zeke pulled the rickety door open and stepped through it into the wind, driving snow swirling around him. Bad Horse Villon was suddenly apprehensive when Zeke hesitated, turning, filling the doorway and fixing his eyes on him.

"Fix the door or don't be here when I get back. Hear me? I ain't cuttin' you no slack, Emile. None. Not a smidgen. Don't you be expectin' none. It'd be a mistake on your part."

Zeke turned in the doorway, snow gusting around him. He disappeared into the gray evening. The driving snow whipped about his legs, tugging at his arms. It was so cold he wondered exactly what he had in mind. Leaning into the storm he was thinking about Bad Horse Villon.

It'll be good to get loose of that son of a bitch. Real good! Ain't nothin' good 'bout keepin' him. Nothin'. I'd of been better off on my own. I surely would.

Better be on the quick. Stay awake. No tellin' what he'll be doin'.

How am I gonna stay in that cabin with that so'n' so?

280

Don't close an eye. Just shoot him and be done with it!

Too easy. Not right. Not gonna just shoot him.

Oh, get on with it.

What does that mean?

Ya know what it means. It means just that. Don't go makin' somethin' out of nothin'.

All right. All right. I won't.

Don't all right me. Get on with it.

I am gettin' on with it. I'll do what needs to be done.

See that ya do.

Not sure what. I know I surely ain't makin' no friends.

Now, that's a fact. Sure as hell. That's a natural fact. Ya oughta bust every bone in Villon's body. Now that's a natural fact.

I'm considerin' it.

CHAPTER 45
Alexandra is 49 miles north by northwest of Zeke on the Greasy Grass

November 4. 1854
Upper Goose Creek
Central Nebraska Territory

Zeke meant to return to the cabin where he'd left Emile Villon breaking up dried sticks, feeding the fire. The difficulty was three horses and Villon's mule standing in a blizzard and the need to retrieve his saddle, the remaining pack saddles, and the three remaining packs. He supposed it would take him fifteen minutes or twenty at the outside but, he had to do something about the livestock; he couldn't leave them standing butts into the storm and the mercury plunging toward twenty below.

Leaning into gale force wind, he trudged toward the horse corral and found neither the horses nor the mule. Immediately he cussed himself for leaving the gate open. But he hadn't. That stumped him. Squinting into the whirling snow, he came to grips with the fact that he didn't have a lot of time. It'd be pitch dark soon: light was diminishing. There was no moon, no stars, just socked in storm clouds. The dropping temperature, a thirty mile an hour wind blowing dry, whirling snow, and the elements whipping themselves into a sizeable ground blizzard made sure of that. To be caught outside was death. And no horses! That was death, too. With the wind driving them, they would be thirty miles away before daybreak. There was nothing stopping them.

But where were they? The corral poles must be down, he thought. *This is real trouble. At least death will sure as hell be quick. No horses. What else could go wrong?*

By the time he reached the gate his fingers were numb; his toes ached; the exposed skin on his forehead was burning; he could barely see. O'Reilly was at his heels, whining: no doubt wondering what was going on. No horses. No mule. The corral empty. Hurriedly, he checked the perimeter; the fence was up rail for rail. Nothing was out of place. There were no holes that he could find. He double checked the gate; it was shut, the latch in place. Visibility was decreasing by the minute; it was down to five yards, if it was an inch.

Emile could have stolen them but he was inside. Who else? What else? In this weather? A blast of frigid air caught him, turning him around. Frantically, he grabbed at a pole in the fence, holding it, waiting for the wind to die. It didn't. He had to either move or die. But the wind strengthened. There was no reprieve from it.

Those damn horses. They had to be there. Somewhere. But where?

Unlatching the gate, he opened it enough to step inside the corral, shutting it behind him. The dog slithered under the bottom rail and followed. As quickly as he could, fighting the wind at every turn, he walked the fence line, double checking the perimeter. It was closed tight. Every rail in place. The gate was tied shut. The western interior of the fenced corral consisted of fifty feet of granite wall, twenty feet high.

They couldn't get through that. Or over it.

He started on the south side, the wind cutting at his legs, whipping past him.

I'll check the other side, he thought. *Better hurry. Can't stay out here much longer. Gotta find them horses. We'll be dead if I don't.*

Quickly he ran his hand along the granite face, pushing himself to the other side of the horse corral where poles and a granite wall met. Suddenly there was no rock face. It was under hand and then it wasn't. Backing up, O'Reilly looking up at him, he turned his back to the wind. Zeke relocated the wall, kept his hand on it, and moved forward. It bent away from him. This time he followed it into the face of the mountain ten feet, snowdrifts hindering him, blocking each step. One second he was fighting the wind, bowing into it, the next he was falling forward onto his hands and knees. The wall had bent back against itself and opened into a large room inside the mountain.

I'll be damned.

Probably.

This is somethin'. Wonder if Villon knows about this?

Getting to his feet, he stepped under an overhang, then followed the wall with his left hand and discovered the horses and the mule staring at him. The walls of the room were solid granite; the ceiling nine feet high in the center, less at the edges. The very back was a flat shelf--in places six feet off the floor and in others, lower, sloping toward the floor. Surprisingly, the room was both warm and dry. His cheeks burning, he suddenly became aware of his fingers tingling. His feet felt like wooden stubs, no feeling at all. But he felt warm. The three horses, and the mule provided the interior heat. Outside it might be forty below but inside it felt like be sixty, a bonafide heat wave.

Certainly it's warmer than the inside of that shanty where that lyin', cheatin' Villon is fixin' the door. If he's fixin' the door. What am I goin' to do with him? Damn near got me killed.

Zeke shivered thinking about it. He patted the wall. It seemed warm to his tingling fingers.

Part of the mountain. Take a while to cool. If ever.

He laughed.

No draft blowin' snow between the cracks here. No cracks.

Got that right.

The entryway provided light, dim though it was. Outside, dark was closing, the evening light diminishing, dying in the howling wind and drifting snow. Already a two-foot drift was closing the entry.

Better get the saddle, packs, or I ain't gonna.

Taking a breath, steeling himself against the wind, Zeke stepped outside, returning with his saddle and the remaining packs, setting them out of the way on the shelf that ran along the back wall. He made two trips. After his final trip, using what was left of the light, he unrolled his bedroll and sheep skin and spread them out on the shelf. Rummaging through his saddlebags, he retrieved some jerky, then crawled onto the shelf and buried himself under his blankets.

I'm sure as hell not goin' out there. Villon's on his own.

Zeke had had enough. Somewhere in the night he woke with a start, listening. What he heard was the quiet of the mountain, and the horses breathing, shifting their weight from one foot to another. He discovered O'Reilly sleeping at his feet, a warm ball of hair.

I'll be damned, he thought and went back to sleep with warm toes, reasonably comfortable with the idea that not one living soul knew where he was. Nevertheless, his fingers were curled around the butt of his Navy Colt. It felt smooth, warm, and safe. One of the horses blew its nose and ground its teeth.

Wonder what the hell's wrong with him?

Zeke woke late. He didn't know it. Not at first for it was dark, the only light coming through the opening. His stomach was empty. He was thirsty. The opening was mostly obstructed by snowdrifts that had accumulated halfway up the rock face and a few feet inside.

Securing his pistol and hat, Zeke pulled his boots on. He and the dog went to see what was outside. Snow was still falling but no wind was blowing. And he could see.

Oh boy, he thought. *How long is this gonna last?*

Across the the horse corral the dugout sat under a two foot blanket of snow, drifts halfway up the walls. He was singularly struck with the fact that there was no smoke drifting out of the chimney. The door was shut; snow had drifted against it and along the log wall. The roof was covered with several feet of accumulation. But no smoke.

What's that idiot doin'? If I'm lucky he's a chunk of ice, frozen solid. That'd solve my problems. The thought of Villon as a chunk of ice make him smile.

Zeke pushed on the door. It gave way grudgingly. Clumps of the snowdrift tumbled inside as he entered the single room. The dog followed him. To his surprise, no one was there.

Where are you, fat man?

Zeke stuck his fingers into the fireplace ashes. Cold. There were no tracks leading out through the doorway. He built a fire, added dry sticks, a log. The dog whined. Zeke glanced at him.

"You wanna go outside?"

The dog didn't move.

"No? Where is he, you think?"

Zeke put another log on the fire, seating it in the growing mound of hot coals.

"Let's find out, dog. See what that fool is up to. Too smelly to be dead. Too ugly. Too old. Wish he was dead. Don't know what I'm gonna do with him."

Pulling the door farther open, he stepped outside, the dog following. Zeke closed the door behind him in an effort to keep the heat inside. Not that it mattered. There was still no chinking to keep the cold out.

The fire will burn half an hour, an hour maybe. A little longer. Where'd that old fool disappear to? Think I should have come back . . . last night? No, that wouldn't have been good seein' what I said to him before I left. Neither one of us would have slept. Especially me.

Zeke glanced at the dog, nodded his head.

"Naw, me, neither. I ain't got a clue where he's gone off to. Damn near got me killed, he did. That lyin' so'n'so. What am I gonna do with him?"

Zeke quickly surveyed the area around the dugout.

"Absolutely no tracks. Musta left last night shortly after I did. Tracks all filled in. Wonder if he was looking for me. Why? If he did . . . it wasn't to do me no good. Where would he have gone? Figure he knew about that hole in the rock? He knew about this place so he'd know about the hole. Probably figured I was gonna kill him. Maybe lookin' to shove a knife in me."

The dog looked at Zeke.

"He could've done that, dog. Maybe he thought I was gonna come back and cut his throat while he was sleepin'. Damn good idea. Maybe he needed firewood. Think he'd do that? He'd need it to last the night. But where would he go?"

Zeke looked about, letting his eyes follow the creek bed. It was mostly covered with snow. There wasn't a living soul.

Must of been lookin' for wood. Where would I go to get wood? In the dark?

Look for trees, dead trees. Probably find him frozen dead.

Probably. How long was he gone? All night?

Possibly. Could be alive. If he was lucky. Probably looked for wood along the creek. That's where I'd go.

But was he lookin' for wood? Did he have somethin' else in mind?

Possibly.

It was O'Reilly who found him. Zeke would have missed him, but not the dog. He stopped in front of a two-foot high mound of snow, a six or seven foot extended drift, and looked back at Zeke and started to whine.

"Whatcha got, dog? What'sa matter with you?"

On the level the snow was at least two feet deep. On top of the roof it was three, in wind driven drifts much deeper. It was deep enough that the dog had to jump to make progress going forward. Zeke followed him and literally stumbled over a body buried under several feet of snow. At first Zeke thought it was a log or a rock. Intending to step through the "drift" he kicked something that gave, something that wasn't rock solid. A second look revealed an arm; brushing away snow, he uncovered a leg.

I'll be damned. That man did commit suicide. He's dead for sure.

Zeke brushed the snow away and uncovered Emile Villon's body, thinking it was frozen solid, that there was no hurry. Surely he was dead. He thought about leaving Emile where he found him. The frozen tundra and the snow would preserve his body, would keep it

286

from rotting. But leaving him wouldn't protect him from coyotes or timber wolves. So he thought better of it.

Grabbing Emile Villon by the collar, he pulled him back to the dugout, through the door, and left him lying on the floor while he rebuilt the fire, adding additional logs and broken branches. Staring at the body, he considered his options.

I don't know; if I keep him inside, he's gonna thaw out. He'll be smellin' worse than he smells already. I suppose I ought to store him outside. I could hoist him up on the roof. He'd be safe there. Makes sense. Wolves probably won't come close. Will they? Not likely, but I don't know.

The dog started whining, as if mistreated.

"What's wrong with you?"

The dog's tail thumped the floor but he looked at Zeke like he was about to be taken behind the barn and taught a lesson.

"I ain't gonna beat you none, dog."

Zeke glanced at Villon's corpse.

"And he ain't gonna hurt you. He's beyond hurtin' himself." Zeke stared at the frozen body, the snow caught in the folds of Villon's clothes.

That ol' boy is a mess.

The index finger on Emile's right hand moved . . . ever so slightly, a mere smidgen. Zeke blinked.

"I'll be damned," he mumbled.

'Did I see that? Did that happen?" Zeke glanced at O'Reilly. "You see that, dog? Or was that just me?"

Zeke knelt beside the "frozen" man, and grabbed his right hand. It felt cold. It felt frozen. He manually moved the fingers back and forth. They moved grudgingly, each time collapsing back to where they'd started. Maybe they weren't frozen like he thought. If they were they'd be brittle, frozen ice solid. Maybe they'd snap off, cracking into a dozen pieces like an icicle if he tugged on them.

Maybe he's alive. Maybe I'm bein' hasty.

Zeke grabbed Emile Villon's coat by the collar and pulled his body across the floor, depositing him on his laid out bedroll. For a moment he stared at him. Emile Villon didn't move. Zeke knelt beside him and slapped him across the face. Emile Villon still didn't move.

Do it again.

He slapped him again. There was still no response.

Do it again.

287

Zeke slapped him harder. But Emile Villon, lying on top of his bedroll, eyes closed, a flat white color to his pallid, bloodless cheeks, moved nary a muscle.

Did I see that? Really? Did he move that finger? Am I seein' this?

Leaving him, Zeke went to the fireplace and threw another log on the fire, glancing from time to time at Villon's body. He looked uncomfortable. But Zeke didn't feel inclined to change Villon's comfort level . . . especially if he was alive. But Villon didn't move.

The dog whined, stretched his scrawny frame, then laid down next to the body. Zeke glanced at him, getting a 'woe is me' look.

"I told you I ain't gonna beat you, dog. You can stop worryin' yourself. Ain't your fault . . . "

For a moment he stared at Villon's body, noting the snow in his baggy pockets, more inside the folds of his clothing, down his shirt, up his sleeves.

'What the hell am I gonna do with you? Suppose I should do somethin'. Keep you from dyin'. But, what? Reckon you'll thaw out plenty soon if I just keep the fire burnin'. Heard my uncle say that you should have the snow rubbed on your skin if you're sufferin' frostbite. Don't seem logical. Seems like it'd be better to bathe you in hot water. Except I ain't bathin' you. I ain't gonna touch you. Reckon I oughta wake you up and get some grits in your belly except we ain't got no grits. Except you ain't wakin' up. Guess I'll just keep the fire goin'. Keep you warm. Maybe you're dead. That'd be good for me."

The fire was burning hot, forcing Zeke to spend time working on replacing chinking, plugging the air leaks with mud mixed with grass. On the outside it froze quickly. On the inside it froze and dried. The net effect was a rise in the inside temperature.

Finished with the chinking, Zeke decided he'd rearrange Emile. He straightened him out on top of his bedroll: pulled his hands and arms tight along his body, brushing away the pockets of unmelted snow. Lastly, he took the cured and tanned buffalo and deer hides that Emile had traded for and draped them over his body. He used the deer hides first, finishing with the heavy buffalo robes. Even if he wanted to, Emile Villon could hardly move.

Zeke found himself talking to a body. He said, "That oughtta warm you up! Now what? Suppose I build a buffalo stew; boil some meat, that way you could get it inside yourself if you wake up. Maybe some black coffee for your belly. You sure look dead to me. Tell the truth, I wish you was dead, if you ain't. Wouldn't have to bother with you. Be the best.

"Wonder if I should pry one eye open to look inside? Reckon not. Don't want to touch you if I can help it. 'Sides, I don't want to waste black coffee. Guess I could drink it myself, you don't wake up. No waste that way. You're the most despicable man I ever laid eyes on. Ever. It's the damnedest thing I gotta help you. You sure as hell ain't deservin'. Best you're dead."

Zeke broke out the boiling pan and the black coffee kettle and filled them both with snow. Every time the snow melted, he refilled both until the meltings were adequate to boil some stew and brew some black coffee.

To Zeke's relief, Emile Villon didn't wake up. He didn't move and Zeke didn't touch him. Instead, Zeke drank the black coffee, then went outside to check on the mule and the three horses. Getting them feed was his next big problem.

How the hell am I gonna do that? He questioned.

Every half an hour he went back inside to rebuild the fire and check on Emile. So far, he hadn't opened an eye and as far as Zeke could tell, he hadn't moved again. He began to hope.

The horses' problem he solved by picketing them out on a flat area, letting them paw at the ground, brushing away the snow until they could get at the foliage underneath. It kept him and the stock busy.

It kept snowing. It snowed all day every day for five days.

On the second day after he'd found Villon buried under the snow, he found Villon laying on his bedroll, not moving, with both eyes wide open, staring into space.

"You awake," Zeke asked. "'Bout time. Thought you was dead."

Emile tried to focus on Zeke, then let his eyes wander around the dimly lit room, flitting from one object to another. He blinked several times and still didn't move.

"Who're you?" he asked after several tries, his lips moving like cold molasses.

Zeke didn't answer.

"Got some stew. Better get yourself around some of it. Found you in a snowdrift. Dog did. Hauled you inside. You ain't been doin' good. 'Bout gave up on you. Gonna pour some of this broth in a coffee cup. Best you try and get it down. If you can."

The man tried to move. He couldn't for the weight of the skins on top of him.

"Here, let me give you a hand. I'll sit you up and give you a cup."

Zeke peeled the hides off Emile Villon, one by one, grabbed him by the shoulders and sat him up, leaning him against the stack of hides. He handed him a cup of broth.

Emile sat staring at the back of his hands. The skin was black. "Lookie there at my hands," he said.

"Looks frostbit. Now take this cup. Get it down you."

"They're black."

"Whadda you expect? Found you in a snowdrift. Take this cup. Take a sip."

"Snowdrift? Was I dead?"

"Damn near. Take a sip."

"I gotta piss."

"Take a sip and I'll get you outside."

"Outside?"

"Don't want you pissin' inside."

Emile Villon attempted to take the cup.

"My fingers ain't workin'," he complained. "What'd ya do ta me?"

"Here, let me help."

Zeke put the cup to Emile's lips, tilted it. Emile attempted to get some in his mouth, trying to swallow. He wasn't entirely successful, getting more down his chest than his throat. Zeke then hoisted him up by an arm and hauled him outside to take a piss. His assistance ended there. There were limits and Zeke had reached them. Emile fumbled around for an extended time, moaning, frustrated with himself. Unsure.

Snow was falling. Thankfully there was no wind.

Emile Villon, wavering on unsteady legs, finally looked in frustration at Zeke, then suddenly pitched forward onto his face into the snow, landing on one knee. Shaking his head in disbelief, Zeke mercifully hauled him back inside and worked on getting more stew inside him. It was a thankless, unwanted task, one which became increasingly onerous.

290

A week later Emile Villon's condition had not improved. He was given to moments of babbling in another language like a lost, starving child. The skin on his face, hands and feet--any part of him that had been exposed directly to snow--was black and started peeling. He smelled like death sipping black coffee, hardly able to stand on his own, unable to hold a cup, hot or cold. Chewing jerked meat was impossible. Any food he got inside himself he drank from a cup. He was too hot, too cold, not warm enough. He'd shake uncontrollably, sleeping in fits and starts, waking himself as he thrashed about emitting moans and shouts that scared the dog.

The snow stopped. Started. Stopped again.

When Zeke wasn't caring for Emile's needs, he was looking after the livestock. The horses and mule ate snow for water. Finding dried grass was next too impossible. The wind became a blessing of sorts. It drifted the snow deep but cleared off the high flat areas, exposing grass and foliage. Picketing them to graze was difficult for the ground was frozen and wouldn't take a picket. Instead, Zeke tied each animal to a section of tree, light enough to drag, using twenty feet of rope. Every night he brought them inside.

It became clear Emile Villon would die if left to his own devices. Trouble was he didn't improve. He couldn't stand on his own feet: too sore, too swollen. He couldn't put his boots on. He'd die without help.

Let him.

Can't do that.

He'd leave ya in a second. Not give it a thought.

Can't.

Sure ya can.

Can't. Can't leave a man defenseless. Not like this.

What about Lexie?

Can't think about her.

Zeke stood at the entry of the stone barn where the horses had taken shelter, where he slept and stewed himself into a dark mood. He gazed north, following the trees that defined where Goose Creek ran back and forth away from the mountain. Somewhere out there Lexie was warming her hands over an open fire. Somewhere. If she was alive. Caught out in this cold, she'd never make it. No one would. He imagined her living in a tipi like the Indians. With the Indians. As an Indian.

Damn it all to hell, I could find her. Ride between the drifts. I could make it to this Greasy Grass Creek. A day's ride. Maybe a little more since I don't know where I'm goin'. What did Emile call it? Little Big Horn? That's right. Little Big Horn. Odd name. If I leave, I'd have to leave the old man.

He ain't old.

He'd sure as hell die. Couldn't fetch himself a bite to eat. Not even if he wanted ta. Starve to death. Freeze. Can't build his own fire. Can't get wood. He'd have no chance. Can't do it.

Sure ya can.

I can. I just won't. But I should. I know I should.

Emile Villon, for many a day, didn't know who Zeke was or what he was doing in his life. Stew? It was something poured down his throat by some kid wearing a sheepskin coat. Where the kid got it he didn't know. He wasn't aware of Zeke carrying him outside to relieve himself. He didn't know who it was that banked the fire, keeping the inside of the dugout warm. He didn't even realize that the inside was warm.

Villon didn't like stew. He preferred tongue roasted over an open fire like his mother had done. He didn't remember her any more than he remembered his dislike for stew. He lost one ear and part of the other; they just fell off the side of his head onto the floor. He lost the little finger on his right hand, two toes on his left foot. For the longest time he couldn't stand. He shed patches of skin off his neck, the backs of both hands: shed it like a snake sheds his hide, growing it back in pink splotches that itched like crazy, driving him to the edge of insanity.

Villon lost forty-six pounds living on buffalo stew. After four and a half months there was nothing to him; his clothes no longer fit. They hung on him like a scarecrow with eyes sunk back in his head, his skin hanging on his bones. He was barely able to move from his bedroll to the fireplace. For some reason the "damn" dog stayed away from him, wouldn't even come into the dugout with the kid. Sometimes he stood at the door, peering at him, growling. He began referring to him as the "Damn dog" wondering if he was good "eatin'"

After four months he could walk, although it was with a limp. The kid brought him some fresh deer meet, cut in strips. He ate it raw. Liked it. He refused to drink any more stew. He shook his head no when it was offered. Two weeks later, early morning, the kid showed up in front of the dugout with a saddled mule. Beside him stood three horses--two with packs in place, one with a saddle.

"Where'd ya get thet mule?" he asked.

"It's yours."

"I gots a mule?"

"Standin' right there."

Emile looked at him, blinking his eyes.

"Am I goin' somewheres?"

"We're goin' to the Greasy Grass."

"I am?"

"Emile, I gotta go. Can't stay here any longer. I can't leave you here. You'll die."

"The Little Big Horn?"

"Yes. The Little Horn. Gotta take you."

"What if I don't want ta go?"

"I know you don't want to go but if I leave you, you'll die. No one to feed you stew. No fresh meat. No wood for your fire. Nothin'. You'll just die. So I'm takin' you with me."

"Leave me."

"Can't. Get on the mule."

"Don't know if I kin."

"You can. Put a foot in the stirrup, grab the horn, and pull yourself up there. I'll catch you if you fall. You won't. Get on."

Emile Villon stared at the mule and started to chew on some raw venison. He swallowed. A minute later he was in the saddle and they were moving north.

He felt better.

CHAPTER 46
Zeke is 49 miles south of Alexandra on Upper Goose Creek

November 5, 1854
Greasy Grass River
Central Nebraska Territory

For Alexandra the first snow in late October had been a starter, a harbinger, a miserable hint of what was to come. It stayed three days and was gone, melting away before a warm wind under the cool November sun, leaving behind the false promise of favorable weather. Six days later came another storm. That storm stayed, bringing deep snow and a cold, driving wind. It was a cold that didn't leave until the snow flowers forced their fat, pink stems up through the snowdrifts in late March. The storm's announcement--the "I'm here" November message--came slowly. It wasn't entirely a surprise for snow and cold always comes in November. Inevitably it stays through December, doesn't leave in January or February, hangs on until the last of March.

After the first snow came and left, a cold, brisk wind blew off the red slate rock ridge, ripping through the grove of leafless aspen moving down the creek bottom, whistling through pine, bending the prairie grass in waves. Alexandra listened to its shrieking, whistling sighs as she laid in her buffalo robes, pulling them tightly around her. It wasn't that she was cold. She wasn't, but the sound of the wind made her feel like she should be. Above her head the breeze played with the bull hide flaps that regulated the size of the smoke hole, twisting the sinew, binding the lodge poles more tightly together.

Within the lodge's walls, she could hear the deep sleep sounds of Bethany and Priscilla, both hidden in their buffalo robes. Alexandra felt so tired yet sleep wouldn't come. She had too much on her mind: fleeting thoughts that ran before the wind, dancing like wood sprites from one idea to another. The sides of the lodge shuddered as the night wind picked up. Involuntarily, as if she sought safety under her coverings, she pulled the robes more tightly about her shoulders, feeling their warmth, taking refuge under their sheer weight.

Outside, in the darkness, snow began to fall. The wind caused it to drift. Inside, the lodge was cold, the fire coals dark, no longer emitting heat of any measure. It was a moonless, starless, hopeless night.

Yesterday, in the late afternoon, the men had come back from raiding or hunting. It was an odd timing for a raid, a war party. It may have been hunting. According to Small Dove raiding was a spring or early summer activity.

She found out later that they were hunting horses, stealing them from the Crow on the north slopes of the Big Horn Mountains. There followed a joyous celebration; no one was injured, no one killed. Thirty four-horses had been acquired from the Crow along the Yellowstone River. Blue Flower, oldest daughter of Standing Bear, had told her where, but Alexandra had never been to the place she described; the disjointed description was not easily recognizable. The dancing, the joyful, celebratory singing, excited chatter, and the soft staccato beating of drums lasted into the evening.

It turned cold long before the celebration was over, a frigid wind blowing in out of the northwest. Alexandra felt so tired she went to bed, wrapping herself in her buffalo robes, staving off the stinging, sorrowful, whining wind. Her sister and Priscilla were already asleep.

Hours later she was vaguely aware of Walking Eagle coming inside, taking his time tying the opening flap, securing it, preventing it from making incessant noise during the night. She listened as he removed his moccasins. He brought with him the smell of sage and pine, the pungent smell of juniper, horse sweat and smoke. He made little noise as he placed his rifle and pistol near to hand. They never left his side. She knew they were loaded; they always were. Always. Such was this horrible man.

Shortly all noise ceased, and she thought he must be asleep. Not her: for her, sleep did not come. Outside in the dark night the wind picked up. She wondered if Walking Eagle returned with someone's scalp: knowing he did. The tangle of blood and hair was so nasty, so despicable. She was grateful the scalps he kept were all from black haired warriors, no women. He was not like his brother, Standing Bear, who kept the scalps of the white women as well. There was Colleen Griffie's long red hair, still braided, and the blond hair of some young woman. It was curly as if she had just put it up in curlers and had wrapped it tightly to dry. Those and many others hung from the lodge poles on a long strip of sinew for all of Standing Bear's friends to see and admire. Besides Colleen, she wondered if she had known the prior owners and tried to think of who she knew with curly, blond hair.

Gratefully, she thought of no one; then, she remembered seeing her mother and father: their dead, vacant eyes, their hair missing, the stark white bone of their skulls shining in the morning light. Fear choked her; her throat ached in sorrow for her loss.

In the midst of this dark, evil reverie she felt a hand on her bare knee, surprisingly warm. It startled her, eliminating any semblance of coherent thought she might have had. The touch may have been warm but was not comforting, not inviting. It was as though she was suddenly facing violent death again. Instantly she could barely breathe, having the vivid mental image of the warrior, Small Dove's uncle, grabbing her father's head by his thinning hair, his knife circling his hair line, peeling the scalp back. She remembered being grateful that he was dead--no longer suffering--wishing she was dead, expecting to be. She remembered the screams, the incessant firing, the horses racing by. The hand moved.

No. Not again. No.

The hand seemed to move of its own volition. Mentally, she shouted at herself to do something: anything to preserve her integrity, her dignity, herself. In spite of her frantic intentions, Alexandra lay frozen, inanimate, a rock lying flat against the buffalo skins that covered the ground, futilely trying to escape without moving. She wanted to scream, but remained mute, fearing for her very life, fearing death from the bloody blade always stuck in Walking Eagle's belt. It was so quiet. Above her the wind played with the skins that covered the lodge poles. Beside her she heard the deep sleep breathing of her sister, the nasal sound of Priscilla. Alexandra fought the impulse to grab Walking Eagle's hand. She wanted to. She wanted to reach for her sister, wanting help, needing help, seeking rescue of any kind. There was none. There was no one.

Please? Please?

She never remembered being so alone, so aware of her own body, in a lodge housing so many people. She couldn't help but think that the calloused fingers touching her were the same fingers, the same hands that ripped the scalps from the heads of her friends, her fellow travelers, from the men she had known and admired. And this night there was no doubt he brought additional scalps back from the raid, more to hang from the lodge poles for everyone to admire.

Bloodthirsty savage—you demon incarnate.

She considered jumping up, running, fleeing outside; instead, she shuddered involuntarily, knowing that her life depended on him for food to eat, to survive, for a lodge to keep warm, to keep dry and out of the rain, to live: for everything. And for Beth and for Pris. He was now at her doorstep, not asking, not seeking permission. Taking. Try as she might to escape, she utterly failed. Her body trembled like a blanket shaking in the wind. She was conscious that he was under her buffalo robes with her.

Hating him, hating herself, she succumbed and did nothing, holding herself still until he was finished and was lying beside her, his right arm across her chest, his breathing normal. The girls hadn't awakened. Nobody had. Alexandra wondered how that was possible for her heart was pounding, racing madly in her chest like a nest of herky-jerky squirrels gone crazy-wild.

The arm didn't move. Above their inert bodies the smoke flaps continued to blow noisily in the ceaseless wind. Beside her, Bethany's breathing was deep and steady. Sleep was not in Alexandra. Outside a camp dog barked. Later the wind stopped and she slept, the man, her captor, holding her body close to his in the dark shadows of his lodge, under his buffalo robes.

Outside, snow was falling, the wind pushing it into drifts. Inside, the last coals of the fire were crusting over with ash. Someone added three juniper logs to the coals. A small tendril of smoke drifted toward the smoke hole.

Alexandra woke with a start. Walking Eagle was gone. In the quiet, suddenly aware of herself, she held herself very, very still, controlling her breathing until the sound of dogs barking pulled her from the warmth of her buffalo robes into the cold, empty mountain air of early morning. It was cold. So cold.

She found her moccasins. The wool socks that her mother had darned had a hole in the heel and a big one in the toe but she put them on anyway, slipping the moccasins over them, feeling the cold from the ground seep into her feet. Tugging at her leggings, she tied them at the knee, then stepped outside to collect firewood for the inside fire. The wind caught the edges of her dress, tugging at her knees. The outside fire pit was filled with drifting snow, the circle of rocks mostly hidden. She didn't bother with it. It was too open, too drafty. Not only would it be hard work, but impossible to get fire burning, for those embers were cold, dead, hidden. It would be the last of March before it burned brightly again.

The snow crunched under foot as her weight compacted it. She built an armload of firewood, then returned to the lodge and the inside fire ring hoping to find some hot coals burning orange hidden under the black ones. For a moment she stood outside the closed opening and looked at the day surrounding her, gray from horizon to horizon, flakes settling in her hair: no stars, no moon, no sun.

No one was coming for her.

No one. Alexandra Wakeford stifled a sob in her chest. It hurt so badly. Everything hurt. Where were her parents? Where was their God? She needed Him, badly. Where did He hide himself? Especially when she needed Him so.

"Where are You hiding?" She said to the sky. "Where?"

There was no answer. There never was an answer. The wind whipped around her face pulling at her hair. She held her breath, waiting for the pain inside her heart to subside, then she opened the entry, stooped, stopped precariously with the wood in her arms, and made her way inside to start a fire.

On the far inside edge, hidden under the weight of buffalo robes and soft deer skin, Morning Flower huddled up against Bethany, one arm clutching the Funson doll, the other across Bethany's stomach. She sighed, mumbling some long unintelligible sound.

It was the first day: the beginning of a long, long, unending winter.

CHAPTER 47
Zeke is 49 miles south of Alexandra on Upper Goose Creek

January 29, 1855
Greasy Grass River
Central Nebraska Territory

The drifts were gigantic, larger, deeper than any that Alexandra had seen. The wind that created them drove everyone inside. They huddled about the fire, keeping it burning. Now Alexandra understood clearly why Small Dove made her move the lodge away from where the north wind piled the snow deep. It would have easily buried the lodge. She wondered how Small Dove knew and was oh, so glad that she did. Such a small thing made all the difference.

The wind blew, the snow fell, fire burned, and work had to be done: wood gathered, food prepared, ice melted. It was odd. Huddling in buffalo robes was a common sight. So was the need to get out and see someone, anyone.

The younger girls had gone with Small Dove a few minutes before, the wind whipping the outer covering from Small Dove's hands as she tried to secure it. Bethany and Priscilla were out getting another armload of wood. They took turns. The fire never stopped eating.

Alexandra never remembered being this cold, for this long. It was the wind, the awful, relentless wind. She had two buffalo robes wrapped around her and would have liked another.

Bethany returned, stamping the snow off her moccasins, sitting down next to the mound of buffalo hides that was her sister. She looked at her.

"Lexie, you don't look so good," Bethany said.

"Beth--" Alexandra paused, looking at her sister, pulling the inner robe closer. "I think I'm with child." The three words seemed to hang in the cool interior of the lodge like a lead weight floating in heavy air.

Bethany sat up straight, her eyes large. "What? With child? Are you sure? How do you know?"

"I know. It's my body. I'd know. I feel sick all the time. And I can't eat. There's no other reason. Trust me, Beth, I know," Alexandra said. "Besides the monthly thing has stopped."

"Oh, Lexie!"

She paused. "This is so terrible."Angry tears streamed down her face. "Oh my God, what should we do? We can't leave. How can we? How can we? It's so cold. We'd freeze to death."

"Beth, calm down. We'll leave. Bet on that. This makes it more complicated. You're right. We can't leave in the middle of the winter, snowdrifts higher than this lodge everywhere. We'd freeze to death. Within minutes."

Bethany buried her face in her hands. Her shoulders shuddered involuntarily.

Alexandra reached out to touch her. "Beth," she murmured, "I'm so sorry. I didn't mean to upset you. I had to tell someone."

"It's all right. I'm all right. I'm glad you did," Bethany said, taking a moment to think. "Does Pris know? Who else knows?"

"Nobody. Just you and me."

"How long have you known?" Bethany asked.

"Two weeks. Remember the last deer that we dressed out? I knew then. I got queasy and wanted to throw up doing something I have done a hundred times. I knew then. I suspected before. I haven't felt well for a long time."

"Oh, Lexie, you knew and you didn't tell me? Why not? I'm your sister."

"Beth, I needed to be sure." Alexandra took a deep breath. "I knew this was coming. It's not like I didn't. I just didn't know when. I was hoping it wouldn't happen. It did. I was hoping we'd get away." Alexandra paused, staring at her sister. "He hasn't bothered you, has he?"

"No. Every time he comes near me, I grab my skinning knife. I keep it right here in my belt." Bethany patted the bone hilt. "He's left me alone."

"What about Pris?"

"Not that I know of. She hasn't mentioned it. Do you think he would?"

"I don't know what he'd do."

The outer covering rattled, shifting as it was untied. Both girls looked and watched Priscilla step through the opening, closing the covering behind her, holding firewood in her arm.

"Oh, my, oh my," Priscilla said, gasping, pausing to hold her

300

breath. "I've never been this cold. I thought I'd die." She glanced at the two girls. "You two look like somebody died."

Bethany turned to Priscilla. "Lexie is with child. She just told me."

"Is this true? Lexie?"

Alexandra nodded.

Priscilla turned, sat down beside her, and hugged her. "Oh, I'm so sorry. So, so sorry. It's all my fault. My fault. We should have been gone."

"Oh, Pris," Bethany said, "stop it, would you? Nobody's blaming you. You know who's responsible. It's not you."

Priscilla didn't respond. Kneeling in front of Alexandra, she said, "Are you okay, Lexie? How can we help you? What can we do?"

Alexandra said, "I am fine. It's not like I didn't expect this. I'm just worried about you two. Has he--?"

Priscilla stopped her. "I don't want to talk about it. I don't want to think about it ever."

Bethany said, "He'd better not, not if he wants to live."

"Jeez, Beth. How'd you get so tough?" Alexandra said.

"I'm not kidding."

"All right. All right. I believe you."

The outer covering was pulled open. She Who Smiles bent over and stepped inside, followed by Morning Flower holding the Funson doll. The girls turned to watch, suddenly quiet. Priscilla started adding more sticks to the fire. "Oh, honey, shut that, please," she said, "before we turn into icicles." The sisters were already closing the opening, snowflakes in their dark hair, not understanding a word Priscilla had said.

Priscilla stared at the two, watching them move inside, then turned to Alexandra. "How long . . . do you think?"

"Three months, I think."

Morning Flower, seeing Bethany, ran around the fire ring in front of the teenager.

"What are you doing, child?"

Bethany flipped open her buffalo robe and wrapped it around the girl, wrapping her up into her arms. Morning Flower stuck the Funson doll into Bethany's neck, laughing.

"You're so cold, you little icicle. Where have you been? Have you been playing outside with your little friends? I'll bet you have.

How can you stand it? It's so cold."

Morning Flower hadn't understood a word Bethany had said, a fact that didn't bother Bethany at all.

Bethany glanced at her sister. "This little girl is my friend. She's all apples and cream." She paused, glancing at her Alexandra. "Wouldn't that be nice? Apple slices dripping in thick cream and maple syrup."

CHAPTER 48

March 28, 1855
Central Nebraska Territory

Spring comes late to the Horn. It always does. It always has. An impatient man wouldn't think it was ever coming: not in March. March was the worst, the thought complicated by the warm winds of April being hours and mere minutes away. But away. April, the month when the buffalo cows drop their calves, wasn't there yet. March is a land still buried in snow, beaten by cold wind, and frozen in deep drifts, with endlessly gray skies. For five long, insufferable months, it is winter.

And March is the worst. It's the time when the last, never-ending storms flow out of the north and firewood is far away from the firepits that were built in late fall. Come March burnable wood is a long, long walk in moccasins and a drafty, doe skin dress. Walking, a heavy buffalo robe wrapped around the shoulders, breathing a white cloud in the crisp morning air, cheeks burning in the wind, warding off frozen death, is a miserable business. Each step is a struggle, toes cold and hurting with April just minutes, hours, days off--so very far away.

Somehow, somewhere, the impossible happens. The day arrives and snow no longer drifts; it begins to melt, crusts over, and steadily recedes. At first, it's hardly noticeable. Then there are patches of open space and a single tiny, insignificant blade of grass sticks its light green shoot out from the frozen sod. It seems insignificant, especially when it freezes every night and the streams are hidden under sheets of ice. But there it is. One blade of grass, then another, and March fades and the prairie turns from brown to a light, vibrant shade of green, a green that will fade all too soon, lost for an entire year, seemingly never to come again.

CHAPTER 49
Zeke is 48 miles south of Alexandra on Upper Goose Creek

April 5, 1855
Greasy Grass Creek
Central Nebraska Territory

"Tomorrow break camp," Small Dove said. "We go this way."
She pointed toward the broken hills.

"North?" Alexandra asked. "Isn't that north?"

Small Dove nodded. "Plenty grass. Much elk. Buffalo. Many. It
good. Tomorrow. That way." Again, she pointed north.

"Good. Hopefully firewood will be easier to find. That's what's
good," Alexandra said. "We're walking a half mile for wood now." She
glanced at her sister, thinking.

*Our escape. This would be a good time for it. Horses will be brought in to
pull the travoises. Extras will go unnoticed, especially at the end just after we take
down the lodge. Or set it up. Good,* she thought.

*Except the meat's almost gone. The parfleches are empty. Two left. That's
bad.   An opportunity, though. Maybe right after we set up the lodge again, while
the horses are still here. Priscilla's ankle is okay. This will be good. Really good.*

Later in the morning, Bethany and Alexandra went with six
other women to gather firewood, leaving Priscilla to keep the two fires
burning: one inside, one out. They were small fires for small fires don't
burn much wood. Not like a big one. It takes more attention to keep
two small fires burning than one big one. For one big one: just throw
on the logs and stand back. Not so with small fires.

They walked upstream following the Greasy Grass a half mile.
The area between had been picked clean, harvested of all dry, burnable
fuel. She Who Likes Bitter Berries was talking about her husband,
describing his antics, the way he ate chokecherry flavored pemmican,
smacking his lips, chasing her on his hands and knees. The women
laughed. She told about him getting under the blanket with her. She
had thrown up her hands, waving her index finger back and forth.
They laughed more.

*Hasn't she any shame? I'd never talk about that even if I liked him.
Hated him. Even if I hated him. I do hate him. I'd never.*

She's funny, though. I've got to say that. Waving her finger like that.

Alexandra glanced east away from the creek; the sun rested in a ten o'clock midmorning sky. The guardians (she thought of them as guardians) were riding about three hundred yards on either side. Small Dove said they were for protection. Just in case. "Absaroka might come," she said. "Or Blackfeet." There were three on either side. Sometimes there were more riders. Today there were six. Their presence made her feel good. Protected. It wasn't that they were close, but they weren't far either. And she was with valued women and her sister.

I suppose we're valued, too.

At the half-mile point, the women began collecting wood, breaking dried limbs into small bundles. She and Bethany started building a stack. Another half an hour and they'd have all she and Bethany could carry. That would be enough for the day. Tomorrow morning they'd need more but they'd be moving.

Alexandra glanced eastward, immediately turning to the west. Something wasn't right. Something was wrong. The outriders had disappeared. The guardians were simply gone. One riderless horse, an Appaloosa, stood in a clearing across the creek, its single rein hanging from its mouth.

"Beth. The outriders?"

"What?"

"There aren't any outriders. They've disappeared."

"I . . ." Bethany looked. She said, "I don't see them," then glanced toward camp.

"Oh, my," Alexandra said. "We're in trouble."

A string of riders broke from the trees on the south, riding at a lope.

Behind them were many riderless horses, pushed by others waving blankets to spook them, keeping them at a run. Even at a distance Alexandra could see these riders' faces were painted with zigzagging streaks of lightning: blue, reds, and white. Some were all one color. Others were not. There seemed to be many.

This isn't good. What should we do?

Do? What can we do?

She felt the baby move. A cry rose from the riders as they bore down upon them, a cry meant to strike fear into the heart. It worked. The riders and horses were upon them: rushing past, a thundering herd. Alexandra heard her sister say, "Ahh shit." She immediately agreed with her analysis.

Bethany stepped closer to her, standing beside her. "This isn't all that good, is it?" she said off handedly. Alexandra didn't answer.

A rider loped up on a thin gray horse, pulling on the bridle, flinging dirt and rocks every which way. He led two horses.

How convenient, Alexandra thought. *They waited for us. This was planned.*

The painted warrior looked as if he had been dipped in war paint for it covered his face, chest, even his bare legs.

You're such a mess, she thought.

Jumping off into the fray, he said something to the girls in another language: harsh sounds, obviously an order, at the same time pointing at the horses. He started toward them, angrily repeating himself as he approached, his right fist around the hilt of a knife tucked in his waistband.

Behind him, She Who Likes Bitter Berries ran, attempting escape. Escape where? Painted warriors were everywhere. Two riders raced up behind the woman, one on either side. She was struck from behind and knocked to the ground, ending in a moaning heap. One, the rider on the left, leaped off his horse, picked up the limp body, and threw it over the back of his mount, swinging up behind her body. Yelling, he kicked the horse in the ribs and proceeded at a gallop toward the creek.

"Get on, Beth, or he'll kill us."

"Get . . . get on?" Bethany said, her hands covering her cheek bones, her eyes wide, and her mouth wide open. Momentarily, she held her breath, glancing about as if thinking of an alternative.

"Yes, do it now. Do you hear me! Do it now. We haven't any choice."

Bethany, all fifteen years of her, stepped forward, grabbed the horse's mane, and swung up on its back. It was the closest horse, a bay with a blaze in the middle of its forehead. Alexandra followed suit. The warrior was screaming, as if increasing the volume would assist them in understanding what he was trying to communicate. It didn't.

Oh, shut up! Alexandra thought, glancing east toward the creek, then west. There was no one familiar. The guardians were nowhere to be seen.   *You've got to be kidding. How can this happen?*

Once they were mounted, the loud mouth rider swung up on his horse, kicking him into motion; the lead ropes were immediately

306

taut, pulling them forward. Almost instantly they were running at a gallop. Without slowing they crossed the Greasy Grass in a plunging spray, then loped up across the west ridge, disappearing into a stand of old cottonwood. Soon they were joined by others.

The two girls had clung frantically to the backs of the plunging animals, their hands wrapped tightly around the horse's manes, their legs squeezing the horses' sides to keep from falling. It happened in an eye blink. In less than a minute they could no longer see camp. Somewhere to the east there were shouts. The riders seemed momentarily disoriented, swirling, then leading off at a canter, south. They moved swiftly, faster than Alexandra thought possible, joined by others. Inside a mile there were approximately fifty of them with what seemed a hundred stolen horses and seven captives, all women except for one small boy clinging behind his mother. They wasted no time, riding south into the hilly country between the Greasy Grass and the big mountain to the south.

Must be Absaroka Crow, Alexandra thought.

Who else? Blackfeet?

Probably not. I really can't believe this. Now what?

And God in Heaven, we might have gotten away. Soon! All three of us. One more day. As if they knew. As if anyone knew.

She glanced around her, behind her.

So many.

What do the Absaroka do with white women dressed in doe skin, their hair in long braids? It's just another 'ahh shit.' Can't anything go right? Just one time? Just once.

Does it matter? What's the difference? Walking Eagle or someone else? Think. Think.

About what? Why bother? I'm pregnant, stupid.

Least we're going in the right direction. South. Right?

Right.

As if that makes a difference.

Think. Get hold of yourself. Do something.

What? Just what? There's too many. Anything I do will get Beth killed. And me.

What difference does it make?

Oh, shut up. You idiot.

So escape! Outrun them!

How? They'll easily catch us, overpower us. I'm so slow.

Maybe not.
So what do we do?
Stay alive. That's what.
I can't take this. Who'd believe it?

Alexandra found herself in the middle of the cavalcade with Bethany a horse's length in front of her. There were six women: their names were She Who Likes Bitter Berries, Ptaaysanwee, meaning White Buffalo Woman, Ehawee or Laughing Girl, Magaskawee, meaning She Who Walks With Grace, Bethany, and Alexandra. She and Bethany had names, too, not all that complimentary. Bethany was named She Who Walks With Hand On Knife. Alexandra was referred to as Angry Woman. All this Alexandra had learned from Small Dove. She was slowly catching on. The language was so difficult.

She Who Likes Bitter Berries looked beat up and was barely staying on the back of her bareback horse. Their captors rode, intent on reaching safety in the Big Horns. It was winter on top of the mountain. She doubted they were going up there.

In the beginning they moved at a canter, then slowed to a fast trot. Sundown came. They kept moving. Night shrouded the land. There was no stopping. Day, night, and day merged. They reached the Tongue River and started a slow ascent into the mountain, riding beside it.

Alexandra resigned herself to the journey, to an unknown ending, to a baby moving inside her.

It's going to be cold up there. She thought. *I hate that. And God only knows what else.*

CHAPTER 50
Zeke is 27 miles from Alexandra on Upper Goose Creek

April 7, 1855
Tongue River
Central Nebraska Territory

A day later, midmorning, a rider appeared on a rise four hundred fifty yards away, maybe more, but not much. He sat his horse, his back to the bald hill behind him; to his right lay the Tongue River and the rush of many waters. He was much too far away for Alexandra to tell who he was, probably another Absaroka waiting to greet the returning war party. Probably he was waiting to celebrate capturing so many horses, six new women, and a boy.

There was something about him, something oddly familiar.

You've seen one, she thought, *you've seen them all.*

The horseman didn't move.

A breeze picked up, twisting Alexandra's hair, pulling it across her lips, covering her eyes. Brushing it aside, she glanced to her left. Bethany, her face somber, had seen him, too. They looked at each other. Bethany's hair was in total disarray, hanging in her face. She sat astride her horse, her dress riding up her thigh past the tops of her leggings.

If she knew how she looked. Alexandra shrugged. *It hardly mattered.* The baby moved. She rested her left hand on her belly.

In the distance the rider sat bareback atop a tall bay horse who, like its rider, was watching the approaching procession.

Lots of men ride bay horses, she thought.

Not like this one. This one simply sat there. Who was he?

Nobody, I suppose. I wouldn't know.

How would I know? Just someone waiting to greet these warriors.

Turning, she glanced behind her, then back at the lone rider. From that distance she could see he wore eagle feathers. Probably three, bound and woven, into his long hair just behind his left ear.

Was it him? Him? Who, him?

Yeah, right. Him. I've had more than enough of him. How would he be here?

He wore no face paint; neither was the bay decorated with

hand prints or lightning bolts. He carried no shield, no bow, no arrows, and no lance. He held a rifle, a Hawkens, in front of him across his body, muzzle pointed slightly upward. Nothing else. One shot and he'd have to reload. That was the trouble with a Hawkens.

How would I know it was a Hawkens?

Just another Absaroka Crow. Probably a scout.

She glanced at her sister then at the river, then back at the rider.

Something is going on.

His demeanor appeared relaxed; he sat easy, his horse standing still, unmoving, silent. On his right and left were tall pine, a dark menace bleeding into a forest. Behind him was the morning and the rising slope of a greening hill climbing steeper as it reached to touch the edges of dark rain clouds.

Her captors kept riding as though they hadn't seen him. But they had.

Just another scout. Someone they know obviously. No one seems concerned. One of them. Who else?

After all, it was one man in a forest of pine. But something had changed. Those riding behind her came up closer to the front of the column. The weapons that were always available seemed more accessible: war shields that had been carried on the backs of warriors suddenly were on their arms. Rifles and pistols were now in hand along with a multitude of spears, bows, arrows, and war clubs. Talking ceased. Their forward movement continued unabated.

This can't be normal.

The rider, closer now, sat easy on the back of the bay as if waiting for stragglers.

The procession did not stop, did not slow, and moved steadily forward.Around the captive women, the collective attention of the raiding party seemed to be elsewhere as though expecting a trap: waiting for it to be sprung. Glancing to her right and left, Alexandra saw nothing that justified such a concern but the men that comprised the raiding party did. Theirs was an assumption, a resignation of the inevitable; a trap was about to be sprung.

What trap? There's just one rider.

She chuckled at the absurdity. But a palpable urgency permeated the air; she could feel it. But there was nothing to justify the conclusion.

It's just one more Indian. One of theirs, undoubtedly.

But something's different. What are they seeing that I don't?

Bethany looked at her. "Who's that?" she asked.

"I don't know. Whoever it is, he seems to have everyone's attention."

"Do you think . . .?"

"I don't know, Beth. But something is about to happen."

The lone horseman, much closer now, started his mount forward at a walk, his rifle pointing straight up into the morning sky. Though he was closer now, she still didn't know who he was; the horse and rider stood in the dark shadows of the pine forest. Odd, how relaxed he appeared. Yet, at the same time, alert.

Out in front, on the rise, the "easy-going" rider suddenly kicked the bay into a trot, descending down the long trail, the short stock of the Hawkens rifle resting on his thigh. The muzzle was pointed up into the azure sky. She imagined the hammer pulled back and locked in place.

It would be if he was attacking. But why would he be attacking his own people? But he isn't Absaroka, is he? Oh, my word. Is this happening? One against so many? This is pure crazy.

There was something oddly familiar about this scene. Three years earlier Alexandra and her grandfather had read in the paper about the charge made by a group of British soldiers, a light brigade. Six hundred men alone against inconceivable odds, riding forward into a line of cannon. It was Christmas time and she'd just celebrated her fifteenth birthday. The story was in the *Boston Herald*. Her grandfather had purchased the paper and was reading it, sitting in her mother's rocking chair, rocking back and forth, muttering to himself. She smiled, thinking about her grandfather. That was so long ago. She wondered if this was how it was, except more men, many more, and cannon on the right and left.

"Volley'd and thunder'd." Wasn't that it?

"Listen to this, girl," her grandfather had said. "These fellows got some real hair on their chests." After saying that, he read the article aloud to her. He'd read a poem written by someone named Alfred Tennyson. It was all in the paper. "How about that?" he'd said. "I've never heard the like."

Neither had she.

So many willing to die. Sort of stupid.

311

An Absaroka warrior riding near Alexandra shouted at the rider, suddenly pulling up, firing his rifle at him. He missed. The rider kept advancing, more quickly now, not bothering to avoid the coming onslaught. Suddenly he kicked the bay into a gallop, thrusting his rifle above his head, shouting something unintelligible, a primal scream. Whatever he said was loud, echoing against the hillside, breaking the silence like an axe on ice. Those around her seemed to understand what he said.

Four Absaroka warriors kicked their mounts forward, racing to meet him, waving their weapons in the air, returning his shout.

What's he doing? Are you kidding me? Is he crazy? He hasn't fired the Hawkens. If it is a Hawkens.

The bay's belly and legs were stretched out, its ears pointed in front of him as it raced toward the four riders. She watched him bring the barrel of his rifle up, stock to his shoulder. A white puff of smoke came from the lock and from the end of the barrel. The rider next to her was knocked "ass over tea cup" off the back of his horse. That's what her grandfather would say: "ass over tea cup." She wondered what it meant.

I mean, really.

"Beth," she screamed. "Beth?"

A sudden commotion erupted in the rear of the column of riders. Alexandra turned to see what it was. Suddenly surrounded by mass confusion, men were rising up on all sides, blood curdling shouts intermingled with Bethany's screams. Horse flesh slammed into horse flesh as attackers rushed the Absaroka war party. Fighting was hand to hand. There were shouts, the swinging of battle axes, the swirl and pounding of horse upon horse, men swinging into action.

There was no quarter for no quarter was asked; none was expected; none was given.

Alexandra turned to see the lone rider break through the midst of the four Absaroka warriors, shooting at one with the Walker Colt, the barrel of the Hawkens rifle in his left hand. She couldn't tell if the shot hit anything. The bay suddenly braced itself, throwing its hind legs beneath his charging body. The rider spun the horse around on its back legs as he tried to club the warrior closest to him with the stock of the rifle. Theys immediately re-engaged, trying to knock one another from the backs of their horses. The bay plunged into the melee, its rider swinging the rifle by the barrel. She recognized the boom of a

312

Walker Colt. Once. Twice.

Walking Eagle! she thought. *Who else? You've got to be kidding.*

Wrong hero. Wrong place. Wrong everything. Just wrong. The evil bastard! This is too much!

Alexandra looked for her sister, only to see her tumbling off her horse, the horse rearing, jerking the lead rope from the hands of the warrior who had held it, Bethany no longer his concern. Alexandra kicked her mount in the ribs, sending it crashing into the warrior in front of her and, at the same time, pushing herself off its back as it bowled forward. She hit the earth, rolled, fell down, and got up. She was knocked down again by something or someone as she struggled to get to Bethany. She grabbed her sister and tried to push her out of the way, a good move except that there was no "out of the way."

Alexandra turned. A huge bay galloped past her at a dead run, slamming into another mounted warrior. Its rider lashed out at the horseman, jabbing with a long spear, then swinging it in an attempt to knock him off his horse. He failed. Around and around they went, ramming into one another, horses rearing, turning, charging. Alexandra dodged to get out of the way. And like her grandfather, she'd never seen the like, standing in the middle of pitch battle in the mountainous northern plains of Nebraska Territory.

She jumped to get out of the way. When she looked back, both riders were on the ground, in mortal battle, a wood handled knife against a rifle stock. The conflict ended abruptly. Walking Eagle shot his opponent with the Walker Colt. He looked at her, and shoved the heavy pistol into this waist belt. Seizing the bay horse's lead rope, he swung up on his back, kicking his sides with the heels of his feet. In a driving flurry he was gone.

Oh my God, she thought.

Behind her she heard She Who Loves Bitter Berries' distinctive voice screaming in terror. Turning, Alexandra saw her hit the ground. An Absaroka warrior had her by the arm, while contending with another. Alexandra recognized the other: the young man that Small Dove described as having a brave heart, fearless, one to be reckoned with. He was advancing, knife in hand, no shield. At the time Small Dove had told her about him, Alexandra had wondered how such despicable people could have a "brave heart," be "fearless," be a "hero." How could the enemy, the slayer of innocent people, be "wonderful" in battle, a power to be reckoned with? The Absaroka

313

warrior was forced to release She Who Loves Bitter Berries to meet the advance of the shirtless Oglala. Alexandra ran to her, seizing her by the arm, pulling her to the relative safety of the fallen pine trunk. Bethany was standing up, a pine club in hand, in complete disarray, screaming at anything and anybody who came close to her. Everyone was busy with his own private Armageddon and paid her no attention.

The Absaroka warrior circled to the younger man's left.

So young. Too young to die. Oh no.

Alarmed, and without thinking, definitely without thinking, Alexandra seized Bethany's club, jerking it out of her hands, then charged through last year's knee high grass, jumping a clump of sage brush. Coming from behind, she struck the Absaroka warrior over the head, the unexpected blow knocking him to his knees. He rolled and came gracefully to his feet, shaking his head.

I hit you, she thought. *I hit you. Why are you . . .? Ahh, shit.*

The Absaroka warrior laughed; he laughed in the middle of pitch battle, amused by the ferocity generated by a white woman in a doe skin dress wielding a wooden club. Unharmed, he glanced at the shirtless one, then grabbed a wandering, bewildered mount, and swung up on his back in one smoothly athletic motion. He was still laughing. Jabbing his newfound horse in the ribs with his heels, horse and rider rushed at the young one who, to save himself, threw himself aside. The shoulder of the horse struck him anyway sending him sprawling.

Alexandra threw her club at the rider, missed, then ran to pick it up, thinking she needed it. She saw neither combatant again that day. The battle surged past her, leaving a flat silence except for the rush of wind through the pine needle forest and the roar of the river, its white waters tumbling across rock and boulders. There was suddenly no one trying to take her life or that of her sister. The Absaroka were gone. The young one and Walking Eagle--all gone.

She picked up a broken spear and the club and hurriedly returned to Bethany. Along the way she found the brave hearted boy and brought him to the old log. Soon she had a group—if five is a group. From the north came shouts, but they were far away, too far for Alexandra to know what was going on. The boy wanted to leave. She told him in broken Oglala, somehow, that the women needed a guardian and these women were his responsibility.

He must have understood her for, reluctantly, he stayed. She gave him the spear she'd picked up. She also found Young Snake; he'd

314

been run through, suffering a stomach wound. At first she didn't know how bad it was. The spear was still in the wound, its obsidian point partially jutting out his back just above the hip bone.

This can't be good., she thought. After a quick second glance she concluded there was nothing that she could do for him, nothing anyone could do for him. *This one's dying, He isn't going to make it.*

"Beth, over here. Over here," she yelled. "Come here. I need you."

When Bethany arrived, she glanced at Alexandra, then at Young Snake, his white fingered hands gripping the shaft of a lance protruding from his belly. She started to shake her head.

Alexandra interrupted. She said, "Sis . . ." her voice trailing off. She paused, as if thinking.

What do you want, Lexie?" Bethany asked. "This one's dying, isn't he? I can tell you that." She cast a furtive glance behind her, then at Alexandra noting the blood leaking from around the protruding spear shaft in Young Snake's belly.

"I know. I see that. It's pretty bad. Should we do something? I mean help him? Make him comfortable?" Alexandra glanced at her sister. "I guess we should."

"No, we shouldn't," Bethany said slowly. "We don't belong here, Lexie. Nobody asked us. What we need to do is get out of here. He's dying so let him alone."

Alexandra nodded in agreement. She asked, "Should we make him comfortable? Get him some water? Maybe we should get that thing out of him. I'll have a look around. You take care of him best you can. I'll be back. I'll see if I can find some horses." She paused, looking at her sister. "Beth?"

"I'm doing it, Lexie. It's just hard . . . so confusing. I'm thinking we should just disappear? Right now? Right now would be a real good time. No one is watching. That's the Big Horn Mountain right there."

Alexandra looked at her sister. "It's winter up there. Beth, we can't get over it and what about Pris? Should we leave her? Forget her? Beth, some of these . . . they need help. We should help. Oh, my God, I hate this. I don't know what to do."

Bethany stared at her, wordless for a moment. She said, "Oh Pris. I forgot about her."

Alexandra was nearly crying. "I . . . ," she began.

315

"All right," Bethany interrupted. "All right. Pris makes it difficult to decide. She sure does. We can't just leave her. You're right. But I do think we should be concerned with ourselves. That's what I think. This sure isn't our fight. This isn't our war. Know what I mean? We shouldn't even be here, Lexie. That's what I think."

"I know. I know. Look, I'm going to look around, see if I can find some horses. Do what you think is best with him." She nodded at Young Snake looking up at them, his skin pale, his lips quivering, and turned to leave.

"Alone? You're leaving me here alone?"

"Beth, that boy is dying. He needs something. See what you can do for him. Okay?" Alexandra was staring at her. She wiped her eyes. "Okay? I'll be back. Then we'll go. Figure out how we're going to get Pris. I don't know. I don't know anymore."

Bethany shook her head in bewilderment and watched her sister's retreat.

"Ahh shit," she said. "Shit, shit, shit. That's what I'm saying." Bethany pursed her lips, then turned and looked at Young Snake.

"What can I do for you?" she asked looking at the distressed boy. "You don't understand a word I'm saying. Do you? My, that is nasty, nasty. Hurt? Of course it hurts. I guess I'll start with cleaning the wound, washing away the blood. Mother said that was the first thing. I need hot water. But there isn't any. So what? Who needs it?" She looked for her sister and couldn't see her. She looked down at the wounded boy. "We need water. So, I'll be back," she said. "Bet you've heard that before. I have. That's all I've heard. That and we're escaping. That's all I've heard. Yet here I am."

Bethany found water, a river full of it. She made use of a water bladder, a buffalo cow stomach, and brought it back to where Young Snake was lying.

"Want some?" she asked, handing him the bladder. After he finished drinking, she poured a small stream on the boy's belly, wiped it off with her fingers, then did it again.

"A rag would be nice. Except there aren't any rags."

Steadily she washed the blood from the boy's stomach: pouring water on, letting it run in little rivulets off his belly. He said something. Bethany glanced at him; she didn't understand a word he spoke.

"Well, there's these leggings. I guess I could use them. Sort of dirty, though. Don't soak up water or blood. Nothing. But . . . " She

316

sat down and removed the legging from her calf. Using it, she dabbed blood from the wound until he seized her hand. She looked at him.

Very big brown eyes, she thought. "I'd have big brown eyes, too if I had a spear sticking out of my belly. What do you want? I can't read your mind . . . especially when it's in another language."

Pulling a knife from his belt, he flipped the blade in one hand and handed it to her bone hilt first.

Surprised by the sudden movement, she paused. "I guess you're not dead, yet," she said. A thought dawned on her; she looked at him, shaking her head. "Ohh, no," she said, "I'm not going to kill you. I'd like to, but no, I won't. This is a bad, bad wound. I'm not going to cut that stick out either. You'll die. Why rush it? If that's of any help. I wish I knew what I was doing."

He still proffered her the knife.

"So what's with the knife?" she asked taking it by the hilt.

His face showed no emotion. He touched the shaft. Pointed to the knife.

"Oh," she said. "Cut it . . . that what you want? I can do that, I guess." Bethany ran the edge along her index finger. "Not the sharpest blade in the bunch, is it? Haven't you ever heard of a whetstone? This thing couldn't cut water if it had a head start."

He touched the shaft again. He stared at her.

Shrugging her shoulders, Bethany began sawing at the shaft, taking small bites out of the wood. Half an hour later she'd cut it half way through. Still no Alexandra. With more effort, more sawing, she was finally able to break the shaft into two parts: the short end protruding from the left side of the boy's lower belly. She tossed the other part behind her and studied the wound.

"Ahh, shit," she said aloud and looked at the young man. "I sure say that a lot, don't I?"

"What did you say?"

Bethany looked up at her sister. "You heard me? Do you want me to repeat myself? Where have you been? He proposed marriage. I had five kids. We have a dog and a mule. Lucky me. Where's the horses? I don't see any horses. How are we going to get out of here?"

"I couldn't find any. You going to pull it through his back? Is that what you're doing? That's why you cut the spear, right? To shorten it? Good idea. I thought you just wanted to let him be."

Bethany looked at her. "It's not my idea. I don't know what

317

I'm doing. He asked me to saw it in two. I think he did. Does it matter? He is dying."

"I don't think you can pull it out the way it went in. Not with that point already sticking out his back. That'd cause more damage."

"Me, neither. I think we should be going. He's going to die. Why are we standing here? Let's go while we can."

"I know what you think. I think that, too. But we're afoot. And I really don't know what to do. Do you? Tell me. Do we walk? Where? Do we wait? Do we hide? We don't know who is coming back from this fight. We don't know who won. We don't know what to do about Pris. We don't know anything. All right. Let's help this boy you started on and figure out what we're going to do."

"Then it might be too late," Bethany said. "Plus that, I don't want to help him."

"What about Pris?" Alexandra said.

"I don't know what to do about her, but we need to do something. We need to do it now."

"We can't leave Pris."

"I agree. We can't. You make it sound like I'm abandoning her.

"I didn't say that. I'm not making you sound like anything."

"I'm not a bad person. I'm not," Bethany said.

"I know you're not."

"How can you say I was?"

"I didn't. Let's finish with what you started here and we'll do whatever you want."

"Whatever I want? I'll remember you said that. Help this boy?" Bethany studied the young man's face. "How old do you think he is?"

Alexandra looked at him. "Fifteen, maybe."

"He is just a boy."

"Same as you."

"Yeah. We're just kids raised in different parts of the country together. I know. I used to watch his baby sister. I actually did that, you know?"

Alexandra nodded and smiled. "Sure you did. Want me to help?" she asked.

"Yeah. Help me get out of here."

Alexandra stared at her.

"Yeah, help me. I don't know what I'm doing. I just hacked the spear in two because he asked me to. I didn't know what I was doing then, either."

"How about I sit him up? You pull it the rest of the way through."

"Do I have to, Lexie? It sounds painful. It sounds awful. He's going to die. Why not just leave him alone?"

"Who else is there? ?"

"Right. Right. Who else is there?"

"I have another idea. Let's turn him on his side. That way we don't have to hold him up. I don't think he wants to be held up. We lay him on his side and you can grab hold of the point. I'll push from the other side."

"Right, Lexie. Right. I'll tug. You push. He dies. What's wrong with that? Don't you get it? He's going to die no matter what."

"We have to do something."

"Lexie, listen to yourself. I don't like him. I want to kill him. For some unfathomable reason you want to save him. What's wrong with that picture?" Bethany said, staring at her sister. Rethinking her words, she immediately said, "Okay. Okay. Let's get it done. He's dying. You know it. I'm tired. Might as well rush it if we can." Bethany looked at her sister. "I didn't mean that," she said.

"I know you didn't."

"Okay," she said. "Let's do something. I think we ought to just let him alone."

"With that thing inside him?"

"Removing it is just going to hurt him. Why do that?" Bethany looked at her sister. "All right," she said, "have it your way."

Alexandra took him by the shoulders and with Bethany's help, rolled him onto his side. He groaned.

Bethany looked at her sister as if to tell her "I told you so," then got behind him and braced her feet against the boy's back. She seized the spear's obsidian point. "You ready, Lexie?"

"No, I'm not."

"On three?"

"On three."

"Okay, but it has to happen first try. He can't take it and I can't take it."

"Right. Right. Let's get on with it." Alexandra paused, then started her count. "One . . . two . . . three."

Bethany pulled on the blood slick obsidian; Alexandra pushed.

To her surprise Bethany pulled the broken spear the rest of the way through the boy's left side and out his back. It slid out and made her a little sick watching the red blood leaking out both sides, front and back, at the same time. First it was a gush, then slowed down to a trickle. Dark, red blood.

The boy gasped, groaned, his face pallid, his eyes rolling into the back of his head. Mercifully, he passed out.

"Ahh, shit," Bethany said again. "We killed him."

"Beth," Alexandra responded, hesitating, "he's still breathing."

"You mean he's not dead? We didn't kill him?"

"He's still breathing."

"I heard you. So now what?"

"Besides washing your mouth out with lye soap?"

"Nobody here knows I said a swear word." Bethany looked at her sister. "Except you."

"Beth?"

"What?"

"I think we need some moss. Lots of it."

"He was bleeding pretty bad, wasn't he? It's slowed. Think he's dying right now? We could just wait."

"Beth. Please."

"Lexie, he can't understand a word I'm saying."

Alexandra nodded. "Maybe bleeding is good," she said. "Maybe it'll clean the wound."

"Maybe."

"Are you getting some moss or what? We need it to soak up the blood and cover the wound. Hurry."

"I'm hurrying," Bethany replied.

"Hey wait. I'll get the moss; you clean the wound."

Bethany cleaned the wound and was relieved when the bleeding stopped. Alexandra brought her handfuls of moss from which they made a poultice, matting the moss over the wound.

Alexandra looked at her sister. "Think that'll work?"

"No, but there it is. At least we didn't kill him. Not right away. But he is dying." Bethany looked at the boy, smiled, then slipped the bloodied blade inside his waistband, hilt sticking out. "He's still breathing. That's something."

"What'd you do that for?"

"What?"

320

"The knife?"

"It's his."

"Oh."

Bethany stood up, addressing the limp body. "Sorry," she said to him. "Hope you get well. Wish you understood what I'm saying. Glad you can't. I'm glad you're not dead." She looked at Alexandra. "Well, I am," she said. "I'm glad. I should say 'Ahh, shit. But you won't let me. Can we go now?"

"Yes. We can go now. There's one thing you have going: he isn't dead."

"Thanks for the vote of confidence. Don't you know I am a graduate of Harvard Medical?"

"You're the graduate of nothing. You never escaped the sixth grade."

"I know. But Grandfather showed me how to cure a sore on a bull's butt. We used tobacco leaf."

"Did it live?"

"Long enough to get butchered. That long enough?"

Alexandra smiled, "Yes, Doctor Wakeford, graduate of bull's butts. At least you lived in the same state as Harvard Medical, your claim to fame."

"Yes, and don't forget the bull lived long enough to die."

"I won't forget. Where are we going to go?"

Bethany looked at her. "You mean without Pris? I don't know."

"Me, either.

The warriors began to return: some across the backs of their horses, some bleeding, some with no scrapes at all.

Alexandra said to her sister, "Beth, do you think they came for us. Are we what this fight was about?"

"No, Lexie, we're not. They came for their horses. They came because they were embarrassed. Their coming had nothing to do with us. We just happened to be here. What's wrong with you? Have you lost your mind? They don't care about us at all."

The boy groaned. The two girls turned to the sound. He was still lying on his side, breathing heavily, the poultices on the entry wound and on the exit wounds bound about him with a vine.

"Well, we did the best we could," Alexandra said.

"Yes, we did."

"I think it looks pretty good."

Several of the returning warrors looked at Young Snake and the girls' handiwork. They talked among themselves.

"What are those men saying?" Bethany asked.

"Which men?"

"Those men."

I don't know. How am I supposed to know?"

"I heard you speaking to them."

"I know how to say hello. What good is that?"

"You said more than that."

"I said 'hello, how are you?' What good is that?"

One approached the two girls interrupting their arguing. He had an ugly wound on his arm that had bled profusely. He started talking and pointed at his arm.

"That's nasty," Bethany said to Alexandra. "What's he want? My congratulations?"

"You know what he wants. He wants it cleaned, bandaged."

"Are we going to? Can I say no?"

"Do you want to say no?"

"You know I do. What if we take care of him and he gets some sort of infection and his arm falls off? What if that boy dies? What, then?"

"Beth, what do you want to do?"

"I want to go home."

"Okay. Me, too. What about right now?"

"I guess we should clean it. A little. That can't hurt. At least it won't hurt me."

"Do you want to sew it together? The skin, I mean."

"How are we going to do that? We don't have any needle and thread."

"How about a porcupine quill and some dried gut? That might work."

"Yes, it might. Who do you think you are? Betsy Ross?" she said, her words dripping with sarcasm. "You do it. I don't sew."

"Right. You don't sew?"

"Not on a live arm, I don't. The bleeding kind."

"There's always a first time."

"Jeez, Lexie. Don't you ever give up? We should have left when I said."

322

"What about Pris?"

"We should have left to go get her. I said I don't know. You're making me look bad. "Betsy Ross?"

They rode and walked all the way back to the Greasy Grass, changing poultices on the wounded as often as possible, doctoring the scrapes and wounds. It took two days. The boy was still alive but not moving much. The way back was different; there were outriders and guards of all kinds. They were never alone. They encountered no trouble.

CHAPTER 51
Zeke is 38 miles south of Alexandra on Upper Goose Creek

April 9, 1855
Greasy Grass Creek
Central Nebraska Territory

Priscilla ran to meet them. "Oh, my God, my God," she cried. I was so worried. I . . . I . . . I'm so glad you're both all right." She was crying.

They stood hugging each other on the edge of Greasy Grass Creek. They arrived at camp with the sun directly overhead and didn't stay long. What little time they remained in winter camp was difficult. Everyone was expecting more trouble from the Absaroka. The guard was doubled; it was tripled at night. Next morning they were moving and moving made all the difference. There were a dozen reasons for it beyond the threat of attack. Principally, the firewood was gone, last year's grass was gone, the dried meat was nearly gone. There were no more dried berries to make pemmican. And lastly, it was spring; it was time to move.

The village fathers' decision to move wasn't difficult. The lodges were already dismantled. Come morning the retrieved horses were ready, the travoises were packed, even the dogs were engaged. Thus, they began the trek north. Somewhere ahead was more of everything. It gave everyone a new hope.

Young Snake had his own travois, his mother leading the pony that pulled it. She concentrated on finding a path that was not littered in rocks and bumps. He was alive but not happy. In spite of it he got better. It was Alexandra who didn't feel well. She thought it might be a cold: hopefully, not dysentery, hopefully, not a dozen other diseases that white people brought to the lodges of the Teton Lakota, killing many people. Fortunately, no one else seemed to be sick except for Young Snake. When they stopped, he tried to walk but his belly hurt. The scar turned a dreadful pink, then purple. At least it wasn't green and it didn't smell.

Bethany announced her opinion after examining his belly. "I'm telling you he's not going to die," she said.

"I hope not," Alexandra replied.

324

"I hope not, too, he being my first patient. Wouldn't look good, I'm thinking." She touched the skinning knife in her waist belt. "If he dies, I might have to defend myself."

"Yes, you might."

Bethany looked at her sister. "You don't look so good, Lexie. Are you all right?"

"I don't feel well."

"What's wrong?"

"I don't know. The baby, maybe. My nose is running. Probably a cold. That's what I'm thinking."

"It isn't pneumonia?"

"I'm not coughing. I'm sure it's just a cold. I'll be all right. I'll get something in my stomach. I'll feel better. The thought of eating jerked meat is sickening all by itself. I really don't want to do that."

Walking Eagle's band of Oglala made their way north. As the crow flies, if there had been a crow and if a crow actually flew in a straight line, it was one hundred and eighty-three miles from the Greasy Grass to the confluence of the Judith River and Dry Wolf Creek, north-central Nebraska Territory. It took sixteen days, averaging between ten and sixteen miles a day. But there weren't any crows, and they had to travel even farther because some mountains must be ridden around and not through; some creeks are rivers and can't be forded just anywhere. It took time: sixteen days.

Two weeks and two days later, camp was pitched where Dry Wolf Creek entered the Judith River a few miles south of the Missouri Breaks and the big river.

CHAPTER 52
Alexandra is 38 miles north of Zeke on Greasy Grass Creek

April 10, 1855
Upper Goose Creek
Central Nebraska Territory

Winters vary. Even over a few miles they are different: some less severe, some more. Behind the dugout cabin it was four miles to the top of the mountain where the snow drifted in twenty-five foot drifts. Some of the drifts were deeper, larger; some, smaller, depending on the wind. On top of the mountain it was colder than hell; hell wouldn't have it any colder. Up there it was cold longer, and was much more intense than where Goose Creek entered the Tongue a few miles away. Ten miles east of the cabin toward the Crazy Woman, the drifts were smaller, prone to melting in a southern breeze.

On the side of the mountain, where the storms marched along the northern slopes of the Big Horn, they left tons of snow and deep drifts. Winter there was longer and more severe than elsewhere. North, thirty-eight miles toward the Greasy Grass, the south wind melted the snow quickly and there generally wasn't as much. On the hills above the creek the prairie grass began to turn green sooner. On the side of the big mountain, Zeke hunted firewood, built fires to keep warm, and waited for spring. On Greasy Grass Creek it had arrived.

On April 10, 1855, when Zeke and Emile Villon left the dugout on Upper Goose Creek, Alexandra was standing in front of Walking Eagle's lodge on the Greasy Grass watching it be dismantled. She felt her baby move, a butterfly fluttering in her belly. Two days later when Zeke reached the Greasy Grass, she was north of him a little less than thirty miles, moving slowly, walking beside a bay horse pulling a travois and carrying some of the dismantled lodge of Walking Eagle. Around her, Spring was advancing; green grass was once again becoming plentiful. Alexandra's pregnancy was pushing towards three and half months. She was continually aware of her changing, evolving body. Placing one foot in front of another, rubbing her belly, she again felt the baby move and wondered, knowing her life had irrevocably changed.

CHAPTER 53
Alexandra is 43 miles north of Zeke on the Musselshell

April 11, 1855
Greasy Grass Creek
North Central Nebraska Territory

"Who's thet?"

Emile Villon stood beside his mule in a shallow depression and watched the cavalcade of riders break the cottonwood trees on the east side of Greasy Grass Creek, then stop. The riders were spread out. Most remained in the protection of the timber.

"Your people?" Zeke asked.

"No. Not my people."

"Look like Injuns to me."

"It's what they are. We shouldn't be standin' talkin'. We gots ta hide. It may be too late."

Villon was talking as if he was the only one listening, using a soft reflective voice, one of resignation. Villon, however, did not move, paying no attention to his own advice.

"Hide? What for? Emile, answer me. Who are they? Why should we hide?"

"Not Lakota."

"Not Lakota?"

"Absaroka."

Zeke stared down the long slow incline to the creek, to the mounted horsemen waiting: some in, some out of the cottonwoods a good five hundred yards away. He looked beyond the creek where the land rose to meet the dark, cloudy sky. It was turning green. The horsemen held his attention. There were at least thirty men, many painted for war; some were wounded. All carried some form of armament: bows, arrows, spears, rifles. Their shields were on their arms, not hanging from their horses' necks or resting on their backs. They did not charge out into the open; instead, they held their position in the greening cottonwoods. After a few minutes two riders rode up the creek and two down. They were looking for someone, something.

This don't look good.

"Absaroka? So, who are they? These Absaroka? Shouldn't we

327

ride down there and talk to 'em? Maybe they know somethin'."

"Ya ride down, ya ain't ridin' back."

Emile Villon and his mule were partially hidden from the riders, standing in a depression. Zeke was beside him, their pack animals ground hitched thirty feet down the slope in a ravine, partially hidden by buck brush and sage. O'Reilly was lying in the shade cast by the bay packhorse.

Emile grunted. He said, "Absaroka . . . the Crow. I know these Injuns. With 'em there's always a fight. We steal theys horses, theys women. They steal our horses, our women. Always countin' plenty coup. It's been this way fer all time."

"They don't look happy."

"Not happy a'tall. They's angry. Must've come from a big fight. See their wounded; they's comin' fer blood, ta count coup, fer a good death. They ain't happy one bit."

This is different.

Zeke glanced at Emile and wondered how much he'd changed, really changed, how much he could trust him, if he could trust him. This was something new, something different. Emile Villon had an actual fear of those riders on the creek. Maybe not fear: maybe it was respect.

"Well, one thing's for sure, we ride out of this hole, they're gonna see us."

"See us?" Emile was staring at Zeke. "They don't need ta see us. They'll know we're here. It'll be a good fight, a good day ta die. We gots ta get ready."

He's serious.

"Seems to me you've already got yourself buried."

"There's too many of 'em fer us ta kill. Not too much of us." He paused. "No matter." Emile was pulling his rifle from the scabbard his mule carried: the old Hawkens. He looked at Zeke. "Sometimes nothin' matters. This time nothin' matters. No place ta hide. Out in the open. We ride out of this place, they'll see us. They've come ta count coup, ta take scalps. For 'em it's about lost honor, lost pride; they gots ta show great bravery. For us, it's ta die . . . die well. We make our deaths good ones. Ones ta remember. Today they'll carry many bodies on the backs of their horses."

Whoa! I didn't know you had it in you, Emile. I'm not sure I'm quite ready to give it all up, though.

328

Zeke looked at his companion. "Hey," he said, "maybe we should just stay put. They ain't seen us. Maybe they won't."

"Kid," Villon said, "ar ya blind? We crossed the creek where they's standin'. Our trail's right in front of 'em. They'll follow us ta where we ar. The Absaroka follow trails. They's careful. Right now, real careful. This place here's where Walking Eagle camped fer the winter." Villon pointed south. "See how many lodge rings they is? The Absaroka knows this. Ya kin expect a big fight. They's lookin' fer Walking Eagle. He's not here. I'd say he left two, three days, maybe four days ago. He's not here. We ar'. The Absaroka ar' followin' Walking Eagle, but they's found us. They's gonna kill us instead. I think maybe you'll need your short guns. We is gonna die today. There's just too many Absaroka. Too many fer us ta kill 'em all."

"They ain't left the creek yet."

"They will."

"I suppose so. But a man never can tell. Before we bury ourselves, let's see what they do. It ain't over 'til it's over and I ain't dead yet. I still gots a round or two in the chamber."

"Ya gots one fer each of 'em?"

"Damn near."

Emile Bad Horse Villon laughed. "You're gonna need 'em, boy."

Half an hour passed. The two men who rode down the creek returned. They stood in the open in front of the cottonwoods, talking. Someone built a fire. They were waiting. Forty-five minutes later those who had ridden up the creek returned, riding slowly. Upon their return, a meeting was held out from the trees twenty yards. The man who'd built the fire was waving his arms as he talked. He was eating something. Another joined him, leading his bay horse out from the trees. The two men on the ground kicked the fire out and mounted. Two warriors, their bodies painted, started away from the trees, riding in the direction of the ravine where Zeke and Emile had concealed themselves. One was studying the ground. The main group rode south, riding up the creek, riding through the lodge rings that Emile had pointed out earlier.

"Emile, now that you got yourself buried--you was raised around here, wasn't you? You was a boy, yes? Right here?"

"Here, yes. A long time ago."

Zeke watched the two riders making their way slowly away

from the creek. "Good. We need a place we can use to protect ourselves that's easy to defend. We need a place with rock on both sides risin' fifteen or twenty feet; higher would be better. A canyon where we can hide. It'd be nice if we could sit at the very end, our backs protected, and these boys havin' to funnel toward us. Get what I'm sayin? We need a place the two of us can defend. You know of such a place? Somewheres close? It'd better be damn close seein' how many there are."

Bad Horse stared at Zeke. "Yeah. Not here."

"How far?"

"Two or three mile. Across the creek, southwest. We ain't never gonna make it."

"We ain't gonna make it less we try. Two or three mile, you think?"

"Three or four, maybe."

"Well, which is it?"

"Don't know. I was a kid. Time and distance meant nothin'. It's a ways."

"A ways?" Zeke repeated. "Maybe three or four mile?"

Zeke turned and looked at Villon. "Get on that mule of yours. Bring my saddle horse and the packhorses. I'm gonna talk to these two. We ain't gonna have much time. So be ready." Zeke smiled at Villon. He checked the loads in the pistol he kept tucked behind his belt buckle.

"I ain't dead yet, my friend. I figure I'm nineteen. Too young to die. The way I see it, we got to make these boys pay a high price for killin' us. Maybe once they figure it, it'll be too high. Nobody is hangin' my hair from his wickiup. Know what I mean? I'm too young. You're too old. This ain't happenin'."

Moving up and away from the creek, one warrior had dismounted and was walking, concentrating on the ground, leading his horse. The other warrior rode slightly behind him.

It's a wonder they ain't seen us.

Behind Zeke, Emile sat his mule. He'd tied the lead ropes to the packhorses to the back of his saddle and was holding the reins to Zeke's saddle horse. Zeke put himself on the rise, lying on his belly, watching. O'Reilly was beside him, his tongue lolling out the side of his mouth. The main group had worked their way up the creek about a half mile. Zeke waited, thinking about Lexie, thinking how it felt when

330

her fingers brushed his, and how she looked up at him and smiled.

I am too damn young, he thought.

Both riders were mounted now, walking their horses up the slope. Zeke rose to his feet and started towards them. For some reason they hadn't seen him. He pulled back the hammers on both pistols. It seemed so surreal. Last year's prairie grass brushed against his boots, the ground soft on the worn soles. In front of him the two painted warriors were studying the ground, still unaware of his intentions.

Look up, you fools!

O'Reilly walked beside him. Zeke stopped. Behind him Emile was walking their animals to the place where Zeke had been lying on his belly, staring at Zeke's back as Zeke walked down the hillside. Emile had the Hawkens lying across the pommel of his saddle. The hammer was eared back. The reins of the black were wrapped loosely around his saddle horn.

The first warrior saw Zeke; his eyes widened. He brought a rifle up, stock to his shoulder, and jabbed his mount in the ribs. He yelled a warning to his companion and raced towards Zeke. He fired without aiming. Zeke felt the slug whip past him, tugging at the fabric in his shirt sleeve. His skin burned something awful.

Dammit.

O'Reilly's head came up; he moved to the side, then raced out to meet the charging horse, barking repeatedly as if chasing a rabbit. Zeke brought his pistol up and fired once, twice. Behind him he heard the Hawkens fire. The second rider flew off the back of his horse as the slow-moving slug struck him dead center. The first rider rushed past Zeke, trying to stay on the back of his horse, his fingers wrapped resolutely around the horse's mane. O'Reilly was barking, nipping at the horse's front hooves; the horse shied to the right away from the dog. In spite of all of his efforts to cling to the horse's back, the warrior was slipping. His horse stumbled; its rider fell to the side, rolled on the ground and laid still. The horse regained his footing and bolted up the hillside, O'Reilly chasing after him.

Zeke shoved one pistol behind his belt buckle and the other into the holster, latching the hammer. Emile came upon Zeke in a rush, throwing the reins of the black at him. He passed him, the horses running without stopping. At the same time he shoved the Hawkens into the boot. Zeke grabbed the horn as the black raced past him, swinging into the saddle, reaching for the flying reins. Up the valley, the main party was turning to the shots fired. Using the reins, Zeke slapped the butt of the trailing packhorse on the hind quarters causing him to jump ahead, running beside the mule.

Down the hillside they raced, O'Reilly out front. They reached the creek, plunging into it, crossing it, racing up the hillside, and turning slightly southwest. Zeke popped the packhorse again, glancing back at the horsemen. They had not yet made the creek. A little over half a mile separated them. He popped the packhorse again, mentally counting how many rounds he had left in the holstered pistol. He was down two. Four remained.

Hope they burn when I need 'em.

Emile was following the ridge line, O'Reilly out front barking excitedly.

Damn dog. He'll wake the dead.

The first of the horsemen reached the creek. Half a mile still separated the two parties. Emile had turned west off the ridge line. Now O'Reilly was behind Zeke, looking at the horsemen charging across the creek. Zeke glanced at Emile's back and the galloping packhorses.

Whatever you do, don't slow down. This ain't the place to take a rest.

Zeke glanced back. All of the horsemen were across the creek and running up the rise. Two of the faster horses were out in front thirty yards, their riders beating their butts with switches.

Don't stop, Emile. Can't get stuck out in the open.

Zeke made up the distance, popping the trailing packhorse on the butt with his reins. The horse leaped forward, his ears back, white foam edging his mouth.

Can they run another ten minutes?

How long has it been?

Zeke glanced over his shoulder. The horsemen were coming off the rise at a gallop. Zeke considered the packhorses. They were a drag, slowing them down. But they had to have them. The riders were gaining.

How far have we gone? Been ten minutes. Two miles? Maybe but not quite. Hope this place ain't no four miles. Might not make four miles. Horses can't take it.

Bad Horse Villon yelled at him; he'd turned abruptly into the mouth of a small canyon, racing up a creek bed, splashing water, the horses and mule plunging forward. He ran the mule up the other side,

332

disappearing momentarily, the packhorses lost in a cloud of dust and flying debris. Zeke looked back; somehow the horsemen had cut the distance to a quarter of a mile.

Too close. Damn them packhorses.

O'Reilly was again out front barking happily as though he was chasing a rabbit, its hindend nearly in his mouth. The black made the rise where the mule and packhorses had disappeared. Zeke rode, leaning forward over the saddle horn, trying to keep those that followed in sight. They disappeared as the black plunged down the other side and into the creek spraying water. Ahead of him twenty yards, Emile had come out of the saddle, slapping the mule on the butt as he galloped on up the canyon, taking the packhorses with him. Emile was busy loading the Hawkens, ramming home the lead projectile. Fifteen seconds later, Zeke was beside him on the ground, his gloved hands full of Navy Colts, waiting.

Oh shit, oh shit. Gotta keep that horse close. He's got my powder. Shit! What was I thinkin'?

Zeke looked behind. The riders had not yet made the rise. He glanced up, seeing that a canyon wall blotted out much of the southern sky.

A man up there could pin us down. But he couldn't get down. He'd have to stay up there. This ain't bad.

"Come on," Emile shouted.

Emile was waving Zeke to follow. He did. The riders still had not made the rise. Not yet. The ground rose on both sides of the canyon to the walls. At the end where the canyon walls came together, was a waterfall; not much water there, but it would be slippery.

"Move. Move," Villon shouted. "Up here. Get up here. Hurry."

Villon was above him standing on a dry ridge. He disappeared from sight. Zeke found him standing under a long ledge. Inside he couldn't see the canyon ridge from either side.

Good. Good. This will do. It's got to.

It wasn't the best but it was a canyon; it forced the attacking force in front of them. The riders could get on the ridges behind them but not to them; they'd have to climb down the walls. They'd be exposed if they did. It was defendable unless they were rushed from the top and the bottom at the same time. Otherwise, they could hold their attackers off indefinitely, depending on how many there were.

"When we was very young, we used ta swim here."

"Swim?"

Villon pointed behind Zeke. A pond opened up twenty feet wide, thirty feet long. It was fed from the water falling off the rim.

"Warm water," Emile said, looking behind Zeke in the direction they'd come. "They's made thet rise above the creek. See thet warrior standin' by the rock? 'Nother in the trees below?"

Zeke looked but didn't see anyone, not at first.

"They's comin'," Emile said.

"I reckon."

"Yor shoulder's bleedin'."

Zeke hadn't noticed. Now he did. "That one got a little close."

"Flesh wound?"

Zeke nodded.

"Better clean it."

"I expect."

"Over there. See thet overhang? Above the water? Build a fire and heat up some water. Clean it 'fore yor arm stiffens up."

"We'd better pull the saddles and those packs before they get around behind us and we can't."

"I'll do that. Ya heat up some of thet water. Make some of thet coffee ya like."

"You want some?"

"No, it's not good. Bitter. The smell of it'll make our friends angry, thinkin' about us, sittin' under this ledge drinkin' thet stuff."

Zeke smiled. "I suppose it will."

Emile made several trips. He carried the packs and saddles to safety under the rock ledge.

"They's on the rim," he said pointing. "This one. Thet one. They ain't gonna wait. They'll be comin' soon."

"Won't they wait us out? That's what I'd do. Nobody gets hurt that way."

"They's too fer from home. They's ain't gots time ta wait. They's want our horses, our hair, and my mule. Too dangerous waitin'. Lakota'll kill 'em, they know they's here. They's gotta take us soon. I'd say they's lookin' fer Walking Eagle. Won't find him. He's gone. I'd say he's already crossed the Yellowstone movin' north. Too far fer 'em. So they's gonna come fer us. We's all they's got. Ain't nobody else."

Zeke listened to Emile. "Somethin's changed about you. Not

long ago you was a regular bastard. Couldn't stand you myself."

Emile Villon stared at Zeke. "Ya saved my life. Didn't have to. Had no reason. I wanted ta kill ya from the first time I saw ya. I planned it. Ya went and saved my life. I don't understand. Ya could've let me freeze ta death. Ya should have. It's what I'd a done." Emile paused. "Somethin' my mother said."

"Your mother? I didn't know you had a mother."

Emile smiled. "I had one. My mother," he said, "was Oglala. My father, French. Villon was his last name. He was a trapper. Married my mother." Emile laughed, thinking about his past. "Paid six horses fer thet woman. He lived with her 'til the Absaroka killed him. My mother raised me after the custom of her people, the Oglala."

"What did your mother say?"

"It don't translate well. She said, 'Be happy. Your people good people. No live like you not related. Related. Not alone. Never alone.' It don't translate good."

Zeke nodded.

"Layin' in thet dugout, unable ta move, I thought about my mother. Do ya know what I remember?"

Zeke shook his head.

Emile looked at him. He said, "It's crazy. I remember my mother liked me."

"She liked you?" Zeke paused. "I don't remember mine at all. She died when I was very young. I lived with my Uncle."

"Related?"

"Yes, related. He picked me up in St Louis, far from here. He put boots on my feet and bought me a hat. I remember that. He fed me beans and buffalo steak. That's what I remember. Beans. Steak. I was so hungry I could hardly spit."

Emile nodded as if he was understanding some secret, unspoken and untold. A shot rang out, echoing up and down the canyon. Neither man moved. Both had expected it.

Nothing happened that afternoon. Both men stayed under the overhang, once in a while creeping out to look at the edges of the canyon walls. They chewed on jerked venison, drank from the creek, and waited. O'Reilly joined them, stretching out in the shade, his hair matted from swimming in the pond. It was after dark when they pulled out their blankets.

Without looking at Emile, Zeke said, "Gonna be a long night. Get some sleep. My arm is hurtin' like hell. Can't sleep anyway, so I'll take the first watch."

Emile Villon nodded, took his blanket, and disappeared into the shadows of the night. Over the next half-hour the fire burned down; Zeke stared into the dark thinking about all of the men around the rim of the small canyon seeking his life. He smiled knowing they were awake too.

The sun came up late in the canyon. Zeke woke with a start, staring up at the scalp of an Absaroka warrior hanging from a staff driven into the ground outside the overhang. Emile had started a fire and was resting on a flat rock under the overhang. Zeke spent some time looking at the scalp, trying to make up his mind what he thought about it, the long bloodied piece of braided hair moving in the breeze.

"What did you do last night?" Zeke asked. "Where'd you get that thing? I don't like it."

"The Absaroka Crow ain't sleepin' now."

"I didn't know they was sleepin'."

"They'll stay awake fer sure. Don't want ta die in their sleep, my knife cuttin' their throat. I'm leavin' it where they kin see, remember what happens in the dark. No sleep. They'll be comin'. The smell of white man's coffee will make 'em angry. When they see the scalp of their friend, there'll be hell ta pay. They'll come . . . angry."

Two days later at ten o'clock in the morning his prophecy came true. They came. Emile had seen them moving up the rise. He ran to cover, crossing the pond, jumping from one stone to another. A shot rang out. A water geyser jumped up in front of him; an arrow caught him in the back of the leg, causing him to fall forward, splashing into the pond water in front of the overhang. Zeke rushed out to grab him, pulling him across the rocks into the relative safety of the rock shelf. Emile was cursing. A shot rang out, striking the stock of Zeke's rifle. Emile had seized the shaft with the fingers of both hands. Blood leaked onto his hands, down his pant leg: not gushing, but leaking at a steady rate.

"Lord, Emile." Zeke looked at him.

"Pull it out," Emile said.

"Now?"

336

"'Fore they get here. "'Fore I die of old age."

Zeke grabbed the shaft and pulled it straight out, jerking it clear. Emile grimaced. Blood flowed immediately. It felt to him like it had been stuck in the large leg bone itself. The blood was bright red, staining his pants, and running into his boot.

Emile cut the pant leg off his trousers and handed it to Zeke. "Hurry," he said, "they're comin'. Cut me a strip thet I kin use ta wrap my leg."

Zeke did so and watched Emile wrap his thigh. Zeke pulled on his leather gloves and readied his pistols, waiting. He had two in his hands, one on the rock in front of him, and one in the holster tied to his right leg. He stared at the bloodied rocks, listening to Emile grunting as he tightened the folded cotton bandage around his leg. The attackers came running all at once, jumping from rock to rock: hiding, waiting, moving again. In the flat surface of the pond he could see the shadow of one standing on top of the rock wall overhead and another on the ridge. A shot rang out: a signal. It must have been a signal for they all seemed to come around both edges of the overhang, running low, hiding behind rocks.

He wasn't ready. He never could have been. Shots fired. His. Theirs. The Hawkens went off. Zeke fired and fired, shooting at form and shadows, at the man who was standing in front of him and then wasn't. He fired until the pistol was empty and he picked up another. He fired, not stepping out from the shelter of the overhang. They seemed to be coming from everywhere. Then there was silence. Hurriedly, Zeke started reloading. Praying for seconds, he popped the spent caps off the nipples, shoved paper cartridges into the chambers, pushing lead slugs hard on top of the paper cartridges, and lastly, replacing the caps. At times he was all thumbs. It was a wonder he loaded any of his firearms. Yet they were loaded and he was waiting.

"Where are they? Didn't we kill anybody?"

The rocks bore streaks of blood. There were no bodies.

Emile was bleeding profusely from the scalp, from his shoulder, from his nose, from his left hand, and from his leg. The loss of blood was affecting him. He was shaking, sitting in the shade provided by the overhang, breathing in short gasps, his face a pale mask. Zeke took stock. He knew he had been hit: he had taken an arrow in the shoulder and the leg, a gunshot wound in the lower arm, a bloodied scrape deep across the shoulder, a cut left by an arrowhead that narrowly missed.

Jeez! It's a wonder I'm still breathin'!

The Absaroka scalp was gone. Someone had removed it. There were no bodies. The running water was dark red with blood. It was quiet. There were no snow birds, no hawks, no camp robbers, no vultures. There were no dead bodies attracting them to the canyon floor.

An hour later Emile came to Zeke and, without asking, grabbed the shafts, one after another, and pulled them from his body, tossing them aside. It wasn't over. The Absaroka were coming back. Zeke began checking and rechecking the loads in each pistol. His body felt numb. Emile managed to reload the Hawkens. He stuck his hunting knife in the earth beside his wounded leg, took a deep breath and waited. Neither spoke, quietly acknowledging they would not survive the next round. It was another calm waiting for another storm: the last one.

Pain is debilitating: each breath difficult, each movement impossible. Zeke's mind wandered. He thought about his uncle: his body lying on the sod, his body riddled by lead slugs, an arrow, his life's blood soaked up by the earth. But he had his hair. He wondered about that, how it happened, why it happened. He thought about Lexie: her fingers brushing his, the wind playing with her hair, the smell of her floating on the evening air.

Gawd, he thought. *Almost. So close. So far.*

But they were still alive. That was a miracle, a phenomena that couldn't be rationally explained. It was an impossibility. Yet there they were: one cradling a Hawkens, the other, his gloved hands wrapped around the butts of two Navy Colts.

Waiting. It was taking so long.

Emile Villon rebuilt the fire, throwing multiple sticks on it to make it hot fast. He stuck the coffee pot in the flame and let it boil, the breeze carrying the aroma down the canyon. He fired the Hawkens at the man on the cliff and missed, but let him know that Bad Horse Emile could see him, that Emile was alive, waiting, daring him to come finish the job.

And so they waited.

The sun hadn't reached noon. It was yet an hour away. Zeke's blood-soaked his shirt, making it cling to his skin. Neither man moved, lost in their separate thoughts. It was dusk before Emile rebuilt the fire

338

the third time that day, reseating the black coffee pot, listening to the water boil.

"Why do you do that?" Zeke asked him. "The coffee, the scalp. I'm not sure it does any good to make 'em so damn angry. Might be better if they wasn't."

Emile looked at the younger man and smiled. "It's me shakin' my fist at 'em, lettin' 'em know thet I'm not afraid, thet I think they's a bunch of old women hidin' from their shadows, shakin' in the lodges of their mothers, afraid."

"Well, I'd say you did a good job. So far, anyways."

O'Reilly came to his feet, stretched, yawned, and walked out into the growing shadows. He lapped some water and stared up at the canyon walls, and in the spirit of the day, growled weakly.

CHAPTER 54
Alexandra is 43 miles north of Zeke on the Musselshell

April 13, 1855
Greasy Grass Creek
North Central Nebraska Territory

"I need paper cartridges."

"What?" Zeke asked weakly. "Sure. In my saddle bags. What for?"

"You."

"Me?"

Emile brought the box of paper cartridges back to Zeke.

"What are you goin' to do?"

"Close 'em wounds."

"What?"

Emile Villon didn't answer. He was breaking the cartridges open and pouring the powder into a tin cup. One, two, three cartridges were broken open, the powder accumulated. From the cup he poured the powder onto the shoulder wound where he'd pulled out the arrow.

"Hold still."

"What's that gonna do? Is that medicine? I ain't never heard of that."

Emile Villon didn't answer. Instead he picked up a burning twig from the fire and touched it to the black powder on Zeke's shoulder. The brilliant flash fire was immediate: the powder ignited--a puff of white smoke and it was out, no longer burning.

Zeke yelled in complete surprise, his eyes wide open in amazement. An all consuming, unending pain bubbled up and overflowed. "My God, I'm on fire! I'm burnin'! Why? What are you doin' to me?" Zeke tried to move but he was far too weak.

Emile studied Zeke's shoulder. "The wound closed," he announced. "I'll do the leg next. Then your arm. It won't kill ya. Doin' nothin' will so, hold still."

"Hold still?"

Emile was paying Zeke no attention, breaking three more paper cartridges, building a pile of black powder to pour onto Zeke's leg. The intense, burning pain was incredible. Zeke didn't cry out, not like he wanted to. He had too much personal pride, refusing to give into the pain. When Emile finished, he stared at Zeke.

"Your turn," Zeke said, wiping the sweat off his brow.

"My turn," Emile replied.

"You'll have to help me break open the cartridges. My fingers don't want to work."

Emile nodded and started opening each cartridge and pouring the black powder into a tin cup.

Zeke wondered if he was going to live; it was that difficult to move. At first the effort left him exhausted. The continuing pain in his shoulder, his leg, and his forearm was formidable. Emile seemed to deal with it better than he.

It was four weeks before Zeke could hobble up the draw to see the horses. It was six weeks before he could walk. Even then, it was with a noticeable limp that hampered his gait, restricting his physical abilities to move laterally, forward, or backward. The forearm took the longest and ultimately was the most important. His hand needed to hold a Navy Colt without wavering. His life may depend on it. His strength wasn't there. Finger control wasn't there. He could squeeze the trigger but couldn't shoot with accuracy. This was a problem that worried him. Six weeks in he started doing finger exercises. At the same time he walked up and down the hill to the horses: six, eight times in the morning, and six, eight times in the afternoon--all the time moving his fingers, clenching his hand into a fist, squeezing, squeezing, squeezing.

On May 30, 1855, they left the canyon for the first time, heading for the Yellowstone River and the Musselshell, the Teton Lakota Indian, Emile Bad Horse Villon, leading the way. Out in front O'Reilly ran back and forth, smelling the ground.

CHAPTER 55
Zeke is 183 miles southeast of Alexandra
on the Greasy Grass

April 28, 1855
Dry Wolf Creek confluence with the Judith River
North Central Nebraska Territory

In 1808 Johann Jakob Astor, a German emigrant, with the permission, support, and encouragement of Tom Jefferson established the American Fur Company. The American Fur Company extended its economic arms to the high plains where it traded for beaver pelts and buffalo hides from the likes of Louis Casabois. Astor opened his little fur shop in New York across the street from his brother's butcher shop and made a stack of money trading furs. His little store front company grew to be the largest company of its kind in North America.

Louis Casabois was not known among the Teton Lakota as Louis Casabois. For one thing, he was fat, and for another, he was French. The Teton Lakota referred to him as the Fat Frenchie. They liked the metal pots and heavy metal axe heads he brought to trade for beaver pelts and cured buffalo hides. Fat Frenchie was built like a green avocado or the alligator pear after which the avocado was first named. His laugh was infectious, matching his girth, and his appetite for pemmican flavored with choke cherries or goose berries was renowned. Knowing this, he was treated with pemmican made from elk grease, elk steak and sometimes buffalo tongue. For such a feast he became the jolly trader, happy to do business.

Fat Frenchie sat in the lodge of Walking Eagle asking first about the chokecherry flavored pemmican which Small Dove, Walking Eagle's sister-in-law, had brought him. It wasn't happenstance. She provided the pemmican at the request of Walking Eagle. Fat Frenchie had trade consisting of four young war ponies, tanned buffalo and elk hides, and a new Sam Walker Colt. The latter weighed four and one half pounds and was fifteen and one half inches long. It lived on black powder. Fat Frenchie had four tins of the best powder that money could buy: a secret concoction of sulfur, charcoal, and potassium nitrate commonly called saltpeter--very explosive, especially if it was kept dry. Fat Frenchie kept his powder dry.

342

Walking Eagle was aware of these things, especially the Sam Walker Colt. He had one and wanted two. Hence, he asked Small Dove to make the chokecherry flavored pemmican for Fat Frenchie. What he didn't know was what Fat Frenchie wanted for the pistol, or even if he could trade him out of it. But he did know that pemmican was a start to a possibly rewarding conversation.

They talked horses; they talked hides. They talked about how good it would be for Walking Eagle to own the second Walker, how much Walking Eagle would enjoy carrying such a pistol into battle against his adversary, the loathed Absaroka Crow. Walking Eagle enjoyed the conversation. So did Fat Frenchie. They spoke in the language of the Oglala, conducting their business in that medium.

"What about this one?" Fat Frenchie pointed to Small Dove. "Her pemmican is very good in the mouth. She'd make her husband happy when he comes home. I trade for her."

Walking Eagle said, "Small Dove has a husband. She doesn't need Fat Frenchie."

Small Dove laughed, agreeing. "I have a man," she said. "I don't need Fat Frenchie. Too many men is not good for a woman."

"I have many horses," he said. "You'd be worth it. I can tell by the taste of your pemmican."

"I have a man," she said again. "I do not need any more."

"I see," said Fat Frenchie.

"You want a woman?" Walking Eagle asked. "Not buffalo skins, not beaver?"

"I was thinking about the white girls."

"My woman?"

"Not her. And not all of them."

It was something Walking Eagle had not considered.

"My woman is not for trade."

"I am not here to trade for her."

"You're not?"

"No. I come offering a big trade for the other one. I am told she is not your wife. I was thinking two horses, the Samuel Walker Colt, and two tins of black gunpower. Not the girl, not the small one. The other young woman–the tall one."

Greed is what it is. It is a weight heavy to bear, hard to conceal. This one wanted a one horse woman and not even a good horse. But two horses? A Sam Walker Colt? Two tins of black gunpowder? Caps?

For the tall one? It would cost Walking Eagle nothing.

Long ago, he'd brought his then future father-in-law, the father of Standing Alone Shaking Her Fist, six horses but she was worth more, much more. He'd have given ten if he'd had them. He did not. Seven was all he had and he'd have given that, but her father had nodded his head with the approval of his daughter's marriage for six horses. Such was the transaction.

The woman that Fat Frenchie sought didn't even speak the language of the people. She was next to worthless. She was no good at cooking. She didn't make pemmican. She wouldn't eat it. She was tall and she was ugly.

Walking Eagle countered with: "Six horses, six tins of powder, caps, paper cartridges. She is beautiful to look at. She is worth much more." The negotiation was set, but the deal not made.

Fat Frenchie took more pemmican in his fingers and put it in his mouth, rolling it around with his tongue. He smiled. He acted as if he was done talking. Both men knew he had more to say.

Finally, he commented to Small Dove. "I can see offering six horses for you. But the tall one? She is a one horse wife at best." He swallowed, took a sip from the water bag, and asked Walking Eagle if he'd had a good year, if he'd gotten many horses from his raids on the Absaroka Crow. He leaned forward slowly as if to get up and leave, signaling that the negotiations may well be finished. Before rising to his feet, he took some more pemmican. Such was his habit.

"This is very good," he said to Small Dove. "Very good." He looked at her and smiled. "I have had a very good year trading with the people," he continued. Walking Eagle knew he would. "The woman is not worth six war ponies. She is not Teton Lakota. She speaks English. I, too, speak English. I offer you three horses. You and I know she is not worth this. Plus four tins of black gunpowder and the Walker Colt. No more. She is worth one horse." Fat Frenchie held up his index finger. "One," he said. "So consider my offer. Talking is over. Too many words. We smoke now. Maybe before we smoke, I'll have more pemmican."

He glanced at Small Dove. "You have skins to trade?" he asked.

Small Dove nodded.

Walking Eagle appeared to be thinking. A new Walker. He would have taken the cans of powder without the pistol. He would have taken one horse, but Fat Frenchie didn't know that.

"All right, it is good," he said to the Frenchman. "All good. I am being cheated by the pemmican-eating Fat Frenchie. The girl is worth much more."

"We have a deal, then?"

"Yes. A deal."

"Let's smoke. You've stolen me blind. I'll be embarrassed to show my face. People will take advantage of me." Both knew Fat Frenchie would have no trouble showing his face. He'd never let someone get the better of him unless it was to his advantage.

They smoked after the custom of the people. They talked of the elk coming down from the Big Horn, sleek and fat. They spoke of the beaver skins being shiny and plentiful and worth so much, of the cow belonging to the Mormon emigrant, killed by High Forehead. They talked of how crazy the white man was and of Conquering Bear offering fine horses in its place only to be shot in the back. It was disgraceful, crazy, stupid. The soldiers with their wagon gun had been killed. Gratton, too. Didn't they know? Bad medicine–that is what it was. Crazy, stupid white men.

Small Dove informed Priscilla of her impending marriage; she told her to pack her things because she was now the wife of Fat Frenchie. She told her that he would be a good husband for he was wealthy: he had many horses, many hides, and was much liked among the people.

"Pack things," she said. "He take you now. Good marriage."

It wasn't that there was actually going to be a marriage. It was an accomplished fact: a union sealed by the exchange of three horses, four tins of black powder, and a heavy Samuel Walker Colt, advertised as new, though the pistol was used.

Upon hearing of her impending nuptials, Priscilla slumped to the lodge floor in shock, moaning as if she'd died, her tenuous world falling apart. All was lost. All hope was gone. All because of her "stupid ankle." If only she hadn't injured it. If only they'd left, escaped like they'd planned so often. Escaped!

CHAPTER 56

Zeke is 183 miles from Alexandra on Upper Goose Creek

April 28, 1855
Missouri Breaks
North-Central Nebraska Territory

"Lexie! Lexie! Lexie!"

Bethany was running, her fifteen year old legs missing clumps of sage, avoiding an old ant hill piled high in sticks and needles, and fresh gopher holes. She had to leap to avoid a long, thick stick of driftwood.

"Lexie," she shouted again. "He's done it. He's done it. Walking Eagle's traded Pris to that Frenchman, that fat trapper. The Frenchman! He gave three horses for her. Can you believe it? She's gone. Just like that! I mean just like that."

Alexandra was slow in responding to Bethany's news. Her initial response was total disbelief.

"What? You're just saying it," she exclaimed.

"I am not."

"You're not?" Alexandra paused. "Where is she?"

"The Frenchman--he's got her. She's already in the saddle. He's leaving. Walking Eagle gave her to him for three horses. Maybe some hides, some deer skins, two buffalo skins, maybe a pistol and some black powder, I think. I don't really know."

Bethany's voice was choking as she spoke, gasping for breath. Distressed, she buried her face in her hands, sitting upon the ground beside Alexandra, mumbling. "Pris . . . she's gone. He traded her like an old saddle. I can't believe it. Poor, poor Pris. I saw her sitting on top of the Frenchman's horse, crying."

"Where is she, Beth? I mean where is she right now?"

"There's nothing you can do, Lexie. She's gone. He traded her for three horses. I can't believe it. Just like that. Can he do that?" Bethany looked at Alexandra and started to weep.

"Beth. Beth, where is she, right now? I mean, exactly. Get hold of yourself. Talk to me."

Bethany glanced at her, squinting, the sun in her eyes. "He Who Hunts Wolves. His lodge. Right in front. The fat one has her in

346

the saddle. She's just sitting looking straight ahead, tears streaming down her face. You know? Poor thing. That man, he keeps patting her on the leg and laughing like he really got something. He does have something, that silly bastard. I can't believe what Walking Eagle did. I think it was all about the pistol. That's what I think."

"Stay here," Alexandra said. Cold, driven by anger and rage, her body awash in adrenaline, she started to run, leaving a surprised Bethany sitting in the grass weeping. Never had Alexandra felt the way she did. For the first time in months she did not doubt herself.

There's no time. I've got to hurry.

She sprang across the creek, not bothering to use stepping stones, her bare feet splashing in the cold water. She tried to imagine the lodge of He Who Hunts Wolves: the people gathering, probably standing around the fur trader. It was the place to be when visitors came. The fat Frenchman would be there. So would the boy who beats on drums and the old Medicine Man, and He who Laughs Loudly.

On the grassy south flat horses were milling as the herdsmen brought them in for the hunters to use. On the hillside on her left, boys were playing with a fur ball, striking it again and again with sticks. Their laughter stuck in her head. Up the creek the older girls were returning with loads of firewood in their arms and the ever present watchmen guarding them from their unseen enemies. Once across the creek, Alexandra dodged through the skunk brush and juniper. Somewhere a meadow lark sang.

Pris. Pris, Pris, she thought. *I'm not letting this happen. Not now. Not ever. I'm coming, Pris. Just wait. You're worth more than a damn pistol. Some black gunpowder.*

Over the rise she fled, past the flat granite stones and the quartz laden rock jutting out of the hillside. The yellow and spotted camp dogs sprang out of her way, whining, barking, retreating. In front of her stood the lodge of Walking Eagle and that of Feather Woman. Beyond that sat the lodge of Black Buffalo Man, and farther still the lodge of He Who Hunts Wolves. Already many people had gathered, some with goods to trade. Alexandra sprang into the lodge of Walking Eagle, jumping across the fire pit. Falling to her knees, she searched for the pistol of Deadman Crying. She found it, flipping open the chamber as she'd seen her father do, checking the loads. She, in her hurry, was not sure what she was looking for, or whether her inspection was relevant. It looked loaded.

She thought, *What am doing? What am I looking for? The loads look okay. Hopefully,* she thought. *Hopefully, they'll work when I need them to work.*

She stumbled back through the entrance, tripping on the door latches. Regaining her balance, she started to sprint across the compound. Four horses stood in front of Walking Eagle's lodge. Alexandra dodged around them, running as fast as her swollen body allowed. Across camp, in front of the lodge of He Who Hunts Wolves, people were gathering; youngsters were bobbing in and around the adults, drawing a loud response, then laughter. It was easy to recognize Fat Frenchie's horses.

I have time, she thought, slowing down to a walk, hiding the old revolver in the folds of her doe skin dress. *I do have time.* She caught her breath and was surprised at how calm she felt.

The Frenchman was tightening the cinch on his saddle horse. He then checked on Priscilla sitting on the saddle horse to his left. Alexandra saw him pat Priscilla's left leg, smiling as she looked away from him. She'd been crying. That was obvious. He laughed. Taking the reins, he stepped into the stirrup, seating himself in the saddle. Someone handed him his Hawkens and the lead ropes to his two packhorses. Balancing the rifle across his lap, he started to tie the leads to the latigo dangling behind his saddle.

Alexandra could see Priscilla clearly. She was slouched over in the saddle perched on the back of a black horse, disconsolate, slumped over like a sack of dried beans, her white-knuckled hands gripping the saddle horn. She was trying to wipe her nose on her sleeve, looking away from Fat Frenchie.

In the crowd of moving people, Alexandra stopped, standing still, feeling the smooth Hickory pistol grip in her fingers, the soft breeze playing with her dress, the grass under her bare feet. The baby moved. She gasped trying to think of what to do . . . exactly.

He'll come this way; he has to go through me. God, I hope he does.
He will.

The Frenchman saw her, and at first paid her no attention, spurring his horse's belly as he brought him around, the lead ropes tightening. Then he saw her the second time, his eyes resting on the heavy four and a half pounds of Walker Colt in her hands. A dark realization formed in his head and he knew she wasn't there to say goodbye and wish his new wife well.

The breeze pulled at her hair. Holding the gun in both hands, she pulled the hammer of the pistol back until it clicked, then stood quietly waiting for what was to happen. Her mind was blank. Nothing mattered except that this marriage or this sale, whatever it was, was not happening--not ever. A child ran past, ducking in front of her, barely missing her and the hands that gripped the heavy pistol.

He saw her clearly now. The Frenchman laughed out loud, a boisterous chuckle that turned heads. It was an "I have her and there is nothing you can do about it" laugh. It was a "you depraved whore" laugh. It was the embodiment of everything evil that had ever happened in Alexandra's life; yet she did not react.

She stared at him. Her glare cold, unwavering, emanating from a solid core belief that she'd come this far and was not going any farther. Except this time there was something she could do, something she did do. Standing right where she was, her feet slightly spread, two hands gripping the butt of the Walker Colt, she said loudly, "Turn her loose, you bastard, or I'll kill you."

It was then that everyone saw the young woman standing in her loose fitting doe skin dress, the heavy pistol no longer hidden. The sight and the sound of her voice turned everyone's head.

The Frenchman was not impressed. He said, "Oh, you will, will you? Just how are you going to do that?" The words, the French accent, were dragged out; he was laughing.

Three of the old ones who were walking beside the French trader turned; they saw Alexandra. In response to her voice they stopped and began to move aside uneasily. It surprised her how quickly they responded. Behind them someone laughed. Abruptly the laughter stopped. Someone called her by name in the language of the people.

"You, woman of Walking Eagle, She Who Stands Angry, get out of the way. Go back to your lodge." Alexandra didn't know who it was that spoke to her.

She could hear Priscilla crying, her sobs falling on Alexandra's ears like summer thunder. Priscilla repeated Alexandra's name over and over, calling for help. Alexandra saw the French trader spurring his horse, trying unsuccessfully to drop packhorse's leads. His mount was shaking his head in frustration, rearing, and leaping forward.

She waited until the horse and man were moving toward her, the Hawkens rifle in his left hand, a triumphant scowl on his lips. She held her breath, then, without hesitation, she brought the Colt up and in one movement brought the pistol barrel down, lining the front sight on the trader's head, and squeezed the trigger. Hammer fell on primer and one slightly misshapen slug tore through the barrel. Milliseconds later it buried itself in the Frenchman's forehead. The second shot dropped the man's horse to its knees. It rolled, kicking its hooves, flailing at the prairie sod.

The packhorses tried to break free. People scattered, trying to get away. Warriors were grabbing weapons. Others turned to look. They saw Walking Eagle's number one first woman walk up to the Frenchman's warm and twitching corpse and put the third slug through his head. They watched her kick his twitching body in the manner of warriors counting coup. They saw her pull the Frenchman's long knife from his waist, securing it behind her belt. She pulled the silver gripped pistol from its holster and picked up the brass mounted Hawkens rifle from where it had come to rest on the sod.

No one moved toward her. She appeared to know what she was doing.

Later, she remembered dogs barking, and people shouting, but no one laughing. She remembered Priscilla's horse trying to pull away when Alexandra grabbed the lead rope. Alexandra saw herself being jerked forward. She remembered calming the horse as Priscilla screamed for her to help her down. But she didn't. Instead she hung the Hawkens rifle by its loop from the saddle horn, and handed Priscilla the second pistol, saying, "Here, hold this." Turning, lead ropes in hand, she walked through swarms of inquisitive people, leading the Frenchman's two packhorses with Priscilla on top of the black, across camp, the heavy Walker Colt heavy in her right hand, her thumb resting on the hammer, her finger on the trigger.

Priscilla stopped sniffling and had grown silent. Then Alexandra heard Priscilla muttering. "Oh, God, Lexie, Oh, God. What are we going to do?" Her voice was a mere whisper. "Please help me down. Please, Lexie."

Alexandra saw him first: Walking Eagle leading four horses, walking toward her, staring at her, wordlessly looking from her to Priscilla. Alexandra stopped in front of him, handed him his old Walker Colt with the three spent chambers, then taking from Priscilla the Frenchman's U.S. North 1819 single shot pistol, fully loaded, she handed that to him as well. Lastly, she took the brass mounted, half-stocked Hawken's rifle from the saddle horn and handed it to him. In doing so, she forced him to drop the leads to the four horses. She kept the Bowie knife. Turning away from him, Alexandra held the saddle horse still while Priscilla slid to the ground, grabbing her to keep her from falling.

She did not harbor a single thought in her mind, no longer caring. With Priscilla standing slightly behind her, she took the lead ropes to the Frenchman's packhorses and placed them in Walking Eagle's already full hands. Then, in the language of the people, in measured words softly, as though each word was a sentence in itself, she said to him, "If you ever try to sell Pris again, ever give her to any man, when you sleep, I'll cut your balls off and hang them from the doorway of the lodge for all to see. Do you understand? Your balls--I will cut them off and hang them with the scalps of your enemies."

Walking Eagle stood very still, the lead ropes to the four horses on the ground behind him, and at his feet the leads to two more. In his hands, he held a Hawkens rifle and two pistols. He said nothing, staring at She Who Stands Angry, glancing at Priscilla behind her. For a moment he looked at the horses, and the saddle and furs that minutes ago belonged to the Frenchman and now were his, a gift from his woman. He glanced at the Sam Walker Colt, hefting it, surprised that a white woman knew how to use it, that she was willing to use it, all the while very much aware of the Bowie knife possessed by Alexandra. The thought of the knife compelled him to take an involuntary step backwards and let Alexandra and Priscilla pass by. As they did, he smiled. It occurred to him that She Who Stands Angry was a ten horse woman if there ever was one.

CHAPTER 57

Zeke is 179 miles from Alexandra just west of
Greasy Grass Creek

May 10, 1855
Judith Trading Post
North Central Nebraska Territory

Shopping in Boston, Massachusetts in 1855 was a grand experience, what with the harbor teaming with ships from all over the known world and shops like Quincy Market, Revere Silver, the outdoor Haymarket, a variety of fancy goods stores, small dry goods stores, and taverns and restaurants where you could eat food you would never get at home. So, too, was St. Louis, Missouri, sitting as it was on the Mississippi River. Huge paddle wheel vessels from far away New Orleans were docked on its shores. Stores of every kind lined Main Street, sporting the latest dresses and fashions out of New York and Paris, as well as Samuel Colt Pistols and Smith and Wesson Volcanic rifles manufactured in such places as New Haven or Norwich, Connecticut.

There were also other shopping centers that serviced tens of thousands of square miles. One such sat on the Judith River a little south of its confluence with the Missouri, the very river that in 1855 brought supplies and furnished mercantile goods by paddle wheel all the way from New Orleans, St. Louis, and Independence, Missouri. It was a trading post, the only one with such connections in northern Nebraska Territory. Paddle wheel vessels unloaded their merchandise at the landing on the south side of the big river. Afterwards the huge wheels of freight wagons hauled the merchandise thirty-six miles along the Judith River to the trading post, pulled by eight and ten horse teams.

"We go trading post," Small Dove informed them.

"Really?" Bethany replied. "Where's this? We can go?" What she meant and what she didn't ask is, You mean Walking Eagle would let us? He isn't afraid we'll be rescued? That we'll escape?

"Where is this trading post?" Bethany asked.

"Up river this way." She pointed. "Not far," she said. "We

352

leave soon. Be there sun high in sky. You come? Yes?"

Why is she asking? Alexandra wondered. *Why now?*

"Sure. You bet. I want to go to a trading post," Bethany said, looking at her sister to see if she agreed.

Small Dove was excited. "Whips The Bear bring horses," she said. "Morning Flower, she come. Trade furs. Many people. You like. Much happy."

Bethany looked again at her sister. "Much happy," she said.

Much happy. Sure. Alexandra nodded, rising to her feet. It seemed so odd. Ironic. Before, they were hidden away from the eyes of white men. *Not counting Fat Frenchie.* Now apparently it didn't matter.

Probably because of my belly.

I haven't told anyone. Except Beth, Pris. They know.

Everyone else knows. It's obvious. All they have to do is look. They aren't blind.

Maybe we can escape. Really escape. Where would we go? We're so far north we're next to lost. But maybe . . . Maybe there'll be white people.

What good is that? That Frenchman was worthless; the three before that wanted to shoot us.

We'll see.

"I want coffee beans," Priscilla announced. "And some rock candy."

"Coffee beans?" Bethany repeated.

"Sure. I can dream, can't I? And I'd like some rock candy. Some sugar sticks like they had in St. Louis. Remember?"

Alexandra glanced at Small Dove. "All right," she said to her. "Let's go. Pris wants some coffee beans."

"Coffee beans?" Small Dove questioned.

"Yes, that's what Beth and I think, too. We'd like some coffee beans and some rock candy."

Small Dove stooped then stepped through the lodge opening, going outside and momentarily disappeared from their sight.

Lowering her voice, Alexandra whispered, "Do you think there will be too many people for us to escape? That they'd know right away if we disappeared? Maybe someone would see us. Maybe we can get a message out. Let someone know we're alive. What do you think?"

"We could just ask for help," Bethany said. "Maybe someone would help us, extend a hand. We could get a message to Arnold. That'd be something. Maybe Arnold would come and get us, or maybe he'd send someone for us. If we could get a message out."

"Let's take care of our business," Priscilla added. "If it happens, it happens. Let's see what the day brings us."

"Are you all right?" Bethany asked Priscilla. "You seem different."

"I'm fine."

Bethany was staring at Priscilla, wondering, not believing her. Something was different.

"Yes, let's see what happens." Alexandra said. "What's that mean exactly?"

"I don't know what it means, Lexie. It sounded good. Especially getting a message out to someone, anyone. Like Beth said, maybe someone will come for us. Maybe we can be rescued. Maybe."

Bethany broke out laughing. "Rescued. Right. I'll keep you posted, Pris. Don't get your hopes up. Nothing has worked so far."

Alexandra shook her head. "All right," she said. "Let's hope. We can do that."

Many of the people gathered. They started for the trading post when the sun was halfway up the sky, riding south in a column along the east side of the Judith River. When they arrived they saw a low-lying log building. Alexandra estimated they'd traveled ten miles. "Not far," as Small Dove had told them. It was noon judging from the ascendancy of the sun.

Dismounting, Alexandra rearranged her clothing, repositioning her skinning knife in her belt as well as Fat Frenchie's heavy Bowie knife. It was heavy, not easy to use, but she took comfort in it wedged inside her belt. Leaving their horses with the older boys, the girls followed Small Dove inside the long log building. Fireplace chimneys occupied both ends. Whips The Bear was at Alexandra's elbow. Morning Flower held Alexandra's right hand; in the other, she clutched the Funson doll, worn and dirty, its yarn hair beginning to fall out. The inside of the trading post felt bigger than it appeared from the outside. It seemed to have everything from bolts of cloth to paper cartridges. There was a swirl of activity around them, people talking excitedly, pointing at this and that.

It didn't take long for the white women to become the object of the residents' gazes, and even those that weren't residents looked them over. Alexandra was grateful.

At least now someone knows we're alive, she thought. *Now to leave a message. It would be nice to have a sheet of paper and a pencil.*

Just ask. Somebody may have some.

Whips The Bear and Morning Flower were standing beside Alexandra gawking. It surprised Alexandra how resolute Morning Flower was for she insisted on holding her hand. There was so much to see and so much to do, yet she firmly gripped Alexandra's hand as though she might become lost.

How to get paper? Something to write with.

"Beth," she whispered. "We need to get something to write on. And a pencil."

"I'll see what I can do."

She's sure changed. Where'd she get all that confidence all of a sudden?

A voice stopped her. It was a sound that had haunted her in a thousand dreams, a voice that caused her to abruptly turn toward its source as if she'd been slapped a stinging blow across the face. The last time she'd heard it was almost a year ago on the high plains north of the Sweetwater. In three months it would be a year.

Alexandra Wakeford's eyes came to rest on a grizzled man leaning against a counter, spittle from chewing tobacco clinging to his salt and pepper mustache, the ends drooping below his smirking lips. Cold anger washed over her, leaving her face tingling, her insides seizing, turning into knots until they felt like they'd explode. His voice brought back a horrifying memory in a rush: three men casually discussing whether to fire a lead ball into her head. She knew, cold as ice in January, unforgiving hatred. In her mind's eye she saw him again: tall, shabby clothes, sitting his horse, a rifle in his hands pointed at Shorty.

Shorty? Whatever happened to him? Is he here, too?

"What did you say?" she said staring at him, squinting in the shadowed room, her blue eyes flashing. It was a demanding voice: a voice that stopped conversation; a voice that commanded attention; that required everyone to stop what they were doing; discontinue what they were saying and look at her.

I know you. I do. Sitting your horse, rifle in your hands. What you did!

Their eyes met; the big man wiped the brown spittle from his mustache with his sleeve. He moved slowly, knowing it bothered her, wanting it to bother her.

"I called that boy of your'n a breed and his mother and that girl

355

Injun whores. Shoulda said a deaf Injun whore." His words were followed by a derisive laugh, the same laugh that had followed Sly's comments as he took her watch fob and her ribbon.

He's referring to Whips The Bear. He thinks these children are mine. But Whips The Bear is old, nearly ten.

Is he blind?

But the boy is clinging to me in this frightening place. He's speaking of Morning Flower. What did she ever do?

He's so evil.

And I know you, she thought. *I know you. My God, it is you!*

I never expected this. You and the other one. . . Sly? What ever happened to him?

And you!

The fellow on the horse. Not the stubby one. That'd be Shorty. Yes.

You're Crease. Sitting on the horse staring at me. I remember. Deciding to kill us, not to kill us. Like we were a sack of old potatoes.

Her voice was cold when she spoke. "You have some gall calling a defenseless child a 'breed!' How dare you? You bastard. I remember you, Crease. It is Crease, right? You were there. I remember. The Oglala came into our camp with their guns and axes, attacking our wagons, killing my father, running my mother through with a lance. They were both scalped in front of me and my sister.

You were there. You were part of it. All of this could have been prevented. All of it. You could have stopped it. You could have helped us. Instead, we were stolen from our people, left for dead--no one even bothering to look for us. Too busy. You were there. Stealing money from the dead white people you killed!"

Her verbal attack was so forceful: so clear, so concise, so filled with rage. If he could have, Crease would have bolted and run fleeing into the night, if there had been any night. There wasn't. He'd have taken back every word he'd spoken, every racist thought he'd entertained. He'd have jumped off the edge of the world and liked it, just to have his words back. He found himself wanting to hide himself from each prying, inquisitive eye that now stared at him. No one was supposed to ever know any of these things. Yet she clearly described to all in a loud voice what was to have remained hidden, secret. In the shadows of that trading post he vividly remembered what Shorty had said over and over. "We gots ta kill 'em . . . they's seen our faces." It is not inaccurate to say he wanted to piss his pants. He knew what was

356

coming. The possibility of him walking out of that log building alive was nil: none at all.

Alexandra paused before answering her own questions, staring at him.

"We were captives. Kidnapped. You were white men. Thieves, killers. You caused it. Leaving us fearing for our lives, expecting to be killed, to die. Because of you we starved, nearly died of thirst, and were soaked wet to the core, facing a winter with no food, no clothes, no blankets, no nothing. And raped." She grabbed her stomach. "Given a baby to carry when I didn't want a baby, didn't need a baby. Because of you! You bloody bastard."

Ah shit. Now everybody knows everything.

Alexandra didn't care.

Crease blinked his eyes, and wiped his mouth, not mentally quick enough to respond, not able to save himself. Everyone had heard her. She was speaking English. He did the only thing he could. He lied.

"I sure as hell wasn't there, lady. Your difficulty ain't none of my concern. I know nothin' 'bout ya. Nothin' a'tall." He was talking, backing up as though he was trying to persuade her. His backing up seemed odd. Not one person in that room believed him. Crease knew it. He didn't believe himself.

"Yes, you were. You and Sly. And that Shorty. Shorty wanting to kill us because we saw you. You were there. You brought the Oglala into camp. You're to blame. I get it. You don't want your friends to know you rode with Indians? That you were part of the party that massacred the Tallasinius company. They know now. They'll hang you by the neck until you're very, very dead. That's what you deserve. Not your fault? You horse's ass."

"Damn right. I ain't had nothin' ta do with that. None of it. I ain't never even heard of that."

Alexandra's tirade continued right along as if he hadn't said a word. "And in your feeble mind what blame does this unborn baby have? Did he choose his parents? You're responsible for everyone who died that morning on the Sweetwater. You weren't there? You lying son of a bitch."

"Everyone!" she announced. "This is Crease. He and Sly and Shorty brought the Oglala to the Sweetwater a year ago. They massacred everyone except for my sister, me, and Priscilla. He did it. This bastard brought them down on us."

357

Turning to him, she continued. "Tell them, Crease. You called me an Indian whore. You were there. You could have prevented it. You could have saved my virtue. But you didn't. So I'm your fault, too."

Alexandra grabbed the blade from the belt of the man standing slightly behind her listening and, before he could prevent her, she'd thrown it, end over end. To her amazement, the blade sunk deep in the post, inches away from Crease's head.

Crease threw his arms up, jumped to the side, swearing in his confusion, taken aback by the sudden aggression of the suntanned white woman dressed in a long doe skin dress, wearing beaded leggings, her hair in long braids after the manner of the Oglala.

In front of him, before he could think of what to do, Alexandra pulled her light skinning knife from her elk hide belt, balancing the blade between her thumb and index finger, holding it tightly. Her voice was an angry hiss.

"You yellow-bellied coward," she screeched. "Who fed me and my sister when we were starving, when we had nothing to eat? When we were cold, who brought us a blanket? When we needed shelter, who took us into their lodge, got us out of the cold north wind? When we were taken by the Crow, thrown over their horses like sacks of potatoes, who came for us? Who faced our enemies and killed them? Was it you? Was it you who helped us when we needed help? Who was it, you miserable camp dog? Who was it? Could it have been the father of this baby you called a breed? Or you? You, who sure as hell are not my hero, you miserable cur."

Crease stood before her, accused, mute, branded with guilt. Already he could feel the rope around his neck, the slack gone out of it.

A deep, male voice interrupted her, cutting her tirade off. "That right, Crease? That you? You done this? What she said?"

"No, it ain't right. Who ya gonna believe, me or this lyin' Injun whore?"

"I don't know, Crease. She ain't got no reason to be lyin'. Seein' there's two more white women standing right there. . . They lyin', too?"

Crease was no longer sure of himself, feeling the barbs of her daggers pierce his soul, the questioning voice interrogating him.

Alexandra Ann Wakeford stepped across the floor, closing the distance between herself and Crease, moving deliberately toward him, her knife held in her left hand now slightly behind her leg. Morning Flower still had hold of her right hand. She was no longer thinking.

"Beth," she said, "take her."

Her sister appeared out of the crowd, seized the little girl up in her arms. "Come with me, sugar," she said. "This is no place for you to be."

The skinning knife switched hands. Alexandra was standing twelve feet away from Crease.

"Lexie," her sister said, the child in her arms, "Lexie, let's get out of here."

"Shut up, Beth. I'll handle this."

"But Lexie . . . you really shouldn't. Lexie, please? Let's get out of here."

"No, Beth! This bastard deserves exactly what he's going to get."

The tall, wiry man found his courage, found his voice, and all his lost bluster. Behind Alexandra, Standing Bear, followed by his brother, came into the room; four others crowded into the space after him. The inside of the trading post was filling up. It was standing room only.

They heard Crease say, "Yeah? You and who else gonna see I gets what I gots comin' ta me?" He reached for his own blade and at the same time he pulled a Navy Colt from his waistband. He'd decided he was not taking any chances; what chances he had left had fled through the open door. It was a move he shouldn't have made. And he knew it the instant his fingers touched the hickory pistol butt.

Alexandra flung her skinning blade, reaching back for all that she was, throwing with all of her body. It flew true, striking him in the throat like a rattler striking a dodging jack rabbit, the blade sinking into the fine bones at the back of his throat. Involuntarily, spasmodically, he dropped the pistol and his knife, the weapons falling through his fingers. In alarm, he grabbed the knife handle of the blade buried in his throat, his involuntary response to jerk it out. He did, slicing his own artery. Even without doing so he would not have lived. Blood squirted into his hands, pulsating down his shirt with each beat of his heart.

"My God," he gurgled, crumbling to his knees, his fingers clutching the errant blade, trying unsuccessfully to stave the flow of blood with his free hand. "My God, ya done kilt me ya . . . ya Injun whore. Ya bitch!" The last words were indistinguishable, a mere gurgle.

"You're right. I did. And you deserved it," she replied. "You doin' what you did. Crease, you bastard." She paused. "Killing babies, old people. Seventy-eight human beings, dead. Stealing what wasn't yours. You'd better remember me. Because I remember you. Crease. Crease?"

He never heard her. He was stone cold dead on the floor, his blood pooling.

For a moment, a fraction of a second, she stood patting hilt of Fat Frenchie's Bowie knife, then she walked across the floor, standing over Crease, removing her skinning knife from his fingers. No one moved, watching her. She picked up Crease's Navy Colt, shoving it into her waistbelt, holding his blade. For a moment she stared at him. "Die, you bastard! Die!" she whispered. She turned to her sister and found her standing with Priscilla, holding Morning Flower in her arms, patting her.

"Beth? Pris? Do you remember him? Do you remember him?"

Priscilla nodded. "I remember him, Lexie."

"I do, too," Bethany answered. "Crease," she said softly, pausing. "I just didn't think you could do that. Jeez, Lexie, how did you do that? I wonder where the other two are? That Sly, that Shorty. Do you think they're here? We better get out of here."

Alexandra started walking across the uneven floor toward Bethany. Behind her, blood was pooling around Crease's throat, running between the cracks. A groan emanated from his chest. He lay still in death but his body betrayed him, jerking spasmodically.

Alexandra said, "Beth? Beth, let's get what we came for and get out of here. We don't belong here."

"We don't belong anywhere, Lexie."

"Maybe. But I need some black powder, some lead balls, and some caps. Pris wants her coffee beans. I aim to have them. I am not leaving here without Pris' beans."

"That's right," Priscilla said, her voice tight and cold. "I get my beans or we're not leaving."

Alexandra glanced at her sister, who pursed her lips, hesitating. Finally she nodded her head.

"Lexie, how did you do that? With the knife, I mean. Twice. I mean, how did you do that twice?"

"Practice," she said as she turned to the counter. "Every day I

360

practice." She leveled her gaze at the man standing behind it. "Lead balls, black powder, and caps. For this." She patted the grip of the Navy Colt stuck in her waistband. "And we want some coffee beans and some rock candy, the stick kind."

"All right," he said. "How are you going to pay for these items, sister?"

"See that dead man on your floor? See him?"

The counter man nodded. "I see him," he said.

"Sell his horse. If he has any hides, sell them. He's paying. That bastard owes me."

The trader smiled. "I see he does."

"Mister?" Bethany said. "Mister, do you know two men named Shorty and Sly? Have you heard of them? Have they been here also? Are they here?"

The trader nodded. "Heard of them but they ain't here."

"Where are they? If you know?"

"Sly is dead. He was shot in a saloon at Fort Laramie. Seems he tried to kill a young man that was better than him. Shorty, he's dead, too. Dead over on the Belle Fourche. Killed by somebody nobody knows. Some say it was the same kid. That's the scuttlebutt. I don't know who kilt 'em but they're dead. That's what I heard."

"By a kid? What's his name?"

"Nobody know'd his name," he said, turning his attention back to Alexandra. "Crease has two horses, a saddle and a pack saddle, and a rifle. I paid him for his skins. Probably has the money on him. Ain't spent it."

"Sell them all. I'll come for the money that I haven't spent. I want the rifle."

"Yes, ma'am," he said, smiling, "I reckon you do."

"Mister," Bethany asked, Morning Flower, in her arms, "do you know what that kid looked like? Was his name Zeke?"

"I don't. I ain't heard that name."

"You haven't heard that name?"

"No, Ma'am, I ain't.."

"Lexie, let's go," Priscilla said. "This is trouble. We should get out of here before we're sunk."

"Soon as I get what I came for. Coffee beans, remember? And rock candy."

"Like we had in St. Louis?"

"Yes. Like St. Louis."

"And coffee beans, Lexie?"

"And coffee beans . . . and Beth wants to get a message to our brother. She needs a pencil, and some paper. Do you have that? Am I asking too much?"

CHAPTER 58
Zeke is 93 miles south of Alexandra on Musselshell Creek

June 13, 1855
Missouri Breaks
North Central Nebraska Territory

In the spring, the Teton Lakota follow the buffalo and the buffalo follow the grass. It is the way it has always been. Walking Eagle's band camped on the south side of the Missouri river between the water's edge and the rugged, chalk white cliffs that rise abruptly, towering into the sky. Across the river Cow Creek drained from the north, its waters having trickled and run thirty-four miles from beginning to end. These are the Missouri Breaks: an irregular collection of canyons, draws, and high chalk cliffs that face the water's edge from both sides of the river. The rough hewn, towering spikes form primeval ridges that tower above the water's edge, casting long shadows. Sometimes they rise rapidly, running straight up from the river below, sometimes not. It is a place of safety. No one goes there to make war. It is said that this land will eat one's enemies, for there is no escaping it.

Grass is plentiful in May and the canyons create massive cliffs over which buffalo can be driven, run to their deaths, falling from the high precipices. If done right, if all the elements join, if everything cooperates, the hunt will be successful and no one will be hurt or killed. That 'if' is huge, for a mature animal can weigh between fifteen hundred and twenty-five hundred pounds. They are a massive, muscular fury, a horned beast without mercy, who, when enraged, can spin on the proverbial dime, and give up the change. In an eye blink they can change directions, attacking, hooking with horn, stomping with hoof, and destroying all who dare come within their path.

Under Walking Eagle's watchful eye the first spring buffalo hunt was planned.

If anything, the use of a buffalo run takes planning, coordination, and a knowledge of the lay of the land. Depending on the configuration of canyon and draw, riders generally start the run from both sides, waving blankets, and yelling. The buffalo slowly start moving: walking faster to avoid the commotion, moving away from the noise, seeking more grass to mollify their enormous appetites. More riders ride up from both sides, waving their blankets in the morning breeze, shouting. Inevitably, the buffalo start to run. First a few, then more. Their pounding hooves begin to shake the ground. Their energy goes kinetic, swallowing everything and everybody in its path.

The more noise there is, the more commotion generated, the more buffalo are running. Moving in a group, in greater and greater numbers, forced by those sheer numbers into a tighter and tighter mass, they move as one flesh. Riders appear, guiding those in front, making a noise, dropping back, dropping away, and reappearing. Suddenly those stampeding animals running in front of the herd simply drop out of sight. There is nothing they can do, pushed by sheer momentum, shoved off a forty-foot cliff, falling to their death. Once it begins, there is no stopping; those in front are forced forward by those behind until the gorge is filled with the dead and dying.

This was done as planned. Afterwards, the women swarm over the warm corpses, cutting their throats so that the buffalo may properly bleed, that the meat may be saved. Afterwards, the butchering begins, followed by great jubilation.

In the evening after the hunt, Walking Eagle did not return. No one had seen him since morning when hunting ponies were selected by the hunters, the blanket wavers. For that matter, no one had seen him since the running of the buffalo. He was there for he'd organized it. In fact, he'd placed the outriders at strategic places; he'd chosen the cliff. He was the architect. His absence wasn't a concern for he was who he was: a known loner, a leader, a shirt wearer. No one took the time to be concerned.

Later, after the sun had set, Small Dove pulled the covering aside and stepped inside Walking Eagle's lodge. For a moment she stood motionless, wordless, in the growing shadows. Alexandra looked up at her. The Wakeford girls were seated together, roasting buffalo tongue, holding fresh pieces of thinly sliced meat impaled on juniper sticks over a small, smokeless fire.

"Small Dove. Come. Sit with us," Bethany said. "As you know, we have plenty. Sit beside me. I'll scoot over."

Small Dove appeared not to hear; she looked like a porcelain doll about to shatter into a thousand pieces.

"Small Dove?" Priscilla said, her voice rising, sensing trouble.

"Are you okay?"

Priscilla stood and walked around the fire, the firelight dancing on her face, her fingers reaching for the small woman. She said, "Small Dove, you look so sad. What's wrong?" Priscilla's arm was about her shoulders. She looked down on the fragile face, the woman's deep brown eyes brimming with tears; their foreheads touched.

Small Dove didn't speak.   Her lips trembled as she opened her mouth. Wordless, she collapsed against Priscilla, the larger girl holding her upright, assisting her, preventing her from falling and hurting herself on the rocks of the fire circle. Bethany and Alexandra immediately joined Priscilla.

"Small Dove," Bethany whispered. "What's wrong?"

A keening sound rose outside. Small Dove commenced a low wail such that the girls had never heard.

"Someone has died," Bethany whispered. "That's the sound. Remember?" The outside keening was mingled with Small Dove's wailing. It sounded as though it came from all around.

"Oh, my," Alexandra whispered. "Do you think it's Small Dove's husband? One of her sons? What shall we do? What are we supposed to do? I mean, if he's dead?"

"I don't know," Priscilla said.

Bethany said, "Remember Tall Woman Standing? Her man was killed by the Absaroka. She had his body in her lodge for four days. A dead man lying there for four whole days. People going in and out. She was beside herself. I thought she'd be stuck with him permanently. I thought he'd begun to smell before they buried him."

"They didn't bury him," Alexandra said.

"I know."

"That's gross," Priscilla said.

"I know it's gross but they don't bury like we do. They keep them for a while."

Priscilla enjoined, "Four days?"

Alexandra squeezed the small woman's shoulders. "Small Dove, Small Dove . . . is it your husband? Who is it? What can we do?"

Priscilla said, "Small Dove, help us help you. We need to know what to do."

The covering was thrown open. The three girls turned to see who it was. A new person appeared, his face framed by the opening, the firelight flickering on his bronze skin. Without being welcomed, he stepped inside and turned to face the opening.

"Ahh, shit," Bethany said in a whisper. "It's Walking Eagle."

"What?" Priscilla said aloud, looking to see the uninvited stranger holding the shoulders of Walking Eagle, his braids dangling to the ground. The man was bringing what was left of Walking Eagle inside, assisted by three others. Alexandra and Bethany moved out of the way, assisting Small Dove. The body was placed on the buffalo blanket closest to the opening.

Walking Eagle was a mess. It looked like he'd suffered multiple fractures to his arms and legs, as though he'd been trampled, stomped by a thousand hooves.

"What happened?" Alexandra asked the stranger in Oglala.

The man, the first to enter and the last to leave, stared at Alexandra. "Tatonka," he said. "His horse stepped in a prairie dog hole, broke his leg, fell. Threw him off. The buffalo ran over him."

"Tatonka," Alexandra repeated, looking at the dead man.

"What?" Bethany said.

"Tatonka," Alexandra said. "Buffalo killed him. He was run down when his horse stepped in a prairie dog hole, broke his leg."

"Run down and run over," Priscilla said softly.

"What do we do, now?" Bethany asked. "When Tall Woman Standing lost her man, they cleaned him up, painted him, put his best clothes on him, and everyone came to see him. Afterwards, they put his body on a scaffold. Sort of like a funeral except we put them in the ground. Better, I think. Do you suppose we do that or does somebody else?"

"Well," Priscilla said speaking low, "this changes everything. Doesn't it?"

"We going to clean him up?" Bethany asked. "I mean wash up a dead man? Is that what we're going to do?"

Both girls turned to look at Bethany.

"I guess so, Beth," Priscilla finally said. "Get some water. I'll find something that looks like a rag. I don't know what we can do with a guy that's all beat up like this. We can just try. Do we want to? He is who he is, you know."

Alexandra stood over the corpse, her hand resting on her extended belly. Immense relief flooded through her. Behind her Small Dove sobbed.

I'm so glad you're dead. So glad. I hate you. I hated you. You're an awful

366

man.

She remembered him on the tall bay horse, holding his Hawkens rifle. Sitting, waiting, coming to rescue her, Bethany. No fear. A warrior.

What am I saying?

I'm saying I hate you. I'm so glad you're dead. I sleep under your blankets. I eat your meat. I have your baby growing in my belly. I hate you. I hate you so much. I wish you'd killed me. I do.

No, I don't.

Alexandra blinked her eyes slowly.

Pris is right. This does change everything.

Small Dove had not ceased crying. She sobbed into the night while the girls worked on the corpse. Alexandra did not. She did not touch him. They discovered he had a broken leg and a broken arm. His ribs were compressed, some broken. His jaw was broken. His ear was torn off. One eye was completely closed. Only his skin held him together. The two girls dressed him in his finest deer skins. Alexandra did not.

On the morning of the second day, the people started coming, one by one, in their finest dress. They came all that day and all the next. It wasn't just those in his immediate band, but others, men and women, children who Alexandra had never seen.

How do they know? Alexandra asked herself. *They just keep coming and coming.*

Some left gifts: tobacco mostly.

Life did not stop. The meat racks were set up; most had been set up on the day that Walking Eagle was killed. The next day they were heavy laden with buffalo meat drying in the sun. A breeze had come up out of the west keeping the flies down and the smoke out of camp.

On the second and third day, all those who were related to Walking Eagle came to build a scaffold. No effort was spared; it was built out of solid pine logs and was over eight feet high. Not that it was measured. It was not. It was built as high as Black Buffalo Man was tall with his hand as high as he could reach. It was built to keep the wolf and the coyote from disturbing Walking Eagle's bones. The place selected was high on the white chalk bluff overlooking the Missouri River, a place that Walking Eagle liked, where he had sought his vision as a young man.

On the fourth day when the sun was at its zenith, the old women came to the lodge of Walking Eagle to collect his body. There were twelve; they brought a painted horse to pull the travois that carried him to the ridge where the scaffold had been erected.

Everyone followed. There were outriders and riders beyond the outriders to guard against possibilities, possibilities that never arose. It was a procession. First came Alexandra, her belly beginning to show, carrying the child of Walking Eagle. With her walked Priscilla, Bethany, and Small Dove, as did her husband and Walking Eagle's younger brother, who no one had seen before. Small Dove knew him. With the girls were his son, Whips The Bear, and Walking Eagle's two daughters, Morning Flower and She Who Smiles, all dressed in their finest, following their father's corpse to the scaffold. His blue painted body lay on the travois, wearing the beaded shirt, the one made to honor a great leader, a man of the people: a shirt wearer.

The body was hoisted up onto the scaffold, his personal things left with him: his war shield, his lance, his bow, a quiver of arrows, and his pipe. Not his two Samuel Walker Colts nor his Hawken's rifle, for they were needed by those remaining, those left behind.

It was said among the old people that truly this day the nation of the seven tribes of the Teton Lakota had lost a great leader, one who could not be replaced, one who had spent his days in service of the people. He had died hunting tatonka, the buffalo, that his people might eat. Had he not ridden with Touch the Clouds, Worm, his young son Crazy Horse, and the great Sitting Bull, leader among the Hunkapapa?

Before leaving the Platte, had he not sat with Conquering Bear, smoked the pipe, and talked of the coming of the white man, and his troubles over a Mormon cow? Had he not brought honor to Conquering Bear's name, avenging the old man's bad death against the whites on the Sweetwater? Sadly, the old man was shot in the back by the long knife soldiers of Fort Laramie who came with their wagon gun, and the drunk Frenchman, an interpreter named Lucienne Auguste. Barely could this one ride, he was so drunk, his crooked words, lies, the whiskey having taken his tongue. Conquering Bear died at their hands because of an old cow, the old man shot in the back, walking away. That, too, was a bad day. Like this one.

Always, this one was fierce in battle, having counted many coup, having ridden his war pony with bravery, protecting his friends, his people with great courage. Was he not the last to leave the field of battle, and never without the wounded? Always, he remembered the aged, those without warriors to guard them, to protect them from their enemies, to hunt for them. Truly, he was a great man whose shadow, even in death, was long. That is what they said, the old people, sitting around the campfires of the Oglala, eating buffalo tongue, talking the stories of the great deeds of Walking Eagle long into the night. Heavy were their hearts. The loss of such a man was great.

"Now what?" Bethany asked after they'd returned from the scaffold.

"Everything has changed," Alexandra said.

"I know you said that. Actually Pris said that but I thought you were talking about Walking Eagle."

"I was."

Priscilla sat down on the buffalo rug. She said, "She means we can leave now, Beth. No one will stop us. There is no Walking Eagle."

"Really? Just like that?"

Alexandra nodded. "Yes, really. I've told Small Dove we will return to our people. That we'd go to the North Platte."

"What did she say?"

"She cried."

"That's so sweet. She's such a good person."

"I think it will take us six days to prepare everything we need. I think we should finish drying the buffalo meat. Say goodbye. We have to prepare She Who Smiles, Morning Flower, and Whips The Bear, also. Make sure they have everything they need. Someone to take care of them." Alexandra stopped. "I'm sorry. Please excuse me. This is what I think we should do . . . unless you have any better ideas. I'm listening. It's just what I think. That's all."

"No. No. Don't stop. It sounds good to me," Priscilla said. "The sooner the better. I don't want to be here another minute."

Bethany sat quietly, tears running down her cheeks.

"Beth, what's wrong?" Priscilla said.

"Nothing. Nothing at all. I'm just going to miss Small Dove, that's all. I don't think I'll see her again. I was just thinking and it made me sad. And then I thought about Morning Flower, She Who Smiles, and Whips The Bear. We won't see them again. It made me sad. And there's Feather Woman. I just . . ." Bethany was crying.

369

CHAPTER 59
Zeke is 5½ miles southwest of Alexandra

June 23, 1855
Judith Basin, thirty miles south-east of Judith Trading Post
North Central Nebraska Territory

They sat in the dark, in a grove of cottonwood trees, waiting for the sun. Their horses were ready, the travois packed. Priscilla had built a small fire out of dead cottonwood branches. The girls were alone. Walking Eagle's band had left the day before, moving south with the buffalo.

"How long do you think it will take?"

Alexandra looked at Bethany. "I don't know. From the Greasy Grass maybe it was two weeks before we got to the Judith River. I really didn't think about it. I should have, but I didn't. I'm guessing."

"It took sixteen days," Priscilla said. "I kept track."

"You did?"

"How did you do that?"

"I notched my walking stick every morning. It was sixteen days. I have it right here." Priscilla held up the broken lance, ran her finger down the notches she'd made. "Sixteen days. See?"

"Good," Alexandra said. "Real good. Sixteen days. The question is do we want to go to the Greasy Grass where . . . you know, or the Belle Fourche? Small Dove said that if we go to the Belle Fourche we won't have to make that climb into the Big Horns then out of the basin. She said if we were going to the Platte it would be shorter through the Belle Fourche and south. Shorter at least in time." Alexandra looked at her sister. "Which way?" she asked.

Bethany answered immediately. "I say Belle Fourche. Only bad thing is we haven't been there and we don't know where we're going. Or what to expect."

"Pris?"

"I agree. Besides, we can change our minds and turn west; go up over the Big Horns through the Canyon of Shells. The Platte River and Fort Laramie is ten days from there. We've been there, though I don't remember much about it."

"Okay. We look for the landmarks and we hold a little more

east and go south. We'll make the Belle Fourche River somewhere around sixteen or seventeen days. I think we can do it faster. There aren't as many of us. No lodges to put up and take down. No meat to dress. No cooking. No stopping to rest for the old people, for the horses. Not as much anyway. I think we should stay out of sight as much as we can. I don't think we should do anything to attract attention."

"We know what you mean, Lexie."

"It's early. Think it's too early to start?" Bethany asked. "I'm sort of anxious."

"No. I don't think it's too early. We can start if we want to. Won't make any difference. We're up. We're awake. Nothing stopping us."

"I'll put out the fire."

"It'll be all right until we leave. Maybe we should let it burn down. We don't want any smoke."

"Yes. Right. Stay hidden."

Priscilla held up her hands. She said, "Okay, we know where we're going. Let's make coffee before we leave. I'm thinking that would be good. I really want some. To celebrate. Besides we have a fire. It's right here. Might as well use it. Don't you think?"

"You and your coffee."

"Want some?"

"I do."

"Lexie?"

"Me, too." Her hands were on her belly. The baby moved. *Ah, shit,* she thought.

"You okay?" Priscilla asked.

Alexandra nodded. "I'm okay. Really, I am."

"Okay. Beth, you get the pot. I'll collect some more dry sticks for the fire. Make a little more heat."

Bethany said, "I'll get the coffee beans."

Alexandra looked past the fire ring to the south, the small orange flames casting a small light, reflecting off her face. In the east the sun had not risen but it was coming. In an hour, maybe a little less, it would poke its head above the horizon.

The baby moved again.

"Okay. Coffee, then let's go," Bethany said. "Let's go up the draw on the east and hold east of that mountain." She pointed. "That's what Small Dove said. I'll lead the bay. One of you two can ride. Lexie, maybe you? The other gets the paint and the travois."

"You don't have to be nice to me, Beth. I can walk. I prefer to walk."

Priscilla looked at her. "That settles it, Lexie will ride. Let's get going."

"One thing," Alexandra said, conceding the issue.

"One?"

"We really have to be careful. We're sort of alone."

Bethany and Priscilla turned to Alexandra.

"Sort of?" Priscilla said.

"We're going to run into trouble no matter what we do. We need to be ready. I think we have to assume everyone is out to hurt us, to stop us."

Bethany nodded.

"You ever shot a Hawkens, Lexie?"

"Once," Alexandra said. "It has a kick."

"Is it loaded?"

"Yes."

"I guess we better make sure we don't miss."

"Don't forget I have Crease's pistol."

"Coffee's ready." Priscilla announced. "Here, you two sit down. Get your cups. I'll pour."

Alexandra and Bethany sat down: one on a log, the other on a rock, and held out their cups for Priscilla to fill. She did so, then filled her own cup, then set the black kettle back in the flames.

"I like the way it smells," Bethany said, "especially in the morning. Like now, before sunrise."

"When everything is quiet," Priscilla observed. She smiled, staring at the cup. "I liked walking with my Poppa, coming up from the barn leading the work horses. I was always in a hurry. Thought they'd step on me with their big hooves. They were so big. Big like water pails and I was so small. Barefoot. That was a long, long time ago."

"Don't start crying, Pris. I don't know if I can handle it," Alexandra said, her hand going to her belly again. "This baby is kicking me," Alexandra said, resting her left hand on her belly, holding the hot, steaming cup in front of her.

Neither Priscilla nor Bethany replied. No one had taken a sip. All were waiting for the liquid to cool.

"Sure is black."

"Wish we had some sugar and cream."

"That'd be nice."

Alexandra smiled. "Zeke liked it pure black with nothing in it. Nothing at all. I asked him once how come he didn't use sugar, or some cream. We had some. You know, dress it up."

"He said, 'Dress up coffee? Why do you want to do that? It comes in a black suit coat and a top hat.'"

Alexandra laughed, her right hand still on her stomach. "I told him it tastes better."

"'Maybe, he says, but it don't look no better.'"

"You're the one that's going to start crying, not me," Priscilla said. "I wish he was here, too, Lexie. Things would be a whole lot better." She blew on the coffee, put the cup to her lips, and inhaled deeply, glancing at Alexandra. "Sorry, Lexie. Really. I didn't mean to open up old wounds."

"It's okay. Sometimes, like right now, I really miss him, that's all. Black coffee, no milk, no sugar, no sun. Reminds me of him. I hope he's okay. Sometimes I wonder if he'd still like me . . . after all this, all that's happened."

Bethany took a small sip, washed the bitter liquid around in her mouth, and swallowed. She never said a word. It was so bitter, so tart, so acidic. So good.

They left the temporary campsite in the early morning of June 23, 1855.

Five and a half miles south, coming north from a slightly westerly direction, having left the Greasy Grass fifteen days before, Zeke stepped into the saddle and, unbeknownst to him, headed right toward Alexandra. It was the closest he'd been to her in eleven months: a mile and a half, separated by a low lying ridge and twenty six minutes. He had no idea. No one did.

CHAPTER 60
Alexandra is 3 ½ miles south of Zeke

June 23, 1855
30 miles southeast of Judith River Trading Post
North Ccentral Nebraska Territory

Zeke stood in the clearing holding the reins to his black horse and the mule that Emile rode. The lead ropes to the two pack animals were attached to the back of Emile's saddle.

Emile had his hands in the ashes, running them through his fingers.

"Ashes still warm," he said. "An hour old. Burnt down. Not wet."

Emile walked around the ash pile, studying the ground, then toward the creek. He nodded to himself, looked east toward the light growing brighter. "Well," he said. "Three riders. Two travois. Another horse. Small feet, all three. Women. No men. Not here, anyway. Women wearin' moccasins. Teton Lakota. They's headin' south. Left an hour ago followin' the creek. We missed 'em. They's movin' east and a little south. Look at this."

"What?"

"Coffee grounds."

"Coffee? I didn't know the Teton Lakota drank coffee."

"They don't."

Three? Number is right. Zeke thought. *But Lexie wouldn't be alone. There'd be men. White women captives wouldn't be left alone. Don't make sense. This couldn't be Lexie. She'd be with this Walking Eagle, Bethany, Pris. Especially if she is his wife. Indian women travelin' south? Alone? And coffee grounds. Guess it ain't impossible. It just don't make sense.*

"Think we need to worry?"

"Three women? Nothin' ta worry about. We don't bother 'em. They won't bother us. They ain't the ones you're lookin' fer."

"Don't think so, either. How far we got to go?"

The first rays of the sun caught the tops of the cottonwood trees. Emile studied the lay of the land warming under the seven o'clock sky.

"Thirty miles," he said. "We'll be on the Judith soon. Dry Wolf

374

Creek is on the other side of the Judith River. They joins up thirty miles from here. That's where they're supposed ta be. There's a tradin' post closer."

"You been there?"

"Four years ago."

Zeke nodded.

Thirty miles. He's right. That ain't far. Not really. He took a deep breath. *Lexie's so close. Thirty miles. Closer every minute. What, then?*

I'll burn that log when I get to it. Hope she ain't forgotten me. Hope she remembers.

She will.

Really?

Yeah, really.

How long's it been? Eleven, 'most twelve months. That's long. I've been doin' this near a year and ain't got no closer.

Most anythin' kin happen.

Well, it hasn't.

Ya don't know. Nobody does.

I'll find her. I said I would. Foolish. I'm simpleton foolish. I could be in Oregon. I should be in Oregon. Stopped this craziness.

Oh, shut up. Get on with it.

What choice would she have really? She's with 'em. She's dressed like 'em. They're all around her. Every day she's doin' what they do. No choice?

Shut up, ya ain't makin' no sense.

Zeke stepped into the saddle. From the seat of his Russian, he handed Emile Villon the reins to his mule.

"Let's go," he said. "We're burnin' daylight."

And so they were.

375

CHAPTER 61
Alexandra is 29 miles southeast of Zeke

June 23, 1855
Judith Trading Post
North Central Nebraska Territory

The Judith Basin Trading Post sat one hundred fifty feet east and away from the river. Some would say not far enough for it was built on the flood plain. Away from the log building half a mile was a long, ten foot high, cut bank. Once long ago, beyond anyone's memory, the river had flooded, running high, and had washed away tons of silt from the sides of the hill, leaving piles of white, exposed rock: white because once they were buried deep in the hillside. Now they were not.

It wasn't as if the men who had constructed the long log cabin had not put some thought into its placement. They had. It was situated away from the Judith River a tolerable distance. A man could easily carry two five gallon pails of water, one in ether hand to the log cabin. It was water to drink and wash the tin plates, forks, knives and spoons, and once in a while, to take a bath. Close enough yet far enough away: that was their thinking. Besides, there hadn't been a bad, "drown in the rain standing up" cloudburst in forever. No one living could remember one, but they knew about the cut bank. It was right there for the most casual of observers to see.

Nothing to worry about.

Emile Villon walked, leading his mule, and a horse packing elk and buffalo hides. He was followed by Zeke. They rode easy, approaching the trading post from the south and found themselves looking down on the building from a hill and a sheer drop of one hundred forty feet to the river bottom and the flood plain. Below them was the trading post; behind it were some horse corrals, a small pole barn, and a stack of timothy hay secure inside an enclosure made of slender pine poles. In front of the cabin were two rows comprised of cords and cords of firewood, some freshly split and stacked. Smokeless chimneys sat at either end of the trading post. Between the two chimneys was a sod roof held up by pine poles, resting on logs, pitched to the north and south.

It was time to sit around a table and chew the proverbial fat, blow foam off a little "made in the back" hooch, and get oneself around some elk steak, baked beans, and some freshly made bread. "Take care of the soul," Eli Tallasinius would say, "by taking care of the body."

Zeke leaned back in the saddle, his feet pushing hard against the stirrups as they plunged off the hillside, their mounts kicking up dust, throwing gravel and rocks.

The front door was on the west side, made of four inch thick ax hewn planks, the top and bottom cut square with a crosscut hand saw. The door was held in the frame by thick leather straps. It would be several years before the door was supported by metal hinges. It had been open for business for eleven years and, as of yet, there was no blacksmith, hence no metal hinges.

Tying their horses and the mule to a pole hitching rail, they stepped inside. Their faces encountered a warm, dry heat that felt good on the skin. Someone was cooking. On the right was the trading business with stacks of wool blankets, barrels of pickles, and wheat, corn, and oats. The counter was made of hewn cottonwood. Behind it were shelves containing bolts of cloth, rope, boxes of ammunition, lead balls, black powder, caps, three navy pistols, two Sharps rifles, and a Volcano lever action. To the left were three shot guns. All for sale.

On the left, built around a fireplace, no fire, was a short bar without stools, six tables, four spittoons, and twelve chairs. Behind the bar was a doorway leading to the kitchen. They could smell fried steak, baked beans, bacon, and coffee. Through the doorway, Zeke could see an iron range, steady smoke from burned grease rising from the surface where buffalo steak was burned to a "well done" perfection. He wondered how the trader got that hunk of iron into the kitchen without tearing down a wall . . . and how he got it to the Judith River. He concluded it must have taken some real doing and four tired horses pulling a freight wagon.

Having glanced toward the saloon, Zeke turned to the trading post and his need for information. Sitting at a table in the corner of the bar would take too long. He didn't have all day. In his mind he had minutes. Lexie was now mere miles away, maybe not even that.

"Afternoon," he said to the counter man, a stooped over individual wearing a blue cotton shirt, dark brown leather suspenders, and faded black denim trousers. He had a full beard extending past the third button on his shirt. His hair was black and pulled back from his forehead and tied in the back, the length of it extending over his collar, hanging down between his shoulder blades. He had small, squinting eyes that seemed to observe everything. His ears were mostly hidden by the full head of hair. He looked at Zeke without returning his greeting.

A tall Lakota was standing in front of the counter and to his left four paces, cradling a Hawkens rifle, wearing moccasins, leather pants, and a breech covering made of tanned, elk hide. He wore nothing in his braided hair. He was looking at Emile Villon and said something to him. Emile nodded.

"Whatcha need?" the counter man asked.

"Information. Maybe some other things if you got 'em."

"What'd that be?"

"I'm partial to rock candy."

"Rock candy, I got. Information? Maybe. Depends on what you need to know."

"I'm lookin' for three white girls: ages fifteen, eighteen, nineteen. Young. Taken captive by the Oglala Sioux eleven or twelve months ago on the Sweetwater. Heard anythin' about 'em? Perhaps you've seen 'em? They're said to be with an Injun name of Walking Eagle. His band is supposed to be around here somewheres."

"You sure pick 'em, boy."

"What does that mean?"

"Just that. No offense intended."

"None taken."

"I seen three white girls. Maybe three-four-five weeks ago. Here. Two were sisters. Wore Lakota dresses. The older one kilt a man right here. Killed him with a knife, then took his knife, his Navy, bought some coffee beans, some rock candy, and left." The trader smiled. "She sold the dead man's traps and came back for the money. Hellava note to tell the truth. Ain't seen the like."

"You say one of 'em killed a man?"

"She did. Without blinkin' an eye. Kilt him dead."

"What was his name? This man she killed?"

"Crease. Got him buried right out there."

"I know'd a Crease. Heard he was a big man."

"This one was that. Don't expect he was thinkin' he could be stabbed in the neck, but he was, expectin' or no."

"And she left?"

"She did, with the Walking Eagle Oglala. Probably three or four weeks ago."

The trader smiled, revealing yellow, black teeth, tobacco stained, and gaps with no teeth. "That Walking Eagle, he ain't to be trifled with. They were his'n, I expect. Well respected by his enemies, he is. Don't have many 'cause they're dead. His band was camped across the Judith where it meets Dry Wolf Creek. I'd say twelve-fifteen miles north of here. They're creatures of habit. Notional. If you know what I mean. It's April." He paused. "Is it April? Damned, if I know. Maybe it's May. Thet Walking Eagle bunch like to summer up there on the Horn. They'll stay in these parts huntin' buff, elk. Maybe he went a little farther north and east, 'most to the Breaks. Depends where the buff are runnin'. I ain't seen 'em in several weeks."

The trader turned to a tall Indian standing in the shadows, an elk robe draped across his shoulders. They spoke in the language of the people.

"Killer, here says they were where I told you but they have moved or are movin' east to the Missouri Breaks. Said they left a week, ten days ago--maybe two weeks. My red brothers don't keep time too good. Somethin' happened that disturbed 'em. Don't know what. Said they're movin'. Probably huntin' buffalo. Said soon as they have a good hunt they intend to head to the Greasy Grass, Goose Creek, then back up on the Big Horn for the rest of the summer. Killer, here, ought to know. He's been livin' with 'em off and on."

"Greasy Grass? We came from there. Didn't see no one."

"Yes, sir, the Greasy Grass. On the 'tuther side of the Musselshell, the Yellowstone. South."

"I know where it is. I was just there ten-fifteen days ago. And they've gone to the Missouri Breaks?"

"Yes, sir. Killer here says ten days, maybe more. Followin' the buff. You lookin' fer those white girls? Lord. That one'll make your hair stand up. She's somethin'. Got everyone a talkin'."

"Think I oughta ride for the Greasy Grass if I'm gonna find 'em?"

The trader looked at Zeke, nodded. "Yes," he said, pausing. "But I'd say first you oughta go to where they are on the Judith, follow 'em, see where they went. Hellsfire, for all we know they might still be there. If'n they ain't, they's leavin' you a trail ta follow." The trader

379

collected the spittle in his mouth and spat into a spittoon behind the counter. "These girls relatives of yourn?"

Zeke shook his head.

The trader paused. "Your woman?"

"Not exactly, but I'm a little sweet on one of 'em."

The trader paused, looked knowingly at Zeke without saying anything.

"I know, I know," Zeke said. "I've heard it before."

The trader smiled, showing his teeth or lack of them. "Know'd some myself. See 'em. Come here time to time. Captives, you know. They're different, let me say that. Livin' with the Injun changes 'em. Reckon it'd change anybody, but women more so. They sorta become Injun. Know what I mean? Ain't no goin' back. The ones I told you about, they's as Injun as I've seen."

"I've heard that."

The trader turned and spoke to the Indian. The second conversation lasted longer.

Finally the trader turned to Zeke. "They're there. With 'em," he said. "He said they live in the lodge of Walking Eagle. After the manner of the people. One is called She With Hand On Her Knife, a younger girl. One is called She Who Is Angry; she's the one that killed ol' Crease. He don't know what the third one is called. Said they are the wives of Walking Eagle. Make his food, live in his lodge, mother his boy, his girls. I reckon you didn't want to hear that."

"I've heard it."

The trader nodded, turned to Emile Villon. "You?"

"Got some skins."

"Where?"

"Out front."

"Let's have a look."

"Take your time," Zeke said. "I'm aimin' to see what's goin' on at your drinkin' establishment. Get myself around some fresh steak, some beans, if you got 'em. Smells like some fresh baked bread, some corn bread. Maybe I'll have some of that before I hit the trail."

"Help yourself," the trader said. "Got plenty."

Zeke found a table in the far corner, and sat down, his back to the wall. He surveyed the room, removed his hat, and set it on the table. He sat there for a moment, resting, listening, smelling the aromas coming from the kitchen, feeling the juices forming in his mouth.

A nice buff steak would be good, he thought. *A cup of black coffee, some corn bread, some beans boiled tender around a ham bone, slices of onions and potato. That'd be good.*

Next to him, ten feet away, were four men sitting around a square table, getting around such an order. They were minding their own business. Zeke wondered what that business might be. He listened.

"That ain't what I heard," said a man wearing a red plaid shirt, top buttons open.

The three turned to look at the speaker.

"Back there at Brothers? You're talkin' Belle Fourche, right? That's not what that fellow said. What's his name? Jacobs? Remember him?"

The fellow in a solid blue denim shirt nodded. "What was it he said?"

"He said that kid was sittin' drinkin' coffee. He'd ate and was talkin' to a couple of fellas at this here corner table. That's what I remember him sayin'."

"Been there a while. If I remembers. Drinkin' coffee and eatin' a buff steak."

"Yeah. That's right."

"And the other fellow, a big man, real short name; he was playin' cards."

"I heard he was losin'. Been losin' all mornin'. That's what upset him."

"That don't explain him shootin' at the kid."

"No, it don't."

"Musta said somethin'."

"You mean the kid?"

"Yeah, but the odd thing is, the kid was just sittin' there. Mindin' his own business."

The three nodded at the same time, apparently remembering the same thing. One poured himself a cup then leaned back in his high-backed chair.

"What'd ya think he said?"

For a moment no one spoke.

"Whatever it was it got that big fella upset."

"Where was this?"

"Laramie."

381

"Laramie? That's ta hell and gone."

"Yeah, it is that but every travelin' soul manages to stop there goin' ta California."

"And Oregon."

"And Oregon."

"Lot of Injuns."

"Musta been three or four thousand camped on the Platte 'bout that time. Damn near the whole tribe."

"Heard that. There was a big government give away and somethin' 'bout some damn milk cow."

"I heard that, too. Injuns butchered and et her. That's what I heard. Damn near started an Injun war."

"Over a milk cow?"

"That's the yarn I heard."

"What'd ya suppose the kid was doin' there?"

"Havin' a drink. What's anybody do there?"

"Well that Simonson says that big fellow, he jumps up like he's been sent for, like somebody poked him in the ass-end with a sharp stick. Starts ta cussin' and swearin', carryin' on."

"What'd he say? I mean the kid. What'd the kid say to him?"

"Don't rightly know."

"But that big feller was all het up just the same. That's fer damn sure."

"Now get this. That big fellow already has his Navy out, thumbin' the hammer. He's got the kid dead to rights. Tries ta kill him sittin' at that damn table. And that kid somehow gets hisself goin' and puts a round through the head and one through the brisket. Just like that. In less time than it takes ta snap your finger. That kid was somethin'. Had folks forever jawin' 'bout what they'd done seen. That fellow, Jacobs, said he ain't seen nothin' like it."

"I heard that myself. That Simonson fella said the big fella put a round into the table where the kid was sittin'. And in the next half a second that kid puts three in him."

"Heard it was two."

"Naw, that Jacobs said it was three and the big fella was dead on his feet. Didn't know it. Said the kid was packin' two irons. Got 'em both out. Didn't bother with no empty. Just yanks 'em irons from outta nowheres and shoots away. Got off three 'fore the fella hits the floor. Sure some shootin'. Said he ain't seen nothin' like it."

"Saw somethin' like that myself once. Down there in Orleans. That's where I seen it."

"The hell you say. Orleans? Ain't never been there myself. Heard it was some town."

"Yeah. It's thet all right."

"I'd like ta seen that."

"What happened to the kid?"

"Don't know."

"Know his name?"

"Jacobs said he simply disappeared."

"Just kid. That's what I heard."

"Kid?"

"Yeah. Damnedest thing. Three rounds the size of a ten dollar gold piece right in the ol' noggin."

The man in the denim shirt sipped on his cup, cradling the warmth in both hands, and stared at the steam swirling off the top.

Emile Villon sat down beside him. "He'll take 'em all. Thet's what he said. This is where we part, kid. This is fer as I go. I figure ta stay here."

"All right," Zeke said. "Want to split up what we got? That what you're sayin'?"

"That's it."

"You got your packhorse, pack saddle, your saddle and that mule you're ridin'. They ain't mine. I got no claim."

Emile Villon nodded, suddenly paying close attention.

Zeke noticed.

"Take it easy, Emile, I ain't takin' advantage of you none. You take the rest of the trade goods. We split even what we get for them pelts. Ain't much trade goods left anyways. You earned 'em. I'll be beholdin' for your help. Sound fair?"

It sounded fair. It sounded too fair.

"That all ya want?" Emile Villon said.

"That's it."

"I reckon it sounds fair. Ya ordered some grits?"

"I ain't."

"Well, let's get somethin' ta take the edge off, cut the dust."

CHAPTER 62
Alexandra is 46 miles southeast of Zeke, heading to
the Belle Fourche River

June 24 , 1855
Judith Trading Post
North Central Nebraska Territory

Come morning the old man Emile 'Bad Horse' Villon was gone. The evening before, he'd sat at Zeke's table in the corner. After the money was divided from the sale of their skins, he ate the beans, steak, and cornbread that Zeke bought him. He drank the corn liquor set at their table. Come morning he was no longer there. He simply vanished. Zeke didn't have even an elemental idea of where he'd gone. There were no goodbyes. No "I'll see you later." He took with him his packhorse, his riding mule, all the remaining supplies Zeke had bought, traded for, and said he could have. In short, everything.

To Zeke it made no difference. Upwind or downwind, he didn't have to smell the old man, didn't have to watch him finger his food, pick his remaining teeth clean, nor scratch himself like some jackass making use of a dead tree. It was just as well. He'd suspected that the old man knew where Lexie was all the time they'd ridden together and stubbornly kept it to himself, never telling Zeke.

With Emile Villon it was always the same old tiresome song and dance played to the same boring tune. He'd said it dozens of times. "It ain't no good ya find her. It ain't no good at all. She's another man's woman. She's that. Sleeps under his buffalo robes, bornin' his babies, eatin' his vittles. She's his'n. Ya ain't got no business gettin' in there. Your life ain't her life. Ya listenin' to me, greenie? Ya ain't got nothin' she needs. Leave 'er be."

Zeke never listened and now he was close to finding Alexandra. He could feel it. He took the trader's advice, for he'd seen her. Come morning, he saddled the black and, trailing his packhorse, followed the Judith River north, looking for the place where it conjoined with Dry Wolf Creek. It took five hours. He found the trail of many people, and the travois marks where they dragged their possessions behind many horses. They were moving east. He followed.

It was evening when he found the place where they'd camped

384

on the Missouri between the water's edge and the white chalk cliffs that towered above him on the south. He followed their trails, taking each to its end: finding the buffalo run and the drying bones of many buffalo, the scaffold of a dead man high on the summit where the white cliffs overlooked the river running slowly east. And when the entire village moved south, he followed them again.

Two days later their trail disappeared under the tracks of several million head of buffalo, any trace beaten into oblivion by sheer numbers. He spent three days unsuccessfully trying to locate any semblance of a trail. It simply wasn't there any longer. Finally he gave up. The best that he could do was assume they continued south intending to end up on the Big Horn Mountain. It was an educated guess based on the information that that was what Walking Eagle's band always did. "Always." That's a long time and invariably it proved to be false.

An exasperated Zeke started south: crossed the Musselshell, the Yellowstone,found the Greasy Grass, and continued south to Goose Creek. He met no one, not a single soul, until he reached Goose Creek. He found Tall Crow, the only Oglala he knew that spoke English, surprised that he was still there He did it by repeating his name Hanska Kangee to everyone he met. He was eventually directed to his lodge on Upper Goose Creek not far from the dugout cabin of Emile Bad Horse Villon. He brought Tall Crow a doe, dressed out. He dropped it on the ground in front of him, then stepped down from the saddle.

"I'm lookin' for Walking Eagle," he said.

"Won't find him."

"No?"

"He's dead."

"Dead?"

Tall Crow looked at him. "Dead," he said again as though Zeke hadn't heard him.

"Where are his people? Have you seen 'em?"

"Not here. On Judith River, Missouri Breaks. Not passed this way. Not on Goose Creek. You look for woman of Walking Eagle?"

Zeke looked at Tall Crow, not wanting to admit that he was looking for another man's woman even if he was dead. He hadn't known that. Still it just seemed wrong. "Yes," he admitted. "I'm still lookin'.""

"No find?"

Zeke shook his head, "No find," he said.

The Indian looked at him for what seemed a long time. He said, "Maybe no good find. She Indian Woman maybe. Her man dead. Maybe find Oglala man. Maybe better."

"Maybe," Zeke said, then stood up, not wanting to hear it. "Thank you," he said. "You've been a great help."

Tall Crow nodded, glanced at the doe carcass and watched Zeke mount his horse.

He pointed at the carcass. "This good," he said. "Tall Crow not work this day. No hunt. My woman fix venison roast. Stay by fire, keep warm." He smiled. "You need woman like that. Find Indian woman."

Zeke nodded. "I sure do, my friend. You wouldn't know where I could find one, would you? I sure as hell have been lookin'.'"

Tall Crow looked at him, glanced at the black horse he'd ridden. Slowly he shook his head no. "I do not," he replied. "Not too many. Maybe you look for Indian woman in blue dress." Tall Crow smiled.

"Yeah, maybe. Maybe I'd get killed if I did that."

"Maybe," Tall Crow said.

Mounting, pulling at the lead rope to the bay packhorse, he nudged the black forward, riding toward lower Goose Creek without looking back, thoughts of Lexie running through his head. Three miles later he pulled up, slid off the horse and dropped the reins. He looked north out over the valley that extended into the haze and shook his head. The trail was ending.

Now what? I've done everythin' I can think to do. Been everywhere and she ain't nowheres. I get gawd awful close and she vanishes like smoke in the wind.

Ya ain't done everythin'.

What do you mean I ain't done everythin'? I sure as hell have. Name one thing that I could do that I ain't done.

Ya ain't found her.

Well, thank you very much. I know that.

Until ya find her ya ain't found her.

Let's take a look at that. She ain't north 'cause she ain't on the Judith no more. She ain't in the Missouri Breaks. She used to be but she ain't no more. I was there ten days ago. I know. She ain't south. Nobody is. Her people ain't been to Goose Creek or on the Big Horn. Not this year. Not yet, anyways.

    Her people? What do ya mean 'her people?'

    What else am I gonna call 'em? They sure as hell ain't mine.

    So where are her people?

    I don't know. They just disappeared into a herd of buffalo. I ain't got a clue.

    They don't just disappear. Ya lost 'em.

    All right, I lost 'em.

    How about east?

    East? I was there last fall. She sure as hell wasn't there. I was. I done kiled a man over there.

    He deserved killin'?

    He sure did.

    Good. Her not bein' there . . . that was then.

    That was then? Ahh, shit.

    Ahh, shit? What's that supposed ta mean?

    It means I'm tired of lookin'.

    Well, quit or get on with it.

    I ain't no quitter.

    Get on with it.

    But east? I sure as hell don't want to go there. Not again.

    What? Ya don't like Clear Creek, Crazy Woman? The Powder?

    I've been there. I been to each one.

    Ya ain't been there lately and ya ain't found her.

    Ahh, shit. I really don't want to hear this.

    Ya done said that. Either get ta lookin' or get the hell out of here.

    All right.

    All right? Don't ya all right me. I ain't in the mood.

    Neither am I.

It was July 8, 1855.

CHAPTER 63

July 9, 1855
Clear Creek
Central Nebraska Territory

His fire was small. Its dim flicker cast indistinct, moving shadows against the rocks that sheltered and concealed it, that held the yellow orange flame cupped away from breeze and draft. The blaze itself was partially hidden behind a tall, dark, blackish, carbon-covered coffee pot, one side dark, black, barely discernable, the other resting in popping, glowing orange coals.

Inside the pot, water bubbles sprang in a steady roll from the fire side and not at all away from the fire. In the middle of the metal container rested an old wool sock, its mate long gone, washed too much, worn too much, all for much too long. Inside the sock were old coffee grounds, beans crushed with the butt of a Navy Colt, then simmered too often for too many mornings, and a handful of new coffee grounds freshly pounded by the same pistol butt fifteen minutes before.

On the west, a granite cliff rose sixty feet, its surface reflecting the hidden glow. On the east, pine trees towered, hiding any light that might have escaped into the early morning dark.

No breeze touched the flame or the rider standing in the shadows, his face partially lit. Pulling an 1851 Navy Colt from its holster, Zeke checked the loads, rotating the cylinder, listening to the metallic clicks: six accounted for, no empties, every cap in place. He checked the loads in the second Navy Colt that he carried stuck behind his belt buckle in his waistband, its walnut grip accessible to his left hand.

He fetched a tin cup from his saddlebag, knocking the dust from the inside by thumping it against the palm of his left hand. For a moment he stood in the shadows and listened, cataloging what he heard: wolves hunting, an owl, a small rodent scurrying in the undergrowth, a pack of coyotes' high pitched singing, chattering among themselves like drunken sailors, a bull buffalo clearing his throat, and the flit of night swallows seeking mosquitoes, snatching them out of the air.

Filling the cup, he set the coffee pot off to the side to cool, wanting the fire to burn itself down and out. No smoke.

The black horse blew its nose, ground its teeth, then started cropping grass. Beyond the black the bay packhorse sniffed at the dog, then stretched its neck, shaking itself from tailbone to nose hair. The rider cupped his hands around the tin cup, feeling the heat permeate into his fingers, warming the joints. He took his time, waiting for the coffee to cool before sipping it. When he did, the taste was bitter, tart, acidic, a product of overboiled coffee grounds. It was awful, sinful, and good. It was a black coffee morning. There had been many, a string of them, and this was going to be another; he could feel it.

It's so useless, he thought *But Lexie is close now. Always close. She has to be. She just has to be.*

The fire had burned down and out. Zeke mounted the black, throwing his leg over the saddle. Why he was traveling east, he didn't know, other than he hadn't been there since last fall. He asked himself *why* again.

It's just somethin' I have to do. Just one more thing. Somethin' to do before I give it all up.

Give up? I can't do that.

What do I do when there's nothin' else to do?

Start over.

Start over? Where? It's like she's avoidin' me.

She can't avoid me if she don't know I'm here. Ain't no way.

Surely, she don't know. How could she?

Of course she don't.

But there ain't no startin' over. There ain't no 'where' to start over. Not even. Wish there were. This is it. There just ain't no never mind. There's this time and this time . . . she's 'bout done.

Zeke patted the black's shoulder, looked as far east as he could see. It wasn't far; the haze prevented it. The black started walking.

All right, let's get after it.

Yesterday was Clear Creek. Next Crazy Woman, the Powder, then Belle Fourche. After that we'll turn south.

"Get that, dog? We'll make Belle Fourche and we'll turn south."

And that will be that.

Sounds awful.

'Cause it is awful.

Zeke rode east into the morning light. Before him lay a long narrow valley running eastward toward the Crazy Woman. He took a deep breath and let it out.

Well, hell, he thought.

"Where are you, Lexie?" he asked aloud. O'Reilly stopped, sat back on his haunches, looked up at him, and scratched, his hind foot a blur. The black walked on by him.

"You could be in so damn many places. Me and the dog, we've been to 'em all. I don't know where to look no more. Don't know where to go." The black's ears laid flat against the horse's head, listening. Zeke noticed.

"Shut up," he said. "You know I don't want to hear from you." He looked down at the dog who'd caught up and was now walking beside the horse. "You, either you worthless hound."

The dog wagged its tail rapidly.

"I hate like hell talkin' to myself," he said glancing at O'Reilly.

"Okay, dog. One more time. We'll take a look at the Belle Fourche. We'll head south."

How can you say that?

How? Easy. There ain't no place else to go.

The dog was out front, running back and forth, its nose to the ground, sniffing. The valley's east end disappeared from Zeke's view but he remembered it from before. From the western most side, on the rise after Clear Creek, he couldn't see the end of it. By the time he'd ridden an hour it had bent around to the north and was going in an entirely different direction. He thought maybe it went clear to Canada. He didn't know, besides he was heading east.

I guess they could have gone east to the Belle Fourche. I guess.

But that ain't likely. Why would anyone do that? I wouldn't.

I'll bet they're wherever that Walking Eagle band ended up. Where would that be? It seems so unlikely that I passed 'em. I'd of seen somethin'. Smoke. Tracks. If I did it was somewheres between the Missouri Breaks and the Greasy Grass. How'd I do that?

That just ain't likely.

Suppose they could have held up on the Yellowstone. That's some creek. All those folks- it'd be hard 'crossin' it. No tellin'. Women, kids. Horses. I guess I could miss 'em.

That ain't likely.

If they did I ought to go north not east, not on some wild goose chase to the Belle Fourche. They sure as hell ain't there. What the hell am I doin' anyways?

Zeke wasn't hungry so he didn't eat. He hadn't bothered fixing breakfast. Except for coffee. Before there was a false dawn he had a cup, then rode right down the middle of the valley. After an hour the haze lifted and he could see six or seven miles.

Someone was out there: three riders a long ways away. At least it looked like three riders. It could have been four. What he saw was three horses: small dots on an open sea of green grass that stretched on and on.

I really ought to turn around and head north. That's where that band was not two weeks ago. That is where I should be goin'. That's where they are if they're anywheres.

Zeke stared at the small figures practically lost in the broad valley.

What if they're Injuns?

What if? What else? Who else? Nobody but Injuns lives out here.

I could ask 'em about three white girls.

Oh, give it up. They're just gone. Probably dead.

Maybe not dead dead.

That liveryman had been right. Just for the wrong reasons.

Right about what?

They's dead. He said.

Well they ain't. I know they ain't.

Why ask 'em? Just kill 'em. After all, they took Lexie and Beth and Pris in the first place. Killin' everybody.

Kill 'em? That's a hellava thing to say. Pure awful. I can't believe I thought that.

I could ask, he thought. *What would that hurt?*

Won't do no good. Whatever they answer, I won't understand. It's useless. What are they doin' out here? Alone?

None of my business. When I get to 'em, I could give 'em somethin' like I was Bad Horse. That's what he'd do. But I ain't got nothin'. What are they doin' out here? Ain't likely they're lost.

He could see them now, much more clearly, though they were still a long ways off. Six miles had become four, then three, then two.

He could see them: a small cavalcade moving slowly up the valley towards him. One was riding; two were walking.

Women? They're just women? And they're alone. Alone? What's this all about? Women ain't never alone.

A shiver went up his spine. Then, just as he'd always known, he knew, he absolutely knew that Lexie was alive, and her sister Beth, and Priscilla were, too. They just had to be.

I just don't know where, but they are alive. I know it.

No. No, the liveryman was right. And the almost old man was right. Lexie is someone else's wife, and her sister, too. They live on the great plains now-- out here somewheres; they probably have children, little black-haired babies, livin' on buffalo and elk, red buffalo berries, and chokecherries.

No, that ain't likely. They ain't had time.

But they can never go home again 'cause they are home. This is home now. They're captives; then they become wives and mothers and their lives are forever changed. Lexie don't want me to find her. She don't want to see me at all. She has a man.

Had a man. He's dead.

It ain't no never mind. That's why I can't find her. She knew I was there and she just disappeared. Hidin'. I should have turned my back a year ago when the liveryman said so. That's what I should have done.

It ain't either. Stop it. Ya know better.

Zeke stepped out of the saddle, pulling the Volcanic from its scabbard, holding it in his right hand.

Gotta be careful no matter what.

The travelers were four hundred yards away and closing. Obviously Indian women. One of the horses—no, two--were pulling travoises. He could see them.

I'll let 'em pass. Wave my hand. Ships passin' in the night, like that Evangeline that Henry Longfellow wrote about. Lexie liked him so much. I won't even bother lookin' at 'em. It won't do no good. I can't speak to 'em anyways.

I will not. I won't do that. I'll talk to 'em. Best I can. See if they need somethin'. They're women.

This is over. I can't do this no more.

It ain't never over.

This is. Laramie. I'll turn and go south to Laramie, catch a wagon group headed to California. A year? A year is enough. I should have done this already. I'm so sorry, Lexie. I should have known that you was gone. Gone for good. I should have known it. I was told. I was told over and over again. I should have listened. It's just that . . . It's just that I told you I'd come for you. And I mean to.

They were two hundred yards away now.

O'Reilly started barking.

Damn dog.

The woman in front was staring at him, her rifle at the ready.

Is she gonna shoot me? he thought. *Looks like she has that in mind. I can see it: a Hawkens. What's she gonna do with that old thing?*

Oh, stop it. She ain't even pointin' at ya.

Be careful.

I'm bein' careful.

The woman's hair was pulled back and tied long on the back of her head. Brown. She was thin and clear complected.

Fifty yards. O'Reilly took off barking, jumping above the grass to see the intruders.

The woman on horseback brought her hands to her mouth. The horse's ears went back. She said something. Something. But it was . . . it sounded like . . . No. She didn't have black hair. Her skin? It was white, tanned brown by sun and wind. She was pointing at him. The other two women were looking in his direction, staring at him.

Zeke touched the skin of his unshaven face with his left hand, still thinking about the woman with the rifle, seeing the rifle, cautious. He turned slightly, bringing himself around, preparing mentally to defend himself, if necessary.

Stop it. Ya fool. Ya ain't gonna do that. It ain't necessary. They's women.

The woman in front dropped the rifle from her hands.

What are you doin'? He thought. *I could be a bad man. You don't go droppin' no rifle.*

Where's that damn dog? What's he doin'?

He thought he heard his name. *No. That couldn't be. No one knows my name. No one anywhere knows that. What's wrong with my ears?*

Why'd she drop that rifle?

Just the wind through the grass.

Somethin' ain't right.

The rider had slipped off her horse. The three girls were standing together looking at him. The rider was talking excitedly, so fast. It wasn't English. Or was it? She fell to the ground in a heap, her head in her hands, long brown hair covering her face.

He looked; the first woman seemed to be weeping.

Weepin'?

393

Ezekiel M. Penrose looked again. Shock washed over him; he leaned back against his horse. His right hand, the one that held the Volcanic was shaking.

"Oh my God," he exclaimed. "Oh my God."

He dropped the Volcanic as if it offended him. The woman who had been out in front leading her horse was walking toward him through the knee high grass, then running. When she got to him she threw her arms around his neck and started sobbing uncontrollably. Another woman, younger, smaller, joined her. But not the woman who had collapsed.

They dragged him, numb with disbelief through the tall grass to where the third woman sat crumpled up like a wet blanket on the prairie sod. They picked her up by the arms, but she was unable to say anything, tears running down her cheeks, her hands still covering her sobbing face.

He grabbed hold of her and hugged her to him. Two people, one sobbing, both clinging to each other in a sea of grass, lost.

"You came," she cried in disbelief sobbing into his neck. "You came."

Zeke could only nod.

The end.

Enjoy G R Howe's next western novel; number seven, if you're counting. Here are the first four pages in hopes that it will whet your appetite and drive you all sorts of crazy.

TENPENNY VOICES

A G. R. HOWE Western

CHAPTER 1

The firing came in quick succession, a staccato barrage of sound that punctuated the silence of the still, morning air. It walloped the sides of the mountain, slapping the slopes and ridges over and over. Houston Tenpenny stood, pushing the kitchen chair back and away from the table. Hurriedly, he stepped through the doorway and outside the two-room log cabin to listen. The initial barrage was followed by three shots which sounded like they were afterthoughts; they, too, slapped the mountain, jerking it awake. Altogether, there were too many to count. He stood for a moment in the midmorning sunlight wondering, feeling apprehensive. Seldom did hunters come to the mountain.

It was early October. The aspens on the slopes of the west Pryor were turning brilliant yellow. There was a cool snap to the air announcing the advent of fall and threatening the coming of winter. Standing on the hard pack in the front yard, he paused, waiting, thinking. There were no elk herds up there, not on the ridges that watched over the head of Crooked Creek. White tail? Mulie? Maybe. But not likely. One shot would suffice, not the number he'd heard. What he heard was a barrage. He smiled. Maybe the white tail were shooting back. This was different: the condensed nature of the shots was hurried, pressing, urgent; as if there was an emergency, something that couldn't be put off another minute. A barrage was certainly not what he'd expect from hunters who knew what they were doing.

One solitary shot had followed the rest: a heavy rifle, a Sharps, or a buffalo rifle, maybe. But there were no buffalo on the south face of the Pryor. It was too dry for buffalo and there was limited grass. He'd never seen a buffalo on the south face in all the time since he'd come to live there: not one. Something was out of kilter. He worried, wondering what it could be. For a moment, he looked south in the direction of the shots. Rifles popping wouldn't matter much except Teddy was out there somewhere. He'd left earlier, wanting to get something fresh to eat---a young buck. He'd left in the early morning to see what he could see. Teddy was eleven, almost twelve: eight years Houston's junior. He was looking for something to feed Wallet.

Wallet? Now that was a big dog: a male wolf. Their father had brought him home as a small two or three-week old pup, fat and tender, so new he had to be bottle fed. Teddy had been a young seven when he took the pup from the gunny sack, fed him from a Jack Daniels whiskey bottle, slept with him--the wolf lying on his chest licking his arm, his face--Teddy laughing and giggling. Teddy played with him; took him on horseback. Teddy's horse wasn't too excited at the dark-haired pup sitting on his haunches, but he got used to it and the pup learned how not to fall off until he got too big. Then the horse wouldn't stand for it. From that time almost three years ago, Teddy and Wallet had been joined at the hip. Teddy learned how to hunt to feed the orphaned pup. The pup grew and grew until he outweighed Teddy. Yet, despite being wild, he never harmed the boy. Teddy was its mother.

Odd how a wild animal could adopt a boy while so young without knowing any better. Certainly Teddy thought the world of the pup. Practically from the beginning the pup only had eyes for the boy. He followed him everywhere, never letting him out his sight, going absolutely crazy when Teddy wandered off. Pops shook his head and kept shaking his head until Wallet pulled Teddy out of the burning lean-to, saving his life. Teddy never thought much about it, but Pops knew Wallet was sent from heaven by Teddy's mother, sent to watch over the boy, knowing Pops wasn't too good at it, knowing she wouldn't be there. That wolf? Fact was that wolf-pup was the closest thing to a mother that Teddy had known.

Standing in the yard, facing the rising sun, Houston listened for more shots but heard only silence and his heart beating. It was quiet again, too quiet. Finally unable to shake the worried anxiousness, he went to the horse corral and caught the bay gelding. He didn't plan on looking for the boy but he didn't plan not to either. What he wanted was to see with his own eyes exactly what was going on. The ache inside his chest told him he'd better do it soon.

Without thinking why, he buckled the pistol belt around his waist. This wasn't unusual. When out he always carried the pistol. Pops had paid twenty dollars for it in 1861. He claimed he paid too much, seeing how long it took him to load, the trouble of having to use paper cartridges and fight with black powder and caps. Houston retrieved the 73 Winchester from behind the door, checking the loads, then cradling it in the crook of his left arm. In his right, he carried a mostly full box of .44-.40 cartridges. Pops liked the brass cartridges a lot better. Everybody did. But Pops hadn't purchased the new Colt, the one that also used .44-.40 brass cartridges. Seventeen dollars was just too much. It would easily take a year to see that much money. Old man Peterson had a couple at the Peterson General. But he was a tricky old bastard; he was asking twenty-five. No one dealt with him. It was a wonder he kept his store open. "Crooked" was what Pops called him. "Damn straight crooked."

Before mounting, Houston checked the loads in the Navy Colts his father left him. He stored the cartridges in his saddle bags, then looked south. The quiet bothered him. There was simply too much of it. He rode east along the crest of the east Pryor, above the ice caves, before he turned south. Cutting Teddy's trail, he followed him and the wolf. For some reason Teddy was walking, leading his horse; the wolf was out in front. Teddy's tracks mostly covered the wolf's. On a knoll above a stand of pine and aspen, he saw where Teddy had sat on a stump eating cornbread, leaving a few crumbs amid the tracks. Wallet's tracks were all about his, no doubt begging. Damn wolf. Two miles farther on, in a grove of aspen and pine, he located the boy's horse, its reins wrapped around a piece of deadfall, an old pine tree lying on its side.

Teddy's tracks started south, the wolf's beside his. They walked maybe a hundred yards before Houston lost his trail. In a clearing he found what was left of the wolf. The ground was broken up and trampled by seven or eight men. There were empty beer bottles, cigarette stubs, and splatterings where someone had spit a chaw of Copenhagen.

Wallet had been shot and skinned, his hide and head removed. Houston figured it was Wallet, although there was nothing left to provide a conclusive identification. Who else or what else could it be? There was no Teddy. Houston's heart beat fast in his chest, his breath coming in short gasps. It wasn't from exertion but abject fear.

Houston steadied himself, then did what he'd been taught. Without further disturbing the ground around the remainder of the wolf's carcass, he circled the outside of the clearing, found Teddy's tracks, and lots of blood. The boy had gotten away, sometimes falling, sometimes crawling, sometimes dragging himself. They were solitary tracks, a story told in the dirt. Wallet was already dead when the boy was there; the boy had been shot. He was doing what was natural: when wounded, seek shelter; avoid the danger; survive.

Backtracking, he found Teddy in a crevasse, barely alive; his body had fallen between two large granite rocks. He'd been shot several times. He'd dragged himself across a flat rock and had fallen into the crevasse. There he stayed, too weak to move and growing weaker, bleeding steadily. His face was pale and drawn. When he perceived Houston bending over him, he grabbed his arm.

"Wallet?" he said.

Houston shook his head, then crawled into the crack, lifting Teddy's head, cradling him in his lap. Teddy started crying, bawling over Wallet. Houston glanced at the boy's wounds, realizing there was nothing he could do. Teddy had been shot at least three times: too many holes to plug. He'd been shot in the upper thigh, the stomach, and the right shoulder. His shirt and pants were soaked in blood.

"Why'd they do that?" Teddy whispered. "Why'd they shoot Wallet? He didn't do nothin'."

Houston didn't answer.

"Why'd they shoot me?"

"I don't know, Teddy. I don't know. Now hold still. Relax if you can. I gotta plug these holes."

Teddy had blood on his lips. Blood was running from the wound in his thigh, his heart pumping it out onto the rock face: so much blood.

"Hooey, I ain't makin' it. I feel sorta tingly."

Houston didn't answer.

"Make 'em pay, Hooey. Make 'em pay for Wallet. Hooey? Hooey I'm scared. I ain't feelin' nothin'. Hooey?" The boy started to explain: as if he had to get it out, as if he had to tell Houston what had happened, as if explaining would make it all go away. He talked in gasps, his chest heaving.

"Hooey, we just walked out in thet clearin'. Followin' deer tracks. Wallet was right there and outta nowhere they starts shootin'. Like they can't see us. I got away. I gots to cover. I gots all bloody. But Wallet . . . They just kept shootin'. Hooey, make 'em pay for Wallet, Hooey. Please, Hooey. It hurts so bad. Make 'em pay."

"They'll pay, Teddy. You and I will make 'em pay."

"Liar." The boy almost smiled, a line of blood forming on his lips.

"I ain't lyin', Teddy. You'll see. We'll make 'em pay." Those were Houston's words but he didn't believe them.

"Hooey, I can't feel nothin'." Teddy started coughing and

coughing made him bleed more. Afterwards, Teddy babbled, talking about Wallet, calling him like he did when he wanted him to come. It was barely a whisper. But Wallet didn't come. And Houston was left sitting below the bare escarpment in a crack in the rock, holding his brother's limp body in his arms, and wondering what to do.

That's the way he remembered it. Somewhere in between babbling and losing coherency, Teddy passed out, his breathing slowed until it stopped. He did not regain consciousness.

And that wolf, that damn wolf. It was like he was right there watching Teddy, looking over him, whining when Teddy didn't respond to Houston calling his name, crying mournfully when Teddy failed to take another breath. There was no Wallet. He knew there was no Wallet, but Houston's heart seemed to stop beating; it was as though he had no heart. In its place was a huge black hole: no bottom, no top, no sides. Just dark emptiness.

About the Author

G. R. Howe was raised in Kane, Wyoming. He graduated from Brigham Young University and received a law degree from John Marshall Law School in Chicago, Illinois. He began practicing in Ventura, California in 1976 and pursued a career in law for the next thirty-four years, after which he and his wife, Joy, retired to Wyoming and began writing western novels. He is an associate member of Western Writers of America.